08- AVM-100

# Not Wicked Enough

## CAROLYN JEWEL

**B**

BERKLEY SENSATION, NEW YORK

**THE BERKLEY PUBLISHING GROUP**
**Published by the Penguin Group**
**Penguin Group (USA) Inc.**
**375 Hudson Street, New York, New York 10014, USA**

Penguin Group (Canada), 90 Eglinton Avenue East, Suite 700, Toronto, Ontario M4P 2Y3, Canada
(a division of Pearson Penguin Canada Inc.)
Penguin Books Ltd., 80 Strand, London WC2R 0RL, England
Penguin Group Ireland, 25 St. Stephen's Green, Dublin 2, Ireland (a division of Penguin Books Ltd.)
Penguin Group (Australia), 250 Camberwell Road, Camberwell, Victoria 3124, Australia
(a division of Pearson Australia Group Pty. Ltd.)
Penguin Books India Pvt. Ltd., 11 Community Centre, Panchsheel Park, New Delhi—110 017, India
Penguin Group (NZ), 67 Apollo Drive, Rosedale, Auckland 0632, New Zealand
(a division of Pearson New Zealand Ltd.)
Penguin Books (South Africa) (Pty.) Ltd., 24 Sturdee Avenue, Rosebank, Johannesburg 2196,
South Africa

Penguin Books Ltd., Registered Offices: 80 Strand, London WC2R 0RL, England

This is a work of fiction. Names, characters, places, and incidents either are the product of the author's imagination or are used fictitiously, and any resemblance to actual persons, living or dead, business establishments, events, or locales is entirely coincidental. The publisher does not have any control over and does not assume any responsibility for author or third-party websites or their content.

NOT WICKED ENOUGH

A Berkley Sensation Book / published by arrangement with the author

PRINTING HISTORY
Berkley Sensation mass-market edition / February 2012

Copyright © 2012 by Carolyn Jewel.
Cover art by Jon Paul.
Cover design by George Long.
Cover hand lettering by Ron Zinn.
Interior text design by Kristin del Rosario.

ISBN: 978-0-425-24660-3

BERKLEY SENSATION®
Berkley Sensation Books are published by The Berkley Publishing Group,
a division of Penguin Group (USA) Inc.,
375 Hudson Street, New York, New York 10014.
BERKLEY SENSATION® is a registered trademark of Penguin Group (USA) Inc.
The "B" design is a trademark of Penguin Group (USA) Inc.

PRINTED IN THE UNITED STATES OF AMERICA

10  9  8  7  6  5  4  3  2  1

*To all the wonderful readers
who've let me know how much they enjoy my books.
Thank you.*

# *Acknowledgments*

To my amazing agent, Kristin Nelson: thank you, thank you, thank you. Similar thanks to my editor, Kate Seaver, and the entire Berkley team.

I'd also like to thank Allen Joslyn of the Antique Doorknob Collectors of America, who pointed me in fruitful directions, which included two of their newsletter issues that were directly on point regarding specifics about doorknob construction in the early nineteenth century. Thanks to Terry Herbert over there in England who uncovered the Staffordshire Hoard. I shamelessly stole your discovery and moved it across time and space. I must also acknowledge the Birmingham Museum & Art Gallery for putting all those astonishing pictures online.

More thanks go out to Nyree Belleville and Jacqueline Yau for the friendship and dinners. I am so glad you guys moved to my part of California. Special thanks to Julie McDermott and Robin Harcher for all the ESC and hours spent talking about academia, romance, books, writing, and reading. You guys keep me sane. Much love to my sister, Marguerite, and my son, Nathaniel, whose skill in the kitchen includes Nutella sandwiches—you're the best! Love to my nephew, Dylan, and my nieces, Lexie and Hannah.

# Chapter One

1:00 AM, Bitterward, seat of the Dukes of Mountjoy, near High Tearing, Sheffieldshire, England, 1816.

LILY WELLSTONE WASN'T THE ONLY ONE TO HAVE been caught in the downpour. She ignored the rain dripping off her bonnet and gazed at the other occupant of the entrance hall.

He was tall with dark hair and an ill-fitting and very wet greatcoat about his broad shoulders. Raindrops darkened his worn boots and glistened in his hair. His eyes were deep-set and private. This was a man who did not share his secrets, a man who could only be unraveled bit-by-tortuous-bit. Not for a moment did she mistake him for a fellow caller, though his clothes were hardly better than something a country squire might wear.

This most fascinating man stood at the opposite side of the room from the front door, near the magnificent arched doorway to the second floor. To the right, if she was correct about Bitterward's architectural integrity, that same archway ended at the butler's pantry. Two sets of crossed swords hung on the wall on either side of the doorway's pointed top.

As the shape of the doorway proved, Bitterward was

Gothic. Legitimately several centuries old and therefore not a reconstitution of the medieval as was the fashion of the recent past. Such follies as the modern Gothic only demonstrated, in her opinion, a failure of imagination.

Her as yet silent companion could have passed for the ghost of one of Bitterward's ancient lords. His present-century clothes spoiled the effect, but notwithstanding that anachronism, the ancient spirit gazing out of his eyes sent a shiver of anticipation through her.

Behind her, a servant pushed the heavy wooden door closed with an ominous *thunk*. The drum of rain diminished. On the table beside the door, a lantern threw her elongated shadow onto the marble floor. The floor was not the original surface, of course, but the marble, laid out in horizontal stripes of *V*s that alternated black and white, was worn enough to be quite old.

The gentleman's wet boot was planted in the shadow of her head. Sensible footwear, those boots. Not even five minutes in the rain, and her slippers were soaked through. The damp from her shoes and the rain dripping off her cloak already penetrated her bones. Neither her shoes nor her coat had proven sufficient protection against this night's weather.

The footman who'd met her carriage and held the umbrella over her head all the way up the front stairs—for all the good it did what with the wind blowing the rain sideways—disappeared through a side exit, umbrella in hand, leaving but one footman with her and the mysterious stranger.

"Welcome to Bitterward," the gentleman said. He did not smile that she could see. The gloom of the entryway made it difficult to tell. Smile or no, the sound of his voice was intimate and very much at odds with the roughness of his clothes. That voice was a thing of dreams, entwining with her emotions, already at a high pitch after too many hours traveling and then this downpour that had her chilled to her marrow.

She resisted the urge to take a step back and instead indulged a fancy that she would be unable to move until he removed his boot from her shadow. She removed her bonnet to stop the water from falling into her face and passed the back of a hand over her forehead. Her glove was too damp, as it turned out, to do much besides redistribute the wet. His gaze followed the motion of her hand. In the dimness, she was forced to guess his age. Thirty, she thought. The prime of life for a gentleman, be he real or ghost.

"Thank you, your grace." She peeled off her gloves. The gentleman did not deny he was entitled to the honorific. She removed her cloak, too, and gave it a shake. Water cascaded onto the floor. Her traveling gown had been spared the worst of the drenching, thank goodness.

The remaining footman stepped forward to take her cloak. She dropped her gloves into the well of her upturned bonnet and handed that over, too. "Thank you." To the duke, she said, "I hope you have ordered your sister and me better weather tomorrow."

He didn't react right away, and she had the impression he was deciding whether she had amused him or convinced him she was a fool. Perhaps a bit of both. Well. She was cold and wet. His boot yet pinned her shadow to the floor, so she remained where she was. Behind him, she caught a glimpse of a stone staircase that quickly narrowed and turned as it spiraled toward the first floor and disappeared into darkness.

Lily pointed to the painting on the wall beside the stairs, a gentleman dressed in the fashion of the Italians from two hundred years ago. "Is that a Gossart?"

"Yes," he said without a glance at the portrait she meant. "It is." He cocked his head. "I am informed my great-granduncle brought it here from the Continent." As everyone knew, the line of descent from the first duke to the fourth was not a straight one. The title had gone into abeyance for a time, and the Crown, she understood, had been poised to take back the lands. Mountjoy had not yet reached his majority when his existence was discovered and his lineage proven. Imagine that. An orphan, living with his younger brother and sister in the home of a maternal uncle. On a farm. On which he himself had labored.

"He had excellent taste." She declined to mention there was now a Gossart in her own house, but wasn't that the oddest coincidence?

His mouth quirked on one side. "Thank you, Miss Wellstone."

The duke might be rough around the edges in respect of his clothes, but there was nothing deficient in his intellect. She curtseyed and caught a glimpse of water stains on her hem. "You're welcome, your grace."

"George," he said to the footman who still held her cloak and bonnet. The silk flowers she had so painstakingly made and affixed to her bonnet might never recover from the damp and, now, from being crushed in the footman's hands. "Do you know which room my sister meant for Miss Wellstone to have?"

"The Lilac room, your grace."

"Lilac?" A wry smile appeared on his mouth. "I'd no idea we had a room with a name like that. I don't know how anyone keeps them straight."

George bowed. "Your grace."

"See to it her trunks are taken there forthwith." He spoke well, with no trace of an accent, a Sheffieldshire one or any other for that matter. "Tell Miss Wellstone's maid she may have a meal in the kitchen once she's seen to her mistress's comfort."

"Your grace." The footman bowed and departed to carry out his employer's instructions, which left Lily wholly alone in the entryway with her friend Ginny's wholly impressive eldest brother. For a man in such inferior clothes, his manners were faultless, but then he'd been some nine years in possession of the dukedom, and nine years was time enough to acquire some polish. Though, apparently, not quite enough.

"You must be exhausted after traveling for so long." He moved toward her, treading further on her shadow. Since she was a tall woman, she preferred men who did not make her feel she was a giant. The duke was quite a bit taller than she. Six feet at least. His mouth curved in the most devastating smile. "In such inclement weather as I had ordered up this evening."

"I forgive you the inconvenience."

His gaze flicked over her, reminding her, forcefully, that she was female to his male. "Will you?"

"Already done, your grace." Now that he'd stepped farther into the light cast by the lantern, she adjusted her opinion of his apparent age. He was younger than she'd thought. Not more than twenty-eight or nine, and with his looks, a good deal more dangerous to a woman's virtue, too. "I will correct you in one respect, your grace, and say that I am not the least tired. I never am at this hour."

"Duly noted."

Ginny was fair-haired and blue-eyed. She'd expected both her friend's brothers to have similar coloring. The duke's hair was dark brown, and his eyes were an extraordinary green with thick, sooty lashes she would have killed to have herself. To say that the duke was handsome, however, would do a disservice to men who actually were.

Lily stayed where she was, meeting his gaze without blinking or looking away. According to the terms she'd set herself, she could not move while he trod on her shadow. The thought made her smile.

The duke didn't look away, either. Nor did he smile in return. The effect was . . . bracing.

"I never fall asleep much before four or five in the morning," she said. "Often as late as six."

"Is that so?" His voice sent a shiver down her spine. He was doing that on purpose. "I would be happy to show you the library. In the event you would like to take something engaging back to your room."

She gazed at her slippers, as ruined as the flowers on her bonnet. When she looked up, she saw a condescending smile flitting about his mouth. But she had indeed understood his double entendre. She smiled as if she had not. "Thank you."

Mountjoy's eyes widened.

Well then. Excellent. She maintained her most innocent expression though, in fact, she was no longer innocent. A spinster she might be, but she was not decrepit yet, thank you. "I do hope you have something thrilling to show me."

## Chapter Two

MOUNTJOY CONSIDERED THE PERMUTATIONS OF WHAT his sister's acquaintance had just said. Regardless of her actual age and experience of life, Miss Lily Wellstone possessed a disconcertingly guileless face. With her dainty, too-pretty features, she looked an innocent incapable of matching wits with anyone, let alone a man experienced with women of all sorts, proper and those not so proper.

Miss Wellstone was young enough to flirt and more than pretty enough to know she had an effect on a gentleman's passions. And she was unmarried. As was he, which she must surely know. Never mind that he was all but engaged to a suitable woman. Until he was actually married, he would be pestered by hopeful parents and girls with ambition.

*I do hope you have something thrilling to show me.*

She was flirting, he decided. He was alarmed to realize he did not feel entirely impervious to her charm. Which was considerable.

Without responding to her comment, he fetched the lantern from the table then held out his arm, and they proceeded up the stairs, with her shockingly bare hand on his sleeve. Her fingers were long, very pale, and slender. She wore two rings, a ruby on her first finger and a diamond on the one next to it. The gems were not gaudy, but they weren't small, either.

When the stairs became too narrow to navigate side by side, he dropped back, allowing her to take the van but holding the lantern high enough to light her way. Her hips swayed as she climbed the stairs. He appreciated the view.

"Aside from the abysmal weather," he said from behind her, "was your journey here a pleasant one?"

"It was, your grace. Until the very moment one of the horses threw a shoe. We were obliged to stop for several hours while we waited for the farrier to assist us." They passed narrow, slitted windows with deep ledges, and she glanced out of each one even though there was nothing to see at this hour. "Your family were Yorkists, I presume," she said as they made another dizzying turn of stairs. "During the War of the Roses."

"Why would you presume such a thing?"

"To my recollection, which I confess might be imperfect, there are no Hamptons listed on Edward IV's Act of Attainder."

At least she wasn't one of those women who pretended they were ignorant. "The Hamptons supported the House of York until after Edward was king. It's how my ancestors eventually became dukes. After that it's less clear. The situation was fluid."

She lifted her skirts higher. Since by happy accident he was looking down, he caught a glimpse of two slender ankles. "Not surprising, if your relative fought valiantly."

"We have been given to understand that he did, Miss Wellstone." He paused, just the merest hesitation before he committed to an inappropriate reply as a test of his theory that she was not as guileless as she appeared. "All we Hampton men have valiant swords."

"Thank goodness," she said without missing a beat and with such artlessness that he frowned. Then she glanced over her shoulder at him, eyes dancing with amusement. "Everyone has need of a valiant sword from time to time. Don't you agree?"

It was all he could do not to laugh out loud. She was an amusing thing, wasn't she? "Some more than others, I daresay."

Outside, the wind shifted and drove the rain against the windows. "The weather," she remarked, "is another reason I was so late getting into Sheffield and then to High Tearing."

"Left at the top."

"Thank you." She reached the landing and went right.

He arrived at the top of the stairs and found she'd not gone far. She was waiting a few feet away. He joined her, holding out his arm for her to take. The air here was cooler, and he saw the skin up and down her arms prickle from the cold. "Left, Miss Wellstone."

She sighed. "I never can tell the difference." She gave him another heart-stopping smile. "Given the nature of my one and only defect, you'd be astonished how rarely I become lost."

"I assure you, I am already astonished."

"At any rate," she went on as he got them headed in the correct direction, "I had thought to beat the rain, but I miscalculated. My coachman ought not to have listened to me. He ought to know better by now."

"Had he a choice?"

"One always has a choice, your grace." She spoke matter-of-factly, and he could feel her experience of life behind the words. "The difficulty comes when one or more of the choices is unpalatable. I'm sure my coachman considered whether his position was worth his silence. He's new to my employ. I'll warrant he does not know I would never dismiss any servant for politely voiced opposition."

"No?"

"Certainly not."

They passed portraits of family members he'd never met and whose names he did not know unless he read the plates on the frames. None of the subjects bore much resemblance to him, but there were two from the sixteenth century that could have been his brother, Nigel. He liked the still lifes better than the portraits. A draft swirled the air around them as they passed a marble statue set into a niche, not Greek, but an Egyptian deity with the head of a jackal. Miss Wellstone shivered.

Without comment, Mountjoy stopped to set down the lantern and remove his greatcoat. He placed it around her shoulders, pulling the garment close around her and holding both sides near the collar until she had a grip on it. Her eyes were the darkest brown he'd ever seen on a woman as blond as she. He stood there, holding his coat around her. He allowed his attention to slide from her eyes to her mouth.

A kissable mouth. He waited to find out whether he might be invited to discover if he was right. He oughtn't be thinking such things. There was Jane, after all, who was, whatever one thought about the weight of everyone's expectations about them, perfectly suited to be a duchess. Miss Wellstone was a guest in his home, a friend of his sister's. No gentleman would dream of seducing a lady under such circumstances.

She cocked her head then took a step back. "Thank you, your grace. That's very kind of you."

He nodded and picked up the lantern and continued walking. This time, because she was holding his greatcoat around her, she did not put her hand on his arm. He led her down a stone corridor beneath an arched and ribbed ceiling. She slowed until he had to stop or leave her behind. He faced her, curious about what had caught her fancy.

"Do you have ghosts here?" she asked.

Good Lord, he hoped she wasn't serious. With that innocent face of hers, he couldn't be sure. "Not to my knowledge," he said.

"You ought to consider it."

He was at sea. One moment he was convinced she was a helpless sort of female, none too bright, the next that she must be daft. Or intelligent beyond what her sex typically allowed a man to guess. There was more than a hint of the contrary about her, and besides, how many unintelligent persons knew about any Act of Attainder? "I beg your pardon?"

She stuck a hand through the opening of his greatcoat so she could wave. As before, her smile transformed her from pretty to ethereal. His breath caught.

"In my experience," she said with a smile still on her lips—so, not entirely serious?—"a ghost improves a residence immeasurably. I have two where I live. I've instructed the staff to relate the stories to visitors on the days when the house is open to the public. They tell their friends, relations, and acquaintances when they return to their homes, and invariably, they visit, too. You ought to do the same."

"Does that not lead to more strangers traipsing through your house?" He began walking again.

She caught up to him. His coat flapped against her legs and dragged on the floor in the back. "I adore visitors. Don't you?"

"No." He opened the door to the library, and, yes, it was in fact the library, one of the few rooms he could regularly find in the labyrinth that was Bitterward. He allowed her to precede him in. "Present company excepted."

"I'm hardly a stranger," she said on her way past him. "Ginny and I are practically sisters."

He stopped walking. "You are not practically a sister to me."

The moment the words were out of his mouth, he realized he ought to have said nothing. Best to think of her as a sister since there must be nothing between them but an acquaintance.

A few feet inside, she turned in a circle, scanning the room but pausing in the motion long enough to face him and say, "I've always wanted a brother."

"I am happy to be a brother to you."

"How lovely." She stopped with her back to him and breathed in. Mountjoy was sorry his coat hid her figure. He crossed to a table by the door, lit another lamp, and the darkness before them receded. He moved so that he could watch her face, studying her while she was not aware he was doing so. Her eyes were closed. She was a woman of delicate beauty with golden blond hair, pale skin, and a slender, elegant figure. He could not imagine why a woman like Miss Wellstone remained unmarried.

"There is nothing quite like the smell of books." She opened her eyes and examined the nearest shelves. "My father is not one to collect books or read much himself. He does not approve of novels." She approached a set of shelves. "When I moved to Syton House, I supplemented my aunt's library with all the books my father forbade me to take from the subscription library. And more."

"Did he not object to your library additions?"

"I'm sure he would have. If he'd known. Now, it's true, he thinks my library is a deliberate offense to him. In a way, I suppose he's right."

He watched her walk, but with his coat around her, he could no longer see the sway of her hips. "There is a famous home called Syton House in Exeter," he said. "Notable for its gardens, if I recall correctly." Eugenia had lived in Exeter with her husband. "Is your Syton House also located there?"

She looked at him over her shoulder, no sign of that breathtaking smile anywhere. "There is only one Syton House, sir, and it is mine."

That shocked him to silence. He didn't remember if Eugenia had mentioned the very interesting fact that her bosom friend Miss Lily Wellstone was bloody rich. "Indeed?"

"Yes." She held a hand toward the shelves. "I can feel the tingle of all those stories waiting to be known to me." She stayed there awhile with her hand outstretched. "Are you absolutely sure you don't have ghosts?"

"Yes."

"I just felt the most mysterious thrill. I would not be surprised to learn you are wrong."

"You are fond of reading?" he asked in a low voice. He

leaned a hip against the table. If she owned Syton House, she had very good connections, and the money to keep company with them. She wasn't much like the women he'd met who came from families with those sorts of connections. Ghosts, for pity's sake.

"Very fond," she said.

"Tell me what books you prefer to read. I could recommend something for you, if you like."

She turned to him, another smile on her lips. He could not imagine a woman more dissimilar to him. She was joy and wit, and, he was sure, the sort of woman who thrived among crowds and at parties. He did not.

"Adventure, your grace." She smiled, and his body reacted with a sexual jolt. "Passion." Though he was sure she exaggerated her emotions to amuse him, he suspected she meant every word. "To have my heart pound until I feel it might burst from my chest."

He continued to gaze at her. She did not break the silence, and in the quiet he felt the pull of attraction. Nothing was wrong with that. He was a man, after all. Men admired women all the time without any intention of seducing them. "You were Eugenia's neighbor. In Exeter."

She blinked. "Yes."

"You were a good friend to her, during her husband's final days."

"I hope I was, sir."

"She spoke highly of you, Miss Wellstone, after I brought her home."

The melancholy in her dark eyes receded. "She was kind to me, too, your grace."

He liked her for that. Very much, indeed. Eugenia deserved that sort of loyalty and regard.

She turned back to the shelves, and he moved the lantern to the other side of the table and placed it so she could see the titles better. She reached for one of the volumes and opened it. In a soft voice she said, "Your sister was always kind to me. Despite everything."

His voice stayed low, too. They were entirely alone here, and the household was asleep. "What would that be, Miss Wellstone? The everything to which you refer?"

She turned, book in hand, close enough to him that he could smell, very faintly, violets. It was a scent he happened to particularly like on a woman. Her expression turned more serious. "You aren't the sort of man one easily deceives."

"No."

With a nod, she clutched the book, and her smile reappeared. "Best not to omit what someone will inevitably discover, I always say." Her mood was oddly bright for a woman with news she seemed to think he would not like to hear. "The *everything* that makes you so curious is that I was once disowned by my father."

He frowned. Her connection to Syton House puzzled him even more. "Once? Do you expect him to disown you again?"

"I can't be sure. My father has always been convinced I am of a wild nature."

"Is he right?"

She replaced her book on the shelf and stood there, her back to him, hand still on the spine of the volume.

"Miss Wellstone?"

"Yes," she said, reaching for another book. "He is. But then you already suspect that of me."

"I am not used to any lady being so forthright."

"Oh, you may rely on that with me." She turned, and he had the impression she had been struggling to hide her emotion. She hadn't entirely succeeded. Her smile was brittle, and it made him want to take her in his arms and promise no one would ever again make her sad. Such was the effect of that angelic face of hers. She hugged a book to her chest. "My father went bankrupt, you see; that was nearly two years ago now. He hasn't a penny left. If he had not come to live with me at Syton House, he'd not have a roof over his head."

"I should think he'd be grateful."

"He resents his circumstances extremely. Indeed, it's why

I have so little time here. I had to promise the servants I would be home before May or I own they would have refused to look after him. I fear he's a difficult man to like. I don't like to have the staff abused, you understand." She opened her book, stared at the pages, then closed it with a sigh. "I can make an excuse, your grace, before Ginny knows I have arrived, if you would rather not have me in your home. I would appreciate, however, the recommendation of a nearby inn. It's far too late to think of driving all the way back to Sheffield."

He considered her offer. He liked an orderly household, and it was plain as anything that Miss Wellstone would disrupt his peaceful country existence. This was not a woman who would sweetly make herself invisible. There was also the fact that she was quite beautiful and an accomplished flirt. He was not impervious to any part of that.

"Your grace?"

"No," he said. He shoved his hands into his coat pockets. "I won't deny my sister the company of someone she recalls so fondly and likes so well as she likes you." This was true. Eugenia had been looking forward to Miss Wellstone's arrival since the day two months ago when the visit had been agreed to. His gaze traveled the length of her, from head to toe. He did like a tall woman. "Nor myself the pleasure of learning why she adores you so unreservedly." His mouth twitched. "Despite everything."

She pulled his greatcoat tighter around her. "My dear duke," she said in a voice of mock sorrow. "It is my sad duty to tell you that I am reformed."

Her smile was an invitation to sin, and he was feeling very much inclined to sin right now. Unthinkable, of course. But knowing all the reasons he should not act on his impulses didn't divert the direction of his thoughts. Not in the least. "That, Miss Wellstone," he said, "is a very great pity."

# Chapter Three

LATE THE NEXT MORNING LILY STOOD IN THE ENTRY-way of Bitterward and slid the rest of the way out of her cloak. She was aware the duke himself had arrived at the door moments after she had and that he now stood behind her. Doyle, the duke's butler, stepped away from her with her cloak in hand. Already, he was reaching to take Mount-joy's gloves, hat, and greatcoat.

She exchanged a glance with Mountjoy. He nodded at her. Say what you would about his grace's undistinguished manner of dress, his servants were efficient and meticulous in their duties.

"Lily!"

Lily looked away from the duke and saw Ginny hurrying down the stairs to the entryway. "Ginny."

"Lily, you're here. Doyle! You should have sent someone to fetch me the instant she arrived." She came down the last steps. "Oh, hullo, Mountjoy. When did you arrive?"

"Last night," the duke said.

"I meant Lily, not you."

"Never mind that," Lily said to her friend. "Let me see you." She raised her hands so that Ginny would stop, which she did. She was not pleased with what she saw. She had expected to see Ginny recovering from the loss of her husband. She wasn't. Sadness inhabited her eyes, and she was too thin in a gown black as night and drab beyond words. "You should be glad no one woke you when I arrived," she said to cover her shock. "It was well after midnight."

"Last night?" Ginny crossed the black-and-white tiles, hands extended. "Good heavens, Lily. So late. You must be exhausted."

"I," said the duke, "am not in the least tired. Thank you for asking after me, Eugenia."

"Couldn't be helped," Lily said. She took Ginny's hands while her friend made a face at her brother. "But I'm here, and I've just come back from a bracing walk and feel ready to face a bit of tea and something to eat. Will you join me? I'll tell you everything that's happened since you left me bereft at Syton House." She glanced at Mountjoy, standing by the door. "You, too, duke."

Ginny enveloped Lily in a hug. Lily breathed in her perfume of roses and citrus. A new scent for Ginny, but she liked it very much. "How wonderful," Ginny said, "that at last you've come to visit after so many months of my pleading with you."

"I ought to have come sooner." Indeed she ought to have. If she'd had any idea the case was so dire, she'd have come immediately. She kissed Ginny's cheek. "You know how I am. Never as organized as one ought to be." Lily tightened her arms around Ginny and softly said, "My darling, you are far too thin." She stepped back and released Ginny.

Mountjoy said, "Doyle, bring us tea, won't you?"

"In the Oldenburg salon," Ginny said.

"Yes. There." The duke gestured. "Something to eat as well."

Lily added, "A substantial something if it's not too much trouble."

"Your grace. Lady Eugenia." The butler bowed at the waist, but he was smiling, which seemed auspicious, though Lily wondered who had decided Ginny was not to be called Mrs. Bryant. "Miss Wellstone."

Ginny put her arm through Lily's and headed for the stairs, ignoring her brother. He followed them despite that. "You have the room next to mine, did you know that?"

"The Lilac room I was told. It's lovely." Heavens, but she was glad to be here. In Exeter, Ginny had become a very dear friend. "I am now determined to have a room with lilac accents when I'm back at Syton House."

"I knew you'd love the view of the garden." They continued walking arm in arm until the stairs were too narrow, and Lily took the lead. She was far too aware of the duke behind them. "They're not the gardens at Syton House," Ginny said. "That goes without saying, but we do very well here, all the same."

Lily walked backward up the stairs so she and Ginny could face each other. His grace continued up the stairs, a pleasantly bland expression on his face. "You were right that I would adore the view. I gazed for several minutes upon the prospect when I arose." After all this time, Ginny still wore black. There was no question Lily was needed here. Ginny must not be allowed to founder here as she had been. "How have you been, my dearest Eugenia?"

"Oh, very well, thank you. Do you still not sleep well at night?"

"Abysmally, I fear." *Oh, Ginny*, she thought, *you should not be so sad*. She touched her left hand to the stone wall and held her skirts out of her way with the other as she continued her backward walk up the stairs.

"We keep country hours here," Mountjoy said.

"I'm sure you do, your grace. Everyone but me keeps them at Syton House. I assure you I'll muddle along whilst I am here." She waved her left hand then returned to skimming the wall with her fingertips. "I always do, don't I, Ginny?"

"Yes, Lily."

She looked past Ginny to her brother. "Don't dream of changing your schedule on my account, your grace."

"I shan't. Right at the top," Mountjoy said.

"Right, is it?" She reached the top of the stairs well ahead of Ginny and her brother and turned. She took several steps before she realized the corridor looked familiar. That couldn't be correct.

"Right," said the duke from somewhere still on the stairs.

"Lily?" Ginny's voice came from behind her. "You've gone left. It's the other way." Lily returned to the stairs and found Ginny and her brother waiting for her. "I should have pointed," Ginny said.

"No harm," she said. "For here I am. Safe and sound."

They reached the Oldenburg salon without further incident. The salon proved to be a smallish room set in a tower at the west end of the house. While not strictly a castle, Bitterward was an old enough structure to have been built with two round towers at the east and west. The Oldenburg salon had the architectural advantage of having windows along the curved outer wall that overlooked the very garden that had attracted her admiration before. The early roses were in bloom, and she wanted to walk outside again just to breathe in the scent.

The salon was charming, with a fireplace mantel of carved mahogany polished to a sheen, as were the paneled walls and ceiling. Very pretty, though she would have preferred if the room had retained more of its Gothic decorations rather than a Tudor character. "This is a newer part of the structure, I presume?"

"Relatively," Ginny said. "I believe this wing was remodeled during the reign of Charles I. Mountjoy would know."

"Yes," the duke said. He tugged on the bottom of his waistcoat, but nothing was going to improve the lay of the fabric except for a pair of scissors and needle and thread. "This wing was extensively redone."

Ginny put her palms on Lily's shoulders and slid her

hands down until they were clasping hands. "She adores ruins, Mountjoy."

"Does she?"

"Yes," Lily said, looking at him from over Ginny's shoulder. "She does."

"After we've eaten," said Ginny, "perhaps you'd like a tour of the church? It's not far, and I've been told it's Anglo-Saxon."

Lily gave Ginny's hands a squeeze before she released her and strolled to a love seat upholstered in dark green velvet. The green would make a striking contrast with her primrose gown. She was never going to marry, for her heart was no longer available for such emotion. But that was no reason not to show herself to advantage when the opportunity arose. Life ought to be lived with due consideration for the beauty of one's surroundings, and that included the elegance of one's attire.

"I should adore that," Lily said.

Ginny sat on an upholstered chair that made her look even more drab and wan than she had in the hall. Lily made a mental note to speak with her brother the duke at her earliest opportunity regarding his lack of attention to his sister. Surely, he had not brought her home to her family only to abandon her to loneliness all these months? She feared he had.

The duke moved a chair nearer his sister and sat. He did not seem much at ease, and yet he was the most vital man she had met in her life. Full of repressed energy.

"I don't know how much we shall see of Mountjoy," Ginny said. "He's the parish magistrate, and the Sessions are on. He's forever doing this and that about the property. Always meeting with someone or attending to business that keeps him from home."

His eyebrows rose. "The responsibilities of an estate like Bitterward are not ones I care to delegate."

"Then I imagine we'll see very little of you, your grace."

He nodded. "To my great regret, of course."

Though she did not say so to Ginny, industrious and useful occupations seemed in keeping with the man. She suspected as well that a man as vital as him had a mistress or a lover or two somewhere not far away.

"He's going to marry the daughter of one of our neighbors. Miss Jane Kirk. You'll meet her by and by. You'll like her exceedingly. She's two younger sisters, both delightful. You won't meet Miss Caroline Kirk, though. She's away just now."

"Congratulations on your upcoming nuptials, your grace."

"Thank you, though your good wishes are premature."

"Come now, Mountjoy, of course you'll marry Jane."

"I will," he said.

Lily leaned against the sofa, stretching an arm along the top and extending one leg. She considered what Ginny had said and the manner of her delivery. "I take it this is one of those situations in which everyone agreed the match was a splendid idea even before you'd met."

"Yes," Mountjoy said. "That's it exactly."

"You love her madly, I hope."

Ginny leaned forward. "Everyone loves Jane."

"I adore a romantic tale. She loves him madly, too, am I right?"

"How can she not? He's Mountjoy, after all. He has a way of getting what he wants."

She looked to the duke. "Indeed, your grace?"

"Yes, Miss Wellstone"—he smiled—"I do."

A servant brought in the tea and refreshments, and while the tray was set on a table near the sofa, Lily used the silence to study her friend. "Ginny." She extended her hand, and after a moment, Ginny took it. Lily drew her to the sofa. "Have you been ill?"

"I enjoy very good health." At twenty-three, Ginny was two years younger than Lily, and though they were both blondes, Ginny's hair was much lighter than hers, and her eyes were blue, not brown.

"I can't say the evidence supports you."

"I don't know what you mean."

"You miss him," Lily said. "I know that." She handed Ginny her handkerchief. Ginny shook her head, but took the handkerchief anyway.

"I do." She pressed the embroidered silk to her eyes.

She understood loss, and Ginny knew that. She glanced at the duke again, meeting his gaze as she spoke. "You have your family to rely on, and that is something fine, Ginny."

"Yes, yes, I do." She balled up the handkerchief. "I do know how fortunate I am." Ginny knew about Lily's estrangement from her father, and that, until her father came to Syton House, she had lived on her own from quite a young age.

When the tea was ready, Ginny, being the excellent hostess that she was, poured while Lily prepared plates of food for herself and the others. Cucumber and watercress sandwiches, cold ham, bread, crackers, and cheese. The butter was stamped with Mountjoy's crest, a swan, wings spread and wearing a duke's coronet with a broken chain around its neck. She arranged and rearranged the food on the plates until she was satisfied with the placement and balance of colors and textures.

"I will engage to fill your mind with happier thoughts," she said when she'd handed out the food and sat with her plate. Though she was hungry, she didn't eat right away. She wanted time to admire the palette of her breakfast plate. "One does not easily recover from the loss of a deep and abiding love."

"No," Ginny said.

"I am proof one can go on and even be happy." She leaned to cup a hand to Ginny's cheek. "We must, you know, even when we've lost the person we love most in all the world."

"Have you suffered such a loss, Miss Wellstone?" The duke set his plate and his tea on a table near him.

"I have, your grace."

"My condolences."

"Thank you."

Ginny covered Lily's hand with hers and gave it a squeeze. "I've told everyone about you. Even Mountjoy, when he was here before."

"Don't change the subject." She cocked her head. Lord, Ginny must get out of black. "What have you said, Ginny?"

His grace sipped his tea then answered for his sister. "That you are wonderful and amusing, and the best friend she could ever have."

"I adore being flattered." She intended to discover why Ginny's brothers had neglected her until she'd become this pale, wan creature devoid of the spirit she so loved about her. Had neither of them seen how heartbroken and unhappy their sister was? Had they even tried to entertain her? To occupy her hours? Introduce her to suitable and compatible gentlemen and women who would befriend her?

"Now that you're here," Ginny said, "we're going to have such a lovely time."

"Oh, indeed we are. Depend upon it." Lily crossed her ankles to one side and ate what proved to be a devilishly good watercress sandwich. The rest of the food was just as superlative, better than what her own cook produced, and he was so French she barely understood a word he said. The crackers were crisp and flavorful, the bread fresh, and the Brie and Stilton first-rate. "Does your dairywoman make a Devonshire cream? If she does and it's as lovely as this, I warn you, I may never leave."

"She does, it is, and you are welcome to stay here for as long as you like."

"You'll regret saying that." Lily ate another sandwich. "If only it were possible."

Ginny picked at her food while Lily eyed another watercress sandwich and wondered if she ought to simply get another plate before she'd finished her first. "I shan't," Ginny said. She gave her brother a defiant look. "In fact, I wish you would live here."

"How sweet of you to say so." The duke ate one of the finger sandwiches. Such a quiet man, and extremely attractive in a visceral manner. Miss Jane Kirk was a lucky woman. "I am very glad to be here." She slathered Brie on a cracker. "You must eat, Ginny. I insist. I won't rest until you have."

Ginny smiled, and that encouraged her. "You needn't ever go home."

"Would you eat more if I agreed?" Lily ate her cracker, and the rich, buttery tang of the cheese spread over her tongue. She closed her eyes in bliss. "Oh, my. I shan't leave until I've spoken with whoever obtains this Brie." Likely the local smugglers supplied the duke's household. "I must know who you get it from."

"You have my leave to inquire of the cook."

"Thank you, your grace. This Brie is astonishingly good. Have some, my dear Ginny."

"I shall, Lily." Ginny made no move to do so.

Lily put down her food and stood, hands on her hips. Stern measures were called for. She was not at all in charity with the Duke of Mountjoy for neglecting his sister. "I see I was too conservative before. I'll fix you a proper plate while you pour more tea." So saying, she returned to the tea table and selected a slice of bread, butter, crackers, a bit of each of the cheeses, and a small portion of ham. No point overwhelming her with too much food. As she had with her own plate, she settled everything into a pleasing combination of shapes and colors. "I still like my tea sweet," she said while she perfected her arrangement of Ginny's plate. She sculpted a pyramid with the butter she put on the plate. "Do be generous with the sugar."

"I haven't forgotten."

Back at the sofa, she accepted her tea and handed Ginny the plate. "Try the Brie."

Ginny gazed at the plate. "You've created a work of art, Lily. This is too lovely to eat."

"*Humph.*" She tapped her foot. Mountjoy snorted, but she ignored him.

"Yes, Mama." Ginny rolled her eyes.

"So long as you eat, I shan't take offense."

While she watched Ginny spread Brie on the corner of a cracker, a blindingly handsome gentleman strolled in. He had Ginny's coloring, with blue eyes and even blonder hair. Unlike his brother, he knew something about how to dress himself. His clothes fit impeccably and complimented his physique and coloring. He was tall, though not as tall as Mountjoy, and possessed a smile that made her like him before she had any right to have come to that decision. He made his way to Ginny and bent to kiss her cheek.

"Good afternoon, Eugenia," he said. "Mountjoy."

"Nigel." Ginny paused with her cracker halfway to her mouth. "Where have you been?"

"Went to see the Misses Kirk. I am commanded to tell you hullo and ask you to come to tea as soon as you can. So, hullo from all the Kirks, Eugenia."

"Tea?" Ginny asked her brother. "The Kirks love my brother. I can't imagine why."

"What?" Lord Nigel put a hand to his heart.

"Perhaps his excellent waistcoats?" Lily said. The garment was a delicious shade of cream silk that perfectly complimented his sober blue coat.

The vision of male beauty quirked his eyebrows in Lily's direction. "You must be Miss Wellstone," he said in the loveliest voice. No country accent, just the crisp syllables of an educated man who spent his time among the Ton.

"I am," she said. His coat fit precisely, and his cravat was neither too plain nor too lacy. She most definitely approved. And good heavens, he was lovely. She would have known him for Ginny's brother anywhere.

"Delightful to meet you at last, Miss Wellstone. Eugenia's praised you to the skies every day for the last month."

"Good heavens, Ginny." She raised her teacup but did not drink. "I fear I will only disappoint your brothers. Do eat that cracker. I can't have another drink of this lovely tea until you do."

The cracker hovered near Ginny's mouth. "I've not told anyone a thing that isn't absolutely true."

"I die of thirst," Lily said, inflecting her words with enough passion and suffering to break the hardest heart. "My throat . . . it is a veritable desert."

Ginny laughed and ate the cracker.

Lord Nigel Hampton smiled fondly at his sister. "According to Eugenia, Miss Wellstone, you are perfection itself."

"She is," Mountjoy said. "As you will soon discover for yourself."

Lily took a sip of her tea and found it acceptably sweet. How odd that she, who admired all things elegant, preferred the duke's looks and manner to his brother's. She said, "Lies, I'm afraid. Shame on you, Ginny."

"You traveled here from Exeter, am I right?"

"Yes, Lord Nigel, I did."

"That's a devilish long trip." He bowed. "But I forget my manners. Nigel Hampton, at your service." His blue eyes lingered on her face. "I'm Eugenia's favorite brother in case she didn't think to praise me."

Lily helped herself to more Brie. "She said something about a pest and bother, but I may be mistaken."

"Oh, Lily!" Ginny laughed, and it was gratifying to hear. "No, no. I said he was a perfect bother." She smiled insincerely at him. "Never a pest, Nigel, dearest."

Having grown up the only child born to her parents, the interactions of siblings had always fascinated her. She loved to imagine what it would have been like to have a brother or sister.

While Mountjoy snorted, Lord Nigel put his hand over his heart, partly turning toward Lily. "You wound me, sister. And you, Mountjoy, you don't defend me? Your only brother?"

"Delighted to meet you, Lord Nigel." Lily gave him her most engaging smile, and Lord Nigel stared. Men often did. She had been told more than once that her smile was beyond lovely, though she'd never quite seen it herself. According to Greer, he'd fallen in love with her smile first. "This Brie is excellent. Tell Ginny she ought to have more."

"Eugenia, do have more of the Brie." Lord Nigel remained

standing. He couldn't be much older than twenty-two. Despite his youth, he had a Town polish. Doubtless because when Mountjoy ascended to the title, Lord Nigel had been young enough to be sent to Eton and then to Oxford. Eugenia did fix herself another cracker and Brie.

"My brother," Mountjoy said dryly, "can be charming when he wishes to be."

Lily extended a hand, and Lord Nigel Hampton bent over it. "Delighted to meet you, Miss Wellstone," he said. He held her gaze longer than was proper. Dear Lord. He was a boy. Beautiful as he was, she had no interest in a boy. "Welcome to Bitterward."

"Thank you, Lord Nigel." She smiled faintly. For good or ill, she was much more interested in the Duke of Mountjoy.

# Chapter Four

NEAR MIDNIGHT, MOUNTJOY LEFT THE STABLES AND headed for the rear entrance that led to his room. He hadn't intended to be gone for so long. He owed his sister an apology for his absence. Eugenia had particularly asked him if he could come home for supper this evening, and he had agreed he would. He ought to have been, given that in the week since their guest's arrival, he'd managed to dine at Bitterward exactly once.

The most direct way to the private entrance took him through the rose garden, a familiar walk now. There was a full moon, and that meant he did not need a lantern to light his way. Finely crushed gravel crunched under his boots as he walked. Once, Bitterward had been a foreign place to him, cold and demanding of his time and attention. Over the years, he'd come to see his legacy as a living thing. He had been required to learn its secrets and shepherd the lands, tenants, staff, and a thousand other dependencies. In return, the estate gave him shelter, food on his table, ready money in his pockets and his brother and sister an income. Properly managed, Bitterward would support his wife, children, and future generations of Hamptons who would one day gaze at his portrait in the gallery hall.

Halfway to the house, he stopped. A woman limned in silver moved with silent grace onto the path ahead of him. Her back was to him, and damned if he didn't wonder if the apparition was entirely of this world. Then she turned her head toward the roses along the path, and he recognized her.

"Miss Wellstone?"

She let out a soft gasp and whirled, a hand to her heart. Moonlight scattered soft prisms of light from the combs in her hair. "Your grace."

He walked to her and, God help him, he was on point, far too aware of her as a woman. He schooled himself against the reaction. "Were you perhaps expecting the gardener?"

Too late, he understood the insult he'd just leveled at her. They spoke at the same time, Miss Wellstone with more than a hint of frost in her tone.

"I was not expecting anyone, your grace."

"Forgive me, Miss Wellstone. That was thoughtless of me."

"It was." Her pale shawl had slipped into the crooks of her elbows, leaving her shoulders and bosom exposed and all the rest of her indefinably luscious in full evening dress.

"I only meant to remark your unexpected appearance out here." He, on the other hand, wore the same clothes he'd put on this morning. While he rarely gave a thought to his appearance, Miss Wellstone made him wonder if he ought to care more. He removed his hat and held it by the brim then thought what his hair must look like. He smoothed a hand over the top of his head. "I intended no insult."

"We hardly know each other, yet here I am giving you my forgiveness again."

Her eyes, Mountjoy thought, gave away the mind behind those innocent, delicate features. Again too late, he realized he was staring and that his silence could be construed as rude. He opened his mouth to speak, too late, of course.

"Twice in an acquaintance seems excessive, don't you think?"

"For a man who is little more than a country oaf? Hardly." Ahead of him the path led to the house. To his right, a narrower walkway lay half in shadow from the roses in full bloom. And in front of him, a vision that made him think of sex and the silk of a woman's form.

"Ridiculous, your grace," she said. Her smile was gentle and inviting and not at all as cold as he deserved from her. "You're no oaf."

"Am I to be forgiven?"

She plucked at her shawl until the two sides were even, then gave him a look from beneath her lashes. "I suppose."

"You are all that is generous, Miss Wellstone." She was a flirt, Miss Wellstone was. A charming, delightful flirt.

"In fact, I am." Moonlight turned her gown silvery gray. "Which you would know if you were ever at home."

"Another failing of mine." He bowed. "I attend to duty before pleasure."

"I expect that of you." She touched one of the roses, a bloom just beyond full. "It's a lovely evening."

He put a hand over his heart. Because he was a damn fool. Because she was beautiful and alluring. "Exactly as ordered."

"For which I sincerely thank you, your grace."

"Might I ask what brought you out here at such an hour?"

"This and that. Ginny and your brother have retired for the night." She tilted her head.

He completely lost his ability to see her as his sister's unmarried friend. Untouchable. Beyond a man's base desires. Before him stood a woman of flesh and blood, and he lusted after that woman.

"I couldn't sleep. I never can this early. I came out here because I wondered if I would still be able to smell the roses." She drew in a deep breath. "I can. I've been standing here these ten minutes or more breathing in the scent of your Gallicas."

Her features were exactly the sort of sweet and delicate form that made men feel a woman must be protected. No darkness or unhappiness should ever enter her life. Women like her were made to be spoiled and coddled and granted their every whim. He felt the urge himself, though he knew she was far from helpless.

"We missed you at supper tonight," she said. "Ginny seemed sure you would join us."

"I sent a note when I realized I would be detained."

"Yes. We received that." She had a narrow nose, perfectly balanced cheekbones, and a tenderly shaped mouth. Head-on or in profile, she was an angel. Her figure only added to his impression that here was a woman too fragile for her own good. His preference was for lovers who wouldn't collapse into a heap at the slightest exertion. He was willing to overlook that with her. "All the same, your grace, that does not mean we were not disappointed."

"I beg your forgiveness again."

"Three times I have been called on to forgive you." She shook her head and gave him a smile of mock ruefulness. "Now that *is* excessive."

Mountjoy moved closer to her. She was not unaware of her appeal, he knew that, but she had not been spoiled by it, as women sometimes were. A gold medallion hung from a long ribbon onto which were knotted several gold beads, spaced every three or four inches. In the dark, it was impossible to tell what color the ribbon was.

"It is." He wasn't awkward around women. He never had been. Even in the days when he'd been merely a farmer with just enough prospects to call him gentry, women liked him, something he'd realized early on. He felt awkward now because he was attracted to her and did not wish to be and suspected he was not going to resist. "I'm sure you would rather enjoy the garden in solitude."

"Actually, no." Her fingerless lace gloves matched the

moonlit silver of her gown. Had she worn those to supper? He found the informality profoundly arousing. "I dislike being alone." She gave him a sideways glance, and Lord, but her eyes were not innocent. She wasn't flirting with him, he understood that. She was a woman, not a girl, and quite plainly knew her own mind and desires. "Would you mind keeping me company? At least for a while."

*God, no.* Still holding his hat, he gave her a half bow. "I should be delighted to."

She laughed. "You poor gentlemen, obliged to accept trivial requests from we ladies even when you'd rather not." She waved him toward the house. "Go on, your grace. I only meant to walk to that hedge and then back. I can tolerate my own company for that long."

Mountjoy stayed where he was. She'd given him an easy way to escape his fate, and he stood there, unable, unwilling to take it. "It's a pleasant enough night."

They said nothing for two heartbeats, a long silence for a man and a woman alone. With no one near. Not even a servant. Mountjoy was far too aware of that fact. Was she? He rather thought she was.

"Ginny said you were at the Sessions," she said.

"I was. Until quite late."

She moved down the path, and Mountjoy followed. When he caught up, he took her arm as if they were relatives or it was broad daylight. As if there was no tension zinging in the air between them.

"Am I keeping you from your supper?" she asked. She did not sound as if she were in any way aware of the impropriety of them being alone here. "Or have you dined?"

Some of her nonchalance transferred to him. There was no reason to be anxious about being alone with her. She was a guest at Bitterward. They must naturally meet, and spend a moment or two in conversation, and without any of the speculation that attended a man's attentions to a woman at a formal social gathering. "With the mayor of High Tearing."

"Does he have pretty daughters?"

"No." The scent of roses carried on the breeze. They walked in silence for several steps while Mountjoy idly and improperly wondered what sort of lover she would be. Not passive, but warm, inviting. Adventurous. How could a woman like her be anything but adventurous in bed?

"Will you believe," Miss Wellstone said, "that until now I've never been farther from Syton House than I can walk in a day?" She let out a breath. "It seems I ought to be able to go home by mere thought alone. Or at least as quickly as a walk over the next hill, rather than a week's travel."

"You prefer the comforts of your home?" Mountjoy said. He'd have assumed a woman like her would be in constant search of entertainment. One party after another and an endless cadre of admiring men, not keeping at home with only herself and her cantankerous father for company.

"Very much, your grace." She shrugged, and the movement of her shoulders was achingly graceful. "I love Syton House. It's been my home since I was nineteen." She looked away from the roses and grinned at him. "All this time I thought I'd be terribly travel sick. I was before. I was so dreading the journey north. For naught, as it turns out."

"When was that?" he asked. "Your previous journey."

Her expression went blank for just a moment, but whatever thought had clouded her eyes vanished. "When I moved to Syton House. It was an unpleasant excursion. I confess, I found the carriage ride to Bitterward by turns dull and exhilarating. But this time, I was never once ill."

"A long journey always has its moments of tedium."

"If it weren't for my father, I'd travel more often." She faced him on the path, and though he was taller, she didn't have to lift her chin to look into his face. "I had an adventure on my way to Bitterward," she said.

His belly hollowed out. "Did you?"

"Shall I tell it to you?"

"Please." They stood close. Enough for him to see the lace that trimmed her gown. Enough to see the rise and fall of her bosom, the smoothness of her skin. She gestured. Her shawl slid down one of her arms, and he reached out to twitch the material into place over her shoulder.

"Thank you."

"Tell me your adventure." The side of his finger brushed her bare shoulder. Neither of them acknowledged the contact. Not yet.

"We'd stopped in Tewkesbury, as I particularly wished to see Tewkesbury Abbey. The nave, I'm told, retains some Norman features, and I hoped to inspect it. I don't know if Ginny told you of my fascination with architecture."

"She did."

Her shawl slipped off her shoulder again. Mountjoy stooped to pick up the trailing end, but instead of handing it to her, he fingered the material. Cashmere, and unutterably soft.

"It's one of the reasons, your grace, that I am so pleased to be here at Bitterward." She clasped her hands behind her back and rocked on her heels. "The house is an excellent example of the Gothic. I'm very much looking forward to exploring and taking some sketches. That's if you don't mind. I hope you don't."

"Draw the entire house if you like." The neckline of her gown was low enough to offer him a view of the curve of her breasts, and, yes, he looked.

"Thank you." She took a step away from him and plucked a leaf from one of the rosebushes. He reminded himself of how improper it would be to close the distance between them. She folded the leaf in half lengthwise then in half again. He had the impression Miss Wellstone was never still for long. Despite her physical delicacy, she was not a languid woman.

"Your adventure?"

She unfolded the leaf and then began again, folding in the opposite direction. "It began when I saved a Gypsy king's dog from certain death."

"A Gypsy?"

"He wore the most colorful clothes. They made me dizzy

with delight and astonishment." The leaf succumbed to the folding and tore. She dropped it at the side of the path. "You never saw a more handsome man in your life. He wasn't as tall as you, but he was well made, with dusky skin and the most languishing eyes."

"Did you fall in love with him?" he asked. He took a step toward her.

"Madly. Desperately. Head-over-heels." Her smile broadened, and Mountjoy thought he'd do anything to see her smile like that again. "If only for a moment. I do believe if he'd asked me, I'd have run away with him and his charming puppy to learn to dance, read fortunes, and live the Gypsy life."

Mountjoy began to understand why her father thought her wild. The idea of her running off with a Gypsy was more than a little arousing, and he suspected she knew that. They were alone. Completely. He did not think only he felt the tension between them. He touched her cheek and began his slide to Hell for what he intended.

"Don't you think that would be a most exciting life, your grace?" She didn't move away from his caress. He wasn't far gone enough not to know he hadn't merely touched her. "I wonder if I ought to have done so."

"Eugenia would have been devastated to miss your visit."

She lifted her chin. "I was only in love for a moment, but what a moment it was." Her laughter was a beguiling thing to hear. No titter or practiced trill, but a full-on burst of amusement. "I had already imagined our ten beautiful children, all of them Gypsy princes and princesses."

"Ten of them?"

"Yes." A breeze came up, and she shivered. She rubbed her palms up and down her arms.

"You're cold."

"Perhaps a little."

Mountjoy arranged her shawl around her shoulders so it didn't droop uselessly down her back. Then he curled his fingers in the cashmere and pulled her toward him. He shouldn't do this, but it seemed he was going to anyway. Because she was beautiful and intriguing, and not at all the innocent he'd imagined when they met. "Will you let me keep you warm?"

She smiled as if she knew a secret, and he wondered just who was seducing whom. He moved her closer to him.

"Better?" he said.

*"Mm."*

He brought both sides of her shawl closer around her. He could not do any of the things on his mind. He couldn't. But if he did? "Since you did not run away with the Gypsy king, there must be more to your adventure. Or was meeting him thrilling enough?"

Their eyes locked, acknowledging what their words did not. "He thanked me profusely and genuinely for rescuing his puppy, which he intended to give to one of his daughters."

Mountjoy kept her close. "If the Gypsy king had a daughter of his own, then he must have already been married, and you could not have run away with him to become his Gypsy queen."

"Well. I suppose you're right." She stood with her head tipped to one side, as if she'd never considered the possibility. Perfect, an absolutely perfect picture of innocent confusion. "It's fortunate I did not run away." Her eyes twinkled. "In any event, he was so grateful he gave me this medallion." She held up the ribbon around her neck, high enough to display a gold circle the size of a guinea that hung from the end of the ribbon. "You see?"

He leaned closer to examine it, taking the metal in his hand, angled so the moonlight illuminated it. One side was engraved with a bow and arrow. He turned it over to show a cherubic face on the obverse.

"The medallion is magic," she said. "He promised me that."

Mountjoy glanced up. They stood quite close. "Will it bring you riches and good health for all your life?"

She took the medallion from his hand and studied it. "He

told me that whoever possesses this charm will be united with the individual with whom she or he will be happiest in love. Ginny says I must sleep with it under my pillow."

Mountjoy said, "Isn't that how such charms work?" Her future husband would take her to bed. He'd cover her body with his and put himself inside her and make love to her. And she would enfold her husband in her arms, kiss him, caress him, and if the man were not a dolt, she would sigh and call out his name.

"Oh, the medallion can't work for me."

He held her gaze. "Why not?"

"I have already met the man I was destined to love."

"The Gypsy king?"

"No." She stood motionless with no sign of her previous animation.

"If you are in love, Miss Wellstone, why haven't you married the man?"

"I meant to. We intended to."

His heart clenched because he remembered too late that she had admitted she'd lost someone dear to her. Whoever he was, she truly had loved the man. He cupped the side of her face. He wanted to stop her from hurting, and he didn't know how. "What happened? What broke your heart?"

"He was a soldier."

"I'm sorry." Not for a moment did he think a man who'd won her love would jilt her. Impossible. "How long ago did he die?"

"Five years."

Briefly, he closed his eyes. "What a terrible loss, Miss Wellstone."

She gave a tiny nod, and he was pleased to see some of her sorrow ease. "So you see, your grace, the medallion can't work for me." She tipped her head into his palm. Only for a moment. He let his hand fall to her shoulder. "I am resigned to my single state. It suits me, for I can't love another like that. I wouldn't wish to ever again." She rubbed one side of the medallion. "It's a pretty thing," she said. "I like it exceedingly."

"Are you sure it won't work?"

"It can't possibly when my heart is incapable of being aroused."

"What if you're wrong?"

"I'm not."

"Can you be sure? Who have you encountered today, Miss Wellstone?" he asked. By some miracle he injected the perfect hint of humor in his voice. She bit back a laugh, but smiled. "Any mysterious gentlemen? Any premonitions or chills along your spine? Perhaps an irresistible urge to demand an introduction to some strapping young fellow?"

She shook her head solemnly, but he could see the laughter in her eyes. "None at all. Unless you count your butler. We nearly collided earlier." She let a beat go by. "Is there, by any chance, a Mrs. Doyle?"

"Yes," Mountjoy said. "There is."

"Ah. A shame."

Mountjoy was horrified by how badly he wanted to kiss her.

And, so, after they'd stood there staring at each other, neither of them moving, he did.

He curled his fingers into her shawl and used that to bring her closer. She came to him with a soft sigh and then lifted her arms to his shoulders. He'd broken, amicably, with his mistress when he was last in London, for no reason other than boredom. Therefore, it had been some weeks since he last held a woman in his arms. He was randy as hell. So he told himself.

Lily Wellstone did not kiss like a virgin.

Jesus, no.

He held back nothing. He was far too wound up for a circumspect kiss. From the moment he touched her without either of them pretending nothing would happen, the possibility of restraint flew from any list of his abilities. The world, it so happened, had just become limited to the two of them. He was lost to every selfish and sexual urge a man might have in respect of a woman and to the scent of her, the taste of her, the feel of her body against his.

She took his hat from him, and if she dropped it to the ground, he surely didn't give a damn because she buried her fingers in his hair and, oh, yes, indeed, she was kissing him back.

Her hips pressed into him, gently against his erection and then the moon disappeared behind some clouds and they stood there in the dark of the garden, still kissing, breathing in each other and the scent of roses.

By the time she drew back, and it was she who did, one of his hands cupped her bottom. The other was curved around the nape of her neck. He took a deep breath, but at the end, though she had put a few inches' distance between them, he leaned toward her and kissed her again. She allowed the kiss to linger, a light touch of their mouths, and then no more.

"Goodness," she said, looking at him from under her lashes. "That was lovely."

"I do know how to properly kiss a woman."

Her secret smile reappeared. "You do, your grace."

He kissed her again. She pressed her hand to his cheek as this kiss lingered, too, but she drew away too soon. Far too soon. She dropped her hand to his chest and kept it there.

"I don't mean for you to get the wrong idea," she said.

"What would the wrong idea be?"

"This." She shook her head. "The two of us."

"It doesn't feel wrong."

She leaned against him, her hand pressed to his chest. "I confess I find you extremely attractive."

"Thank you."

She pushed on his chest and stepped away. "This is not wise, your grace. We can't. Much as I like . . . all that— Well. You understand."

"What do you like?"

"Don't be obtuse. You know precisely what I like. Kissing you." She placed a finger across his lips. "Touching you. You're so very lovely, which I am sure you know, but it would be unwise to continue this when more is impossible between us."

He wrapped his fingers around her wrist. "Are you certain?"

"Your sister is my dear friend," she said. "And you are to be married."

"I am aware," he said. Lord, yes, he was aware now. He hadn't been when he was kissing her.

They stood there, in the darkened garden. Lily looked away, and he bent to retrieve his hat from the path, and there they stood again, mere inches apart. She looked like a woman who'd been kissed. Thoroughly.

She let out a short breath. "Despite what you must think of me, I'm not a woman of loose morals."

He nodded his agreement.

She met his gaze. "I wanted to kiss you." She brushed a hand over her face, then to her throat. "I suppose that makes me wicked. Wanting you to kiss me. Then allowing you to do so."

"It doesn't." He reached out and took her Gypsy medallion between his fingers. "I blame this," he said.

She laughed, and the sound lightened his heart. "Of course." She plucked another leaf. "That must be the cause. We had no power to resist the magic."

"You see? We are not at fault here."

"Better you than Doyle, I daresay."

He let go of the medallion and laughed outright. Quiet descended, and during the silence, she adjusted her shawl over her shoulders and closed the distance between them. Mountjoy slid an arm around her waist, and the tension was back, singing through him. But all she did was lean in to kiss his cheek.

"I'll tell you good night, your grace, and see myself inside." She touched his cheek. "Thank you for your company."

He didn't let her go. Not until she cleared her throat. "The pleasure was mine, I assure you."

She curtseyed to him and then left him. Alone.

He watched her walk away, and since the moon had come out from behind the clouds he had no trouble discerning the sway of her hips until, at last, the shadows hid even that.

She was right. They couldn't when nothing would come of it. He was going to marry Jane. He could not seduce his sister's friend. Affairs always ended. Eugenia would never forgive him when their inevitable break cost her Lily's friendship. His sister had few enough friends as it was.

He wanted to, though.

# Chapter Five

Just before Lily blew out the candle at her bedside, she took off the Gypsy's medallion and slipped it underneath her pillow. Not that she believed in the power of the medallion; she just didn't want to lie to Ginny about whether she had done so, and Ginny would ask. She marked her place in her novel with an ivory bookmark and set it on the table beside her. The candle was barely an inch tall. Her inability to sleep at night meant she would have to ask the housekeeper to see that there were extra candles in her room.

Dawn was just touching the windows as she pulled the covers to her shoulders. The room was no longer dark, and at last, sleep dragged her eyes closed. Her sheets smelled of lavender, and while she breathed in the scent, she imagined the coolness of the Gypsy's medallion lay not beneath her pillow but beneath her fingers. She could still feel the duke's mouth on hers, the solidity of his body. The taste of him. The bewildering response of her body to him. He was not Greer, and she could not help feeling she'd betrayed the man she loved. And yet, to be held like that. Kissed like that. She tried to summon Greer's beloved face and she couldn't, and her heart broke anew.

She fell asleep as the first light of morning filled her room, turning dark shadows to gray, and gray to palest lilac. She dreamed. Vividly. She was outside, a spade in her hand, looking into a hole in the ground. In her dream, she knew she was searching for treasure.

Footmen stood around her, wilting in the afternoon heat, soon dirty and sweaty from the work of digging the trench. They'd cast off their coats and rolled up their sleeves, though it was she who held the shovel. Ginny and the so very young and handsome Lord Nigel Hampton stood to her right. Across from her, on the other side of the trench, stood the Duke of Mountjoy, his eyes green as moss.

Their gazes connected, hers and the duke's, and her heart beat hard in her chest. He wasn't as lovely as his brother, but there was a look in his eyes, a certainty about him that appealed to her immensely. Surely, she thought, he would not ask more of her than she had in her to give.

She broke from his gaze and returned to her digging. After turning a few spadefuls of dirt, her shovel hit something that was not dirt. Carefully, she reached in to scrape away the dirt. Gold gleamed from the shadowed trench. She bent closer and the shadows resolved into an iron pot full of gold coins that, even in her dreaming state, she thought looked suspiciously like her medallion. Why, with these, the whole unmarried population of High Tearing would be able to find their truest and happiest loves.

The footmen applauded as she bent to touch the coins, and she grinned with triumph. She stood up, the pot in her arms, and no one, least of all herself, remarked that such a pot would be too heavy for her to lift, though she held it easily. She gave everyone present one of the discs. Except for the duke, who stood on the other side of the excavation, his arms crossed over his chest. Refusing to accept one.

She walked the perimeter of the trench until she reached Mountjoy. There, she handed him the pot of coins. "You see? We succeeded. Look at your sister." Ginny stood beside Lord Nigel, wearing a sky blue frock instead of a black one. "Do you see how happy she is? She ought to wear colors all the time."

"Yes," he said. "She ought to." Mountjoy turned away from the crowd, but she followed him, and they were soon in the library, quite alone. The coin-filled pot sat on the largest table. Each disc in the pot exactly resembled her medallion. She smoothed one of them between her fingers. They were heavy enough to be solid gold and therefore must be worth a fortune.

Mountjoy stood beside her, silent. Brooding.

"Are you angry, your grace?" she asked.

"No."

She gave him a disc and this time, he accepted it.

"Thank you, Lily."

In her dream, his voice sent a shiver down her spine. Yes, the man did have the loveliest voice, edged with smoke and silk. She touched his coat, poorly cut for a man whose shoulders were so broad. Mountjoy was an active man and his body reflected that. One heard things, if one paid even the least attention. On occasion, the duke worked alongside his tenants, and the plain truth was that with his advice, crop yields were up. He had a reputation as a horseman able to turn even the most bad-tempered mount into an obedient ride. He was not considered an approachable man, but his neighbors solicited his opinion about horses and farming. The Duke of Mountjoy was, if not well liked, then well respected.

"You ought to hire me on as your valet." She was perfectly serious, and Mountjoy took it as such.

His eyes stayed on her face. Such a pure and intense green, framed by dark, thick lashes and a tilt at the edges that made her think of his kisses. Her pulse raced out of control so that she could scarcely breathe. "I won't pay you more than twenty pounds per annum."

"So long as I have room and board, that is acceptable."

Since she would be working for the duke, she'd have to close Syton House, though the garden tours must continue. Syton House was famous for its gardens and that brought visitors who spent money at the local establishments. If enough of her staff agreed to stay on even though she no longer lived there, the public tours of the house could continue. The moment she had the chance, she'd write to her steward to put that into motion.

"Then the position is yours," the duke said just as if there was nothing unusual about hiring a woman as his valet. "You'll start immediately."

"Excellent, your grace, since you require an entirely new wardrobe."

He picked up one of the discs and spun it on its edge. "Do I?"

"Indeed, sir, you do. You won't regret it. I'll make you the envy of every man in England. Everyone will beg to know the name of your tailor."

"Make it so, Wellstone."

She laughed, tickled that he should have fallen immediately into calling her by her last name. Oh, yes, she would be the most excellent valet in the Empire and the Duke of Mountjoy would be her triumph.

"Wellstone." He caught the still spinning coin between his fingers.

"Yes?"

"There is one other duty you'll have."

"Yes?"

"This."

Then he kissed her, and she was not an inexperienced girl who could only guess at the passion possible between a man and a woman. He kissed her the way he had in the garden. Tenderly then passionately, holding nothing back, and beneath her fingers she felt the strength and warmth of his body, and she wanted more than anything to touch him when he was nude. To slide her fingers over his magnificent physique, over the muscles that formed his body, to touch and taste and tell him how astonishingly lovely he was.

Her body betrayed her memory of Greer, because she clung to Mountjoy as if no one else had ever mattered to her. In her wicked, wicked dream she kissed him back, and it was wonderful to feel a shiver of arousal when his arms slid around her, the soft touch of his mouth. He pulled back to look at her, his eyes a deep and unfathomable green, and the world dropped away.

She held his face between her hands, sweeping her thumbs underneath his eyes. His skin was warm and alive. She'd felt like this the first time Greer touched her. Shaky, full of anticipation, nervous, aroused, and completely without doubt that they were right to do this. To hold each other, to kiss, to enjoy the physical. Mountjoy's arms tightened around her as the chasm that was her grief opened up and threatened to swallow her whole.

"You work for me now," he told her in a gruff voice. "No one but me."

"Yes."

"I shan't ask you to forget him. Never that." His hands moved over her, caressing, sliding along her shoulders, over the curve of her breasts, her bottom, and everywhere else he could reach and in between he pressed kisses on her, and she melted a little at each one. "Eugenia is right. You can find happiness with another man."

In her dream, she wondered for the first time if that might actually be possible for her.

## Chapter Six

MOUNTJOY CAME HOME TO A QUIET HOUSE EVEN though it was early afternoon. He thought nothing of it, supposing, erroneously as it turned out, that Nigel was visiting the Kirks again, and his sister and her friend were shopping or making calls. He admitted to a certain disappointment at the empty house because Lily Wellstone was a sensual pleasure to watch. She was his secret and guilty pleasure. Addicting, actually. She was in his thoughts too often and, lately, in his dreams, too.

They had succeeded, however, in putting aside that mad incident in the garden. He stayed away from home more than he might have otherwise, and if they happened to meet, they were cordial to each other and nothing more, whatever his private thoughts might be.

He nudged aside the guilty thought that he ought to take the opportunity to call on the Kirks himself. One day, Miss Jane Kirk would make him as suitable a wife as any woman of his acquaintance. Her father had made it clear an offer from him would be welcome, and most of High Tearing behaved as if their marriage was inevitable. He should get the thing done and propose to her. As soon as the time was right. When he had a moment to breathe amid his duties. When more of his affairs were settled. When he did marry, he wanted the thing to be done right, with all the sincerity and sobriety the marriage deserved.

In his room, he put on fresh clothes, breaking his valet's heart yet again by ignoring his suggestions as to alternate attire. The man took every opportunity to suggest, by deed or look or allusion—Mountjoy had forbidden overt remarks on the subject of his clothes—that his wardrobe was deficient. Why should he mind his clothes when he was in his own home and no one was here? He wasn't one of those noblemen born into money and position, and he saw no reason to behave as if he had been.

Dressed in his most comfortable clothes, he left Elliot to his incipient despair and went downstairs in search of a bite to eat. He passed one of the salons on his way and heard voices and laughter, the deeper tones of a man and then a woman's laugh. Two women, he thought.

The salon door was ajar, though not enough for him to see what was going on. His ability to keep the names and functions of the various rooms in the house straight wasn't improving, in part because he didn't care and in part because he'd grown to manhood in his aunt and uncle's home, a house with two floors and seven rooms, including the kitchen and servants' rooms.

Why did anyone need four salons? Or was it five? He could not recall if this salon had a particular use or name. The music room? He pushed open the door and looked in. He didn't think he'd been in it more than a dozen times since he came to Bitterward with his sister and brother in tow.

He did not see musical instruments.

What he did see was Nigel standing by a table, his back to the door, one hand on the top rail of a chair occupied by Miss Lily Wellstone. A paisley shawl draped down her back. Nigel was bent over her shoulder, intently watching something. Eugenia and Miss Jane Kirk were here, too, as intent as Nigel on the table. Jane sat enough to one side that if she were to look up, she'd see the door. And him. Her gloved hands were pressed together and her cheek rested on her uppermost hand. He was struck by what a pretty woman Jane was. He could not do better for his duchess. Like Nigel, Eugenia and Miss Kirk were absorbed in whatever Miss Wellstone was doing.

As best he could tell, Miss Wellstone appeared to be writing or perhaps drawing. Sketching the room as she liked to do? Her intention, she'd said, was to draw the entire house before she departed. Rather than continue in and interrupt them, he leaned against the door and drank in the sight of Lily. He remembered how she'd melted in his arms, the taste of her, the touch of her lips, the roar of passion through him.

She laughed in that heartfelt way of hers, and Eugenia leaned closer to look. His sister giggled. So did Jane, for that matter. Miss Wellstone reached forward with one hand, did something, then drew back. An action consistent with dipping a quill into ink. So. She was writing or drawing something.

"Have a care," Nigel said.

Miss Wellstone spared his brother a quick glance. "I am being very careful. Honestly, Lord Nigel. Has disaster struck yet?"

"No. But you're tipping it."

She did something with whatever they were looking at. "That's because you distracted me." She wrote or drew something. "Don't distract me, my dear young man, and all will be well."

Eugenia propped her chin on a fist this time and said, "What are you going to write next?"

Jane craned her neck to look. Her dark hair contrasted with the blond of the others. She would do well as his duchess. Very well indeed. He wondered if they had decided to write a play. There were enough young people in the environs of High Tearing to put on a creditable production. Lord, he hoped they did not intend to perform their creation at Bitterward. The house would be overrun, and he'd be forced to lock himself in his office to escape the agony.

"Something dramatic," Miss Wellstone said. "Something to pull at our hearts. Unless anyone wants to compose an extempore poem, a line from Shakespeare I think. *Out damn spot!*" She made a flourish in the air then returned to her paper and wrote something down. "Out, out, you dreadful lout."

Nigel guffawed. "Oh, poetess!"

On the other hand, Mountjoy was convinced Miss Wellstone would prove an adept actress. It would be amusing to watch her in a dramatic role. If they were writing a play, he would not object to having the performance here despite the disruption to his schedule. So long as they did not disturb him with their rehearsals.

"'Yet who would have thought the old man to have had so much blood in him?'" Miss Wellstone did a creditable Lady Macbeth, full of fearful lunacy.

Nigel said, "Write something else."

"Such as?"

"I don't know. 'The weather is fine today'?"

"No," Jane said. "Write, 'Mountjoy has not smiled these seven years.'"

Nigel gave her a quick look. Miss Wellstone continued writing, pausing frequently to dip her pen in what Mountjoy presumed was an inkpot. "Why would I write that?"

"Because it's true," Jane said. "Isn't it, Lord Nigel?"

"He has a great many duties, Miss Kirk, to occupy his thoughts. Though it's true, he does not smile often," Nigel said.

"Not unless he thinks he has to," Jane said.

"I don't think that's so," said Miss Wellstone. She kept writing.

Mountjoy pushed off the doorway and headed for the table. Best join them before they said something about him that would embarrass them all.

Jane looked up, and her eyes met Mountjoy's. Her cheeks flushed pink. She stood and squeaked out a set of nonsense syllables he presumed was meant to be his name. Good God. Did he actually frighten her?

Nigel and Eugenia continued unaware, and Miss Wellstone was too absorbed in writing out her sentence to notice Jane's reaction or the reason for it.

"I'm not going to write something that isn't true," Miss Wellstone was saying. She looked at Nigel instead of Eugenia or Jane. "How about 'The Duke of Mountjoy is in dire need of a new wardrobe'?"

Eugenia saw him, and she started. She cleared her throat and got out the words that had stuck there. "Mountjoy. Whatever are *you* doing here?"

Miss Wellstone froze.

Nigel looked over his shoulder, saw him, and turned the color of old porridge. "You."

"Good afternoon, Nigel," he said as if he'd overheard nothing. "Eugenia. Miss Kirk." He headed for the other side of Miss Wellstone's chair so as to have a view of the table. There was no reason on earth for Jane Kirk to be afraid of him or believe he never smiled. None. "What has you four so occupied?" he asked. He was near enough now to see a sheet of paper on the table. Unlikely as it seemed, the words glowed a sickly yellow. He made out the lines from Macbeth. She had not, it appeared, gotten around to writing down Nigel's little ditty about him nor her own suggestion. "What the devil?"

"Your grace," Miss Wellstone said with a brilliant smile that left him momentarily witless. "Good afternoon." She held a quill in her right hand and in her left a phial of water. There was a small pot on the table, capped. The tip of her quill appeared to be wet.

He was aware that Nigel, Eugenia, and Jane had gone quiet, but in that silence he forgot how to breathe. Because Lily Wellstone, when she smiled like that, was quite literally breathtaking.

"We are engaged in a scientific experiment." She gestured with the hand that held the quill. He did not think he was mistaken that the point of the quill was emitting the same eerie yellowish light as the words on her sheet of paper.

"An experiment?"

"Indeed, your grace." She lifted the paper. "Behold!"

He hadn't been wrong. The words were glowing.

"If the room were dark," she went on, "I'm sure the effect would be even more dramatic. I was about to ask Lord Nigel to draw the curtains. Do you mind if he does?"

"What is that?"

She used the quill to point to a book that had not yet been bound. The cover was still the ashy blue cardboard sheets. He could not read the label pasted on the spine. "A book I bought shortly before I left for Sheffieldshire. *The New Family Receipt Book*. It's filled with the most fascinating information and advice. Invaluable to household management. If you're interested, I'd be happy to provide your cook with a recipe for coffee made with acorns."

"Acorns." She kissed like an angel.

"Or potatoes."

"Coffee from potatoes?" He shot a glance at Jane. She sat with her hands clasped on her lap, and she did look terrified. He smiled at her before returning his attention to Lily. "Forgive me, Miss Wellstone, but that's vile."

Her lips pressed together and she managed, somehow, to look down her nose at him even though she was sitting and he was standing.

"You think it's not vile?"

"I think it's narrow-minded of you to judge without evidence. It is an ingenious receipt." She waved the quill again. "Think of the savings."

He rocked back on his heels and smiled again. "The household can yet bear the expense of actual coffee. There's no need for substitutes."

"Perhaps you'd like to give your cook a better method of stuffing a goose."

He gazed at her, torn between thoughts of kissing her senseless and informing her that his household ran perfectly well under his supervision and Doyle's.

"No?" she said. "Another means of making excellent ink? There are several, and I mean to try them in any event so it's no trouble at all." She smiled again. "I'm happy to report the results to you and recommend the best."

Nigel fidgeted and said, "Miss Wellstone?"

"What experiment are you performing?" Mountjoy asked. Some of his wits returned, and he realized everyone except Lily was wary.

"Ah. Yes." She stopped waving the quill and held it up between them. "A phosphorus pencil."

"Phosphorus?"

"Miss Wellstone!"

She turned on her chair. "How may I assist you, Lord Nigel?"

"The quill must be kept wet."

Mountjoy saw her blink and glance at the phial of water in her other hand. He frowned. "A phosphorus pencil? Are you mad?"

"Oh." She blinked again. "Lord Nigel, I do thank you for the reminder. Your grace, I'm quite sane, but thank you all the same for your concern."

"The water," Nigel said.

"Yes, yes. Phosphorus, as I am sure you know, your grace, ignites on contact with air. Hence the precaution of keeping the quill wet. The instructions were quite explicit on that point."

Mountjoy watched her hand. The hair on the back of his neck prickled. "I am well—"

Light flashed at the head of the quill. Nigel shouted and that made Miss Wellstone startle. Her reflexive jerk sent sparks showering over the sheet of paper. At the same time, she dropped the phial of water. The container struck the edge of the table and broke, scattering glass and the contents onto the rug. His Axminster rug, valued at several hundred pounds in the most recent inventory and originally installed by the second Duke of Mountjoy.

"Miss Wellstone!" Nigel leaned in, reaching for the burning quill. Ominous dark spots appeared on the paper.

Eugenia and Jane cried out.

"Good God." Mountjoy swept up the smoldering paper and threw it into a large Chinese vase fortuitously within his reach.

"The pencil!" Nigel said.

Mountjoy stopped Nigel from snatching away the quill. "You'll burn yourself, you fool." He whipped off his coat, prepared to wrap Miss Wellstone's arm and the now flaming quill in the garment.

"There is no need for panic." Miss Wellstone, holding the quill by the feathered tip, walked briskly to the vase. The paper he'd tossed into it had fully caught. A strong smell of smoke and burning phosphorus permeated the air. The light was intense as flames appeared above the rim of the vase and continued to burn all out of proportion to a single sheet of paper. Miss Wellstone tossed the burning quill before she quite reached the vase.

Not that he blamed her for doing so since she might otherwise have severely injured her hand. But Mountjoy, with visions of the quill missing the vase and setting fire to the carpet and thence to the room, roared, "No!"

The quill, half in flames, seemed to dance through the air. It made a graceful arc and landed.

In the vase. The flames and light intensified, and they all held their breath while they waited to see if the fire would stop or continue to a conflagration that required an evacuation of the house. The flames sputtered, then died down.

No one said anything. Except for Miss Wellstone, who had her back to him and could not see his black expression as could Nigel and the others. She dusted off her hands. "That's that, then."

# Chapter Seven

"MISS WELLSTONE."

Lily turned. Without his coat, the Duke of Mountjoy was both physically magnificent—there was no disguising the perfection of his form—and a sartorial disappointment. His waistcoat bagged at the sides, and his cravat was a horror. One might as well not even bother having suits made. Did his tailor not know how to cut fabric for such a specimen as Mountjoy? Did not his valet understand how to properly starch and fold a neckcloth?

"Do you know, your grace, if *I* were your valet, I wouldn't permit you to step foot outside your dressing room with a cravat like that."

"I beg your pardon?"

Lord Nigel said, "I've told him so many a time, Miss Wellstone. Perhaps he'll listen to you."

"You do not appear to be happy, your grace. It's only a poorly tied cravat. Easily remedied."

"How observant of you, Miss Wellstone."

"Yes, well. Who could be happy wearing such inferior attire?"

"I am. Might I point out that you are not my valet, Wellstone?"

Her heart did a flip, but no one, including the duke, seemed to notice what he had called her. "More's the pity, I say."

He glowered at her, actually, and she hadn't done anything to merit such a glare. She gave him a quick smile. True, there had been a moment when the fire might have done more than singe the interior of the vase, but nothing worse had happened. He squeezed his coat, which he held in one hand. "Did you burn yourself?"

She shook her head, flattered that he was worried on her behalf, yet cautious on account of his dark expression. "There was never any danger of that."

"Your phosphorus pencil was on fire." Their relations since their encounter in the garden had been, if not warm, then at least distantly cordial. She understood the reason for his reserve. They had transgressed propriety that night. One could not help but expect a certain discomfort as a result. But that did not warrant his present behavior. His fingers tightened around the coat. If it were a living thing, the garment would be dead by now. With that happy thought, she was forced to look anywhere but at his hand lest she imagine him choking the life from some poor, innocent creature.

"Well, yes, sir, it was on fire. A little."

"A little."

"You distracted me, and the tip dried out. If you hadn't interrupted, we would still be writing out glowing words from the immortal bard. It was great fun. It's a pity we didn't finish."

" 'The weather is fine today'?" he said. At least his tone was milder. " 'Mountjoy has not smiled these seven years'?"

"No one wrote those words."

He arched his eyebrows and glanced at the vase. "The proof of that is nothing but ashes."

"I don't see that I need to prove anything." She licked her lower lip. He didn't seem to be any happier. "Would you like to try for yourself? There's plenty more phosphorus."

"Where?"

"Just here, your grace. We are fully outfitted for a lengthy experiment." She was aware the man was angry, but she wasn't about to let him get away with spoiling their afternoon. "This is excellent. Your participation in our adventure is most unexpected, I must say." She half turned. "Lord Nigel, have you another quill?"

Lord Nigel, pale as a sheet, gripped the back of the chair she'd been sitting on. His knuckles were white as bone. "No, Miss Wellstone, I haven't."

She knew perfectly well he did, but Ginny was as ashen as her younger brother and Miss Kirk was far too somber. She herself, having never had relations of any degree who acknowledged her existence, did not know what it was like to have a brother. For all she knew, everyone feared one's eldest brother. She doubted that, though.

"I'm sure," she said, turning back to the duke, "that we could send for another quill." She walked toward the bell-pull. She no longer permitted anyone to bully her, and that included noblemen of any rank. "Shall I do that?"

"No," the duke said in a pleasant voice that nevertheless frosted her ears. "You shall not. I meant, Wellstone, where is the phosphorus?"

"On the table." She pointed. His eyes darted that direction, and she knew instantly what he intended. She took a step back and to the side, placing herself in front of the table and between the duke and her phosphorus, arms outspread. "It's mine, sir. I purchased it at the apothecary earlier today. I'm afraid I cannot allow you to take my property."

"Mountjoy—" his brother said.

"And I"—the duke spoke with deceptive calmness—

"cannot permit anyone to continue in possession of a substance capable of burning down my home."

Lord Nigel spoke up again, loudly. "See here, Mountjoy. You've no call to address her like that."

The duke could glower all he liked. She would march to her doom willingly and alone. Brave to the very end.

"You and I will speak later," Mountjoy said to Lord Nigel.

Lily looked at Lord Nigel and then at Ginny and Miss Kirk. Lord Nigel was still pale, but his eyes were fiery. He'd taken a step toward Jane, and Lily silently applauded his instinct to protect the young woman and his sister. Ginny stood with her hands to her mouth and was blinking rapidly. Jane, very sensibly, sat quite still, but she was not holding up well either. There would be tears any moment, and Lily would not stand for that.

"If there is blame to apportion, it belongs to me alone," Lily said. "I proposed the experiment. I convinced the others. And I acquired all the necessary materials." She picked up the container of phosphorus. "Might we discuss this in private, your grace?"

"No."

She fixed him with a glower she hoped was every bit as intimidating as his. "But, your grace," she said. There wasn't enough sugar in the world to match her sweetness. "I require a word in private with you." She walked to him and put her arm through his free arm—he still had his coat in a choke hold in the other—and headed for the door. "Ginny, I'll meet you and Miss Kirk in the Oldenburg salon in a quarter of an hour. Twenty minutes, at the most." She glanced at the duke and amended her estimate. "Perhaps half an hour. And you, as well, Lord Nigel. I expect tea will be as lovely as always."

She tightened her fingers on Mountjoy's arm and said in a voice pitched low, "Do come along."

Mountjoy did. She wasn't surprised. She'd found over the

years that men responded to decisive action, perhaps especially from a woman. Nursemaids trained them to obedience from an early age.

Lily strolled out of the room with Mountjoy at her side. "Which way?"

"Left."

"Thank you." She marched down the hall only to have him refuse to follow.

He drawled, "The other left, Miss Wellstone."

"Never mind then." She opened the nearest door. "This room will do."

Mountjoy reached around her in time to hold the door for her. When she'd swept in, he followed, holding out a hand after they ended up facing each other. He continued strangling his coat with the other.

"The phosphorus, Wellstone."

"I told you, it's mine." She crossed her arms, but she was distracted by the breadth of his coatless shoulders. He wasn't a huge man, but there was substance to his frame and none of it to spare. "You'll think me bold and impertinent, your grace, and you will be right."

"I always am." His voice was steel and smoke, but there was something else there, too. Something hungry that sent a frisson of anticipation racing down her spine.

"Do please put on your coat," she said. "I don't think I can bear to look at your waistcoat another minute."

The duke drew in a long, slow breath. "Forgive me."

"Again?"

He put on his coat and rapidly buttoned it. "An improvement, I hope."

"No." She examined him from head to toe. "Your valet ought to be dismissed."

"So you've said, Wellstone."

"I don't think I have."

"You have in my dreams."

She braced herself against showing how his remark

startled her. "I swoon, your grace, to think I have been honored to appear in your dreams."

"Did I say dreams? I meant nightmares."

"Your coat, sir, is as atrocious as your waistcoat. But I did not ask for this interview to chastise you for your attire."

"No?" A note of something wild curled around the edges of his voice.

She sat on a sofa with a large harp set at an angle to one end and gestured for him to take the chair across from her. As he did, she slid a finger over the strings of the harp. The instrument was out of tune. "For a time, in my extreme youth, I had harp lessons. I did not enjoy them."

"I thought all young ladies enjoyed their music lessons."

"Did you enjoy yours?"

"Farmers do not have the luxury of a musical education."

"You're not a farmer."

"Did you mean to ask me if I could play you a song on the harp? I can't."

She set the phosphorus beside her. Mountjoy eyed the jar. "It's tightly sealed, your grace."

"It had better be."

"It is. I assure you. But please. It's your sister I wish to speak to you about. I knew her when her husband was alive, how happy and in love she was. I saw her in her grief when he died. When you came to take her home, I thought, thank goodness. She'll have someone to look after her. Family upon whom to rely."

"She has that," he said.

Lily sniffed then glanced down and winced. The man was in need of a decent bootmaker, too. "My God," she said in a low voice. "Those boots." No amount of polish or oil could save his footwear. She shook her head. "Now that I am here, your grace, it is my particular aim to see your sister amused." She folded her hands on her lap. "It's something you and Lord Nigel have failed to do. You ought both of you to be ashamed. I intend to continue to encourage her to leave the house, make calls, and engage in divers recreation that will refresh her heart."

"Wellstone, please believe that I do not for a moment doubt your devotion to my sister—"

"If writing sentences with a phosphorus pencil amuses your sister, and it did, sir, then how can you object to that?"

His eyes widened. "Because it is dangerous."

"Oh, pshaw. We'd been writing for some time before you interrupted us. In fact, Lord Nigel, Miss Kirk, and your sister had already had their turn."

"I object to my house burning down."

She lifted her hands, palms up, and looked from side to side. "Your house has not burned down."

He spread his thighs and propped his hands on his knees as he leaned forward. "Pure luck."

"Hardly."

"The quill burst into flames. You might have brought the house down."

She snorted. "Tell me, do you come home every day and say to yourself, 'Thank God, today I was not savaged by wolves'? Or 'killed by a runaway carriage'?"

He yanked on his cravat. There was at least no way to make it look any worse. He would be passionate in bed, she was certain. Capable of gentleness, but more than able to set tenderness aside if the moment called for more. "There are no wolves in England."

"Precisely my point."

"But there are runaway carriages, and when I am in the presence of one, yes, I am grateful to continue among the living." He leaned back on his chair and raked his fingers through his hair. Such beautiful, thick hair. She wanted to run her fingers through his hair again. "Phosphorus is a dangerous substance."

"So is gunpowder. Have you removed every trace of it from your estate?"

"Of course not. There are precautions, Miss Wellstone."

"Thank you for making my point."

He stared at her. Lily stared back, and the heat between them had nothing to do with phosphorus pencils. "I've never covered a quill in the stuff and thrust it into the flames."

"What an absurd thing to say, your grace. Did you see me do that?"

"Tell me, Wellstone." He leaned back, arms crossed over his chest, legs apart. "If you were to survive a fall from a twenty-foot cliff, would you then presume you would be unharmed when you jumped the second time?"

"Argument by analogy is hardly logically sound."

"Yes it is." His eyes flashed. "But allow me to speak without resort to analogy. What I mean for you to understand is that this is my home, and I consider phosphorus to be an element so dangerous that I do not wish to have it present. With or without precautions. I don't want Eugenia, Miss Kirk, or Nigel to be injured. Or you, Lily." He spread his arms. "Is that unreasonable?"

"No, sir. It's not." She tapped her chin. She was aware that she'd been outmaneuvered and could not help admiring him for it. "I cannot disagree it must have been alarming to you to enter upon such a scene."

"Indeed."

"Without knowing the various precautions we followed."

"They were not sufficient."

"I admit that phosphorus is volatile." She fingered her medallion, smoothing a finger over the surface as was becoming a habit with her. "We followed the instructions almost without deviation. Lord Nigel was there, and if there had been any danger, I am confident he would have acted quickly to prevent harm from befalling anyone." She gestured. "It was a lark, your grace. You must have seen your sister. Before our phosphorus pencil caught fire, that is."

He nodded.

"She was laughing. How often have you seen her laugh since she came home? The entire project amused her, and that can only be good."

The duke relaxed a little on his chair, and Lily began to

hope she'd brought him round to her point of view. He fell silent a moment. "I've not seen her laugh like that for far too long."

"You see?" She leaned over far enough to pat his knee, and it was no surprise that his attention followed her bosom. Or that she felt that shivery sense of anticipation. "We do agree on something. That's lovely, isn't it?"

"It seems we do." Mountjoy stared at his thigh. And then at her, turning the full force of his gaze on her. She'd kissed him, and she wanted to again even though he wasn't Greer. She hadn't in all this time thought of another man in that way. So intimately.

"Can we not be friends?" she asked.

He did not answer straightaway. "Would you be as loyal to me as you are to my sister?"

Her heart tripped because his voice had gone softer. Not sweet so much as silky. It was the voice she heard in her dreams. That shivery sensation climbed inside her again, and she was hard-pressed not to melt in her seat. "If I find you deserving, yes, absolutely."

"I will endeavor to deserve your devotion, Wellstone."

Lily looked at him sideways. His face was perfectly bland. "You should not call me that."

"I would prefer, Wellstone," he went on in a voice that was oh so slightly less silky, "that you give the phosphorus to me for safekeeping. I will return it to you when your visit has concluded."

"You were not present to see the care we took."

He kept his thighs spread. "You failed to keep the quill wet."

"Lord Nigel reminded me." She reached for the jar and held it out to him. He had a point. This was his home and surely a man expected to make the rules in his own home. "Consider it a gift, your grace."

His eyebrows lifted. "A gift?"

"You needn't return it. I can always buy more when I am back at Syton House."

"I pray there is a local firefighting association."

"As a matter of fact there is. I donated the very newest engine."

He took the jar from her and slipped it into his pocket. She rose and he, too, stood. He offered her his arm. "Now that we have settled matters between us, may I escort you to the Oldenburg salon?"

Lily tucked her hand under his upper arm so that her fingers rested lightly on his biceps. If she kissed him again, would it be as wonderful? "You'll just have time to change before tea."

"I've already changed."

She very nearly laughed, but she had the good fortune to look at his face in time to stop herself. He was serious. "Do you mean to tell me, sir, that these are your best clothes?"

They reached the door before he answered. "No. These are among my most comfortable clothes."

"You have the oddest notion that fashionable clothes are necessarily uncomfortable ones. You are wrong." The duke reached for the knob. "A properly fitted suit not only makes the most of a man's assets, and yours are considerable, but it is also comfortable. Because it fits."

"I am perfectly at ease in these clothes."

"You're serious."

"Why wouldn't I be?"

"You really ought to hire me as your valet."

"Perhaps I ought."

She gestured at him, and he took a step nearer her. Away from the door. "As bad as that?" he said in that silky voice.

"Worse," she said. She grabbed a handful of his cravat and pulled his head to hers. His lips caught at hers, slanted over her mouth, and he parted her lips or, perhaps, he didn't have to.

Not a kiss between friends. Not at all.

Mountjoy's arm snaked around her waist, and he pulled her close. She ended up with her back pressed against the door and his forearms on either side of her head while they kissed each other as madly as they had before. More.

He wasn't gentle this time, and she was swept along, and by the time they separated, they were both breathing hard and she was weak behind the knees. "We can't do this, Wellstone," he said, his mouth inches from hers.

"No. Positively not," she whispered.

"Go. Go have tea, and give my regrets to Eugenia and Miss Kirk." He didn't release her, but even if he had, she wouldn't have moved.

"I'd rather stay here."

"Impossible." He pressed a kiss to her ear.

"It's the medallion," she said, arching her throat to give him the access he wanted. His lips slid along her shoulder. "We have no power to resist."

He rested his forehead on hers but managed to reach behind her and pull the door open enough that they had no choice but to move. "Damned magic."

"At the moment, I find it rather thrilling."

Mountjoy gave a low laugh. "It is at that. Go or I won't answer for the consequences."

# Chapter Eight

TWO DAYS LATER, LILY SAT WITH GINNY AT THE FAR
side of the Kirks' salon, listening to Miss Caroline Kirk play
the piano. Lily wore a gown of pale pink satin while Ginny
wore a frock that was at least not quite black. One took small
steps. There was no point in asking more of Ginny than she
was yet prepared to give. Gray, even a very dark gray, was
a triumph.

Jane Kirk sat beside her sister, turning pages. The middle
of the Kirk sisters, Miss Caroline, had only yesterday
returned from a visit to relatives in the north of England.
This gathering was a welcome-home for her. Most of the
High Tearing gentry were here on her behalf. Lord Nigel
sat a few rows nearer the front while Mountjoy sat closer to
the door, beside Mr. Kirk, who would one day be his
father-in-law. All in all, Lily thought the connection would
be a good one for both families. At the moment, Jane was
rather outmatched by Mountjoy, but that would change.

Miss Caroline was a better than excellent musician, and
Lily was glad that the room was comparatively quiet while

she played. She'd chosen a difficult piece by Scarlatti, and such was her talent that Lily had some time ago stopped worrying about whether she would make a mistake and was simply enjoying the music.

The salon door opened to admit a late arrival, but the butler, wisely, did not announce him. Nevertheless, Lily and several other guests turned for a better look at the latecomer. From the whispers, she gathered he was someone important. He looked to be in his late twenties, quite handsome and distinguished, but with a decidedly cold air about him. He reminded her of someone, but she couldn't think who.

The new arrival elected to stand near the door, well within her view as it happened. He surveyed the room as if he were searching for someone. Whoever he was, she approved of his taste in clothes. Heartily. Mountjoy could learn a thing or two from this stranger's example.

Whoever he was, though he took no sartorial risks, his clothes fit him to perfection. Even from where she sat, she could tell the fabrics were first-rate. The very best grade of wool and silk, the finest lawn for his shirt. His cravat was subdued yet folded and knotted to perfection. His boots gleamed and though there were no tassels, she felt the lack suited him. If his attire was a trifle severe, he'd relieved the effect by wearing an embroidered fob of an overly cheerful yellow. An intriguing whimsy.

When Caroline had done playing and the applause had not yet died down, Lily leaned to Ginny and whispered, "Don't be obvious"—she held Ginny's forearm to prevent her from turning around—"but do you know who that is? The gentleman who's just come in."

Under cover of adjusting her gown, Ginny glanced across the room. "Who?"

"With the yellow fob."

"I don't see anyone with a yellow fob."

"There. By the door. I've the strangest feeling I've met him before, but I can't think where."

Ginny frowned. "What's *he* doing here?"

"You *do* know who he is."

Ginny straightened. "Yes." Her lips thinned. "Lord Fenris."

Lily's heart frosted over. "Fenris, you say."

"Yes. He's Camber's heir."

"The Duke of Camber?"

Ginny rolled her eyes and huffed. "I don't know how anyone stands him."

"Camber?" Lily put her fingers over her mouth, then immediately lowered both her hands so that Ginny would not see her trembling.

"No, Lily. Fenris." Ginny looked over her shoulder and frowned in the man's direction. "Though I hear Camber is no better."

"Does Lord Fenris know one of the Kirks, do you suppose?"

Ginny turned her back on the man. "Mr. Kirk wouldn't keep a connection like that quiet. He'd have told Jane to marry Fenris instead of Mountjoy. Better if your son-in-law is to be the ten thousandth duke than merely the fourth."

"Perhaps he met Caroline while she was away, and she invited him?"

Ginny sniffed. "Poor Caroline Kirk if that's the case."

Feeling she needed to proceed carefully, she said, "Miss Caroline Kirk is an attractive girl. He might be here on her account, don't you think?"

"Fenris?" Ginny made a face. "Marry a Kirk? A mere Miss? He'd never stoop so low."

"I take it you don't like the man." Lily didn't know whether to feel she'd been vindicated or not.

"No," she said. She adjusted her shawl. "I'm sorry, I don't. Don't let his looks fool you, Lily." Ginny lowered her voice. "He's handsome enough, I'll grant you that, but Lord Fenris is a judgmental bore."

Lily glanced in Fenris's direction. "I wasn't aware you knew him well enough to have any opinion at all."

"I do," Ginny said with more passion than Lily had seen

from her since she'd arrived. "You can't go falling in love with him. You can't." She paused and then lowered her voice again. "I don't care how perfect his clothes or how handsome you think he is."

"In love?"

"Don't admit to a fault around that man unless you want a lecture on the evils of imperfect comportment. He once told Miss Abigail Archer she ought to think more and laugh less, and Abigail Archer is an absolutely delightful young lady."

"I'm sorry to hear that." Lily clasped her hands on her lap.

"What does it matter if she's prone to laugh too often? It's charming, if you ask me." She sniffed. "I wonder what he's doing here?"

"If he's no prior acquaintance with any of the Kirks, I fear there is only one possible reason for his presence here."

"Oh?" Ginny said.

Lily nodded soberly. Her heart remained frozen solid. "I expect he's here on account of me."

"But you didn't even know who he was." Ginny started to say something more, but a footman walked by with a tray, and she held back her comment.

People were leaving their seats and heading for the back of the room where servants were setting out food. Lily watched a footman enter with a salver of strawberries, but her attention returned to Fenris. Now that she could study him, there could be no doubt he was searching for someone.

"I am very much afraid Lord Fenris and his father mean to wrest control of my fortune from me."

"I don't understand," Ginny said. "Why would they want to do that?"

Fenris continued scanning the room, and Lily's heart thumped when she realized he was now looking over the area where she and Ginny sat. He did look at them, and she did not think she was mistaken that his attention paused, but whether he was looking at her, whom he had never in his life met, or at Ginny, whom he did know, was impossible to say.

He headed across the salon, but the flow of guests to the food impeded his progress. He hadn't got far when Mrs. Kirk intercepted him. He took her hand and bowed over it, and the cadences of their exchange, if not the specific words, floated over the sound of conversation. His manners were impeccable, she had to grant him that. Fenris broke free of Mrs. Kirk, and this time she could not doubt that he was headed toward her and Ginny.

Lily jumped up, grabbed Ginny's hand, and pulled her along to the back of the room, hoping to blend in with the crowd.

"Lily," Ginny said. "What on earth?"

From the corner of her eye, Lily saw Fenris adjust course. She zigged through the crowd and when she peeked again, Fenris had done the same. "What if he knows who I am? What if someone described me to him?"

"Good heavens. You're afraid of him." Ginny pulled on Lily's hand and they stopped. "Honestly afraid. If you're worried about Lord Fenris's intentions toward you, we ought to tell my brother. He will help you. He will."

"Lord Fenris and his father are my concern. Not his. Or yours."

"Lily." Ginny pressed her hand. "Lily, you are not alone. If Lord Fenris has made himself odious to you, Mountjoy will intervene on your behalf."

"Your brother has more important matters to deal with."

"He's just there." She glanced in Mountjoy's direction. "Tell him, Lily. He won't leave you to that odious man's mercy. You'll see."

Her heart stayed cold as ice. "If only he could help."

"But he will. I know he will. Why wouldn't he?"

"Because Lord Fenris is my cousin. One of my few relations, actually."

Ginny's mouth opened and for a moment no sound came

out. "Fenris? Is your cousin?" She groped behind her for a chair, found one, and sat down. "But how?"

She stayed close to Ginny, keeping her voice low. "The previous Duke of Camber was my mother's father."

Her eyes widened. "Your grandfather?"

"The present duke is my uncle. And that, I fear, makes Lord Fenris my cousin."

Ginny put a hand to her heart, her hand pale against the gray of her gown. "Lord Fenris? Your cousin?"

"My aunt Lily, I've told you about her—"

"She left you Syton House."

"To me, instead of Camber." The subject of her relation to the Duke of Camber was painful. She had years ago stopped thinking they would ever meet under any circumstances but unpleasant ones. "Aunt Lily was a Talbot before she married." Talbot being the Duke of Camber's family name.

Ginny, no fool she, tilted her head. "Ah."

Yes, Ginny understood. "Precisely."

"You poor thing, to be related to such a man."

Lily remained on her feet. They were only partially hidden by the guests, but for the moment at least, Fenris seemed to have lost sight of them, for he was now looking in the opposite direction from where they were. Because, she realized, Ginny was sitting down. She looked down at her friend. Wasn't that interesting? Was it possible her cousin was following Ginny and not her?

"Ginny, my dear. How is it you know Lord Fenris?"

Ginny's mouth thinned. "He was Robert's friend. Before we married."

"But not after?"

She looked at Lily and passion flashed in her eyes. "He did his best to stop Robert marrying me. He did not approve of me, you see. My brother, after all, was nothing but a farmer who, in his opinion, didn't deserve his title. And me? Why, I was only an ignorant country girl with designs on his friend."

"Much worse than a judgmental bore," Lily said with a nod.

"Why didn't you tell me"—Ginny twisted on her chair and looked behind them—"that such a hateful man is your relation?"

She shrugged. "I've never met my mother's family. They've never wanted to meet me. Camber and Fenris disapprove of me, too, you see. Because my father had married so far above his station. My father, they believe, did not deserve my mother. Just as Fenris believed you did not deserve Robert."

"Judgmental bores the lot of those Talbot men," Ginny said fiercely. "Well, whatever he's planning, he's not going to succeed." She squeezed Lily's hand again. "Don't look, but he's coming this way."

Lily froze. The idea of meeting her cousin when she was so thoroughly unprepared and with no notion of his immediate intentions unsettled her. If there was to be an unpleasant confrontation, let it not be here, in front of Ginny's friends. "Fenris?"

"No, Lily." Ginny touched Lily's arm. "Mountjoy. Behind you."

"Eugenia." Mountjoy's voice wound around Lily's senses. "Miss Wellstone."

She turned and curtseyed to the duke. His coat was the wrong color of blue for his waistcoat. "Your grace."

Without warning, Ginny shot from her chair and threw an arm around Lily's shoulder, putting her mouth by Lily's ear. "Pretend you are about to faint."

"I've never swooned in my life."

"Didn't you say you once wanted to be an actress?" Ginny looked over her shoulder again. "Swoon, Lily, or you will meet Fenris now and there will be an awful scene. Do you want that here? In front of everyone?"

Lily believed in action with conviction. Half measures only made things worse. Therefore, she grabbed the back of a chair and went limp with the intention of landing, ever so delicately and safely, on the chair.

"Mountjoy," Ginny said. "Thank goodness you're here. Help."

Lily found herself not on the chair but enfolded by the duke's arms. There was nothing for it now but to see the thing through.

"Oh, dear!" Ginny spoke too loudly. "She needs fresh air, Mountjoy. Do help her outside."

Mountjoy, already supporting her, swung Lily into his arms. She willed herself boneless in his embrace. Her head lolled back, and one arm dangled toward the floor.

"Mrs. Kirk," Lily heard Ginny say as Mountjoy carried her out. "Yes, yes. I know. I don't know. Thank goodness my brother was here. The crowd, you understand. Stifling. So many people in the room. A little fresh air, I think . . ."

Ginny's voice faded. By the time Mountjoy had carried her out of the salon, however, Ginny had caught up with them. Lily cracked open one eye and caught a glimpse of Ginny's gray gown as the duke moved away from the gathering. She opened a door for her brother. In an excess of caution, in case they were followed, God forbid, by the hateful Lord Fenris, Lily remained limp against Mountjoy's broad chest until they were inside.

Mountjoy said, "Eugenia?"

Lily bestirred herself and, still in Mountjoy's arms, reached for Ginny's hand. "Thank you, Ginny. You are a good friend. The very best."

"As are you, Lily." Ginny patted her brother's shoulder. "Look after her, Mountjoy. Do not under any circumstances leave her alone. I'll be back as soon as possible." Ginny left, pulling the door closed behind her. Mountjoy looked down, and Lily blinked at him.

They were alone. The door was closed, and Lily was far too aware of the impropriety of that. The duke drew in a breath and put her down on a small and infernally maroon sofa. He took a step back. "Have you a vinaigrette?"

She looked around and shuddered. "I am wearing entirely the wrong colors to be in this room. My God, whoever thought maroon was anything but a hue with which to accent?"

"A mystery," Mountjoy said.

"Indeed, sir." She left the sofa for the window but stood sideways so she could see Mountjoy. He was so very handsome, and she could not stop thinking that they were alone. *Alone.*

"If you're not well, are you certain you should be on your feet?"

She pushed aside the curtains to get a better view of the garden. "You know perfectly well there's nothing wrong with me."

He crossed his arms over his chest. "You could have a career on the stage, Miss Wellstone. I was convinced you'd lost your senses."

She turned her head to glare at him, but his comment was so beautifully double-edged that she couldn't help but be impressed. And amused. "I would have been ashamed if you had not been. At my father's home when I was a girl, I mean, not Syton House. I was renowned for my Ophelia. I had her every line memorized before I was ten. I did Lady Macbeth, too. My father lived in fear of my running away whenever a traveling troupe came into town."

The curtains, the same unfortunate maroon as the sofa, were giving her a headache. The view, on the other hand, was spectacular. She thought of Ginny, facing Lord Fenris on her own. She was a Wellstone and not ashamed of her family or herself. Let him stare down his aristocratic nose at her and tell the world she was non compos mentis or whatever nefarious scheme he planned to carry out.

"If there's nothing wrong with you, dare I ask, Miss Wellstone, what your most impressive swoon was meant to achieve?"

"I wished to avoid Lord Fenris." She smoothed her skirts and gazed out the window. She would never be free of the hatred between the Talbots and the Wellstones if she ran at the first possibility of a confrontation.

"I meant to warn Eugenia he was here," he said, "but it seems that's unnecessary." Mountjoy joined her, standing behind her, too close if anyone should see them, and not close enough. "I know my sister has no reason to like the man, but has he done something to upset you as well?"

"You might say so."

"Will you?"

"Your grace." She put her back to the window and told him the history between her and Lord Fenris. She could see him making all sorts of mental leaps of logic. "Naturally my father objected to my correspondence with my mother's sister. He never forgets a slight done him. Speak a word to him in anger and twenty years later he will repeat to you the exact circumstances of the offense. He regularly reminds me of all of mine, and there were many." She looked up at the duke. "I am now more than a quarter of a century old, and he has held a grudge against my mother's relations since before I was born. I can only marvel, sir, at his tenacity. My maternal grandfather is no longer living, and my father cannot and, I assure you, will never forgive any relative of the man who disowned my mother for marrying him."

"Ah."

"I could not tell him my mother had maintained a secret correspondence with my great-aunt any more than I could confess I'd carried on as she did. If he had known, he would have forbidden it, and I would know nothing of my mother's life."

"And he would never forgive you."

"No. He would not. And does not." She crossed her arms and tapped one finger on her upper arm. "Even so, I was betrayed. After a fashion."

"How so?"

"She meant me no harm, you understand. Quite the opposite. But when Aunt Lily passed on, she left me Syton House. My father was furious. That I had been rewarded for my treachery only made it worse, you see."

His expression stayed thoughtful. "Her legacy to you cost you your father. The only family you had left."

The enormity of his understanding shook her. No one, not even Ginny, had understood what it had meant to lose her father, even though he'd never been the sort of loving family she knew Ginny had grown up with. All she could do was nod.

"Syton House." Mountjoy rubbed one cheek. "Quite a legacy, I'd say."

"The disaster was total. She left me everything and destroyed Camber's hopes of combining her fortune with his."

"Everything?"

She sighed. "Eighty-six thousand pounds and two estates besides Syton House. One in Scotland, a castle near Edinburgh, and another estate in Kent."

His eyebrows rose.

"They are leased with fifty more years remaining. I make a tidy sum on them both. I don't have any expectation that I will be forgiven for that from any quarter. I do believe my father would be a happier man if I were reduced to living under a tree."

"Why would you ever go home to him? Why not travel the world until he passes to his reward? Let him live in another of your houses."

She shrugged. "He is my father, and the only person I know who remembers my mother. Sometimes he'll even tell me about her. Things I never knew because I can hardly remember her. When he does, I begin to understand why she married him, for he loved her beyond life. There was room for only one love in his life; my mother. Just as Greer was the only love for me."

Mountjoy cocked his head and, after considering her a moment, said, "Shall I ask Lord Fenris to leave? Or would you prefer I take you home?" He put a hand on her shoulder, and Lily's senses focused on that contact between them. His fingers curved over her, touching her gown and bare skin, too. Her heart beat too fast. "To Bitterward, I mean." She faced him, and in so doing, his hand fell away from her. He meant nothing by that casual touch. They were close enough to touch again. But neither of them moved. "What are you thinking?" Mountjoy asked.

She could not remember a time when any man had made her so relentlessly aware that she was a woman. The man made the back of her knees positively weak. "Nothing."

He laughed, and her belly tightened. "Wellstone. The day you are thinking of nothing is the day the world ends."

"Very well." She shook her head, amused by him. "I am imagining myself calmly telling Lord Fenris that I am indeed his cousin and that if he chooses to withdraw from High Tearing on account of my being an unwanted connection, that is his choice to make. He will leave, mortified and secretly happy with his narrow escape, and that will be that."

"Begging your pardon, but that does not sound like you. Or Fenris."

"No?" She resisted the urge to touch him. "More likely, he'll accuse me of stealing his watch. Or his gloves. Or perhaps his horse. That's a hanging offense."

Mountjoy snorted. "I very much doubt he plans that."

"You know what he's like. What he did to Ginny. Or nearly did. Why else would he be here, if not to pursue his family's vendetta against mine?"

"Coincidence?"

"My attorney once warned me Camber might try to declare me mentally incompetent."

Mountjoy frowned.

"Camber wants Aunt Lily's legacy. He thinks it should have gone to him. Or to Fenris."

"My God, you're serious."

"You've no idea the rancor he holds toward me. I didn't think he'd ever give up." She glanced away. "I don't think he did. Not really. He's been biding his time." She laughed

softly. "Thank goodness Camber never spoke to my father.
If he had, he might have found grounds."

He frowned again. "Would your father allow such a thing
to happen?"

"Perhaps not deliberately."

Mountjoy didn't answer right away, but he continued to
frown. "I can take you home if you'd rather not meet Fenris
today."

"Thank you, your grace." She touched his sleeve. "That's
kind of you. But not necessary."

He cocked his head, a thoughtful expression on his face.
"It might be wiser to meet him at Bitterward where you are
surrounded by friends and people he cannot bully as easily
as he must hope to bully you."

At first, she thought that by *friends* he meant Ginny, but
then she realized he meant more than that. Just as Ginny
had promised, he was extending an offer of his personal
support. In all her life, she had never had anywhere to look
for assistance but to herself and those whom she hired to
act on her behalf. The idea that Mountjoy intended to help
her was as disconcerting as it was astonishing. "You mean
that."

He regarded her in silence. Lily held her breath, expecting any moment that he would withdraw his offer or chastise
her for putting him to such an inconvenience.

"I do," he said. "You are my sister's friend. My friend as
well, if I am permitted to be so bold. Even if you were not,
I would not leave any woman to the mercy of Lord Fenris.
Certainly not you." He smoothed the front of his coat. Not
that it did any good. Nothing would improve the appearance
of his coat. "Not while you are under my roof. Even if you
weren't, I should hope you'd know you could appeal to me
for assistance."

Lily swallowed the lump in her throat. She didn't care if
he dressed as if he'd never set foot in a tailor's shop. His
support touched her deeply. "Thank you, your grace." She

swallowed the lump in her throat. "But I think I ought to meet him now, if only to give him a face to go with the devil's spawn he's been imagining all these years."

"I'll go with you. To make the introduction."

Tears jammed up in her throat and further words were impossible. All she could do was nod her agreement.

"We will present him a united front of persons of whom he can disapprove all he likes and to no avail."

She wanted to thank him, but if she spoke she'd sound as if she were crying, and she never cried. Instead, she nodded.

"Very well then." Mountjoy headed for the door, but Lily, having mastered herself, stopped him from opening it. To know that she was not alone made more difference to her than she would have believed.

"Best let me go first," she said.

He nodded, and she reached for the door. As she pulled it toward her, the metal knob came off in her hand. She didn't understand at first what had happened, only that the door remained closed. "How odd."

"What is it?" Mountjoy said from behind her.

She showed him the doorknob. "I've broken the door."

# Chapter Nine

"BROKEN? HOW CAN THE DOOR BE BROKEN?" Mount-joy took the bit of metal she handed him in answer. While he examined it, Miss Wellstone tried again to open the door.

"I've never seen anything like it," he said. The metal had sheared clean off, leaving only the brass plate affixed to the door. He looked up when she let out a frustrated huff. "What?"

"I am unable to open the door."

His first inkling of disaster hit. He clutched the broken doorknob. "What do you mean?"

"I mean, my dear Duke," Miss Wellstone said a bit too evenly, "that when Ginny left, she closed the door, and with the knob no longer attached, there is no way to open it."

"Allow me." Mountjoy dropped the doorknob into his pocket and examined the faceplate. The metal was smooth except where the knob had been attached, and only the smallest bits of twisted metal remained behind. She was right. Without the broken-off knob, there would be no easy way to pull the door open.

"My hands are smaller than yours. Perhaps I can grasp a bit of the metal." She stripped off her gloves, and he took them from her while she bent to the door. Her tongue appeared at the corner of her mouth.

"Caution, Wellstone. It's sharp."

"Thank you for that reminder of the obvious." She arranged her fingers over the spot where the knob had been attached and pulled. The door moved forward an infinitesimal amount, then her fingers slipped. "Drat."

Mountjoy didn't think anything except that she had failed to open the door until she hissed and caught her left hand in her right. Blood welled between her fingers. "You've hurt yourself."

"It's nothing." She looked at him, eyes wide, features so impossibly delicate, now ashen because she had hurt herself and was trying to hide it. His chest tightened.

"It's not nothing." He reached for her hand. "How bad is it?"

"I don't know," she said.

"Let me see." He caught her injured hand in his. The moment she released her grip on her fingers, blood flowed even faster from a cut along the side and across the pad of her index finger, covering her skin in brilliant red. He pulled out his handkerchief and wrapped it around her fingers. Blood soaked through almost immediately. "I ought not have let you near the door."

"I am an experienced door opener, I'll have you know."

He glared at the door. There were other reasons to get them out of here as quickly as possible, but her injury was the most pressing at the moment. "Do you see the key anywhere? I might be able to use that as a lever to pull the door forward enough to open it."

"Brilliant idea."

The key, however, was nowhere by the door, and they both looked.

Mountjoy scowled. "If it fell from the lock, I'm dashed if I can see where it landed."

"Do you suppose it could be in a drawer somewhere?"

If they weren't able to open the door in the next five minutes, he was going to have to call for help with all the unpleasant ramifications that such a public action entailed. Jesus, the house was full of people. And that prig Fenris, who probably already thought the worst of Lily, would have his prejudices confirmed. Should they be discovered alone, in a room that had been closed against intruders, scandal would be the inevitable result. At least he liked her well enough. More than well enough. He got on well with Lily. If it came to that.

*If.*

"Why," he said with more tartness than was required, "would someone put the key anywhere but in the door?"

"Look around you, your grace, what do you see?"

He was helpless to act except in a way that would not please either of them, and he was not a man prone to help-lessness in anything. "Furniture. A window. An average room."

"Are you blind?" She winced and brought her hand closer to her body. "The room is maroon, sir."

"What's that to do with anything?" The handkerchief around her hand was more red than white now. He stripped off his gloves and tried to get some kind of leverage on the decorative metal plate, but his hands were too big and the bits left of the doorknob were far too small and razor sharp besides.

"I regret to say," she said in a thin voice, "that anyone who would decorate a room with such a singular lack of consideration to what is pleasing and restful to the eye is not likely to have been sensible about where the key ought to be kept. You'd best pray Miss Kirk has better taste than her mother."

He ignored the dig, but, Lord, the thought of anyone having a hand in making over Bitterward gave him the shivers. "I'll look again, then." He walked to a highboy and opened a drawer at about his waist height on the theory that the key wouldn't be kept inconveniently high or low. "How is your hand?"

"Better." From the corner of his eyes, he saw her study the room, gripping her handkerchief-wrapped fingers and tapping her toe. "It wouldn't have to be the key to the door would it?" she asked.

"Of course it would."

Lily walked to a secretaire. "Why? The door is not locked. All we need is leverage. Any key, any object capable of catching in the lock will do."

He shut another drawer of the highboy and acknowledged that with a tight nod. "Quite so."

With both hands, she pointed to the key sticking in the upper lock of the desk. "This one will do nicely I should think."

If he did have to marry her, he was unlikely to be bored anytime soon. Exasperated, yes. Amused, often. But bored? Never. "Quick thinking, Wellstone. Please"—he strode to her—"don't use your hand. I'll get it." He extracted the key from the secretaire. A tassel of reddish purple silk hung from the end. He didn't like the color much himself, but what did he know? As he wriggled the key into the lock, someone knocked on the door.

Lily understood the seriousness of the moment, for she stood beside him, quite still and silent. Not that it mattered who it was. At this point, his duty was to get her out of here to have her injury looked after and never mind explaining why he had been closeted away with an unmarried lady.

"Lily?"

That was Eugenia's voice. Thank God.

"Yes, Ginny, I'm here."

"Is everything all right?"

"Yes, yes. Tell me, Ginny, is anyone there with you? Or are you alone?"

"I am not alone."

He and Lily exchanged a look. "It can't be helped, Wellstone," he said in a low voice.

"Ah," Lily said for Eugenia's benefit. Her somber nod of understanding was for his benefit. "If you wouldn't mind opening the door, there's been a malfunction of some sort. We are not currently able to open it from this side."

"Oh, dear."

Mountjoy put an arm around Lily's waist and drew her away. "Be so good as to open the door, Eugenia."

The door rattled, then moved smoothly inward, and Eugenia walked in, one hand on the side of the door. Lord Fenris and Mr. Kirk came in behind her. Eugenia took one look at Lily's hand and blanched. "What happened?" She whirled to him. "Mountjoy, what happened?"

"Shall I fetch a doctor?" Fenris asked. He pulled out his handkerchief and, as Mountjoy had done, handed it to Lily.

"Thank you, my lord." Lily gave him a nod and wrapped Fenris's handkerchief around her hand.

"That's blood," Mr. Kirk said. "Blood all over your hand."

"Yes, sir, it is. I had the misfortune of doing myself an injury."

Mr. Kirk turned the color of chalk. His eyes rolled up in his head. He wasn't a tall man, but he made considerable noise when he hit the floor and landed at Lily's feet.

"Someone had best call a doctor," she said, staring down at the insensible Mr. Kirk.

"Dr. Longfield is here somewhere," Eugenia said. "Perhaps we ought to fetch him."

Lord Fenris crouched and patted Mr. Kirk's cheek. The man did not respond. "An excellent notion, Mrs. Bryant. I'll see to him until the doctor has looked after Miss Wellstone."

"Thank you," Lily said. "That's very kind of you." She walked briskly past Fenris and Kirk. "You can't imagine how badly it hurts, Ginny." Her voice trembled, though Mountjoy could not help the impression that she was, at last, exaggerating her injury and the pain she was in. Eugenia put an arm around her shoulders. Lily shuddered. "Imagine the horror if blood had gotten on my gown. And yes, let's do find Dr. Longfield. Quickly. I believe I'm feeling faint."

Mountjoy watched Lily and Eugenia walk down the hallway, their heads together. "Thank God the man passed out," Fenris said from his position at Kirk's side.

"Why is that?"

"I suspect he'll not recall that you were alone with Miss Wellstone." He stood. Slowly. "I, however, will not."

He gazed at the marquess. "Nothing happened, Fenris."

Fenris ran the bottom of his thumb over his fingernails. "That's never the point where scandal is concerned, is it? Your grace."

"I don't give a bloody damn what rumors you start, Fenris."

"Gossip can be quite vicious."

"I'll marry her if I must."

The marquess flinched. "Where I am concerned, you are, for now, both safe from that fate." Kirk moaned, and Fenris hauled him to his feet. "You might wish to make yourself scarce."

Mountjoy walked away and waited in another corridor where he counted to one hundred before he returned to the salon. On the way there, he stopped a servant and ordered his carriage to be brought around. He found Nigel and let him know they would be returning to Bitterward.

Not long after Mountjoy's unexceptional return to the salon, there was a commotion that proved to be Lily returning with Dr. Longfield. Her injured finger was done up in a plaster. Eugenia walked at her side, an arm around her waist. He met them halfway.

"She'll have an aching finger tonight, your grace," Dr. Longfield said. "A glass of your best sherry will go a long way to relieving her discomfort."

"Thank you."

Longfield continued to address Mountjoy. "I'll call in a day or two to confirm everything's going well with my most beautiful patient. Put a fresh plaster on it tomorrow and don't hesitate to send for me if anything seems amiss."

Mountjoy nodded. "I will."

The doctor left to attend to Mr. Kirk, and Mountjoy took that opportunity to tell them he'd ordered the carriage. Lily said nothing, but he thought both women looked relieved to have avoided another encounter with Fenris. Their good luck did not last, for just as they reached the stairs that would lead to the entrance hall, Fenris intercepted them.

"Your grace," he said, bowing to Mountjoy. For a man who had done nothing to make himself agreeable to Mountjoy or his siblings, he had some nerve accosting them. Fenris looked between Eugenia and Miss Wellstone, but his attention lingered on Eugenia. Mountjoy, well aware of the role Fenris had played in attempting to convince Robert Bryant not to marry Eugenia, silently counted to ten. The urge to plant his fist in the man's face did not fade. "Mrs. Bryant."

Eugenia, whom Mountjoy had never in his life seen cut anyone, turned her back on Fenris. Lily said nothing. Fenris blanched, but that was the only sign that he was affected by Eugenia's refusal to acknowledge him. Could he truly have expected anything else from her when his offense against her was so grave?

The marquess bowed to Lily. "Cousin."

Mountjoy kept his hand on Lily's elbow. He didn't like the man, and now that he knew of his relationship to Lily, he liked him even less. "We are on our way out, Fenris."

"I shan't detain you long," he replied.

A flash of irritation passed over Eugenia's face. "Mountjoy, we ought to go now. Lily is not well at all. She's had a shock."

Fenris took an abortive step forward. "Miss Wellstone," he said quickly. "Did you know you look very much like your grandmother? And mine."

"How would I know such a thing?" Lily said, her words clipped.

Fenris paled.

"Enough is enough, my lord." Mountjoy shifted so that he stood between Lily and her cousin. "Another time you might be welcome. But not now."

The marquess gave them both a curt nod and once again, his gaze slid from Lily to linger on Eugenia. Did the man still resent her for her marriage to Robert Bryant? Mountjoy found himself making a fist of his free hand. He would not allow anyone to cause Eugenia any more pain. Most especially not this man. Bloody officious prig.

Fenris bowed again. "Your leave, Mrs. Bryant. Mountjoy." He hesitated, as close as Mountjoy had ever seen to uncertainty. "Cousin Lily."

"Good day," Mountjoy said.

They left Fenris standing at the top of the stairs. Quite alone.

At the front door, Mountjoy took the doorknob out of his pocket and handed it to the Kirks' butler. "You'll want to have this repaired."

Lord Fenris, Mountjoy thought as he handed his sister and Lily into his carriage, had not behaved like a man who despised his estranged cousin. Quite the opposite.

# Chapter Ten

HAVING FINISHED VOLUME ONE OF THE NOVEL SHE'D
selected the night of her arrival, Lily made her way to the
library in search of the second volume. She carried a lantern
in one hand and the first volume of her novel in the other.
She had not bothered yet to dress for bed and still wore the
gown she'd worn at supper, a sumptuous white silk trimmed
with lace she'd tatted herself last winter at Syton House.
Amid the lace were gold gauze flowers no larger than her
littlest fingernail that she'd spent most of one Easter week
making. Similar flowers around the hem complimented the
burgundy bodice. Her slippers were white satin embroidered
with matching burgundy flowers picked with tiny gold
accents.

Pearls were her jewelry of choice tonight: at her ears, her
throat, and even a strand wound through her hair and one on
the first finger of her left hand. Her injured hand was not yet
healed enough for jewelry. She'd changed the ribbon of her
Gypsy medallion to a white silk that matched her ensemble.
Her shawl was white cashmere embroidered with gold silk

and gold accents to match her slippers. Even at four-thirty in the morning, one ought to look one's best.

In the library, she set the lantern on the table nearest the bookcase where the novels were shelved. She kept her volume in hand while she admired the room. The ceiling, though not visible at its highest point, was the original Gothic structure, vaulted with structural ribs that supported the central dome. One of these days she would add a sketch of this library to her growing collection of architecturally interesting structures and rooms. There were no windows here, and what walls were not covered with shelves were carved stone. In one such corner stood a suit of armor, supported by a stand and polished to a sheen. Upon closer inspection, she found some wag had placed a book of poetry in its upraised steel hand.

She stood before the armor, rapt. Which ancestor of the duke's had last covered himself in all that metal and ridden to battle? A dent marred the chest plate, a small defect near where the man's ribs must have been. She imagined Mountjoy's ancestor standing beside his destrier, sword in his hand, defending himself—no—attacking his enemy.

Footsteps echoed in the corridor. She recognized that determined stride, having by now heard it on those occasions when the duke was home. She was therefore prepared when she faced the doorway. The shiver down her spine was familiar, too.

Mountjoy appeared in the doorway but stopped without stepping over the threshold.

"Good evening, your grace," she said.

He leaned against the side of the doorway, looking, for once, especially dashing in a luxurious midnight blue silk banyan. Gold embroidery of Arabian flair decorated the fabric. The banyan was nipped in close around his arms and chest, though he'd not closed the garment but left it open to show his waistcoat and shirt. The silk fell to the tops of his shoes, draping in a way that came only from superior workmanship. And the colors. Blue and gold were luscious on him. His waistcoat was a match for the banyan, with the same fabric and embroidery, by which she assumed banyan and waistcoat had been purchased as a set.

"Wellstone."

She wanted to drink him in, caress that gorgeous fabric, and tell him how very lovely he looked. Instead, she pointed to the corner. "Do you know, sir, when that suit of armor was last worn?"

His eyes followed the direction of her arm. "March the twenty-ninth, fourteen and sixty-one."

"The Battle of Towton?"

He nodded. "It was." He used his shoulder to push himself upright. "You know your history."

"I do, your grace." She didn't say so, but she appreciated that he was not bothered by her historical knowledge. It had been her unhappy experience that some men disliked the mere hint of erudition in a woman. As a child, there had been little for her to do but read what books were in her father's library. Books of history, for the most part. And a great many treatises on architecture. She had become expert in both subjects. Had it not been for the housekeeper taking pity on her she might never have learned more feminine occupations.

"An ancestor of mine fought at Towton. He took an arrow in the thigh."

"Was he badly hurt?"

"Not enough to keep him from continuing to fight. He was loyal to King Edward." He walked in. "Up late as usual I see."

His coming so near set off tingles in her chest and the backs of her knees. One of the inappropriate dreams she'd begun having, now for several nights running, had as its setting this very library.

"You don't sleep well," he said in his smoke-edged tenor. "Why is that?"

"Why does the sun rise in the morning and set at night? Because the world is made that way." She shrugged. "I am not made to sleep at night. Since I shall be up one or two more hours at least, I've come down to fetch the next volume of the novel I selected the night I arrived."

"You are enjoying the story?"

"Very much. It's quite exciting."

"Then you did take something thrilling from the library that night."

"I did, sir." She wasn't sure whether she ought to respond to the suggestion that lurked in his comment. "The heroine, Miss Quince, has been attacked by banditti whilst escaping from her uncle who wishes to force her to marry his odious son. She is in love, sir, with a poor young man who possesses a noble brow. I suspect the author's use of *noble* is no accident and that he is a prince in disguise. Or else unaware of his heritage."

"And vast fortune."

"Indeed." She smiled, pleased to have him join in. "I further suspect that the captain of the banditti is the brother she believes was lost at sea when she was a girl."

He kept walking toward her. She did enjoy watching him move. He was a graceful man. The most shocking notions came to mind while she did, and really, where those thoughts came from did not bear examination. Him nude, bending to kiss a woman, moments from sliding into her willing body. As he had slid into hers in her dreams. More than once.

Her experience with Greer had taught her just how much she adored the male physique. Even though she'd not been with anyone since, there were times she longed for intimacy, for the pleasure a man's body could give. There had been occasions when she'd thought even a man she did not love would do. The Duke of Mountjoy put just those sorts of thoughts into her head.

"What *are* you thinking, Wellstone?" His banyan shimmered in the light. This was the sort of fabric he ought to wear all the time, rich and flattering to his coloring and features.

"Nothing I will confess to you, sir."

He was now in front of the suit of armor and mere inches from her. Lily was nearly five feet and ten inches, and

Mountjoy was at least two inches taller than she. He gazed at her.

More wicked thoughts occurred to her, more images from her dream, more forbidden longings. Whatever might happen, she would be safe. The Duke of Mountjoy was a decent man who had no expectations of her outside of this room. Her fortune was of no consequence to him. To him, her family connections meant nothing. Before much longer she would go home to Syton House, and if she had lovely memories of Mountjoy to add to her visit, then she would be a lucky woman indeed.

"Dr. Longfield is right. Your eyes are very fine. Full of life and spirit."

"Good heavens," she managed, somehow, to reply in a cool voice. She did not feel about him the way she'd felt about Greer, and he had no deep feelings for her, either. They could flirt in this way that was not innocent and have no fear of unwanted entanglements. "Was that a compliment buried in there?"

"Yes."

"Thank you. To you and Dr. Longfield." Her belly tightened. She'd worked so hard to suppress her attraction to him and all that simply vanished. He filled the room with his presence. She wanted to touch him. Yearned to touch him. To taste his skin, his mouth, feel his hair beneath her fingers, his breath warm against her skin.

"When I was in town this afternoon I happened to see him. He asked after you."

"I hope you told him I'm well."

"I did. He then described your eyes to me at length, but he was certain they were black."

"Why on earth would he say anything at all about my eyes?" She walked away from him, heading for the shelves. "It was my finger he treated."

"I've no idea. But one wants to know such things precisely," he said. "When one is forced to listen to a man prattle on for the better part of half an hour about a woman's eyes. Could my memory be faulty, and your eyes are black? Or some other color entirely?"

She clutched her book. He had a way of making even a large room feel small. "Five minutes or twenty-five, I observe that he did not trouble himself to discover their actual color."

"I grant you that." He didn't quite smile, but there was a lightening of his countenance that suggested he might. She resisted taking a step back when the duke took a step forward. Under no circumstances would she retreat from this spot. She intended to stand here as if her slippers were glued to the floor. "What color are they? Let me see, Wellstone."

She lifted her chin and opened her eyes as wide as she could. "As you can see, a very common brown, your grace."

He took her book from her while she blinked to recover her vision. What he did with the book she had no notion whatever. "There's nothing common about you."

Since he was so close, she put her hands on his chest. She knew immediately she oughtn't have. Because everything changed. Her world was no longer safe. Mountjoy tensed, but he didn't move away. He stayed just where he was, his moss green eyes on her face. The silk beneath her palms was as rich as she'd imagined.

"This is lovely," she said, stroking the material. "You look a god in this."

"A god?" His low voice sent a thrill through her, a warmth that centered in her belly.

"Yes." She left her hand on his chest. "Arrayed in gold befitting your status as a deity."

"It was a gift from a friend who traveled to Anatolia."

What could he mean but a former lover? Of course he had had lovers in his life. A man of his great physicality must have lovers. "Was she very beautiful?"

The distance between them became smaller yet, and that made her pulse leap. A hint of citrus clung to his skin. "Why do you assume it was a woman?"

She curled her fingers around the lapels of his banyan, just beneath his chin, and that was the moment that sealed her fate, because he still did not move away. And she didn't want to. She didn't. Because she wanted to kiss Mountjoy. And more. The anticipation was delicious. "Wasn't it?"

"No." He smiled, and it killed her to see the curve of his mouth, the tender shape of his lower lip. He had kissed other women. Taken them in his arms and whispered endearments to them.

"I hate them all," she said. "Your previous lovers. All the women you've held and loved."

"You shouldn't."

She leaned forward, dizzy with the images in her head and the longing for him to do . . . something.

"The friend who gave me this was a man," he said. "I met him not long after I came into my title. He was in the army at the time and was soon after deployed near Constantinople. He's only recently retired to the English countryside where he lives a very dull existence, so he tells me."

"He has exquisite taste." She stroked the silk, traced one of the sumptuous patterns embroidered in the fabric of his waistcoat. "You need more clothes like this."

"My valet, Wellstone, says much the same thing." He didn't move. Neither did she. "He's in raptures whenever I wear this."

He was going to kiss her. She knew it and wanted it. Desired his mouth on hers beyond anything. Lily tightened her hands on his lapels. His head came nearer to hers, and she made sure to meet him. She closed her eyes in anticipation. But there was no brush of his lips against her, and she looked at him through her lashes.

One of his hands cupped the nape of her neck. So warm. His thumb slid toward her jaw. "Horrible man," she whispered.

His hand moved along her jaw, and then his thumb brushed the line of her lower lip. "Are you sure?"

"Yes. You're horrible." She rolled her eyes. "I shan't fall in love with you, your grace."

"I don't expect you will," the duke said in a soft voice.

She wouldn't. She couldn't. Her heart had died with Greer. "You won't fall in love with me, either."

"No." He laughed. "Given our mutual defects in respect of our hearts, tell me, what would you like to happen between us?"

"I've been thinking about that these ten minutes at least."

His arm tightened around her. "Something shocking?"

She leaned closer. "You don't strike me as a man easily shocked."

He laughed, low and throaty. "I swoon, Wellstone." He continued touching her face, but his other hand now rested on her waist, very near her hip. "But I shall endeavor to bear up."

"I want you to make love to me."

There. She'd put words to the feelings building in her.

His hand had moved up to cover the side of her face and then angled down until his first three fingers were underneath her chin. His eyes stayed locked with hers. "You relieve my mind."

"Indeed?"

"I'd begun to think I'd put on this banyan for nothing."

"You wore this for me?"

A grin pulled at his mouth. "You are welcome to see the matter in that light, yes."

"Oh, you are horrible." She tugged on his lapels. "I wish you weren't so tall," she said. "I thought I liked that about you, but I don't. Not in the least."

"Is this better?" He lowered his head to hers.

At last.

At last his mouth brushed hers.

Lily opened her mouth and kissed him, and he made a sound in the back of his throat and kissed her back. Before she was quite ready for the contact to end, she pushed him back. "Aren't you worried we'll end badly?"

"Yes." He pulled her closer. "But right now I don't give a farthing for that."

She didn't either.

## Chapter Eleven

AS A LOVER—POTENTIAL LOVER—LILY WAS UNFA-
miliar to him and he was, quite honestly, overcome with
sensation. The entire time he was sticking his tongue down
her throat and sliding his hands over all the parts of a lady
a gentleman never touched, he understood he was crossing
a line that shouldn't be crossed. The knowledge aroused him
even more.

Her skin was warm and her mouth hot beneath his, the
shape of her body against his undeniably feminine. She
tasted good and smelled even better, violets again, sweet
and delicate.

No, at the moment, he didn't give a damn that he shouldn't
be doing this. He wanted her, and he meant to have her.

She kissed him just as hungrily as he kissed her, and
when both his hands cupped her arse, she tightened her arms
around him and pressed harder against him, as if she
couldn't get enough either.

He entertained thoughts of laying her on the table, throwing up her skirts, and getting himself between her legs.

Would she object? Would she let him take her right here? Now? With just this desperate kissing and touching before they got there?

Then she moved back a step, not far because she was still kissing him like the angel she resembled. Heavenly. She removed a hand from his shoulders, and he prepared himself for an end to whatever was going on between them. Only he didn't want to stop kissing her yet. Not yet.

Her hand slipped between them, inside his banyan that she so admired and then along the fall of his trousers. Her fingers, damn the woman, slid very deliberately over the top of his cock, tracing the shape, and it just couldn't be his good fortune that she was touching him there. Like that.

Miss Lily Wellstone couldn't possibly be a virgin.

Neither was he.

Wasn't that a happy coincidence?

Indeed, yes.

Her fingers curved around his cock, pressing gently, stroking up, then down, and he could feel his eyes crossing behind his closed lids. When a woman caressed a man's prick like that, surely she was at least thinking about fucking him. Please, God, let her want to fuck him here and now. He took her head between his hands and tilted her face toward his to get a better angle on her mouth. There wasn't anything refined about the way he was kissing her. Or she him.

She unfastened one of the buttons at the fall of his trousers and then another, and the whole time she did that, part of him was thinking he really shouldn't let his happen, not with his sister's friend, but more of him was thinking he'd come to the library for reasons that weren't pure and he was lucky, lucky, lucky for that. Then all such thoughts faded to nothing because now he thought if she stopped he'd go out of his mind.

Mountjoy sucked in a breath when her bare fingers touched his belly and then, God help him, curled around his member. He nipped at her mouth, but his concentration was on what was going on with his prick and her hand. Little else existed. At some point he became aware she was pushing him back, toward the table, and he went along with that, kissing her the entire time.

Out of control. Beyond wicked. Bloody arousing.

He ended up sitting on the reading table with her standing between his spread thighs. She drew her head back from his and looked at the disarray of his trousers. His eyes fixed on the tops of her breasts, and Lord, he wanted to see her body laid bare to his every desire. At the moment, he was perfectly willing to let her take the lead because, damnation, she was good with her hands.

Angelic, oh so innocent, delicate, and fragile Miss Lily Wellstone unfastened enough of his trouser buttons to expose his cock, and he did nothing to discourage her. In fact, he spread his thighs wider.

"My, your grace," she said in a gratifyingly breathless voice while she put her hand on him. Around him. He threw back his head and concentrated on what she was doing to him. "How beautiful you are."

Eyes on her face for now, he put a palm on the table and let that arm take his weight while he leaned back to give her better access. Though he had, of course, been complimented any number of times, he could not recall any past lover specifically calling his prick beautiful. If one had, then she hadn't sounded half as earnest as Miss Wellstone. No one could mistake the look on her face for anything but heartfelt sincerity.

"I adore a man's body," she said in that same breathless and admiring voice. Sultry, that was what she looked like and sounded like. Reverent, even, and it made him even harder, even more aroused. Her fingers swept down and caressed his balls before sliding back up his shaft. "But you, your grace, you are simply magnificent." Lord, but he loved the glitter in her eyes. "Do you find that too wicked of me?"

Once he realized she wasn't asking him a rhetorical question, he said, "Very wicked, Wellstone. Pray continue." And she did. God, yes, she did. The first shivers of incipient orgasm built, promising him bliss. He cupped his other hand around her elbow.

He tightened his fingers on her arm, and then around her hand so she'd know what he needed from her. She caught on, and he released her hand to grip the back of her neck. He wanted to kiss her, but he was incapable of anything but pushing his cock harder into her palm. "Jesus."

"There's no need to take the Lord's name in vain," she said. Her fingertips touched his sac. "*Lily* will suffice."

"Lily." His breath hitched in his chest, caught there as he began to peak. "Finish me."

She leaned in, her hand gripping him, sliding up and then down his shaft from the base of him to the crown. He rocked his hips into her hand, and when he was teetering at the edge of spending, with him not giving a damn about the mess or anything but getting to his release, she came in close enough to kiss his throat, just by his jaw.

His hand, still on her nape, gripped her hard, and as his eyes fluttered closed, she said, "I don't want to ruin that lovely waistcoat of yours, your grace. You're going to have to stand up."

He tried to focus on her, but his brain was incapable of thinking of much besides impending orgasm. Fortunately, she took him in hand. Because he was already there, in a manner of speaking. He stood, not really understanding what she wanted from him. "I don't give a damn about the waistcoat," he said.

"But I do." And then she went down on her knees and the next thing he knew her mouth was around him, and her tongue was licking the head of his cock, then his shaft and, hell, just hell, he was deep in her mouth, and he buried his fingers in her hair and held her head. He didn't need but a few strokes of her tongue along his length before his crisis was on him.

Too fast. He was going to come too fast and not have the time to savor her mouth. God. "Lily."

One of her hands spread over his belly. The other stayed around his cock. Jesus. Jesus, Jesus. Her fingers curled over the waistband of his breeches, just by the fastening of his braces, and he came. Lord, he came hard, his cock pulsed and he thrust forward and cried out, some incoherent sound, and he had never in his life had a mistress who made him believe without question that she loved having him in her mouth, but he believed it of Lily.

When he had the presence of mind to let go of her head, and he'd withdrawn from her, he slid his fingers beneath her chin and tilted her head so that he could look into her eyes. Her hand remained around him. And then, very daintily, she leaned forward and kissed his prick and proceeded to put his clothes to rights. He let her because he liked seeing her on her knees. Because apparently he was a base rogue without any tender feelings toward a woman, a lady, who was a guest in his house, whom he'd just debauched. And hoped to further debauch in as short a time as possible.

He did, however, extend a hand to help her up when she was done. Except just as she was putting her hand in his to rise, the sound of someone walking down the corridor, humming something out of tune, froze them both before she was on her feet.

Whoever it was came into the library.

"Oh," said a woman. The word itself was a squeak of alarm.

Mountjoy lifted a hand to Lily, signaling her to stay where she was. The table was between them and the door, and his banyan was open. Chances were good Lily would not be seen if she stayed where she was. His eyes met hers. So dark and beguiling. Hers were wide open, but she crouched down more, making sure her head was not in sight. He turned enough to see the door and the maid who had stopped several steps into the room. She clutched a bucket in one hand.

"You may tend to the fire here later," he said as easily as he could under the circumstances. The girl curtseyed. From the look on her face she was frightened half to death.

"Your grace," she said, hardly audible.

"Thank you. Stay there," he said to Lily in a soft voice when the servant had gone.

Mountjoy adjusted his trousers then walked to the library door and closed it. He did not think the maid had seen Lily. The girl hadn't looked scandalized, only shocked to have come across her employer. But what if she had? He didn't care to think of making a spectacle of himself in front of the servants, and even less about publically compromising Lily. Privately, of course, the deed was done.

When he faced the table, Lily was standing up, and she looked . . . stunningly pretty. Her hair was disheveled, but in a way that made him think about her mouth on him again. Or him covering her while he fucked them both out of their minds. He wasn't engaged yet, he told himself. He'd made no promises to anyone yet, not to Jane and not to her father.

Her eyebrows drew together. "That was . . . more excitement than even I had anticipated." She cleared her throat. "Perhaps I ought to retire, your grace."

He nodded, but didn't move when she walked toward the door. He caught her arm as she passed. He had no idea, none at all, what this meant to her. An interlude she'd sooner forget or one she wanted again?

"Yes?" she said coolly.

"Lily."

"*Lily*," she said with a frown.

"Am I not permitted to call you Lily?"

"You may, certainly. When we are private. But isn't it odd that I prefer when you call me Wellstone?"

"It's what I call you in my dreams."

"How odd." She tilted her head. "It's what you call me in mine."

He drew her close and kissed her again. Just once. But it was a kiss that curled his toes. And she did respond to him. He drew away, not much because she looped an arm around his neck and then her hand slid into his hair. "Thank you."

"Lovely, lovely man." She pulled away. "We must do that again."

"Yes," he said.

"Good night, your grace. Or, rather, good morning."

"Sweet dreams. Wellstone."

He watched her all the way out the door and wondered how his dreams would change now that he knew for certain what her mouth was like.

## Chapter Twelve

MOUNTJOY HAD NEVER BEEN MORE VISCERALLY AWARE of a woman than he was of Lily Wellstone at this moment. This morning he'd awakened having dreamed even more scandalous things about her than he'd yet done so far. Shocking dreams that had him satisfying his lust on his own.

He hadn't explicitly intended to see her so soon. This morning, he *could* have left the house as he did most days. He hadn't. Even before Eugenia had asked him to drive her and Miss Wellstone into town, with Miss Wellstone standing quietly to one side watching him as if she expected to be disappointed, he'd known he would agree.

Of course he was going to agree. She wasn't going to be here much longer, after all, and it would be a shame if they did not explore more of what had happened between them in the library while they could.

Besides, Lily believed he neglected his sister, which he did not do any more than could be helped given the demands on his time; and in the time remaining for her stay, he intended to prove to her that he didn't. He also wanted Lily's company, and that meant that the words *I would be delighted, Eugenia* had actually passed his lips despite a long list of appointments and tasks he had before him.

Even though he wasn't delighted. At all. He'd said so anyway. He could ill afford the time away from the management of his estate. His state of anxious desire was nigh onto intolerable and all he wanted was to have Lily in his arms again. To be in her arms again.

"Eugenia," he said when the two women came downstairs. "I don't recognize you. I surely do not." He bowed. "I'd forgotten what you look like in colors."

Lily speared him with a meaningful gaze. "She's lovely, don't you agree, your grace?"

"Yes, Miss Wellstone. She is." It was true. His sister was transformed. "That shade of green looks very well on you, Eugenia."

"You see, Ginny? I told you so."

He helped the two into the carriage and frowned as it occurred to him, now that he was actually looking at Eugenia, that his sister was only a year or two older than Jane. How odd that he'd come to think of her as a matron of no particular interest to men, when she surely would be. Surely must be. It did not speak well of him that he'd allowed that conviction to creep into his mind and stay there.

Was there some truth to Lily's accusation that he overlooked or even neglected Eugenia?

When they reached High Tearing, Lily walked at his side, her hand on his arm, as cool and collected as if last night's encounter had never happened while he could scarcely think of anything but that. He told himself that one encounter between them could be blamed on the lateness of the night, or on his poor judgment, or his moral weakness. He could not, however, say he hadn't seduced her, because, in point of fact, he had. He'd done nothing to avoid their meeting or what happened afterward and a great deal to bring it about. All of it.

Her visit to Bitterward would soon be over, but as long as she was here and there was this heat between them, why not indulge? Why not? While they walked, his mind was occupied with all the ways he might get his sister's friend on her knees again. And then on her back with him driving into her. Lord, he hoped she wanted more of what had happened between them because it would be a crime against nature to leave that passion unexplored.

*How soon?* became a drumbeat in his head. How soon could he get her alone? Eugenia waved and the motion jostled him out of his thoughts. Thank God.

"Nigel!" She waved again. "Look, Mountjoy, it's Nigel and the Misses Kirk."

Indeed, Nigel was walking in the opposite direction on the opposite side of the street, with Jane and Caroline Kirk on either side of him. Mountjoy waited with Eugenia and Lily for Nigel to safely escort the Kirk sisters across the street.

Nigel greeted them with, "You'll never guess who I met. Completely by luck, of course. I met them coming from the stationer's."

Eugenia looked gravely around her and said, "By any chance was it the Misses Jane and Caroline Kirk?"

There were fond greetings between the women, compliments for Eugenia's appearance, and then, without Mountjoy knowing how it had happened, they were walking, all of them, to the milliner's.

For God's sake, the milliner's.

Inside the shop, which reminded him of a closet in which bits of a woman's wardrobe had exploded, the ladies carried on an animated discussion of the wares. Their conversation slid past him. He didn't retain a single word they said between them, not even when they spoke directly to him or Nigel. Nigel had no trouble offering his opinion, requested or not. He *had* neglected Eugenia, he thought. He had allowed his sister to fall into her grief and stay there. She'd lived here so quietly, managing all the things a woman managed for a household, and he had let her wthout a thought to the consequences for her isolation. Shouldn't he have remembered before now that Eugenia had once been more like Lily than him? Happy and quick to laugh. His sister had not always been content to keep to herself the way he was.

He had the presence of mind to step to the counter when Eugenia approached the clerk with the ribbons she'd selected. They were white, pink, and yellow, and for several seconds he wondered why that seemed odd. It was, he realized, because they weren't black.

"I hope, Eugenia," he said, "that this means we shall soon see you in matching gowns?"

"Perhaps you shall," Eugenia said. She smiled, and he was reminded of the way she used to smile before.

Lily leaned her forearms on the counter. Last night, only an untimely interruption had prevented him from taking her on the library table. "I daresay we might, your grace," she said. She picked up the pink ribbon. "This is an excellent color for you, Ginny. What do you think?"

"Have a gown made in that color," he said. "Yellow, too. And blue. I remember how well you look in blue." He paid for Eugenia's ribbons, aware that Lily was smiling in his direction as if nothing indecent had happened between them. "It's time," he said. "No more black, Eugenia."

Eugenia glanced at Jane. "What about you, Mountjoy?"

"No pink for his grace," Lily said. "It is not his color." Enough laughter followed that he was not obliged to respond to his sister's hint about the state of matters between him and Jane.

Nigel insisted on paying for the Kirk sisters' selections. Jane had chosen green and lavender, and Mountjoy duly admired them when she showed them to him afterward. He wasn't without sensibility. Admiring her ribbons was nothing more than any soon-to-be-engaged man would do. It was about time he behaved as if he were. In any event, if she was pleased with her ribbons, that was exactly what she ought to be. Caroline Kirk slipped her packet into her reticule.

Lily approached the counter with a batch of ribbons and gewgaws of the sort that ended up on ladies' hats and gowns, and Mountjoy hesitated to approach the counter again.

He'd bought ribbons for ladies before that damned attorney called on him and changed his life. But he had not done so since. He'd understood very early on after he came into the title that his attentions to a woman, particularly a young, unmarried woman, created expectations he was not ready or willing to fulfill.

Lily didn't have those sorts of expectations. No one would think anything of it if he paid for her ribbons. Everyone, including Lily, knew he was going to marry Jane.

Nigel reached again for his wallet and the paper money there. "Allow me, Miss Wellstone," his brother said before Mountjoy could act.

"How kind, Lord Nigel, but not necessary." She lifted a hand and dazzled the clerk with a smile.

After which commenced one of the most ruthless bargaining sessions he'd witnessed in some time. She never lost her smile and she did not denigrate the merchandise other than, perhaps, to frown as she fingered a bit of fabric. She relentlessly made it clear that without a discounted price, she could buy nothing. Why not add another length of ribbon since she was buying so much, and by the way, if anyone asked, she'd instantly tell them where she'd obtained the items that adorned her gowns. There was to be dancing at Bitterward, you know. A Spring Ball, everyone would be there.

She had her coins counted out and on the counter before he or Nigel could even attempt to pay for her purchases.

They left the shop, Jane on Nigel's left, Caroline beside her while Lily took Nigel's right. He took Eugenia's arm and they made their way to the confectioner's for chocolate and perhaps some candies and tortes, so the ladies declared. They were nearly there when Lily released Nigel's arm.

"Oh," she said. From her tone, one imagined that the world had just come to an end.

Everyone stopped to see what was the matter.

She stood motionless. "Disaster has struck."

"What is it?" Jane asked. "Are you unwell?"

"I knew I should have worn the half boots. You know the ones I mean, Ginny. With that darling fold by the ankle. But these slippers are such a perfect match for this gown that I thought the risk worth it."

"What's happened?" Caroline asked.

"My slipper has come unlaced." Her shoulders tipped as, Mountjoy surmised, she balanced on one foot. "Not just unlaced, I fear, but damaged." She made a shooing motion. "Pray don't wait for me. I will attempt to effect a repair and rejoin you as soon as possible." She waved them off. "Lord Nigel, take Ginny and the Misses Kirk to the confectioner's. If my slipper cannot be repaired, I'll send Mountjoy for the carriage. Oh, do please, go," she said, forestalling objection. "I'll feel just awful to have spoiled our outing."

"Ought we to return home?" Eugenia asked.

"By no means," Lily said. "I won't hear of it."

"I would be happy to fetch the carriage if required," Mountjoy said.

"Go on, Ginny." Lily waved them on. "See that you drink an entire chocolate for me."

Once the others had moved off, she hopped on one foot to the side of the shop where they'd stopped. Mountjoy was both resigned to his fate and on edge with anticipation.

"Give me your arm, your grace," she said. He did so, and she actually blushed as she stooped, one hand gripping his arm for balance. A moment later, she had her slipper in hand. "Dear. Much worse than I feared." One of the ribbons that tied around her ankle had shredded where it was affixed to the inside of the slipper. "You'll have to fetch the carriage," she said so mournfully his heart actually dropped. "I did so want a cup of chocolate."

He held out his hand, palm up. "Allow me?"

"It won't fit you, sir."

"I am crushed, Miss Wellstone. Crushed."

She put the slipper on his palm and continued to hold on to his arm. "I can't walk without it fastened, as you can well imagine. It will never stay on."

She was entirely correct about that. The slipper was hardly more than a leather sole with a bit of fabric attached.

"I'll wait here for you to return with the carriage."

Mountjoy pulled the sapphire stickpin from his cravat and held it up. "With your permission, I think I can make a temporary repair." He wanted to pull her into his arms and cover her with kisses. "In the alternative, I can carry you to the confectioner's where you can wait in comfort with the others while I take your slipper to the cobbler two streets over."

Her eyes widened. "Oh, you clever, clever man. Do you think you can? I should hate for your stickpin to be damaged."

He smiled and did his best not to think of her on her knees. "We can but make the attempt. Shall I?"

"Please."

"I'll need both hands. And the ribbon."

"Oh, yes. Naturally." She gave him the ribbon. "Do be careful, your grace. I shouldn't like for you to be injured."

Mountjoy met her gaze. "For you," he heard himself say, "I would slay dragons."

Her smile struck him dumb, and the truly astonishing thing was that she appeared genuinely touched. Why? A woman like her had to have heard such nonsense from dozens of other men ever before he uttered such an inanity.

"How gallant of you to offer. But I require only my slipper."

His idea was a complete success. Her slipper was made of a material more than fine enough to pierce through with the added thickness of a folded section of the ribbon. The pin itself was long enough and sturdy enough that he fully expected it would hold until they returned to Bitterward.

"Voilà." He held up her slipper, pinned side toward her. "You are rescued."

Her smile threatened to stop his heart. They stayed where they were, gazes locked. She lifted a hand to his face but stopped short of touching him, while he wished she hadn't. She whispered, "What a lovely beast you are."

"Lovely, I can't agree. But a beast?" He leaned closer. "There are all manner of beastly things I wish to do with you."

He knelt at her feet. She pulled up her skirts and obligingly extended her stockinged foot. Her ankle was slim and her arch delicate, and he wrapped his hand around the back of her ankle, sliding a finger over the lace clocking along the outward side of her silk stocking. She slid her foot forward. They were in public, he reminded himself. Not someplace where he could lock the door and to hell with what was right and proper. He slid his smallest finger upward, to her calf. Lily remained still. He didn't dare more.

Neither of them spoke while he retied her slipper. When he was done he stood and stared at her mouth, and in his head was the image of her on her knees before him. She gazed back. Quiet. Serene.

"Shall we, then?" he said. There were a dozen possible meanings, and he meant every bloody one. Was there a man alive who could look at that angelic face and not think of what it would be like to have her beneath him? He wanted to touch her, caress her, and he had to fist his hands to prevent himself from doing just that. It was bad enough to have compromised her in private. To do so in public would be reprehensible.

"Yes," she said with a decidedly wicked grin. "I think we should."

He held her gaze while he extended his arm and walked, metaphorically speaking, through the gates of Hell. "Excellent, Wellstone."

"Oh. I'm Wellstone now?"

"You know very well you are. Come along." The confectioner's was yet twenty yards distant, at once too far and not far enough away. She was tall enough to keep pace with his longer stride, but he maintained a slow walk out of concern for the repair to her slipper.

"What sort of beastly things were you thinking?" she asked.

"Do not provoke me, Wellstone." He glanced at her and found her watching him. He had a mad desire to drag her into some dark corner of High Tearing and kiss her, to lift her skirts and take her up against a wall or find a private room anywhere he could and get her on her back. She knew what he was thinking, too. He watched her front teeth press into her lower lip.

"Will you think me terribly wicked if I ask you a favor now?" she said.

He forced himself to look away from her mouth. He shouldn't rise to that delectable bait, but he did. "I should like it if you did," he said. "Your favors are quite rousing as I recall."

"Not that." Her cheeks pinked up. "I would like your assistance with a project that I think will engage your sister's spirits."

"That's all?"

She nodded.

"Does it by chance involve flaming pencils?"

"No, your grace." She laughed, and he felt unduly proud to have amused her. He was not known as a man who amused people. "But I daresay you won't like my idea."

"What?" He wanted to put her on her back right now, having stripped her naked and then himself.

"You heard me mention a ball at Bitterward when we were buying ribbons."

"Did I?"

"You know you did." Her fingers tightened on his arm, a gentle reproof. "I was perfectly serious about a ball. I was astonished to learn you've never had dancing in all the time you've lived at Bitterward."

"For most of that time, I did not have a hostess." Not that his single state was an excuse. "When Eugenia came home, she was in mourning."

"You ought to have had a ball before now." They continued walking. Slowly. They were neither of them in a hurry. "If only for the ladies of the parish. All those beautiful Kirk sisters, and you've never given a ball. For shame, sir, when Bitterward has a splendid ballroom."

"Are you asking for permission now?" he asked. "I'll

wager you've already invited most of High Tearing." They weren't walking very fast, but they were nearly to the confectioner's.

"Yes, I am." She gave him a narrow look, full of suspicion. "Do you mean to refuse? Could you be that heartless?"

"I surely am, Wellstone." True. "I am heartless as you well know. But I am also selfish. Any favor that puts you in my debt is one I mean to grant."

"Is 'thank you' the correct reply?"

"It is. Have whatever parties you like. I'll tell the staff you are to be accommodated in your every requirement in that regard."

She stopped walking. "Do you mean it?"

"Why wouldn't I? So long as you inform me of expenses over fifty pounds before they are incurred. Or if your expenses exceed two hundred pounds in total."

"Tyrant." They started walking again. Even more slowly than before.

"A solvent one, Wellstone."

"I trust you will engage to attend." They'd reached the confectioner's and now stood only a few steps from the door.

He sighed. Through the low shop window, he saw Eugenia and both the Misses Kirk at a table, each with cups of something to drink. The fabled chocolate no doubt. Nigel had his back to the door but appeared to be dancing attendance on the ladies. Another gentleman in the shop sat with his back to the windows. "So long as you tell me when and where I am to be."

"I will slip a note amongst the bills."

"Be certain you inform my secretary. He keeps my appointment calendar."

"I will do so, your grace. Now, I have another project in mind."

"Two favors will cost you dearly."

"Wretch." She grinned at him and they stood there, not daring to stand closer. He did want her. Quite badly. "No phosphorus is required."

"You relieve my mind." He laughed and didn't care who

saw. He was doing his duty to his family, and he was damned if he'd feel guilty for enjoying himself. "What is the project you really want me to approve?"

"Too clever by half, your grace."

"I am the eldest brother. I am required to be clever simply to survive two devious siblings such as I have. What is your project?"

"Treasure."

He stood in front of the window. Nigel, facing the window but with his attention entirely on the ladies, put a hand on the back of Jane's chair and bent to whisper something in her ear that made her laugh. He wondered if Jane had refused other suitors because everyone, including him, expected he would marry her. Had other men declined to court her as a result? "I beg your pardon?"

"You and Jane suit you know."

He nodded and looked away from the window. He did not want to think about Jane just now. "What is your favor?"

"I've been having the most astonishing dreams. About finding treasure at Bitterward. And I thought, why not?"

"Why not what?"

"Why, why not search for treasure? My project, your grace, my brilliant notion to amuse your sister and recover her spirits, is to find buried treasure somewhere on Bitterward lands."

"Treasure." He frowned. "Am I expected to conjure up this treasure you've dreamed about?"

"I misspoke, your grace." She clasped her hands behind her back. "Not treasure. A treasure hunt."

"You seem convinced you'll find it."

"I have the very highest hopes for success. It happens all the time, some farmer . . ." She hesitated, he knew, because she was remembering that he had once been a farmer. "An earnest farmer toiling among his parsnips uncovers an ancient artifact. A cache of Roman coins, part of an ancient road, pots, a sword or poleax, or jewelry, all having been buried for hundreds of years. We shall search for treasure, Ginny and I. After all, the Romans were here in the north. We'll survey the property, make maps of suspicious mounds or likely caves. Why, you might be engaged for weeks with the project, long after I've gone home."

"Does not a search for treasure require that someone dig holes in the ground?" The idea gave him a chill since he vividly recalled dreams in which he stood with her at the edge of a wide trench, surrounded by servants who'd been digging in the ground. Three of his footmen, staring at him from across a hole. And Lily. Beautiful, alluring Lily Wellstone.

"Unavoidable, I should think." They remained partially in view of the shop window. Nigel had not noticed them, but Jane had. She was pretending she hadn't, but her eyes flickered to the window too often, sliding away when otherwise she might have looked directly at Mountjoy. "My plan is to have two or three burly footmen do the digging."

"Three?"

"That seems a proper number to me. Perhaps several energetic boys if you can't spare us assistance from your staff, or I can hire men from High Tearing."

"Have you reason to think there might be treasure of any kind on the property?"

"None at all." She grinned. "But why shouldn't there be? Sheffieldshire is rich in history, as you well know."

"Someone will break a leg in one of those holes you dig."

She rolled her eyes. "We'll have them filled in. You'll never know anyone put a spade to the earth. I promise you."

He ought to refuse, but aside from his disinclination to allow anyone to dig holes in the ground, he could think of no objection she wouldn't quickly dismantle. "So long as you fill in the holes after you have dug them, you are free to search for treasure anywhere on Bitterward lands."

"Excellent." She smiled again, that private, personal, incandescent transformation that made his heart thump against his chest. "Have you a survey map of the estate? I should like to copy it."

"I will make a copy available to you."

"Thank you." She leaned in to kiss his cheek, then checked herself. He knew why. Because her instinct wasn't innocent. Like lovers determined to hide an affair, they didn't dare touch in public.

She was precisely the kind of tonnish woman he preferred to avoid, except she wasn't. She wasn't like the women he met in London, no matter her exquisite clothes and her managing ways. "Have you considered the effect of your eventual disappointment when you fail to uncover treasure?"

Lily waved a hand. "We'll never finish before I go home, so who's to say we failed?" She reached past him, opened the door herself, and swept inside. "Ginny," she said in response to the greetings. "Jane. Caroline. Two hearty huzzahs for the duke. My slipper is repaired."

As he followed her inside, the gentleman with his back to the window rose. Mountjoy passed him on his way to the table where Lily now stood. Nigel held a chair for her. The two Kirk girls smiled, but Eugenia kept a stony silence, one hand curled around her cup of chocolate.

The man who'd stood turned to Mountjoy and bowed to him. "Your grace."

No wonder Eugenia had gone so quiet. And Lily. "Lord Fenris."

The marquess nodded to each of the Kirk sisters, studying them with a cold eye. "Ladies. Miss Wellstone. Mrs. Bryant."

Eugenia stared into her cup.

Lily gave him a cool look. "Good afternoon, my lord."

Lord Fenris let a hand drift to their table. Just his fingertips touched the surface. "I hope I have found you in good health, Miss Wellstone."

Lily inched closer to Eugenia and put a hand on her shoulder. "I'd offer my wishes for your health, but I don't think they'd be well received."

"On the contrary," he replied.

The edge of Lily's mouth twitched. "Then do accept my wishes for your continued health."

He bowed. "Thank you."

"Good day, sir."

There was a moment's awkward silence until Fenris removed his hand from the table. "Ladies." He bowed again, his gaze sliding to Eugenia. "Mrs. Bryant."

Eugenia took a sip of her chocolate and stared in the direction of Nigel's shoulder. On his way out, Fenris placed a coin on his table and, after one more bow, left.

Into another awkward silence, Nigel said, "May I fetch you a chocolate, Miss Wellstone?"

"Chocolate would be delightful, Lord Nigel. And some sugared walnuts, if it's not too much trouble. I adore them. Don't you, Miss Kirk?"

"Yes, thank you, I do." Jane smiled and Mountjoy had not the slightest reaction, even though Jane was pretty when she smiled. "Very much, Miss Wellstone."

"The ones here are particularly good," Lily said. "It is my goal to convince the proprietor to give me the recipe."

"Sit down, Nigel. I'll order for myself and Miss Wellstone." Mountjoy headed for the counter.

While Nigel did so, Lily put her hands on the table. "About our ball," she said.

He stood at the counter, staring at the table where Fenris had been sitting, wondering why a man whose family wanted nothing to do with their relative had come all the way to Sheffieldshire. And stayed.

"I am considering a Venetian theme," he heard Lily say. "What do you think, ladies?" From where he stood, Mountjoy saw her prop her elbows on the table. "Shall we flood the ballroom and do our dancing via gondola?"

Mountjoy said nothing. He was preoccupied with the realization that Lord Fenris had not come here to exact some sort of petty revenge on Lily. He was here to mend fences with her.

## Chapter Thirteen

LILY PACED BEFORE THE FIREPLACE IN HER ROOM. IT was three o'clock in the morning, hours before she would be able to sleep. There was no moon out or she might have thrown on her cloak and gone for a walk. What she wanted to do was wander the house until she met with Mountjoy. Handsome, magnificent Mountjoy.

She hated feeling she was confined to her room when she wanted to be moving. To be doing something. Anything. Anything to take her mind off Ginny's brother. She did so hate to be alone with nothing to divert her from her thoughts.

She plucked her shawl off the chair where she'd left it after she'd retired to read and discovered she could not concentrate. Her situation was desperate indeed if she found no solace or distraction in a book. She knew the reason for that. There was no point denying she was infatuated with Mountjoy or that her attraction to him was the cause of her current unrest.

Even now, so many hours after their return from High Tearing, she felt the warmth of his fingers on her ankle, sliding, caressing, that quick slip of his fingers along her calf. If she closed her eyes she could see again the flash of heat in his eyes.

Thoughts like hers were not appropriate for a lady. Her father had once told her she'd been born wicked, and she suspected he was right. What proper lady, never married, took a lover, regretted nothing, and dreamed of taking another? Even as a girl, she'd dreamed of men who fell in love with her and to whom, in those dreams, she yielded all. Until Greer, naturally, her imaginings had been vague on the details of her surrender to passion.

Now that she'd kissed Mountjoy, touched him, tasted him, heard him groan in the passion she'd brought him to, she wanted more. Solitary enjoyments no longer sufficed. She wanted to caress him, to stroke his body and see his face when he reached his pleasure. Even more, she wanted the duke to touch her and kiss her and, yes, do some of those beastly things he'd alluded to when he'd fixed her slipper.

Mountjoy was nothing like Greer. He hadn't Greer's easy manner or his passion for history or his flights of fancy. Not his way with words either. The duke did not and would never love her the way Greer had, and she would never feel about Mountjoy the way she'd felt about Greer. She would always have that place in her heart where Greer still lived, and all the joy and happiness and the black despair of his loss remained locked away there. Safely guarded.

The only sounds in the house were the typical ones heard in a large and very old building. Syton House had inured her to such creaks and groans, the distant sound of the wind. She faced the door to the corridor, and tried to breathe, but the stale and thin air was suffocating in here.

She walked away from the door to unlatch and open the window. Night air whooshed over her, damp with the promise of rain. The hooting of owls stopped then started up again. She breathed in deep draughts of air and still felt she could not pull enough into her lungs and that she would never be able to catch her breath.

The sky was utterly dark. No moon, no stars, and no

promise of dawn, and that wet heaviness of impending rain. She leaned out the window and let the breeze riffle through her hair. Her skin rippled from the chill. It was spring, for God's sake. Not winter.

She stayed at the window until she could bear the cold no longer. Or the solitude. She could not stay here with the walls closing in on her and the air going away and her wicked, wicked mind whispering that she could find Mountjoy's room and settle entirely the question of what it would be like to make love to someone other than Greer. If she remained with nothing here capable of distracting her, she would reach a point where staying became intolerable, and she then really might search out Mountjoy's room.

Self-denial, she'd found, was the unfailing precursor to overindulgence in the very thing one sought to avoid. Her father excelled at denying himself and those around him, and she had always rebelled against his strictures.

She closed the window and pressed a palm to one of the panes of glass until the cold seeped into the bones of her hand. Hers was not an aesthete's character. That was, frankly, a truth to which she had long ago been reconciled. Her nature was, quite simply, not a proper one for a woman.

Lily picked up her sketchbook, pencil, and an oil lamp. She would wander the house looking for architectural details to sketch for her collection of oddities and grotesqueries and if, by chance or purpose, she and Mountjoy met? Well.

The moment she stepped into the corridor, the tightness in her chest released. Thank God. She walked to the Armory Hall, so called because the walls were hung with medieval weapons and there were at least ten separate suits of armor, including one for a horse. The door she'd entered through was at one of the short ends of the rectangular room. Three double-branched candelabra decorated a long oak table in the middle of the hall, gleaming silver in the lamplight. There were twenty-two chairs around the table and overhead a crystal chandelier, though with just the light of her lamp, there were no prisms of color to be seen.

A sideboard sat in the middle of the wall opposite the windows, but all along the rest of this long side were the suits of armor, in various attitudes of martial valor as was possible through the clever use of wire. Some held weapons: a sword, a dirk, or a pike. Another had a mace at its feet, yet another an axe.

According to Ginny, the Armory Hall was sometimes called into use as an informal dining room. The knights faced the windowed wall, and she fancied they had each come to know their separate views quite well. Every few feet opposite the knights were tall, multipaned windows inset in a bowed area topped by a small dome. Each dome contained a different carved ivory medallion: a face, a medieval beast, an open book with an inscription in Latin. One of the medallions was a swan with a broken chain around its neck, the very beast from Mountjoy's coat of arms.

To a careless glance, the last wall appeared to be nothing more than a wall that ended without a passage into yet another room. But Ginny had shown her the concealed doorway there that opened if one knew just where to press.

She set her light on the table and considered sketching each of the windows. There were seven. Enough for one a night for a week. Or, perhaps she'd sketch one of the suits of armor. There were eleven of them. As she was deciding that she would begin with a sketch of the swan, the hair on the back of her neck prickled.

She turned in time to see the concealed door swing open.

Lily's breath caught in her throat. Mountjoy had denied there were ghosts here, but if ever a house ought to have a ghost or two, it was Bitterward. But it wasn't a ghost that entered the hall. It was far, far worse than any spectral apparition.

The duke halted when he saw her, and they stood there, she fancied, in mutual disbelief that they should meet. Again. At this hour. When they had agreed they must avoid each other at such times as this.

"You," he said.

She curtseyed. "Your grace."

He wasn't wearing that lovely banyan of his. Alas, tonight he was dressed in his usual inelegantly fitted clothes. He put down his candle and pointed at the frescoed ceiling that, at the moment, was not possible to see. "Doyle tells me that in fourteen hundred something, my ancestor hired an Italian master to paint the ceiling."

She looked up as if she could see that far in the darkened room. She did recall from her previous tour that the paintings were sublime. Her heart thudded in her ears.

Why encounter him now when she was not feeling at all virtuous? On a night when she'd been entertaining salacious thoughts about the man across from her? She was already weak where he was concerned. "Do you know who he engaged?"

"Family legend is that it was Fra Angelico, but I've seen nothing to prove that. The claim seems suspect at best."

Lily stood close enough to the table to put her hand on it. The wooden surface had been polished until she could see her reflection. In her room, she had imagined herself taking actions that she was now barely able to contemplate. Not with the duke here in the flesh, with his guarded eyes and somber expression.

It seemed another time and place entirely that she had unfastened his trousers and his fingers had been buried in her hair.

But then, disaster.

Mountjoy left his candle where it was and crossed the room to her. He ended standing mere inches from her.

Oddly enough, her nerves settled. "Your grace."

"I have decided," he said in the manner of a man who was used to deciding a great many things, "concluded, that we cannot be lovers." He drew a fingertip along the line of her shoulder. "I'm sorry," he said softly. "I'm sorry, but it just can't be. You and I."

She leaned in to him, and his eyes swept downward to fix on her bosom, which she found a gratifying reaction.

"I'm sorry, too." She curled an arm around his neck, which required that her upper torso press against his chest. His arm snaked around her waist, and she gave a little tug of her arm and just like that, his mouth was in reach. She kissed the side of his jaw.

Mountjoy laughed, a low, velvet sound of ironic mirth, and he dipped his head toward hers. In return, she brushed her lips across his. So soft, his lips were. Again, nearly a kiss this time.

And then a kiss.

That was all the two of them needed. She'd known the moment he'd come in that she hadn't the strength to continue in a ladylike manner. He was here, and she wanted him to stay.

His lips parted, and he nipped at her mouth, soft kisses that turned into heated kisses, and Lily melted against him. She adored the way he kissed. The Duke of Mountjoy knew what he was about. His other arm went around her waist, too, pulling her tight against him. His tongue dipped into her mouth, caressed, beguiled, turned her bones to jelly.

He lifted her up, and she did not know what he intended until she was sitting on the table, close enough to the edge that had he not stood between her legs she would have worried about falling off. He planted his hands on either side of her thighs and returned to kissing her mindless. Which he did very, very well.

Lily returned his passion, accepted everything he did, and tightened her arms around his neck. She pushed her fingers into his hair. She gave a moan of protest when he lifted her up a second time, but as she learned, it was only to lift her skirts and set her down with her bare bottom on the table. Cool against her skin. Thrilling. One of his hands ended up on her knee. Just above her garter.

"Lily," he said, shaking his head. "You and that damned medallion. You're constantly in my thoughts. My dreams. I can't keep my damned hands off you."

His fingers curved around her leg as potent proof of that.

Her belly tensed and a quiver of arousal spread upward from her breasts to her throat, and lower, too, between her legs. She felt her need for him there especially.

She gasped when his fingers slid higher. Oh, heavens, higher yet, until he was touching her exactly there. She was wet and slick, and he knew where and how to stroke her, and she angled herself into his hand. They weren't kissing anymore; she hadn't the breath for it now. For a time, he watched her face while his fingers were busy.

Mountjoy leaned in to kiss her once. Just once before he slid his mouth downward, along her jaw and then back to her mouth. He drew away, then kissed her ear and said, very low, in nearly a growl, "We can't be lovers, but it wouldn't be gentlemanly of me if I did not repay the favor you recently did me."

"That's so," she managed to say. He knew what to do with his hands. He'd found that place that made her weak with need. Not weak, she thought, strong. Stronger because of her need and her determination to satisfy it, and stronger because he was so very close to fetching her. Stronger because she trusted her body and its reactions and welcomed the pleasure. Stronger because her feelings and reactions were true. She pulled him toward her, tightened her arms around his shoulders.

"You *are* wild," he whispered. "Wild and lovely beyond words. I worship you for that. I thank God for that." He slid a finger inside her, and this, this was the moment to allow her control to slip away. "You're hot around me, Lily," he whispered. He beguiled. Seduced, except she'd been seduced from the very moment she'd set eyes on him. A second finger joined the first, and while he stroked his fingers in her, he managed to keep contact with that spot that made her grateful for her wildness. "Every time I looked at you today I thought of your mouth fetching me."

She could barely speak, but she managed to say, "I, too."

He lay her back and, though she wanted to touch him and could not, except to touch his head and thread her fingers through his hair, he used his mouth instead of his fingers. He kissed her sex, and that was not something Greer had ever done for her.

She would go mad. No woman would survive what his mouth demanded of her. One of his hands stroked her thigh, and she felt the coolness of the air on her skin, the warmth of his hands, the pounding of her heart when his fingers and palm followed the curve of her leg. She did not last long. His tongue flicked over her, and she was done. Climax washed over her, swept her away.

His name fell from her lips, but only his title, *Mountjoy*. Because that's all she knew as she clutched his head and gave herself over to sensation. Pleasure rolled through her, wrung her out, and then, when she thought there was nothing more, when he'd slowed and then stopped, and she was breathing again, he blew on her, and it electrified her. He licked and waited, then kissed her there again, and she wasn't finished after all. She came again, and she was his in that moment, his utterly, for as long as her heart continued to beat.

When she could think again, she opened her eyes and saw Mountjoy standing over her, one hand on her belly and the other resting on the outside of her thigh, and his green, so green eyes watching her. "What a shame," she said, and she actually did mean every word, "that we cannot be lovers."

# Chapter Fourteen

MOUNTJOY USUALLY TOOK THE SAME ROUTE WHEN he returned to the house after riding out, but today he changed his mind. His horse, Fervent, fancied a gallop, so rather than take the road from High Tearing to Bitterward upon reaching the edges of the estate lands, he took Fervent over the stone fence into the field and let him have his head.

He was delaying the inevitable return home, he understood that, but it was also true that Fervent wanted a run. Since it was their mutual decision that they should not pursue an affair, he preferred to avoid Lily when possible. Fervent therefore got his way.

For a quarter mile, he and Fervent flew, taking a line that followed the river Tear and curved past the woods, and he hardly thought at all about her skin, the taste of her, the way she kissed, or the sound of her calling his name when she came. He and Fervent were both breathing hard when he slowed down. He put his horse into a trot and headed more or less in the direction of Bitterward.

Lately, whenever he stayed at Bitterward he missed London

less and less, and he'd never missed Town all that much. He wasn't a proper duke; he never had been and probably never would be. He'd much rather be in the country than sitting in the Lords or whatever Mayfair gentlemen's club would have him for a member. If there weren't duties in Town that required his presence there, he'd be content to stay here the rest of his days. Every time his presence in London was required, he missed Bitterward more and more. He belonged in the country with his sleeves rolled up and his hands full of dirt.

He took the climb to the last substantial field before the more manicured lawns at a walk. At the crest of the slope he had a view of Bitterward to his right, and to his left, the Saxon church that was still in near pristine condition. The view, as always, took his breath. Everything within his sight belonged to him. Unless he married and begot himself a son or two, one day Bitterward and all the rest of his inheritance would belong to Nigel or Nigel's sons. The dukedom was his by right of birth. He worked and managed the estates with his own sweat and blood, and he wanted to raise a son of his own to step into the role of Mountjoy.

He had no business chasing after a woman who did not want what he did from life. Tomorrow, he thought. He would offer for Jane tomorrow, and he would then be obligated to put Lily out of his thoughts. He would settle down to the business of ensuring his line endured.

As he neared the church, he saw there was a veritable crowd outside the doors. This was so even though, according to Doyle, the last services held there had occurred when the centuries were still in three digits. He rode closer and saw a woman marching away from the stone building in a deliberate, measured stride. Was she counting off steps? And why?

Nigel stood near Eugenia, whom he did not immediately recognize because she was wearing colors again. Jane was a few feet away, watching Lily pacing away from the church. Lily stopped her marching and faced Nigel and the others.

He continued riding toward them, and his heart sped up

even though there could be nothing more between him and Lily. This was, however, an opportunity for him to begin a formal courtship of Jane. He came close enough to see that Lily wore a blue riding habit that flattered her figure extremely. A round hat perched jauntily on her head. For her, it seemed, every day was an adventure for which she must be exquisitely attired. She had a leather case under one arm, and as he approached, she opened the case, took out a sheet of paper that rattled in the breeze, and made a notation with a pencil.

By now, all three of them had heard his approach and turned. Lily, farther away from him than the others, stayed where she was, a hand lifted to shade her eyes. He remained on his horse, aware, as he had rather not be, that Nigel was as beautifully clothed as Lily and his sister.

"Eugenia." He nodded to her, and it was as if he hadn't seen his sister in months. His heart turned over. She was too thin. Far too thin, and he ought to be hanged for not having noticed before. "You look lovely again."

"Thank you, Mountjoy."

"It's good to see you in colors, Eugenia." He was very much aware of Lily several feet distant from them. And of Jane, of course. His future duchess. He dismounted and handed the reins to the footman who held the other horses. The ground was soft from the recent rains. Lily remained standing several yards from the church, still engaged in writing something down on her paper, using her leather case as a makeshift table. "Miss Kirk," he said. "Good afternoon."

Her cheeks turned pink, a reaction she attempted to hide by ducking her head while she curtseyed to him. "Your grace."

"I hope you're well today."

Jane's eyes went wide. "Yes, sir."

Good Lord, he terrified the girl. That must be remedied as soon as possible. He smiled at her, but it didn't seem to help.

Lily, meanwhile, had finished with her writing. She tucked her pencil away and strode toward them without the deliberation that had so marked her walk away from the church.

"Your grace," Lily said when she reached them. She extended a gloved hand as if she were a queen and he a mere flunky. Her gaze traveled him from head to toe, and he did not think, alas, that she had in mind her remarks about him being a splendid animal. In fact, that was a shudder when her attention reached his neckcloth, which he had yanked loose during his gallop. His clothes, so comfortable, felt even more inadequate. His damned grooms looked better than he did. He wondered what Jane thought of his appearance and realized he had no idea what she thought about anything.

"Lovely to see you, sir," Lily said.

"A pleasure to see you, too, Miss Wellstone." Mountjoy bowed over her hand and stepped back. He hadn't ridden out expecting to escort their guest on a tour of the property. And yet, ridiculously, he wished he'd not worn his oldest riding clothes or his battered greatcoat that, this morning, had seemed just the thing.

"We've been examining your church." Her eyes sparkled. "Did you know the baptismal font is still in place?"

"Is it?"

"I've made a detailed sketch, but really, there's simply no way to capture the sense of all those ancient hands that must have touched that stone." She put a hand on her head to keep the breeze from whipping off her hat. "How lucky you are to have such a splendidly preserved example of Anglo-Saxon architecture on your property. Lord Nigel didn't know when the church was last used, but I'd say it must be centuries, and yet so wonderfully intact. Down to the sundial!"

"Your enthusiasm inspires, Miss Wellstone." He knew what she tasted like. He knew what she looked like when she came. He knew her skin was soft and her limbs sleek. He wanted to know the rest.

"I've made a note of all the likely spots hereabouts." She held up her leather case as if that explained all.

"Likely spots?"

She walked the rest of the way to where he stood with Eugenia, Jane, and Nigel, her leather case under one arm. He watched the sway of her hips as she walked. Mud dotted the hem of her riding habit and clung to her boots, but this was England in spring, and they had been subjected to frequent storms, some of them with the chill of the past winter at the edges. Her cheeks were rosy from her brisk walk. "For finding treasure, of course."

"Treasure."

"You did agree to our searching." She gave him another of those head-to-toe looks, and this time he knew she wasn't thinking about the fit of his coat. "Don't tell me you've forgotten."

"Not at all." Last night—this morning, rather, he'd held her bottom in his hands, and he was, say what you would about him not being a proper duke, thinking it would be better than pleasant to do so again. Never mind what was proper. If she was willing, if she had no more expectations of him than he had of her, why not?

"Who knows what we might find? At home, my neighbor, Mr. Bardiwill, was hunting in a corner of his property when he came across an entire cache of Roman coins partially dug up by one of his spaniels. They'd been stored in an amphora, but alas, his servants broke the vessel whilst they were digging it out. It would have been wonderful to see the amphora intact."

"You expect to find Roman coins?" In London, on those occasions when he was looking to spend a few hours in a woman's arms, he appeared in those places frequented by women looking for lovers and the thing was done. He never pursued married women. He'd only once become involved with a widow, and she had not been a woman of the Ton. His past lovers were never women like Lily. She was unique among females. He took a step nearer Jane but found his brother had already offered Jane his arm. "What else, dare I ask?"

"Who knows?" She grinned, losing herself in her enthusiasm. "The foundation of an ancient Roman garrison. A Viking ship."

"This far from the shore?" Eugenia said.

"A hoard of gold, then." She gestured with her free hand, then put it back on her head to prevent her hat from blowing away. "Goodness, the wind. At any rate, your grace, one never knows. We might find anything at all."

"I suppose that's true."

"In the meantime, I, for one, am famished. Aren't you, Ginny? Miss Kirk? Shall we return to Bitterward for tea?" She headed for her horse, a very fine mare, Mountjoy noted, that she must have brought with her as it was not an animal from his stables. "Were you on your way home, your grace?" Her eyes pierced him and killed the denial on his lips. "Or had you business elsewhere when you saw us?"

He could tell her yes, that he had business away from Bitterward. But he didn't. He frowned to see Nigel whispering something to Jane. "On my way home. Miss Kirk," he said. "May I assist you to your horse?"

Jane turned pink as a sunrise. "Yes, your grace."

While he did so, with Nigel stepping aside, one of the grooms bent to offer Lily a hand up. She looked over her shoulder at him. "If you're on your way home, your grace, we should adore your company."

"Thank you."

He looked into Lily's eyes, and he could have sworn he lost a little part of himself to the joy he saw there.

"Will you hold this for me, please?" She handed her leather case to Mountjoy, and he, being closer to her than anyone else, accepted it with a nod. She set her booted foot on the footman's cupped hands and mounted gracefully. She sat her mare with complete confidence. He wondered if her father had given her lessons when she was young or if her skill was more recently acquired.

"Thank you, your grace." She leaned down to collect her case, and he handed it to her.

"You're welcome, Miss Wellstone." There. What could be more proper than that?

With a glance at Eugenia and Jane, both of whom were now mounted, Lily gave him a smile that bedazzled. She gave absolutely no sign that he'd brought her to climax only a few hours ago. "Talk with Miss Kirk, won't you, your grace? She'll be pleased if you do."

He nodded again, afraid that if he spoke or stayed where he was even a moment longer he would give himself, and Lily, away.

"Lord Nigel," she called. "Come tell me everything you know about the church. And is it true there are caves on the property?"

She'd managed them all. Nigel. Eugenia. Jane. Him, too, and not even for the first time. In the normal course of things he did not care for women who wanted to manage him. With Lily, he wasn't at all sure he minded. He remounted and, as instructed, dropped back to accompany Jane. Nigel, Eugenia, and Miss Wellstone rode ahead.

Mountjoy discovered his impression that Jane was terrified of him was an accurate one. He kept to safe topics such as the weather, her family, and, in a moment of daring, phosphorus pencils, and she said hardly a word. They spent the entire return to Bitterward in this utterly boring and safe manner. Once there, Jane declined tea, claiming a prior engagement. He suspected she was afraid of being trapped in conversation with him again.

He would have insisted on escorting her home, but Doyle came down the front stairs, a letter in his hand. "Your grace, the messenger has been instructed to wait for your immediate reply."

The letter was from Mr. Thomas Plummer, the vice-chancellor. Indeed, his immediate attention was warranted. "Nigel," he said. "Would you be so kind as to see Miss Kirk home?"

"Of course."

When Mountjoy came downstairs sometime later, he was late for tea but his response to the vice-chancellor was on its way back to London. He'd refused to give in to his desire to dress with more than his usual attention to his appearance. For whose benefit would he do such a thing? This was his home, and if there was anywhere a man ought to be comfortable, it was in his own home.

The moment he walked into the Oldenburg salon, he regretted his stubborn refusal to give in to his valet's hints that perhaps *this* time he might attempt something new in his dress.

Eugenia presided over the tea while Lily sat at a table, a pencil in one hand and a rectangle of paper before her. Nigel had one hand on the table and was bending over Lily's shoulder. A familiar scene. But there was no phosphorus, thank the Lord, and the pencil was a normal pencil of the sort anyone could use to write with no danger of flames engulfing the house.

"Your grace," Lily said with a smile when he came in. She rose to curtsey, but he lifted a hand.

"No formality between us."

"That's very kind of you." She sat again. She'd changed from her riding habit—of course—and now wore white muslin trimmed with pale blue. Some sort of cap perched atop her hair, plain enough not to interfere with anything. The colors suited her. She wore a chain of silver beads that reached to the middle of her stomach, and her medallion on a velvet ribbon of the palest blue.

She looked, as she always did, very well. Devilishly pretty with her golden hair and chocolate eyes. He'd known a few women who were more beautiful, but he'd begun to believe he'd never known any woman more alluring than her.

"Eugenia," he said. "You're well, I trust."

"Yes, Mountjoy." She looked at him with a smile. "I'm so glad you could join us." Once again, he was taken aback at seeing her in colors. How had he forgotten what she'd been like before her husband's death? Happy, he recalled. Smiling. Intelligent, that was a Hampton trait. "We thought you might not."

"I'm famished," he said. "And in dire need of tea."

"Lily's brought some Lapsang Souchong for us to try. Will you have some of that?"

"Yes, thank you." He went to the table where there were laid out several cheeses, some biscuits, bread, butter, a yellow cake, various jellies and preserves, and Devonshire cream. There were apples and grapes, too, as well as some early strawberries. "May I bring you anything, Eugenia?"

"No thank you, Mountjoy."

He gathered a plate for himself. "Miss Wellstone?"

"Are there more grapes?" She did not look up from her paper. "I should love more grapes."

Nigel said, "I'll get them for you."

"Lord Nigel," Lily said sternly. She barely looked at Nigel. "Your brother is half an inch from the food. He can trouble himself to bring both of us grapes and perhaps a slice of that cake." She glanced in his direction, but her attention was directed more at the food than at him. "And a bit of that delectable Devonshire cream."

"I should be delighted, Miss Wellstone." He only just stopped himself from rolling his eyes in self-disgust. Was that now his favorite phrase? *I should be delighted.* Lily Wellstone had his life turned upside down.

He brought her and Nigel plates with the requested items, then accepted his tea from Eugenia, which he took with him to study the paper Lily had spread over the desk. No one could think anything of his doing so since Nigel was doing the same.

"What do you think?" Lily asked him. She smelled good. Just enough of violets to be pleasant and to remind him of the scent rising from her skin, the taste of her flesh, and the sound of her sexual release.

"I can't make heads or tails of what that is." He nodded at her paper.

Nigel laughed at him. "She meant the tea, Mountjoy. What do you think of the tea?"

"Did she?" He took another sip, slowly because it was hot and Lily was watching him. "I still can't make heads or tails of that." There was a smokiness to the tea that he liked. The flavor hovered on the edge of too much. "It's quite strong."

"It is a bold tea," Lily said. "And therefore not for everyone." She put her elbow on the table and her chin on her hand. "I suspected you might like it."

"Why?"

"You are like this tea. Bold. Opinionated." Her lips quirked in a smile. "And something of an acquired taste."

Nigel gave a yelp of laughter.

"Few people have acquired that particular taste," Mountjoy said.

Lily met his gaze. "Perhaps they've not given you a sufficient chance."

"Where do you get this?" No one could blame him for staring at her. Her smile could resurrect a dead man. "I should like to have a supply laid by."

She reached across the table for another sheet of paper and wrote on it. "The name of the tea, and the tea merchant my steward swears by. If you write to him and tell him that I particularly recommended you to him, I'm sure he'll sell you some."

Mountjoy had been duke long enough to know he was unlikely to need any introduction or recommendation. His name would be more than enough. "It's quite good."

"But not a tea everyone cares for." Lily sat at the table like a queen, in command of them all. "I recognize that and for that reason bring my own personal supply. Ginny, for example, did not care for the taste, and your brother, I fear, only pretends that he does."

Nigel hastened to say, "There's no pretense, Miss Wellstone." He took another sip of his tea but it was obvious to all he was restraining a grimace. "Perhaps a bit," he said with a shake of his head. "I have hopes it will grow on me. Like Mountjoy eventually did."

"So very amusing, Nigel," Mountjoy said.

"Don't quarrel," Lily said. She looked between him and Nigel, touchingly anxious. "Not on my account."

"If I didn't mercilessly tease him over something like that," Nigel said, "he'd wonder what was wrong with me."

"My dear brother, I have no need to wonder." Mountjoy sipped his tea again. "I've known for years what's wrong with you."

"Gratifying to hear." She gave the paper to Mountjoy. "I'll write to my steward and have him send more. That way you will have some of your own after I'm gone and while we hope that Mr. Philby agrees to take you on as a client."

"Whyever should he not?" Nigel asked. His eyebrows soared upward. "I can't think of many merchants who would refuse my brother's custom."

"Mr. Philby is exceedingly particular. My great-aunt transacted all her tea-related affairs through him, and I suspect he only deals with me because he feels a sense of obligation to her memory. It's rather sweet of him, actually."

Mountjoy drank more of his tea. He did like the taste. If Lily had met Mr. Philby in person he knew exactly why she was his customer. One look at her, and only the most hardhearted man could refuse her. "I hope your good word will persuade him to my side."

She looked at him, and when their eyes met, she did not look away. Nor did he. The sexual thrill was familiar. Compelling. Addicting. She looked at the papers before her, and he felt in some absurd way that he'd won. "One hopes, your grace. One hopes."

"May I ask what you are doing with these papers here?"

"An excellent question, sir. Marking down the likeliest spots for us to find ancient treasure. Your sister and I have done a preliminary survey of the property and determined where we believe some ancient tribe or Roman Legion might have had occasion to travel or live."

"It's all very scientific," Nigel said. Mountjoy remembered the way Nigel had been leaning over Lily when he came in. Was it possible Nigel was developing tender feelings toward Lily?

"I am sure it is," he replied.

Lily ate a grape, eyes closed, savoring the flavor as if she'd never tasted anything sweeter in her life. "They are ever so faintly chilled. Your cook keeps these on ice, I presume." Slowly, she opened her eyes. Mountjoy was aware of his brother's stare at Lily, and of his own. His gaze met hers, and he thought of sex. Hot, passionate, blood-burning sex. "Do you know," she said, "that once I ate some grapes that had been frozen through? They were wonderful. Ginny, my darling"—she turned on her chair—"have you ever eaten frozen grapes?"

"I don't believe so."

She plucked another grape from the bunch Mountjoy had set on her plate. "I think I'll write to Mr. Stevens and tell him I am quite settled that this year we shall have a new icehouse built. Our ice never lasts the summer. Late August becomes intolerable with nothing cold to drink."

"And Mr. Stevens is?" Nigel asked too quickly.

She ate another grape, languidly and with as much single-minded attention as before. Mountjoy had the wicked image of her stretched out naked on a bed—his bed—enjoying grapes while he stripped to his skin and joined her.

"My steward," she said, unaware of his wayward thoughts. "He's absolutely devoted to me."

And who, Mountjoy wondered, was not eventually absolutely devoted to her?

# Chapter Fifteen

LILY STOPPED WALKING WHEN SHE HEARD THE ECHO
of footsteps on the stone floor. Her pulse jumped with
anticipation. She waited and, as she knew would happen,
moments later the duke appeared from around the far corner.
He held a shielded candle, and when he saw her he, too,
stopped.

Of course the duke.

From habit, her fingers closed around her medallion.
Who but the duke would she meet at this dark-of-night hour?

"Your grace." She curtseyed to him, and he nodded and
crossed the remaining distance between them. They were
in a gallery hall of sorts, though it contained no paintings,
with original-to-the-structure Gothic arched windows along
one wall and a bare stone wall opposite. The ceiling was
ribbed and domed in the Gothic fashion. Light from the
duke's candle and hers flickered off the walls and the window glass. Had it been daylight she would have been able
to enjoy sunlight rippling through the thick panes of glass
instead of reflected candlelight.

"Wellstone." He gave her a half grin that sent her heart pounding. "Imagine us meeting like this."

"I'm not sure it's entirely safe," she said.

He gave her an inscrutable look then held up his candle to illuminate the windows. "Have you sketched this part of the house yet?"

"Several pages of my notebook are dedicated to this passageway." Half a notebook, actually. "The masonry and stonework are exemplary. And quite beautiful."

"What will you do with all your drawings?" Mountjoy stayed where he was. As did she. And yet, the connection between them tugged at her. She was more flustered by him than she cared to admit.

She shrugged. "Assemble them into a book I should think. I'll call it *A Study of England's Ancient Homes, Volume the First*, and publish under a man's name. Professor L. Carter Farnsworth. What do you think of that for a scholar's name?"

Mountjoy smiled. She did love the shape of his mouth. "That Professor Farnsworth cannot fail to find a publisher for such a work. There must be upward of half a dozen people in the whole of His Majesty's Empire who would put such a book in pride of place in their library."

"Would you?" She cocked her head. "Acquire me for your library?"

"My dear Wellstone, I would love to have you in my library."

"Between the royal quarto sheets, your grace?"

He didn't answer right away because he was trying not to laugh. "But of course."

Lily was close enough to the wall to stroke one of the stone ribs that lined the windows. "I think this corridor is my favorite in the whole of Bitterward."

The edge of his mouth twitched with a suppressed smile. "Yes. Just now this corridor is my favorite, too."

"I can feel the past here. Can't you?"

"No." He reached out and tapped one of the windowpanes. "But I can feel someone calculating my window tax."

She gave him a sideways look. "If ever there was a place to encounter a ghost, this precise spot is it." In the quiet, she gestured toward the windows. "Sometimes when I find myself in a place like this, I feel as if the world is weary of we humans."

"I as well."

"Whenever I walk here, I imagine knights and their ladies, feudal lords walking past these windows on their way to the Great Hall for a meal where the food is flavored with salt and saffron and pepper that costs half a year's income. I see Jesuits with prayer books in hand on their way to Matins."

"I don't believe Bitterward ever housed Jesuits."

"That does not signify, your grace. That is what I imagine. I hear them speaking in Latin as they walk."

"What an eccentric mind you have."

"It's an odd fascination of mine, I admit," she said. His coat was atrocious, yet she itched to put a hand on his chest.

"Born in your father's library."

"Yes. And come of age after I moved to Syton House." Her father's housekeeper, the woman who had, in effect, raised her after her mother died, had not accepted Lily's invitation to come with her. She had a husband and children who kept her there. "I found myself solely alone and in want of occupation in my free hours." She smoothed a wrinkle from her skirt. She was glad she still wore her evening gown. One did so want to look one's best at a time like this. "Out of sheer boredom, I inspected the house from top to bottom. I discovered the foundation was built on a Roman villa, or if not a villa, some such structure at any rate. There is a Roman bath belowstairs."

"I should like to see that."

Lily hesitated, on the brink of telling him that he must come to visit. She couldn't say such a thing. That presumed too much. Far too much for them both, for it assumed the sort of friendship from which one could not simply walk away.

"Given your interests, Miss Wellstone, there is a room here I think might well send you into raptures."

"Indeed?" She kept her hands buried in her skirts or she really would touch him. "Other than the east tower, I thought I'd been in every room in Bitterward." A portion of that part of the house was inaccessible. When she had asked Doyle about the locked door that blocked her access, he had politely informed her that he did not have a key, which she had taken, sensibly enough, to mean that Mountjoy did not wish anyone to enter that part of the tower.

"Yes." He held her gaze.

"Your grace. If you have a room in which to give me raptures, I should very much like to see it."

"Lily," he said, laughing at last. "Lily, you'll drive me mad."

"I don't see why."

"May I show you?"

She nodded, fully aware that she was agreeing to more than a tour of a usually inaccessible part of the house. "I should like that."

"Come along then."

She followed the duke out of the stone gallery hall. They turned a corner, then another, and at the end of that passage was a plain wooden door with a threshold worn to a curve in the middle from all the feet that had passed over it. Decorative ironwork covered the door from the hinges to the latch. Beside the door was an empty niche the height of her two hands with a scallop design carved into the stone above it. She took his candle while he fit a key to the lock and opened the door.

Mountjoy stepped across the threshold, his back to the door, keeping it open for her. Narrow stone stairs spiraled upward. As she went in, he pulled the door closed, and she said, "Do keep the key safe, your grace."

"I will." He took the lead in climbing to the very top of the tower. The passageway narrowed as they ascended. At the top was a door with no landing, just a stone threshold curved in the center simply from centuries of feet stopping there. Mountjoy opened that door, too. The latch operated by a simple rope one pulled to lift the bar on the interior of the door. He took his candle from her and they went in.

"I came across this room shortly after we moved here," he said. Lily set her candle on a stone table by the door while the duke set his candle next to hers. The air inside was cool. She could not see much beyond a few feet, though she could tell the room was round and that there were windows in the opposite wall.

With a flint he took from the stone table just by the door, he lit a lantern. "Nigel was at Rugby by then," he continued. "I don't recall where Eugenia was. Visiting our aunt and uncle in Haltwhistle, I think." He snuffed out their candles and lifted the lantern. "Mind your step," he said. He walked farther in.

Lily, too, walked into the center of the tower room. "Oh." The walls were bare stone, and it seemed that every inch was carved with fanciful figures, grotesqueries, and scrollwork.

"What do you think?" he asked.

She put a hand to her heart and found she could barely speak. "Magnificent." She spared him a glance before she craned her neck to see the ceiling. "Thank you. Thank you for bringing me here."

"You're welcome." Mountjoy crossed the circular room, which was not large, and lit a second lamp. Here, the windows were deep wells that narrowed to panes of glass. An archer could have stood in the well, before the glass had been installed, aiming at advancing hordes. But it was the carved stone in between the windows that caused her stunned admiration.

Mountjoy cleared his throat. "My apologies if you are offended."

"I'm not offended." She stifled the urge to giggle. "What a marvelous sense of humor the stonemasons must have had."

"They're lewd, Wellstone, not comic."

"A fine line, sir. Very fine." She took a step closer. "Marvelously fine."

"In that case, I'll give you a key so that you may take sketches at your leisure." She could hear the smile in his voice. "For Professor Farnsworth, you understand."

"Yes, thank you." She looked at him from over her shoulder and returned his grin. "I think you'll find him very grateful."

His gaze traveled slowly from her head to her toes. "I hope so, Wellstone."

She went to stand beside him at one of the windows. "The view from here must be breathtaking during the day."

"It is."

She examined the room, aware that Mountjoy was watching her. The ceiling, too, was covered with stone figures and yes, some of the figures were engaged in sexual acts. "This is astonishing," she said. She turned in a circle, slowly, taking in as much detail as she could.

"I hoped you might appreciate it."

Absurdly touched that he'd thought to bring her here, to a room that was so plainly a private retreat, she could barely speak. There were Turkish carpets on the floor and blankets piled on a chest against the wall because with no fireplace the air here would certainly never be very warm. There was one chair that looked quite comfortable to sit on, and beside that a table with several books and near that a chaise that couldn't be more than a few years old. On the table beside the door were a decanter, a humidor, a flint, glasses, and several bottles.

"Thank you," she whispered.

"I don't allow anyone in here but a few trusted servants."

Lily put a hand on his arm. "I'm honored you've shown me. It needn't go in the professor's book, you know. It's enough that I've seen this."

He gave her a sheepish grin. "I was quite a young man when I came to Bitterward. You can suppose the effect this room had on someone of my tender years. I kept it secret from Nigel and Eugenia. They were far too young to see . . ." He gestured at a vaguely bearlike creature in congress with a centaur.

"I understand completely."

"Before I knew it, this room was the only place where I could escape my fate."

"Sanctuary." She tilted her head, her hand still touching his arm. "I have a similar retreat at Syton House. Without the stonework, alas. I am green with envy that you have monsters and gargoyles."

"By all means study them."

"I will." She turned to the wall and drank in the cavorting beasts and monsters.

From behind her, Mountjoy said, "I remember the day the attorney came to Haltwhistle, that's where Eugenia, Nigel, and I were living at the time, with our mother's sister. He sat at the best table in the only parlor we had and showed me the family lines that led to me. I made him go over and over it, and each time, he ended up at our branch of the Hamptons. With me." He let out a breath. "He'd been researching five years, he said, on behalf of the dukedom. Following the branches. They'd somehow lost track of my father's branch for a while. I suppose in those earlier days they thought us too remote. The attorney, it happens, had set out to prove the line was extinguished. Instead, he found me. Each time we went over what he claimed was incontrovertible proof, I thought sure he'd find he'd made a mistake, that if anyone was to be the next Mountjoy, it would not be me."

She turned just enough to see him. "Yet, here you are."

The duke shrugged. "There was no time to air out the country smell or knock the dirt from my boots." Lily went still when he came to stand behind her. She found it difficult to concentrate on anything but him. Why, oh why, had he been so kind as to show her a room like this? He would break her heart. He truly would. "I went from Haltwhistle to the house in London, then Bitterward and a seat in the Lords with hardly a breath in between."

"Who doesn't dream of one day discovering one is secretly royalty?" To her left stone animals cavorted above and between the windows; a stag, a bear, a boar, and even a swan. She could make out the broken chain that identified the creature as representing the Hampton family sigil that had found its way into the Mountjoy coat of arms, with the later addition of the ducal coronet.

He leaned a shoulder against the wall where there was a smooth space between the window-well and the carved stone forest. His mouth twitched. She did so like the way he looked when he was trying not to smile. "I never did. Never once."

"Well, I can assure you I grew up convinced I was a princess."

"You would."

Lily's stomach did a flip. They stood so close. So close. "Hidden away for safety while my father bravely and in secret fought against our country's enemies. I was to have married a prince and taken my place on the throne of my beloved subjects."

"Where you would prove yourself a fair and benevolent ruler."

"Precisely. Alas, no one ever came to the house with papers to prove my true identity. My father is my true father. Not that I'd want any other. I love him. Despite everything."

"I've not met the man, but I'll own I do not care for what I've heard." He frowned. "He neglected you when you were a girl. He abuses your generosity now that you are a woman. Was there no one besides you and your father in the house? A governess to see to your education?"

She tipped her head to one side. "Our housekeeper taught me to read and do figures. To sew and knit, too, and how to cut fabric. She was a genius with scissors and a needle."

"And she taught you to run a household."

Her urge to touch him rose up again, threatening to overwhelm her. "Skills that have stood me in good stead all these many years, I must say."

"Could your father not spare twenty pounds to educate you?"

"Why would he, when I was so wicked that my education would surely have been a waste?"

He backed up a step to allow her to advance along the wall and continue her study. "Because he was your father. Did he never sing to you or read you stories?"

"Others are not as lucky in their families as you were."

"I'm no prince, but I was indeed fortunate in my parents."

"There's still hope that someone will inform me that I am a princess and much beloved by my subjects who long to have me back in my rightful place as a gentle and benevolent ruler."

He grinned. "You'll tell me the moment that happens, won't you?"

"Oh, certainly."

Mountjoy put a hand on a smooth bit of the wall by the window. "I was fortunate in my aunt and uncle, too, that they took in a family of orphans. We might have been split up, you know, Eugenia, Nigel, and I." He smiled, but his eyes stayed serious. She did not speak into the silence. The quiet went on too long. With his other hand, he touched a rabbit carved at his eye level. "My good fortune persists, Lily, for you came here. To Bitterward."

"You flatter me, your grace."

"Flattery?" He drew a finger along the stone back of a gargoyle having sexual relations with a nymph, and she, God help her, watched the slow movement of his finger. "Have you any notion, Lily, of the effect you have on men?"

"Some. I'm not a fool about that."

"You walk into a room, and no one can think of anyone but you. Where before there was tedium, now there is life. We all want that warmth and joy for ourselves."

"We?"

"Dr. Longfield. My brother. Every man to cross your path."

"You?" she asked.

His eyes pierced her through. "Beautiful. Elegant. Never wearing anything that isn't the height of fashion and exquisitely made."

"I spent too many years deprived of elegant attire, forbidden anything pretty." She licked her lower lip. "Now that I am free of that, I refuse to live my life without fashion or beauty. When I'm old and wrinkled and breathing my last, I won't be sorry for having lived a life with beauty in it."

"Your damned father. You shouldn't go back to him."

"I must. You know that. Besides, if I were to stay here, you'd soon reach a point where you wished me gone. Best to leave while your hosts still like you, that's what I've always felt." She breached the space between them to touch his cravat. "You could do with a little of my conceit. Don't deny you aren't aware of *your* appeal."

"Tonight," he said, "I deny nothing." He stepped forward and put his hands on her shoulders. His thumbs brushed along her collarbones. "Not you. And not me."

The world vanished from beneath her feet.

## Chapter Sixteen

In the back of his mind, Mountjoy knew he still had a chance to stop this from happening. He could step away from her and turn the conversation to her plans for treasure hunting or to bloody architecture. Lily, being the intelligent creature that she was, would know he'd lost his nerve.

To be honest, though, whatever guilt he might feel over involving himself with a woman besides the one he was supposed to marry, he could tuck away very far from this particular moment. He stayed where he was, his hands on her shoulders and his thumbs sweeping over her soft skin. Her eyes stayed on his face, and he could see she was deciding what she would allow to happen.

There was no telling what she would decide about the two of them.

Without letting go of her he said, "I dreamed about you last night."

"I'm not responsible for your dreams."

"No, but that damned medallion of yours might be." He

reached out and touched the metal. "What if that Gypsy's magic works and that's why I can't get you out of my head or my dreams?"

She burst out laughing. "Oh, it doesn't, and well you know it."

"Are you certain?" He dropped the medallion and moved closer. She retreated, but that put the wall at her back.

"Very," she said. "There's no such thing as magic."

Their eyes locked, and he smiled because of the challenge there. Beyond anything, he wanted her in his arms. "Last night," he said, "my dreams were filled with you."

"Proper dreams, I hope."

"Not very."

"How odd, your grace. For I dreamed of you last night."

"Was yours a proper dream?"

She lifted her chin. "You kissed me."

"On the cheek, I presume?" He held her gaze. He wanted to be sure he would leave this room having stripped them both naked and left no passion unexplored between them. The uncertainty of gaining what he wanted aroused him. She was so maddeningly forthright and in control of herself. She might well tell him no.

"No, your grace. That was not where you kissed me."

"Perhaps it was your forehead I kissed. I might have done that."

She put her hands behind her back and shook her head. "Not there either."

He arched his eyebrows. "Your hand?"

"No."

"I confess myself baffled." He moved close enough to draw a finger along the top of her shoulder. "Such warm skin, Lily. Soft beneath my touch." He continued stroking her. Caressing her. He trailed the backs of his fingers along her collarbone. "Yours is skin a farmer or a duke would enjoy beneath his own."

She pushed away from the wall and walked past him to the table. She turned with a motion that sent the fabric of her skirts snapping. Her eyes swept over him from head to toe. "I do believe you are being deliberately wicked, your grace."

"Do you object?" He walked to her, and he took her in his arms and turned so they ended with him backed up to the table and her with a hand on his chest.

"Wickedness does not become you."

"I think it does," he said. "But in any event, I cannot help my dreams." He resisted the urge to pull her into his arms. Lord, but she was astonishingly pretty. "Or what you do in them. And you have done things in my dreams, Wellstone. Such things."

"Infamous, your grace, that you lay the fault at my feet."

He gripped the edge of the table on either side of his legs. He was mad. Mad to be pursuing this. He could not imagine doing anything but this. "In your dream, where did I kiss you?"

A grin flashed over her face. "Where else but in the library?"

He'd brought her here, where they would not be interrupted, and if it was not a bedroom, that hardly mattered. They were alone. He leaned forward, still holding on to the edge of the table. He was very much aware that he was responsible for what was happening between them. He wanted to fuck her, and she knew it and had come here with him. "That's not where I kissed you in *my* dream. Shall I show you?"

She touched a finger to his chin. "Let me guess."

Once, he thought. Once with her would be enough, though if this alluring, fascinating woman wasn't averse to an affair, well, then. His life would become much more interesting for as long as they lasted. "Try."

"Only if it would please you, your grace."

"I'll tell you if you don't."

She took a step closer and went up on her toes. His stomach bottomed out. He saw her lips part just as his eyes closed. She put her hand to his cheek and slid the cool tips of her fingers across his skin. She kissed his chin and drew back.

He stayed just where he was, leaning slightly forward. He opened his eyes. "How disappointing."

"In what way?"

"That's not where you kissed me."

Her eyes glinted with humor. "I'm sure it's where I meant to kiss you."

They weren't far apart. He leaned forward another inch or two and brushed his mouth over hers. She went still. Only for a moment, but enough that his heart gave a lurch. Then her palm cupped the side of his face, and she kissed him, and he let her. He invited her to kiss him, and she closed the distance between them until she stood between his spread thighs, and her torso pressed against his.

He leaned into the kiss and opened his mouth over hers, and she did reciprocate. Her hands moved to the back of his neck and her fingers pulled his head to hers. Lily Wellstone kissed the way she lived. Boldly. According to her taste. With conviction. Never married, and she kissed like this? Like a courtesan.

For all that she was bold and taking exactly what she wanted, she wasn't a courtesan or his mistress. He knew better than this and didn't give a damn.

His hands disengaged from the table, and he was holding her tight against him. Bringing her closer, closer. Jesus, not close enough. The hell with holding anything back. No man in his right mind would hold back with her.

She made a small sound in the back of her throat, and his tongue was in her mouth, and hers met his, touched, swept away, and her hands cupped his face as if he were precious to her, when, how could he be?

She did not break the kiss but gentled it. So tender, and he was content with that, too. Part of his mind was engaged with imagining her naked and accepting the pleasure her body afforded. They'd burn to ashes, the two of them, if things progressed to that.

At last, she drew away. Her hands stayed around his shoulders. He left his arms around her waist. "*Mmm*," she said, low and throaty. Gratified. She ran her fingertips under-neath his eyes, along the line of his cheek, his nose and jaw. And his mouth. "I suppose your other lovers tell you how much they adore kissing you."

*Other lovers.* He wanted that to mean she now considered herself a member of that cadre. "Not in so many words."

She smiled. "Well, you're a lovely, lovely man, and I adore kissing you."

"But not enough to make you lose your head?"

"Or you yours," she said.

"It was a near thing, I promise." He lowered his head to hers, his lips hovering above hers. "Perhaps we ought to try again. See if we can discover where we went wrong."

"Perhaps we should." She drew away, but he closed his thighs, trapping her gently between his legs. She could move away if she wished. "I wanted to kiss you tonight, and now I have."

"And?"

Her eyes lost their glitter of humor, but he didn't dare ask her what made that vanish. Not yet. "And," she said, "I quite enjoyed it. Did you?"

"You know the answer to that." He brought her close. The smile that curved her mouth made him mad to know what she was thinking, what she intended. Had she decided what would happen here? Between the two of them?

"I don't think I do."

They ended up looking at each other, and Mountjoy didn't know what to do or say in response. So he kissed her again, and she melted against him and damn him to Hell if he wasn't even more aroused. He took the lead this time and, yes, her kisses drove him mad. Wonderfully mad.

When they broke apart again, his brain must have been addled because he heard himself say, "Have you been to bed with a man before?"

That pert smile of hers danced on her mouth. "Have you been to bed with a woman?"

He stared at her lips and then looked into her eyes. She

was a passionate woman, but unmarried, and whatever else had happened between them, she might not be as experienced as he'd assumed. "Several times. Have you? Been to bed with a man?"

"Of course."

"Your soldier."

"Does that bother you?"

He brought her closer. "That you've been with a man before? Not at all." A half-truth. He was jealous of her previous lover, of the way he'd captured her heart. "But if this was to be your first time, I'd be more careful. That's the only reason I asked."

"How thoughtful." She leaned closer. "If this were your first time, I promise I would have been gentle with you."

She never failed to amuse him at the most unexpected times. "Thank God I'm no virgin."

"I should say so."

He touched the medallion around her neck. "In my dream," he said, "you wore this." He smoothed a finger over the scrollwork etched in the metal. "Strange that I recall that detail so vividly."

"You have a labyrinth of a brain, sir."

"I parted ways with my mistress before I came here from London."

"Why?"

He shrugged. "No reason other than she no longer interested me, and I had a friend who was enamored of her. As well let her move on to a lover inclined to be more generous than I was."

"Are you stingy with your lovers?" Her smile knew too much, but then Lily was unique among the ladies he knew. "That surprises me."

He traced the line of her lower lip with his finger. "I am generous. But not as generous as a new lover is apt to be."

"Did you enjoy making love to her?" Her voice was languid, warm silk, inviting, appreciative, and underneath a taste of need that resonated in her words, her half-shuttered gaze, the curve of her body against his. He brought his hands to the side of her throat and slid them down, fingers spread over her skin, along the curve of her bosom. She tipped her head back, and he wanted to bask in his reaction to her. He understood the mystery that was Lily, knew the contradiction between the sweetness of her face and the sharp wit behind it.

"I did. But then as you know, I am a man of country appetites." He dropped a kiss at the corner of her mouth. He kissed her again, and she melted against him. She responded with a soft moan and a step forward that brought her torso even closer against his. His hands wandered down her corseted back to the softness of that dip of her spine just before the swell of her bottom. The contact turned raw and needy, and he was halfway to climax already. The tingle of arousal centered in his nether parts, and he wanted that climax, the sweetness of completion in a woman's body.

Lord, but this was the kind of kiss that led to naked bodies. He drew back, but kept his arms around her and only enough to say, "How far. How far are you willing to let this go? More than just a kiss? More than your mouth on me or mine on you?"

Her eyes fluttered down, lashes dark against the pale skin of her cheek. "Two kisses, I think." She looked at him through her lashes. "Someplace convenient."

"Two kisses seems a paltry number on which to decide." He tightened his arms around her. "There ought to be a third, don't you agree?"

"There ought to be a sufficient sample."

"Four?"

"Four seems excessive to me."

"Wellstone." He trailed his thumbs along the inner curve of her breasts then pushed his fingers into her hair. A few pins came loose and he picked them out and kept going until her hair fell around her shoulders in golden waves, and it was wicked, seeing her with her hair down. Forbidden. As if she'd stepped from her boudoir. And not one word of protest passed her lips. "I'll take whatever you offer me."

He waited while she drew in a breath and slowly let it out. He stood straight, moving them away from the table but still holding her head between his hands.

"Tell me what you want, your grace. Is it only a few kisses? Or is there more?"

"I want to see you in your bare skin. Lily. Will you do that for me? Every inch of you nude for my eyes to devour?"

## Chapter Seventeen

WOULD SHE? LILY COULD SCARCELY THINK, SO DRUGGED was she from his kisses and the wicked promise of his voice. Lord, what wouldn't she do for him? His request was outrageous. Brazen. If she were a proper sort of woman, she'd swoon with outrage. If she were a proper sort of woman, she wouldn't be here with him. Alone.

She couldn't imagine telling him no, even though she ought to.

There was no pretense between them in respect of physical desires, and that was at once frightening and exhilarating. She had been on her own, directing her own life for long enough to have gotten used to that. Tonight, he would be the perfect lover, if things went that far, this man who made her heart race for the first time since she'd lost Greer.

"Lily?" His thumbs brushed over her cheeks. His hands stayed in her hair, holding her in place, and all Lily could think was that this beautiful and fierce man wanted her. He wasn't after her fortune, which other men certainly had been. He didn't *want* her in any way but the carnal sense, and that meant he wanted her. Only her. Only for what she was right now. He wanted nothing of her besides greedy pleasure. Best yet, he was indulging her love of words and play, a patient man. Thoughtful.

Lily leaned toward him. The sight of him, the scent of him, the warmth of his hands on her made her imagine the moment when he would push inside her body, and just that made her shiver with longing. He must know how much she wanted him.

"You are the most unusual creature I've ever met," he said. "What the devil *are* you thinking?"

She could let this happen and if afterward the situation became uncomfortable or went badly, she could retreat to her solitude at Syton House, and she would be safe. No one would know she'd been wicked because Mountjoy would never tell a soul.

"I am thinking," she said slowly, "how improper it would be for me to remove my clothes."

"Very." His mouth twitched.

"A gentleman would not ask it of me."

He took her medallion between the fingers of one hand and rubbed the surface. "I am aware."

She put a finger to his lips to still his smile then put that same finger across hers. She studied him. "If I agree, your grace, I have a requirement."

"Oh?"

"Just one."

"I'm a generous man." His smile was an invitation to sin, but she could see caution flickering around the edges of his mouth. He was a duke, after all, and women must surely have schemed with demands of him before. "Within reason."

She managed to hold off a smile. She wanted him to suffer. He deserved it before she ceded the very last bit of power she had over him. "That's a pity because I think you'll find my request unreasonable."

"Then why make it?" That was frank curiosity on his part.

"Because it is the one requirement I have before I give up everything." She took a step back, and he released her.

"Put me out of my misery, Lily, and tell me what you want from me so that we either proceed or go our separate ways."

"It's a simple thing."

"You say."

"It is. I promise." He arched his eyebrows at her. "Allow me to take your wardrobe in hand."

He gaped at her, and she reached with her free hand and tapped the underside of his chin. A laugh burst from him, and he let go of her hand to rake his fingers through his hair. "My wardrobe?"

"Give me an hour with your tailor, two if he is a stupid man, and I can manage your clothes no matter where I am. From Syton House if need be." She drew off a glove, slowly. He watched. She dangled it from one hand. "I make your wardrobe a condition because I don't know how much longer I can stand to see you dressed as if you don't care a fig what you look like."

"I don't."

She sighed. "Such a disappointment, your grace." She looked at her glove. "Should I put this back on?"

"Witch," he said. "Temptress."

"Lord, I hope so." She crossed her arms beneath her bosom and tapped her toe on the carpet. "One's appearance matters. One ought to take pride in looking well. You are a duke. You ought to dress as if you believe it of yourself." She fingered the bottom hem of his coat. "Look at this. It's only a decent fit. And your shirts ought to be made of a finer material." She took another step back and worked her fingers free of her other glove. "I'm not suggesting anything but that you ought to care how you look. It affects Ginny and your brother, you know."

Mountjoy snorted. "They're more affected by the fact that I can afford to pay their debts and expenses and put a better than decent roof over all our heads."

"No one disputes that. Not for a moment. But, your grace, you are such a lovely man. I'm not suggesting you set fashion, though I think with my assistance you would. I am suggesting that you wear colors that flatter you and clothes that fit your magnificent body. Clothes that make others think, here is a man worth knowing." She touched his cheek. "Because it's true. Not to mention, you might have more success with Miss Jane Kirk if you dressed the part of a duke."

For some time he regarded her with a solemn expression, and she really had no idea what he was thinking. She thought of all the colors she could put him in that would accentuate his green eyes and take advantage of the drama of all that thick, dark hair.

"If I accede to this requirement of yours, I want you to take off every stitch you have on right now." Lily looked him up and down, and Mountjoy waited while she did that.

"Everything, you say?"

"Yes." Mountjoy walked over to the side table and filled a glass with two fingers from one of the decanters there. "I have a decent Madeira. Port, as well, if you'd like something to drink."

"No, thank you." Stubborn, stubborn man.

He walked back to her but stopped halfway to tug on his coat and take a sip from his glass. "What's wrong with my coat?"

"The pattern is unimaginative, it doesn't suit a man of your size and form, and the cloth is inferior wool." She waved a hand at him. "The color, my God, what am I to call that color? Mud? Ditchwater? You're fortunate you're handsome."

"You are aggravating in the extreme." He took a drink. "Has anyone told you that before?"

"Many times."

He walked toward her until he stood an arm's length away, this time with the cut-glass tumbler in one hand. His eyes scoured her. "My wardrobe?" he said in a low, silky voice. "Is that really all you ask?"

"You told me what you wanted," she said. "I told you what would convince me to agree to such an outrageous and improper request as yours."

"Every stitch, Lily?"

"I think you made yourself plain."

His expression turned so subtly wicked she could have sworn the room got warmer just from the effect. "That's not all I want."

"It's no concern of mine if you failed to clearly convey your request."

"I want to touch you. And, forgive me if I use a country term, *cover you*."

She adored his willingness to draw out their wordplay. "I believe *fornicate* is the more accurate term."

"I suppose it is." He took another drink, but not in time to hide the twitch of his mouth. "So?"

"You know my terms." She shook her hair behind her shoulders.

His gaze lingered on her mouth before dropping to her bosom. "Done. I put myself into your hands."

Her stomach dropped. Too late now to back out. She'd made her pact with the devil.

He set his drink on the table. "Lily," he said very softly. So softly she could barely hear him.

"*Yes?*"

His gaze raked her up and down. "I've agreed to everything you asked of me."

"So you have, your grace."

She turned her back to him. She could not see out any of the narrow windows, just bits of faint reflections in the glass. Mountjoy came close enough to work the fastenings down the back of her bodice. His fingers brushed her skin from time to time. Or lingered there, on her back. She managed the tapes herself when the time came. Her petticoat rustled to the floor. She caught her gown when it was loose enough for her to step free of it, though she didn't. She turned and found Mountjoy's attention on her, gaze traveling over her.

One must do the outrageous with style. With élan. With complete conviction.

Lily dropped her gown. It caught on her hips, and she reached down to push the fabric free. She turned her back to him again. "Unlace my corset?"

"Of course." His fingers nimbly worked the lace, and when it was loose enough, he drew it over her head. He stepped away. She wore just her chemise now, and her slippers and stockings. "Turn around, Lily."

She did, and watched him watch her. He stood with his eyes half closed, one loosely fisted hand held to his lips. He lowered his hand enough for her to see his mouth.

She unfastened her garters, one then the other, and shed her stockings and now she stood before him in her chemise.

"Go on," he said.

Lily threw herself over the brink. She drew off the chemise, and when the linen came over her head, the room fell utterly silent. She kept her eyes open because she was no coward. Not that it mattered. Mountjoy wasn't looking at her face.

Lily stood in the froth of her gown and petticoats around her calves, holding her chemise in one hand. Cool air washed over her skin. She was aroused and abashed at the same time, and yet there was also a shiver of anticipation. She was exactly as she was meant to be.

The duke reached behind him for his tumbler and drank half the contents. Glass in hand, he walked toward her. "Stay just as you are," he said. He paced a circle around her. Slowly. When she could see him again, he returned his drink to the table behind him. "Simply ravishing."

"Thank you." She knew, of course, that she was not unattractive and that her figure was one men admired, but she knew nothing of how her body compared with any other woman's when a man experienced in sin was thinking of indulging in more.

He held out his hand, and after a moment's hesitation she put her bare palm on his. With his assistance, she stepped over her clothes and found that without her shoes she had to tilt her chin to look at him. He made no move to touch her beyond the contact of their hands; he just continued to inspect her. "So very lovely," he whispered. "I could look at you all night."

"Is that all?"

With his other hand, he cupped the back of her head, fingers spread out on her skull, tipping her head to his. "I told you what else I wanted." She adored the gruffness of his voice. "Tell me what will convince you to agree to that. Diamonds for your fingers? Sapphires around the column of your throat? Ropes of pearls? I assure you, my taste in jewelry is exemplary."

"I don't need any of that."

"What do you need?"

She met his gaze. "To know you want me."

"Do you doubt it?" His voice roughened, and she found herself pulled against him, her bare skin against his torso. "Christ, how can you doubt it?"

"Easily enough, as here I stand without any finery to hide my flaws. You want sex, but do you want me?"

"What flaws? It's you I want. Lily Wellstone. No one else will do for me and therefore, if there are flaws, I want those, too." The fingers of one hand glided down her shoulders, along her spine, and to the small of her back and lower. "Your skin is unconscionably soft, and that, my dear Wellstone, is no flaw."

"Thank you."

"Are we too near the windows? I don't want you to be cold."

"I'm not."

"Good. That's very good." Both his hands slicked up her body. He picked her up and carried her to the chaise longue, and the very first thing he did after he'd laid her down was say, "Shall we see how convincing I can be?"

# Chapter Eighteen

❦

HE WAS MAD TO BE DOING THIS. UTTERLY MAD. JUST now, he'd not trade madness for sanity, not for the world. She was nude, and he had never in his life wanted a woman as much as he wanted Lily right now.

So here he was, sitting beside her on the chaise, and she was in her bare skin. The little witch had seduced him with that pert smile of hers and her quick wit and by shocking him out of his usual dour habits and left him with nothing but need. She'd beguiled him and aroused him, and now at this moment, if she were to ask him for carte blanche in return for allowing him to touch her, he might actually agree, he was that far gone with lust.

Because, good God, Lily Wellstone had the face of an angel, the body of a goddess, and the spirit of the devil glinting from her eyes. She was a woman worth losing his soul for. Mountjoy thought he'd never in his life seen a more erotic sight than her stretched out naked the way she was. The chaise longue was dark blue, and her skin was smooth and alabaster white against the fabric. Her Gypsy medallion glittered gold against the upper part of her stomach, not far below her breasts, and her hair spread out in golden waves.

"What a lovely body you have," he said. She was not familiar to him like this, her lush curves bared to his examination, her eyes soft on him, her will, at the moment, in abeyance. Patient. Waiting for him. No matter her boldness and passion, she was not, he thought, as experienced as lovers he'd taken in the past, though he did not doubt for a moment that she knew what she wanted. "I've wondered what you would look like. Dreamed about that."

He took his time studying her, his Venus. Her smile widened while he did, but there was a reserve to her expression that puzzled him. He lifted a hand along the line of her leg, but did not touch her. Not yet. Anticipation was almost enough. The thought of having even a moment of mastery over her, fleeting though any such moment might be, was unbearably luscious.

"You've seen me almost every day since I came here." She shifted a little, stretching, not in the least shy. And yet, there was a center of quiet in her that made him think she was not as sanguine as she appeared.

"True," he said. "I have. But not like are you now." Lily was a frustrating delight to be around. She challenged everything he believed about himself, and more than once through her reactions to him or through his reactions to her, there was reflected back to him a man he barely recognized as Mountjoy. A stranger whom he thought he might actually like. "I do like a woman with long legs," he said. "Most of your height is in your legs."

"Then I am fortunate, your grace," she said.

He cocked his head, tracing with his eyes the curve of her breasts, the slope of her waist. "I've always preferred brunettes. And women who do not look as if I'd break them. And here you are, with your golden hair." He touched one of her curls. "And your slender figure and a face that makes me think you must be protected from the world, let alone from me, and I cannot imagine any woman I want more than you."

"Good fortune rains upon me."

"You're no delicate flower to be cosseted and pampered." She tipped her head. "Not even a little?"

He touched her hip, curved his fingers around the outside of her there, and the room got smaller. The world held just the two of them, with hardly room for his desire. "You'd be bored in a week if I did, Lily."

"All the same, a little pampering would not go amiss."

He was aware that there was more to the pitch of his arousal than *what* she was, which right now was stark-naked and gazing at him from half-lidded eyes. This was Lily, a confident, curiously independent woman who fascinated him, challenged him, and wasn't ashamed to admit her passions. There was also, quite undeniably, the lure of the forbidden. He really shouldn't. They shouldn't. But he was far beyond denying himself anything Lily would consent to do with him.

She adjusted herself on the chaise longue, on her back, with one knee raised, an arm underneath her head, and all her beautiful curls spilling onto the fabric beneath her. Mountjoy wondered for a moment if he would last long enough to get inside her, if she agreed to that. She might not, though he was determined to convince her.

He knelt on the floor beside her and put one hand on the far side of the chaise, near her rib cage. He lowered his head to her belly but kept his eyes on her face. A man didn't need a title to be a good lover. Even before he was Mountjoy, he'd learned how not to be a fumbling boor when he took a woman to bed. "What would you say if I asked permission to kiss you here?"

"I would ask you why you'd want to do such a thing."

"To see if your skin is as soft as it looks." He bent closer. "Why else would I want to do such a thing to a beautiful woman?"

"I admit I'm curious to know the answer."

"Allow me to discover for us both." He kissed her right below the spot where her medallion lay. The scent of violets was sweet near her skin, and he kissed his way upward until he reached her breasts. She'd denied she was cold, but her skin rippled with a chill and was cool to touch.

"Liar," he whispered.

Her hand fluttered onto his shoulder. "Your grace, I protest." Her dark eyes were mischievous. "I almost never lie."

"But you are cold." He dipped his head to her stomach, and in a moment of pure whimsy, kissed her Gypsy medallion, too. She arched toward him, and he worked his way to her navel, dipping his tongue in and out of the indentation.

"I'm feeling much warmer now."

"Your skin is indeed very soft." He moved back up and hovered over her breasts. "But what about here? Are you sensitive here? If I kissed you here, would that give you pleasure?"

"I confess I wonder that myself."

"Allow me, then, to help us discover the answer."

"In a spirit of inquiry, I think you ought."

Her breast fit his cupped hand, and, oh, so pretty. As lovely as the rest of her. He flicked his tongue over her nipple, and she made a soft noise of appreciation. He closed his mouth over her while he cupped the outer curve of her breast. Lord, but she was soft, and the way she filled the curve of his palm was going to drive him mad. Her nipple tightened in his mouth, and that aroused him even more.

He did the same to her other breast, then kissed his way down again, and though he'd thought about pressing kisses along her legs, what he did was part her thighs and set himself to the task of finding out what would fetch her. What touch did she prefer? Did she like to have her breasts stroked, held, or gently pinched? What other parts of her body intensified her physical reactions?

He gave no quarter because after what she'd done to him she didn't deserve any. At one point, he replaced his mouth with his fingers and watched her face, and that was that for him. Her lips were parted, her eyes looking inward, the middle of her back arched off the chaise, and then he found the rhythm she needed, and he stopped long enough to earn him a fiery look.

"Rogue," she said. "Horrible man."

"I've been called worse." But he did himself and her the courtesy of finishing her with his mouth. Her hands clutched his head, and after just a moment longer, there, she shuddered and cried out.

She held nothing back. His name broke from her as she broke, and the sight, her reaction and his, was everything he'd imagined and more. While she came down from her orgasm he kissed the inside of her thighs, one then the other, and drew his fingers along the length of her outside leg.

Her eyes fluttered open. "Oh, my," she said in a low voice. "You are a very talented man."

Next to her, Mountjoy turned onto his side, half sitting to unfasten his breeches and free his stone-hard cock from his clothes, and she held out her arms to him and like that, in a smooth transition he was over her body, sliding himself inside her.

Oh God. Inside her. Warm and soft, and it was like he'd never been with a woman before, as if this were his first time and had no idea what to expect. He lost his ability to speak from the very first thrust into her, and she moaned long and deep and wrapped her legs around his hips and her arms around his shoulders.

He could barely open his eyes or focus when he did; all he could do was try to keep up with the sensation. God help him, this was Lily at last, warm and soft beneath him, hot and slick around him, her breath on his skin. Her arms holding him close, her body moving with his, meeting him. Matching him. Her fingers pressed into him, urging him deeper.

After they'd let the wonder settle between them, she worked the buttons of his coat, and he paused long enough to shrug it off, because if that's what she wanted, he wasn't going to deny her, and then he went back to fucking her. Her hands stayed busy removing his cravat then opening his waistcoat, and he had to stop again to remove that hindrance to her pleasure, and then pull out of her long enough to shrug off his braces and pull his shirt over his head. Where the hell that landed he didn't know and didn't care.

"I want to see you," she said. She sat up and ran her palms over his chest, along his shoulders, and down his spine to the curve of his behind.

"Later."

"Now." She grabbed his head with both hands. "You beautiful man, I want to see you. And feel your skin against mine."

Maybe the delay to remove the rest of his clothes wasn't so bad, because he'd been very close to climax, and not nearly ready to be done. He pulled off his boots and stockings and when he stood to shuck his breeches and small-clothes, she leaned on one elbow and gave him a look that melted him. He put his hands on his hips and gazed at her.

"Come here, your grace," she said after she'd thoroughly examined him. She held out a hand. "I'll catch my death otherwise."

"We can't have that." He rejoined her on the chaise, and she was right. They were skin to skin now, and her body was warm against his, her breasts soft against his chest, and he kissed her until she pushed him back, palms on his chest, until he was on his back.

She stroked him, trailed her fingers down his chest and to his belly, and he couldn't take his eyes off her. "I knew you would be lovely to look at." She drew in a breath. "But I didn't know I'd want to lick you from head to toe."

"Deny yourself nothing." He pushed his fingers into her hair.

She laughed and bent to kiss his chest, and when her tongue flicked over his nipple he groaned. The entire time she was doing this, pressing kisses on his body, her hand wandered toward his belly, along his thigh, and, Christ, yes, to his cock. He held his breath, hoping for her mouth, though her hand around him, then on his sac was enough to make him hiss with pleasure.

She looked up at him, and said, "Am I too wicked, your grace?"

"My love, if I may be honest—"

"Please."

"You're not wicked enough."

Her eyes widened, and slowly, she smiled. "Tell me what would be wicked enough. Better yet, show me."

His fingers tightened in her hair and he gently pushed her in the direction of his sex. "Use your mouth on my prick. The way you did before."

And she did. He about went out of his mind. Her tongue traced the length of him, then followed the head of his cock, moved down to his bollocks, and she'd have kept going until he came in her mouth if he hadn't stopped her.

"Why?" she asked.

"I don't want to come yet."

Her fingers remained lightly wrapped around him. "I adore your cock. He's lovely and awe-inspiring."

Mountjoy laughed. "Do go on."

"He tastes delicious, and I love the sound you make when I kiss him."

He took her upper arms and pulled her up until she lay on him. "Sit," he said. She ended up straddling his belly. "Like so. I want to look at you some more."

"I'd rather kiss your cock, your grace."

"Madam," he said. Lord, she was an unmarried woman, not a widow or a courtesan. But she was no innocent, either. "Another time you'll take me to completion that way again, but not tonight."

She gave him another melting look. "Do you promise?"

"I do." He covered her breasts and levered himself up enough to kiss the tips and run his hands along her stomach, all that soft, smooth skin under his fingertips. He put her under him again and while he entered her, slowly this time,

as every moment passed he wondered why he didn't feel
that he was at all mastering her. The more he tried to think
about fucking, the more images of her flashed through his
head. The way she smiled, her in the breakfast room making
Eugenia laugh. In the library, facing him with that insouci-
ant smile of hers.

Eventually, he pushed up on his hands and watched her,
watched their bodies. Her face, the depths of her eyes. The
sound of their breathing, the slide of him inside her. Her
legs wrapped around him, her hips moving against his, and
this was heaven for him for quite some time.

He withdrew again and, with no words between them,
he turned her over and, a firm grip on her hips, came into
her from behind. He had the idea that he had surprised her,
but she adjusted. Her round bottom pressed against his groin
and for a time he was content to take in the curve of her hips
to her waist, and glide the flat of his hand along her spine.
Then he started to move in her again, and the quiver of his
sexual completion stayed just enough out of reach that he
was confident of lasting awhile longer, and yet close enough,
intense enough, that he wanted to find out sooner than later
just how high that peak would be.

They ended up on the floor, her torso and arms on the
chaise, him still behind her until his orgasm was too close.
She understood the urgency, and he had her on her back
again with her gorgeous legs around his waist, and he drove
hard, and she met him, thrust for thrust.

His body raced toward a pleasure that seemed just out of
reach, but he couldn't be so selfish as to not bring her again
when he knew she was close, too. He reached between them
and stroked her, once, again, and she shattered again. Her
arms tightened around him and she said in a low, fierce
voice, "Harder."

He obliged her. Of course he did. He could deny her nothing. It seemed a miracle to him that he was able to withdraw
in time, and even so, even not finishing inside her, his climax
roared through him, and she wasn't squeamish about the

result, but rather took him in hand and in that moment, he ceased to exist.

When he had his wits and his breath back, he said, "Next time, I will procure a *baudruche*."

To which she replied, "What is that?"

"A sheath. To cover me. So that when next we do this, I can finish inside you." And then he remembered that he'd just fucked his sister's best friend within an inch of both their lives. And promised to do so again soon.

He didn't feel at all guilty.

## Chapter Nineteen

LILY THOUGHT IT A MIRACLE THAT SHE WAS OUT OF bed and outdoors two monstrous hours before noon. Had someone told her she'd ever be out of bed before one in the afternoon, she'd have laughed herself silly.

Yet here she was at not even half past ten, standing midway between the back of the house and the stables. She wore a cotton muslin walking dress two shades darker than her eyes, the better to hide the dirt that would inevitably stain her hem whilst she tromped about in the fields. Her dark gold spencer was trimmed with gold braid and epaulettes, and there was a gold silk bow tied beneath her bosom.

After some internal debate, she'd elected not to wear the turban that went with the gown, but, rather, a toffee-colored top hat with an egret plume. The turban would have been more adventurous but she hadn't the heart to forgo the match of the top hat that, with its gold trim, was a twin to the braid on her spencer. Her walking coat she left open because it was warm. Who would have guessed a spring morning would be anything but cool? Not that it mattered. It would have been a pity to hide her frock when everything coordinated so wonderfully. Her sole reservation was that she had on her second-best boots, but since that was her only concession to the reality of mud, all in all, she had achieved the perfect ensemble for a morning to be spent searching for Roman treasure.

They were taking two dogcarts to the location Lily and Ginny had ranked first on their map of likely locations for uncovering treasure. The site had clear signs of ancient habitation. It was her intention to excavate the foundations of what she hoped would prove to be the remains of a Roman garrison. A few well-placed questions around High Tearing had uncovered tales of coins, glassware, and bits of pottery having been found by people who hiked along the river Tear until they decided to take the shortcut into the village, which shortcut ran, not coincidentally, through Mountjoy's field and past their excavation spot.

Would not a Roman Legion have made the same trek? Perhaps even on their way to and from their barracks.

Lily supervised the loading of the cart that would transport the shovels, spades, and three footmen enlisted to dig, ticking off items on her list as they were placed on the carts. No point driving all that way only to learn something crucial had been omitted from the supplies. One needed the planning skills of a general and a quartermaster's talents of organization for such an endeavor as this.

While she counted shovels, picks, rakes, and sorting baskets, another cart, loaded with an awning, folding chairs, tables, and hampers containing refreshments, started on its way, carrying as well two serving maids, one of the undercooks, two more footmen, and grooms to manage the horses.

The morning was a fine one without a single cloud in the sky. A breeze kept the heat from becoming unbearable, but for anyone who stood in the sun, she imagined one would soon be uncomfortably warm. Lily stopped a footman on his way back to the house. "See that there's plenty for all of you to drink, won't you?"

He bowed. "Yes, miss. I'll speak with Mr. Doyle right away."

"Thank you." She intended to do some digging herself, of course, but it was the footmen with their brawn who would do the brunt of the work. They were all of them in for a day of what would likely be the tedious labor of uncovering the foundation of the structure she hoped was there.

Before long, the second cart went on its way, too, fully laden with all the implements required for her excavation. Lily brushed off her skirt. Excitement for the day's adventure curled in her stomach. Bronze oil-paper parasol in one hand and her map in the other so that she could finalize her approach to the area she'd chosen to start their digging, Lily headed for the front of the house. There, she found Ginny and Lord Nigel waiting underneath the portico for the carriage that would transport them to the site.

"A most thrilling morning, don't you agree, Ginny?" she said as she joined them. Ginny was very pretty in pale rose muslin and sarcenet and a delightful cap pinned slantways on her head. The ensemble was one of the gowns Lily had offered in the hope of tempting Ginny into remaking it for herself. Though impractical for an outing, did it matter when she looked so lovely? She put her arm through Ginny's. "It's unlikely we'll find anything the first day out, but we might. We just might."

"What do you think, Nigel?" Ginny asked. "Will we have good luck and find treasure straightaway?"

Lord Nigel took off his hat and bowed. "The first day?" He smiled a bit too heartily. Lily narrowed her eyes at him. "I don't see why we won't find something."

"We mustn't forget Lily's Gypsy magic," Ginny said. "That's bound to help us."

Lily pressed Ginny's arm. "Magic or no, we shall stand firm and not give up even if we are disappointed today. I'm sure we'll have work for the better part of a month before we've excavated whatever building is there."

"Of course." Ginny patted Lily's arm just as a groom brought the carriage around. "We stand firm."

Thank goodness there would be plenty of food and drink to sustain them through the afternoon. She had no worries about Ginny's fortitude, but she did not expect Lord Nigel to have her enthusiasm nor to withstand the inevitable tedium of an endeavor such as this.

"You ought to make a good luck wish on your medallion before we go," Ginny said.

"Excellent notion, my dear." Standing beside the carriage, she held her medallion, closed her eyes and counted to three, throwing in a hasty wish for good fortune and lots of treasure—no harm in that—and then opened her eyes. How odd that the metal was warm against her fingers. Had she been in the sun long enough to heat the gold? "There. All done. Shall we go?"

She accepted Lord Nigel's hand up into the carriage. "Come, Ginny." She patted the seat. When Ginny was seated, Lily held up her medallion. "You ought to wish for good fortune as well."

"Do you think it will work?"

How wonderful to see Ginny smile. "It can't hurt."

"Is there a best form?"

She rubbed the medallion between her fingers. "I think it's sufficient if you close your eyes and wish wholeheartedly, but whatever you feel is efficacious would be much appreciated."

Lord Nigel, now perched in the driver's box, snorted. Ginny stuck out her tongue at her brother's back. Then she closed her eyes, medallion in her hands. "There," she said. "I've wished for us to find a treasure trove."

From the driver's box, Lord Nigel snorted again.

"You ought to wish for good fortune as well, Lord Nigel."

"I do," he said. "I do."

"Well. That's that then." She leaned back. Lord Nigel snapped the reins and they were off. He was perfectly put together. It was a pity, really, that she did not like blond men and that he was, in any event, far too young for her. She did admire the cut of his driving coat. If only Mountjoy had a coat that fit his marvelous form as perfectly as Lord Nigel's coat fit him. Of course, very shortly, he would.

When the day came that Mountjoy dressed in clothes worthy of his physique, no woman would be able to resist him. To be fair, she doubted many women resisted him now. There were times when his eyes positively smoldered. What woman could deny a man who gazed at her with such open passion?

As they drove, Lily kept her map spread over her lap, studying her sketch. She didn't believe for a moment they would find any artifacts, not the first day, but she saw no reason not to apply her intellect to the matter of exposing a building, whether it once housed Roman Legionnaires, medieval serfs, or a family of Angles or Jutes.

She set aside her study of the map when Ginny said, "I've been thinking, Lily, about what we should serve for our spring fete."

"Have you?"

"Yes. I've been wondering about a menu."

Lily took out her notebook and pencil and found a blank page. "What do you think?"

"We ought to have pheasant."

"Yes, I think we should."

"I'll ask the cook if any is laid by."

As best she could given they were driving the carriage over a road rutted from the season's late rain, Lily made a note about the pheasant. "Duck, too, don't you agree?"

"Jane says to ask her father if we haven't any. He hunts every season, and she says there's always an abundance."

She noted that, too. She wondered when Mountjoy would offer for Miss Kirk. Not until after she left Bitterward, she hoped. She and Mountjoy had no future beyond her stay here, yet the thought of his eventual marriage felt bittersweet to her. Her preference would be to read of the engagement in a letter from Eugenia, not witness it personally. "Duck Mr. Kirk."

"Cakes, too," Ginny said. "And other sweets from the confectioner's in High Tearing."

"Oh, certainly. We ought to meet with the cook tomorrow. To plan a menu." She made a note of that, too.

Ginny sat sideways on the seat, a smile on her face, and Lily was strongly reminded of the woman who had become her friend in Exeter, before the heartbreaking loss of her husband. "We should have music and dancing for the young people, don't you agree?"

"Heavens, yes. We must have dancing for everyone who wishes to. Including you, my dear."

"If you will, I will. If anyone asks, that is."

"You may be assured of that."

"I haven't danced for ages and ages, Lily. I'm not sure I remember how."

"Everything will come back to you as soon as you hear the music." Lily waited for the carriage to pass over another rut before she made that note. "Is there a local orchestra you can recommend or should we send to Sheffield?"

"We've a very good one here." Ginny leaned in and pointed at Lily's notebook. "Put down that I'll hire them."

And so it went until Lord Nigel slowed the horses and looked over his shoulder at them. "We're here. The awning isn't up yet so now's the time to say something if this isn't the spot you meant, Miss Wellstone."

She looked around. They were on the northeast corner of the property at the rock-strewn meadow she and Ginny had felt was the most promising. The field was no more than a thirty-minute walk from the ruins of the Norman church and within sight of the river Tear. A likely place, as she'd thought from the very first, for a fortress.

"Yes," she said. "This is the place."

Lord Nigel put on the brake and secured the reins before getting down to assist his sister and then her. Interesting, she thought, that the degree of Lord Nigel's attentions to her could be predicted by whether his brother was present. In the former case, she could count on Lord Nigel flirting a little too much. But without Mountjoy? He was merely a very polite young man.

By the time they'd crossed the meadow, the servants had put up the awning and were arranging table and chairs underneath. Farther away, the rest of the men were unloading the shovels and other excavation implements.

Lily put up her parasol and walked smartly to the spot she thought was the place to begin. Lord Nigel and Ginny came along. The ground was strewn with rocks, most smaller than her fist, though a few were larger. She strongly suspected and hoped to confirm that the rocks were all that was left of a Roman garrison. Larger stones that would have once formed the walls had likely been long ago scavenged for fences or homes elsewhere. Like Lily, Ginny held a parasol over her head to ward off the sun. The day was really quite warm. Lord Nigel's hat did not provide him sufficient shade. He'd be brown as toast before long.

"See there?" She pointed for Lord Nigel's benefit as he had not been present when she and Ginny first examined the site. "Those impressions in the ground along there and there? They are too straight to be natural and surely mark the location of an ancient structure. Ginny and I noticed that the first time we came here."

"You think it might be Roman?" Lord Nigel said, a bit too jovially.

She gave him a sideways look. "Perhaps."

"Or Viking," Ginny said. "Or Norman. Or whoever was here before that."

Lord Nigel suppressed a grin. "Or after."

"Given the Roman artifacts so often found around here," Lily said, "I have high hopes this was the site of a garrison." She squinted to narrow her field of focus to the outline of the foundation. On which side should they begin?

"Cromwell might have done that," Lord Nigel said. "Leveled a building. He was mucking about here with his cannons. Or it might have been our great-great-granduncle—or was he a cousin several times removed?—the first duke. Any one of the ancestors who preceded Mountjoy, actually."

Lily, who didn't want to dampen anyone's spirits, continued her study of the foundation lines. She pointed at another series of furrows barely visible in the grass. "Could there have been two buildings here?"

The footmen with their shovels, picks, and spades had reached them and were now awaiting instructions. "Do you mean for us to dig here, miss?" the eldest of them asked. He wasn't more than twenty-five and looked a strapping man. He nodded at Lord Nigel. "Perhaps we ought to dig by the river. That's a likelier spot than this one, I say."

Lord Nigel, it seemed to her, made a particular point of looking away from the fellow. And now she rather thought Lord Nigel and the footman were both trying to hide a smirk.

"Is it?" she said. The ground by the river hadn't even the faintest sign of human habitation. Flooding over the years would have washed away any structure built so foolishly near the water.

"Yes, Miss Wellstone. It is."

She didn't like the way the eldest servant looked at Lord Nigel, nor Lord Nigel's overly hearty tone of voice.

Something was afoot, and she meant to discover what it was.

*Chapter Twenty*

LILY THOROUGHLY STUDIED THE THREE FOOTMEN
Mountjoy had been kind enough to allow on this adventure.
The eldest was Walter, she learned. A smile continued to
twitch at the corners of Walter's mouth. Lord Nigel had
interfered in some way. She was sure the two of them were
partners in some plot.

"You recommend we start near the river?" she asked the
young man. She smiled at him quite deliberately. He gog-
gled, but only for a moment because another of the footmen
poked him in the back.

"Aye."

"May I ask why?"

"Heard tales about it when I was a lad." Walter nodded
as if that were of vital importance. As if, perhaps, he'd
rehearsed the words. "Romansford, it was called. Isn't that
so, boys?"

*Romansford.* Oh, for pity's sake. The two hadn't even
bothered to come up with a believable name. "Is that so?"
Lily asked dryly.

"It was?" Ginny asked. "How odd. I don't think I ever—"

"Eugenia." Lord Nigel, standing a bit behind his sister, grabbed her by the shoulders and leaned on her in a hearty manner. "Romansford. Everybody calls it that. How could you fail to remember that? Mountjoy and I were out here the Easter after we moved to Bitterward, and we found an entire cache of coins along the banks. I remember it as if it were yesterday."

Ginny shook her head, craning her neck to look at him. "I don't recall that."

"Aye, milady." Walter nodded with enthusiasm. "I found a wee coin there once." He nudged one of his companions. "Didn't I?"

"You did, Walter," the young man said.

"Mountjoy still has them, Eugenia. Ask him if you don't believe me."

"I don't think you found any coins at all," Ginny said, one hand on her hip.

"Did too."

"In fact, I'll wager anything you like that you can't produce a single one of them," Ginny said.

Lily slowly turned her parasol in a circle over her head. She was highly tempted to close it and give Lord Nigel a sharp rap over his head. "Can you, Lord Nigel?"

"I don't know precisely where they are. Somewhere in the house."

"Nigel." Ginny shook her head.

Lord Nigel put his hands in his coat pockets and looked sheepish. He cleared his throat. "Just because I don't know where they are now doesn't mean we didn't find them."

Ginny rolled her eyes.

"Do you remember the winter I built a model trebuchet? The year before you were married." He held his hands about two feet apart. "About that big."

"Yes," Ginny said, looking at him with her arms crossed over her chest.

"I tested it."

"Mountjoy told you not to. He said you'd break a window if you did."

Lord Nigel drew himself up. "That's why I used the coins instead of pebbles. I shot most of them off the west tower roof."

"What about the rest?"

"Into the lake."

"Does Mountjoy know?"

"Good God, no, Eugenia. He'd have skinned me alive if he'd found out."

"Allow me to understand," Ginny said. "By your own admission, my dear little brother, the coins you claim you found, if ever they existed, are stuck in the gutters at Bitterward or sunk to the bottom of the lake."

"Yes."

"Do you really expect us to believe any of that?"

"Yes."

"Rubbish, Nigel."

"It's not."

Ginny snorted. "If you've interfered with our adventure, Nigel, Lily and I are going to be peeved with you. Very peeved."

He lifted his hands in protest. "This is the thanks I get for trying to help?"

"Thank you, Lord Nigel," Lily said in a firm voice. "That is indeed helpful information. Very kind of you to share, and so important to the cause." She rested the handle of her parasol on her shoulder and braced it underneath her forearm so as to have both hands free to hold her map and consult the sketches and notes she'd made. "That clump of rocks is intriguing, don't you think?" She pointed away from the river. "Perhaps the threshold of the garrison building."

"The riverside, miss," Walter said. Again, too heartily. "You'll want the river. It's the best spot."

"Shall we toss a coin?" Lord Nigel reached into a pocket and came out with a coin, which he flipped into the air and caught on the back of his hand. "Heads it's the river, tails, your meadow of rocks there."

Ginny scanned the meadow as Lily had done. "I think Lily's medallion ought to determine where we start."

"Brilliant idea," Lily said. One never did want to accuse one's host of cheating, but she was convinced, among other things, that Lord Nigel Hampton had rigged his toss of the coin. Or else so thoroughly seeded the area with "treasure" that her project was hopelessly compromised. "You are clever beyond words, my dear Ginny."

Lord Nigel lifted his hand, but tilted it so she couldn't see the coin. "Heads." He glanced at her. "Right then. The river it is."

While Lord Nigel was still looking at her, she clapped a hand to her chest and stared to her right. "Good Lord!" She added a hint of alarm to her words. "What on earth is that?"

Lord Nigel looked.

She snatched the coin off his hand, placing a finger over the side that had been facing up. "Just as I thought." She sniffed and handed back the coin. "Tails, sir. Not heads."

Lord Nigel had the grace to look abashed, but in the end, he shrugged. "Does it matter?" He pointed. "The ground is softer by the river. Why make these poor fellows dig among the rocks when the day promises to be so warm?"

"Do you find it warm?" she asked. "I do not. It's rather cool out in my opinion."

"Romansford it is," Walter said. He pushed off on his shovel, ready to go. The other two propped their shovels and picks on their shoulders and prepared to follow him to the river.

"I do not care for luck that is no luck at all," Lily said with a meaningful look at Lord Nigel. "Ginny's idea appeals to me." She smiled. "Let's have my medallion choose."

"Give it a spin," Ginny said, "and whichever part of the face is nearest the two locations, the river or the foundation, why, we'll start there."

Lily met Lord Nigel's eye. There was not the slightest hint of flirtation in his gaze. There never was unless Mount-joy was around. Which she found interesting. "Gypsy magic is useful for any endeavor involving a search for treasure." She patted Ginny's shoulder. "I ought to have thought of it myself."

Lord Nigel snorted. "Toss a coin, spin your medallion, what difference does it make? It's only chance."

"I agree with the principle, but only when others are not actively attempting to influence the outcome. Or when magic is involved."

"Magic?" Lord Nigel said, hands on his hips.

"Magic," she said. She pulled the ribbon over her head. "I can think of no better cause in which to call upon Gypsy magic than this. Can you?"

"Several, but go on." Lord Nigel gestured for her to continue.

She spun the medallion and they watched the ribbon twist, reach a point at which it could turn no more, and then spin again in the opposite direction, untwisting the ribbon. She waved a hand around the spinning disc. "I call on your magic to help me find that which I most desire."

Ginny giggled.

She cocked an eyebrow at her friend. "Do not mock the mysterious forces at work here. It's unbecoming of you and disruptive to the power of the medallion."

"Oh, I should never mock." But Ginny couldn't stop grinning. Lord Nigel was doing the same.

The medallion slowed.

Lord Nigel looked past them. "Blast."

Lily sniffed. "You won't fool me with that trick. Honestly. Do you take me for a fool?"

"No. But I mean it. Blast."

"Oh, dear," Ginny said in a way that reminded her of how Mountjoy had surprised them all during their experiment with the phosphorus pencil. The man was stealthy when he wanted to be.

Lily gazed at the slowly turning medallion, willing it to stop before it made her too dizzy to stand. "Is there an apparition?" Wouldn't that be rousing, to think the medallion had called up a specter to point them in the direction of treasure? "The ghost of a Legionnaire, perhaps?"

"No," Lord Nigel said. "Something much more terrifying than that."

"What could be more terrifying than the ghost of an ancient warrior?" Her stomach was feeling a bit tender, what with watching the spinning medallion.

"Mountjoy."

Lily's stomach somersaulted, but this time the sensation had nothing to do with the spinning medallion. She turned in the direction Lord Nigel meant, clutching the ribbon of the medallion in one hand and her parasol in the other. It was indeed Mountjoy. Her heart thumped.

He rode his chestnut gelding and, truly, was there ever a man to sit a horse the way he did? She didn't move because the sight of the Duke of Mountjoy had frozen her in place. An invisible line connected them and pulled on her heart. *Yanked* might be a more apt description of the sensation. She forgot, utterly, the business with the medallion.

When he reached them, he pushed back the brim of his hat. "Nigel." He nodded at his brother. "Eugenia." There was nothing untoward about his greeting. He sounded bored, as he so often did. "Miss Wellstone."

Ginny curtseyed. "Mountjoy."

Lily did the same. She was never nervous around others, but she was now. How did one behave with a man with whom one had been illicitly intimate? Her time with Greer had been so short and private. Those final days and hours had been spent alone, exactly as if they'd been husband and wife just married, and then he'd gone off to war and she'd never seen him again.

From atop his horse, Mountjoy gazed at them, careful, so careful, not to look at her any longer than was polite. Possibly his gaze lasted less than was polite. His coat was indifferently cut, and his cravat had not survived whatever journey he'd been on. The folds were now uneven though, knowing him, he'd probably started his day with his cravat tied like that. "You are about to dig up my field, aren't you?" he said.

"Yes." Lily smiled because anything else might give away the state of her nerves. Their encounters so far did not mean they were engaged in an affair. They weren't lovers yet. They might never be. How could they when she would not be at Bitterward much longer? Her heart was not involved. Nor was his. So why, then, was her pulse racing so?

"Where will you start?" he asked.

"We'll dig here." She pointed at Mountjoy. "If you wouldn't mind moving aside, your grace? We have a Roman garrison to uncover."

Lord Nigel said, "Isn't this the site of the old stables? I remember hearing somewhere that the second duke tore down the original house and rebuilt where Bitterward now stands."

"Not another word from you, Lord Nigel."

"What about at Romansford?" Ginny said, all sweetness and innocence.

"Romansford?"

"You remember, Mountjoy. Where you and Nigel found the coins?" Ginny spoke without the slightest indication she believed the story was a false one. "Over there, by those rocks. You remember, don't you, Mountjoy? The Easter after we came here from Haltwhistle."

Mountjoy frowned. "Was it there?" He gave a more convincing performance than his brother. "No, it was closer to the river than that, wasn't it, Nigel?"

"Infamous, your grace," Lily said.

His eyebrows rose in that infuriating way he had. "I beg your pardon?"

"You're in on the plot with your devious brother."

He dismounted and dropped the reins to the ground. His mount flicked its tail and nudged a clump of grass under its nose. Its back hoof dislodged a small rock. Lily stared at the rock and the too square bottom surface. That was no naturally occurring shape. He turned, one hand resting on his saddle. "Nigel, take Eugenia to the awning to await the excavation of the Romansford Garrison. I need a word in private with Miss Wellstone." After his brother and sister left them in relative privacy, he looked her up and down with a gaze that would have broken a woman of weaker will than her. "What plot would that be, Wellstone?"

She did not bother hiding her annoyance. "You and your brother have colluded to be sure we dig by the river and not here."

Mountjoy returned his attention to her, and her stomach took flight again. "Why would we do that?"

"So we find the artifacts you buried for us to discover."

The duke scanned the area before he replied. "The ground would be softer by the river, and it is where Nigel and I once found some Roman coins."

"You, sir, are incorrigible."

He returned his attention to her. He crossed his arms over his chest, and it did not matter to her one bit that his waistcoat had no style whatever or that his coat and buckskin breeches both should have long ago been handed over to his valet for disposal. He met her gaze, and her stomach went spinning away. They had been intimate. He'd been inside her. She knew what he looked and sounded like when he climaxed.

"I don't think you can produce a single Roman coin, your grace. In fact, if you can produce even one of the coins you claim you found, why, why . . ."

"Yes?"

"Why, I'll wait on you hand and foot for an entire day, that's what."

"And if I cannot?"

"You will do the same for me." She held out her hand and met his gaze straight on. "Be forewarned, your grace. I am without mercy."

His mouth curled into a smile that made her too giddy to

think straight. She wanted her hands on him again. Her mouth. Her tongue. She wanted to feel the weight of his body over hers. More than anything she wanted to look into his eyes when he slid inside her. "Bloodthirsty girl, aren't you?"

"You've no idea."

With that devastating smile still hovering around his mouth, Mountjoy tapped his riding whip against his open palm. "I never make a wager I am not confident of winning."

"Nor do I, your grace." Was it possible he wanted her with the same intensity? Heavens, she hoped so. "Do you accept?"

"Done." Mountjoy clasped her hand.

"Prepare to grovel, your grace, for when *I* win our wager, I'll have you on your knees to me."

"Delightful as that sounds, Wellstone," Mountjoy said far more evenly than she liked to hear from him, "I never grovel."

"I am adding, Mountjoy, to my very long list of tasks I will demand you perform. I hope you enjoy dancing."

"I abhor dancing," he said.

Lily took her notebook and her pencil from her pocket and prepared to write. "Item the first," she said to herself. "Dan . . . cing . . . duke." She made a flourish underneath the words. "There."

"When I win," he said in a low voice, "I'll have *you* on your hands and knees. Again. Tonight, I hope."

She licked her lower lip. "Best go, your grace, and join your brother and sister. I've serious work to do."

Mountjoy bowed, and while he walked away, she returned the notebook and pencil to her pocket. Coolly as she could, she walked to where Walter and the other footmen waited. "If you would," she said, closing her parasol and using it to indicate the area she meant, "dig a trench from here to about there. At least two feet deep, I should think. More, if possible. Do not, under any circumstances, disturb the foundation when you've reached it. The goal is to uncover what remains and leave it in place. We are not here to salvage the stones."

Walter bobbed his head. "Miss."

She would stay here, valiantly supervising the work. She opened her parasol again, shading herself from the sun and, incidentally, hiding her face from Mountjoy, who was by now back at the awning. She stayed near the footmen as they worked and soaked in the scent of fresh earth, the *shick* of a spade biting into the dirt, the soft comments from time to time between the men. She kept her parasol over her head, but the sun beat down unmercifully, as hot as Lord Nigel had predicted.

Half an hour later, Ginny called to her from the awning. "Lily, darling. Do come have something to drink."

"No, thank you." She waved. A trickle of sweat ran down her spine. "Would you be so good as to have someone bring the men something to drink?"

Refreshment was duly brought to the men, who leaned on their shovels while they drank from the clay jars brought to them. In the meantime, Lily fidgeted. She never wanted to sit or stay still when she was outside. She wanted to walk, to explore. To see the world around her and breathe it all in. She wanted to be alone with Mountjoy.

She walked to the edge of the hole and looked in. As yet, there was no sign of a foundation.

"What do you see?" Ginny called from the edge of the awning.

"A great amount of dirt." She turned. Underneath the awning, a maid handed Mountjoy a glass of lemonade. Ginny cooled herself with an ivory fan. She held a glass in the other.

The footmen dug steadily, leaning over more and more as the trench became deeper and longer. There was nothing but dirt down there, and it was unrelentingly dark and dampish from the spring storms. Perhaps her idea of digging for treasure had a flaw. Days and days of uncovering nothing but dirt wasn't so very adventurous. Oh, perhaps they'd uncover the occasional root or rock, but the predominant finding was going to be dirt.

She ignored the entreaties from the others to come out of the sun or to have a cool, refreshing glass of lemonade. There was a minor bit of excitement when one of the men uncovered a bit of metal, but examination proved the object to be a horseshoe nail.

The sun climbed higher in the sky. More sweat rolled down her back and beaded at her temples. She blinked because for a moment, she was sure she saw something that wasn't the color of dirt. After all this time, even a rock would be a thrill. The merest hint of the foundation would be lovely. Even if it was all that remained of a stable.

One of the servants brought up a clump of something on his shovel, but after another bit of excitement, the object turned out to be a piece of broken slate and yet another horseshoe nail. Ginny called her again, and Lily turned just enough to see her.

"Strawberries," Ginny said, holding up a plate. "They are excellent. Will you come have one?"

She waved a refusal. "How good of you to ask, but no, thank you." She ought to sit under the awning with the others, drinking lemonade and eating strawberries. In the shade. She could admire Mountjoy's shoulders and imagine him naked. Bother with her commitment to the tedium of treasure hunting.

In the trench, Walter emptied his shovel of dirt and went back for another. The shovel made an odd sound, and he stopped before the bottom of his stroke down. Another of the footmen stopped digging, too, arrested by the sound.

"What is it?" Lily asked. Had they reached the foundation at last? Or had they found a horseshoe to go with their collection of nails?

"A root, miss," Walter said.

A root. She could practically hear him thinking how much he'd rather be digging by the river.

"Have you found something?" Lord Nigel called.

Lily waved a dismissive hand. "Carry on," she said to the footmen. They did, all three in a line and all of them more miserably hot than she was.

"Walter," said the man at the far end of the trench. "Give me the smaller shovel?"

The implement was duly handed over and Walter tossed the larger one onto the lip of the trench. Lily considered walking to the awning. The shade would feel delicious.

"Oi!" Walter waved one arm over his head. "Oi there, miss!"

She arrived at that end of the trench in time to see the other footman drop to his knees and reach into the hole. "Have you reached the foundation?"

When his hand came out, by some trick of the sun, his fingers glittered with gold.

# Chapter Twenty-one

Mountjoy accompanied Eugenia and Nigel to see what was causing the fuss, but hung back when they reached the edge of the trench. The scene was eerily familiar. All three of the footmen had taken off their coats and hats and rolled up their sleeves. As in his dream, one stood at the rim of the trench, leaning on his shovel and staring down into the trench they'd dug. The other two stood in the excavated area. Lily, on the other side of the excavation, stared at something in the trench. Her parasol was closed and on the ground at her feet, exactly as he'd dreamed.

He'd known for days about the treasure hunting project and that it would involve digging. Therefore, his dreams about this weren't so unusual. Women commonly had parasols outside. The details of Lily and her treasure hunting were hardly earth-shattering, and yet, the hair on his arms prickled.

The servant nearest to Lily held out a bit of twisted, dirt-encrusted metal. The piece wasn't much larger than his palm but he'd scraped off enough dirt to expose the unmistakable gleam of gold. There appeared to be flashes of red, too. The man grinned as if he'd just been handed a fortune of his own.

Mindful of Lily's accusation that the field had been seeded with treasure, Mountjoy looked at Nigel, but his brother looked as shocked as everyone else. If this was whatever Nigel had buried here himself, which he suspected his brother had done, Nigel was a better actor than Mountjoy thought.

He walked to the lip of the trench and peered down. A jumble of objects, all of them covered and encrusted with dirt to the point where he could not form the shapes into anything recognizable, lay at the bottom. Most appeared to be quite small. He didn't see anything that looked like pots or glassware or the sorts of jars that turned up in areas where the Romans had established forts or cities. Another of the footmen crouched in the trench, bringing out what looked at first glance like more dirt-covered rubbish.

Every so often, gold glittered from beneath the dirt, and some of the bits of metal that could be glimpsed were obviously of exquisite workmanship. If whatever these things were had once been contained in something, that material had long ago rotted away. He looked at his brother again. Was Nigel responsible for the find? If so, he'd gone to a great deal of trouble by burying them so bloody deep and making the items look as if they genuinely had been underground for seven or eight hundred years. He frowned because he didn't see how or why or where anyone could have acquired unidentifiable items in order to perpetrate a fraud. It made no sense. Yet.

On the opposite side of the trench, Lily knelt and tucked her outer coat underneath her knees. It was too warm a day for a coat, he thought. She moved her parasol out of her way and used one hand to brace herself so she could reach down with the other. They'd dug down three feet in some places. The man nearest her in the trench extended a hand to steady her before he placed a dirty lump on her palm.

"Gold, miss," he said in awed tones.

Lily clutched the object and speared Nigel with her gaze. "Are you responsible for this?"

"No, Miss Wellstone." He raised his hands, palms out. "I assure you I am not."

She glanced at the eldest of the three footmen. "Walter, fetch the baskets, please."

"Right, miss." Without bothering to put on his coat—it was too warm for a man who'd been laboring in the sun these past hours—the young man jumped out of the trench and hurried toward the dogcarts.

The servant who'd steadied Lily bent down and handed her a second lump of dirt. "Another one, miss."

Lily leaned back and gently scraped debris off the object. It was button shaped, domed on top, but too large to actually be a button. Like the other piece, it shone gold and red where she'd dislodged enough of the dirt.

"Whatever is it?" Eugenia asked. She held her parasol over her head.

Lily scrubbed at the object then held up the bit of metal. An elongated, U-shaped stem made the button look vaguely mushroomlike. She brushed away more dirt. "My dear Ginny," she said in reverent tones, "I do believe it's the top bit from the pommel of a sword. A decorative button."

"Where's the sword, then?" Eugenia asked. She peered in the trench, and Mountjoy did, too. Everyone did. He saw nothing that looked like a sword.

Lily sat back on her heels, the button in her gloved hand. She'd removed more of the dirt and just then the sun hit a bit of the red material. It shimmered. "Oh," she said. "It's lovely." She wiped her forehead with the back of her gloved hand before she held up the object. "Do you see?" Sunlight reflected off the now cleaner edges of the metal she held. "How beautiful this will be when it's been washed."

Walter returned with the baskets and Lily supervised the transfer of objects from the trench to the baskets. There were hundreds of them, few of them of any decent size.

This was scavenged metal, Mountjoy thought. Bits of

metal torn from fallen warriors, the remnants of bridles, armor, anything that could be quickly carried from a battle-field. Now that he understood what he was looking at, he could see there were buckles and brooches, broken finials, tabs and buttons, twisted shards of gold torn from whatever they had been attached to. There were gems, too, cabochons that had fallen out of their metal settings. One of the last items pulled from the dirt, though, was a set of daggers, then the decaying metal bits of a scabbard, and a sword.

After nearly an hour with the sun continuing to climb in the sky, Lily agreed they would find no more buried objects without considerably expanding the trench. Mountjoy, who by now happened to be standing nearest her, helped Lily to her feet. He steadied her when she wavered on her feet. With a laugh that sounded too feeble for someone like her, she bent to brush the dirt and grass off her skirt.

Her cheeks were pink, and Mountjoy wondered if she'd gotten too much sun or if that was just the flush of excite-ment. "Eugenia," he said, "kindly bring Miss Wellstone some lemonade."

Eugenia took a step forward. "Lily?" Her voice rattled with worry. "Lily?" Lily swayed, and if he hadn't grabbed her arm she might have fallen. "Oh, Mountjoy, help! She's going to faint."

"Nonsense," Lily said in a shaky voice. "I never faint."

Mountjoy caught her around the waist because Eugenia was right, and he did so not a moment too soon. Lily's legs crumpled beneath her. With Nigel at his side, he carried her to the awning and set her down on a chair. "Eugenia," he said. "Fetch that lemonade now."

She did. Moments later she pressed a glass into Lily's hands.

"Thank you, Ginny, dear," Lily said. She drank deeply and then pressed the cup to her face. Her cheeks remained flushed while the rest of her skin was chalky white. She closed her eyes and swayed on the chair.

"Take off that blasted coat," Mountjoy said. He helped

her out of the garment and scowled to find her skin clammy to touch. "Whatever possessed you to wear such a thing on a day like this?"

"It goes with my gown." She looked at him without her usual penetrating gaze. "How was I to know the day would be so dreadfully warm?"

If he hadn't had a hand on her upper arm, he might not have noticed she was trembling. He didn't like her flushed cheeks and too bright eyes. "Have you a fan, Miss Wellstone?"

She shook her head. "I tell you, this is why I prefer to sleep through mornings." Her voice faltered, as if she couldn't spare the breath for words.

"Have you one, Eugenia?" Mountjoy said. He put out a hand when his sister nodded. Eugenia pulled a fan from her reticule and moved close enough to fan Lily's face. "Wellstone, drink more of that lemonade." He made sure she did, then made eye contact with one of the serving girls. "Another lemonade for Miss Wellstone, if you please. And fetch a damp cloth, as cold as you can get it."

Nigel hovered nearby, silent. The servants had gone quiet, too.

"Thank you, Eugenia." He was grateful for his sister's quick action. "Better, Miss Wellstone?"

She closed her eyes and touched her hand to the side of her head. "I've the most awful megrim coming on."

"Nigel," Mountjoy said. "See that the carriage is ready to go. She needs to get home. Inside. Where it's cool."

Lily opened her eyes. "Don't make a fuss." Her voice remained indistinct. "I promise not to be a bother. I need a moment is all."

He grabbed her hand and yanked off her glove. Her palms were damp with perspiration. He removed her other glove, too, and let it drop to the ground. "You're too warm."

"Give me back my gloves. Those are the very finest kid."

"I've seen this happen before," Mountjoy said. "To a man in the heat too long."

"What happened?" Eugenia continued to fan Lily.

A maid handed him a damp cloth, and he took it. Mountjoy gave his sister a look and shook his head. The man had died. He'd been much worse off than Lily was right now, but then Lily was a delicate woman, not a man inured to labor, and there was no knowing how badly she'd react. He wiped her face and pressed the cloth to the back of her neck. She wasn't reviving as she ought to. Instead of protesting, she bowed her head and groaned.

"More lemonade," he said, pressing another glass into her hand.

Nigel returned. "Carriage is ready," he said. "How is she?"

Mountjoy looked past Nigel. "Put the top up." While Nigel did so, a maid brought a second dampened cloth. He wiped her wrists and face again.

"Perfectly fine," Lily said.

"You're not."

She opened her eyes and gazed at him. Her eyes were unfocused. She stood, but swayed once on her feet. "I won't be a bother."

"You of all people ought to know I am always correct," he said. He pushed her back onto the chair. "I'm going to carry you to the carriage. I wouldn't object if I were you. Things will go badly for you if you do." She opened her mouth to protest, but he forestalled her by gathering her into his arms. Wonder of wonders, she sighed and rested her head against his shoulder.

"Adorable man," she whispered.

Mountjoy stood, seeing the concern on the faces of the gathered servants. Eugenia gave no sign she'd overheard Lily's endearment, thank God. Then again, he could not see her face while she bent for Lily's parasol and gloves. When he could, though, and Eugenia had the parasol shading Lily from the sun, he saw nothing but concern from her. From any of them. She hurried beside him, keeping the parasol over them while Mountjoy strode to the carriage with Lily inert in his arms.

# Chapter Twenty-two

MOUNTJOY CLIMBED INTO THE CARRIAGE WITH LILY while Nigel helped Eugenia up before leaping into the driver's box. He settled Lily on the seat between them. She went limp, as boneless as her garments permitted. He and Eugenia exchanged a look. Lily turned her head toward him and set a bare hand on his cheek. Her skin was warm and clammy. "Such a lovely man, Mountjoy. Have I told you that?"

"Thank you, Miss Wellstone." He didn't look at his sister to see what she thought of Lily's boldness. Best pretend there was nothing untoward about it or that he believed she was not entirely in her right mind. "She's still got on too damn many clothes," he told Eugenia. "Help me get this off, will you?"

"Yes, of course." Eugenia assisted in the removal of Lily's spencer, a process that required some contortions from them all. That done, Eugenia began fanning Lily again, briskly enough to lift strands of his hair.

"Ah." Lily sighed. "That does feel good. Thank you, my dear Ginny."

"How are you?" Eugenia smoothed Lily's hair. "Feeling any better?"

"You're such a dear, Ginny, to look after me."

"Is your megrim improved?"

"Some." Lily rested her head against the back of the seat, eyes closed. Every so often Mountjoy wiped her still-flushed face with the damp cloth he'd kept for the purpose. The carriage bounced over a rut, and Eugenia braced herself on the seat.

A few minutes later, Lily tried to sit up and adjust her gown. "None of that," he said. He put a hand on her shoulder and gently pushed her back. "You'll rest until the doctor's examined you and agreed you're well."

"My gown will be wrinkled."

"Oh, Lily—" Eugenia said.

"Damn the gown," Mountjoy said. Lily tried to sit up again, and this time he leaned over her, put a hand on her shoulder, and growled. "Pray do not exert yourself. I insist."

"Beastly man."

He said, "If your frock cannot be restored to its original splendor, Lily, I will buy you a new one."

Eugenia coughed softly, and he realized what he'd said. What could he do but pretend he'd not called her by her Christian name?

"My God, Ginny, he's threatening me." Lily grasped Eugenia's free hand and pretended to swoon. "In my weakened condition, no less. It's a wonder I don't have a relapse." She gave him a look that went a way toward relieving his mind about her condition. "Besides, look at your brother's coat. I wouldn't trust him to buy me an apron, let alone a frock."

"I know how to buy a woman an extravagant gift." At least she was feeling better. His attention flicked downward, and Lily noticed. Probably Eugenia noticed, too, but he was beyond caring anymore. Lily leaned against the seat, gazing at him from under her lashes.

"Buying a gift is simple," she said, with a lift of her chin. "It's choosing one that's fraught with danger."

"Don't lecture *me* about buying a woman gifts. I assure you I've done it often."

"Mountjoy," Eugenia said, more a whisper than anything else. "Really."

"I've bought you many a gift, Eugenia, and never heard you complain."

"Well, no, but, then I am your sister."

"Were you dissatisfied?"

"No, Mountjoy. But that's hardly the same as telling Lily you'll buy her a gown. That's not . . . proper."

"Then you buy it for her, so long as the woman stops thinking a deuced frock is more important than her health."

"Better Ginny than you," Lily said. Eugenia laughed at the rejoinder and, well, if the laugh was at his expense, at least Eugenia had been distracted from his inappropriate remarks.

In the ensuing silence, he traced lazy circles on Lily's palm. He *did* know how to choose an extravagant gift. Several minutes passed before he realized that all this time he'd been holding Lily's hand. He ought to let go, but that would only draw attention to the fact that he'd been doing so all this time. Eugenia didn't appear to have noticed.

By the time they reached the turn to Bitterward, Lily had improved to the point of taking the fan away from Eugenia and declaring she had half a mind to break it lest she turn into a block of ice.

Another carriage waited at the head of the driveway. A groom—not one of Mountjoy's servants—held the bridle of the lead pair. A Bitterward footman had a hand on the carriage door, ready to open it as Nigel brought the coach to a halt as near to the door as he could manage.

Mountjoy got out, and, while he reached to take Lily in his arms, from the corner of his eye he saw the occupant of the other carriage emerge. Fenris. The bloody Duke of Camber's heir. Nigel stayed in the coachman's seat and called down, "I'll fetch Longfield."

He spared his brother a glance. "Thank you."

Fenris approached, eyes wide and fixed on Lily. "My God, Mountjoy, what's happened?" He succeeded by look and words in implying that Mountjoy had injured Lily himself. "Is she badly hurt? Is there anything I can do?"

"Fenris—"

Fenris pulled up short. "Where is your sister, Mountjoy? Has something happened to her?"

He hardly had time to register the sharpness of that last question before Fenris glanced away and saw Eugenia ready to step from the coach. He moved smoothly to the carriage door and held out his hand, cutting off the groom ready to assist Eugenia. "I'll see to Mrs. Bryant," Fenris said. "Mountjoy, take my cousin inside. And do try not to do her further injury."

"Lily," he said in a low voice as he climbed the front stairs with her in his arms. "You would be easier to carry if you didn't behave as if you'd rather leap to your death than touch me."

"What if someone should see us?"

"They will assume I am carrying you to your room so that you may be properly looked after." She turned her head away from him, but she did slip an arm around his shoulder. "Thank you," he said. Doyle opened the door and Mountjoy strode inside.

She rested her head against his upper shoulder, and, well. Her bodice gaped and the shift in her position provided ample evidence of the curves he wanted so much to caress again. "I'm sorry to be a bother," she said.

"You are not a bother. Which way is your room?"

At the top of the stairs, Lily pointed right and said, "Left here."

He went left and moments later he'd found Lily's room. The Lilac room. The predominant color was indeed lilac, from the canopy over the bed to the pattern in the wallpaper. He laid her down on the bed and stepped back. "You see? I did not drop you."

They gazed at each other, and Lord, he thought he might

go up in flames. This was her room. The bed in which she slept. What would happen if he locked the door, with him still inside?

Her lips parted, and she licked her lower lip. "I didn't think you would."

"Nor ravish you," he said in a low voice. He could hear someone, a servant or perhaps Eugenia, moving down the corridor. Close. Too close to risk anything.

"Were you at least tempted?" She lifted one knee, only a few inches, but that movement was enough to expose a slender ankle.

As Eugenia came in, Mountjoy held her gaze, not hiding a thing from her, and said, "Yes." To his sister he said, "Is Fenris still here?"

"I gave him leave to depart." Eugenia went to the wash-stand. A moment later, she came to the bed with a basin and a cloth. She gave him a peculiar look and said, "Go on, Mountjoy. You're not wanted here anymore."

He cleared his throat and bowed to her and then to Lily. "I leave you in my sister's capable hands, Miss Wellstone. Please accept my hopes that you recover enough to join us for supper."

"A cool bath will be just the thing," Eugenia said. "Very refreshing."

His gaze slid from Lily's ankle to her face. While he'd been engaged with thoughts of her legs and regions north, she'd slipped a hand underneath her head. His eyes locked with hers again. That she understood the carnal nature of his perusal of her was no fault of hers. Or, no more than it was his. He didn't look away when he ought to have. Neither did she, and he felt a burn of desire start up in his belly.

Christ. He wanted her still. Again. More. Much, much more. More than any woman he could recall, he wanted Lily Wellstone, fascinating, desirable, infuriating creature, in his bed as often as he could convince her to join him there.

"Shoo, Mountjoy," Eugenia said. She put a hand on his shoulder and pushed him toward the door. Was that amusement in her voice? "She needs a bath and to rest and you aren't helping by standing there like you've turned to stone."

"Ginny? Are you saying I am Medusa?"

"No, Lily. Of course not." Eugenia threw him a last glance. "Go, Mountjoy. I'll have a word with you later."

"As you wish."

In the hallway after Eugenia closed the door behind him, he wondered what the hell had happened to his formerly regulated life. He had only himself to blame. Lily wasn't chasing after him. He knew what it was like to be chased after. He was the one pushing matters between them. He'd done that. Him. Because he wanted to take her to bed, and now that he had, he wanted to do so again. If he wasn't careful, he was going to care more for her than was safe. This was a first for him with a woman—the worry that he might want more than she did.

He left the hallway and ensconced himself in his office and did a pisspoor job of responding to the correspondence his secretary had left for him to go through. Hours and hours went by, except when he looked at his watch, it had been exactly fifty-seven minutes since he'd sat down. Just over an hour since he'd carried Lily to her room. A little more since he'd come home to find that damned Fenris waiting. He returned to his letters and another eternity.

Someone tapped on the door.

Mountjoy muttered, "Thank God," and threw the letter he was reading onto the top of the pile of correspondence he would have to read again.

It was Doyle, with Dr. Longfield, whom Nigel had brought to the house to look after Lily. Mountjoy stayed at his desk and waved the doctor to a seat, privately glad of the interruption. Doyle retreated. Mountjoy was very good at appearing to be busy and engaged in important matters. Matters of State, even. "How is Miss Wellstone?"

The doctor perched on the edge of the chair across from his desk. "Quite a remarkable woman, as I'm sure you know."

"Do you think so?"

"Delightful smile and—*ahem*—extremely beautiful woman. Very well formed, I must say. Brilliant mind, too, if one can say that of a female."

He quirked one eyebrow.

"Very spirited and amusing, which I'm sure your grace has noticed."

Mountjoy tapped a finger on the table. He recognized in the doctor all the symptoms of infatuation with Lily Wellstone. "Since you found her spirited, am I permitted to assume that her health is no longer a matter of concern?"

"Her finger is well healed, I was pleased to note."

"Excellent." He forced a smile, but it wasn't her bloody finger that worried him.

Dr. Longfield grabbed the top of one knee and rocked on his chair. "How is it she's unmarried? A puzzling thing that at her age no man should have snapped her up."

Mountjoy moved a pile of correspondence from one side of his desk to the other. He didn't trust himself to look the doctor in the eye, torn as he was between wanting to laugh out loud or tell the man if he so much as breathed Lily's name he'd find himself outside of the house looking in. "Ought we to be more concerned with her present health than with her marital status, doctor?"

"Provided she does not overexert herself, she's as well as can be expected, which is well enough, your grace. And so I told her."

Mountjoy stood abruptly. Ten more seconds of this prattle and he'd go stark raving mad. "You see no need for concern?"

"Very little."

"Then thank you for coming here on such short notice."

"I've warned her she's far too delicate to stand in the sun as she did."

Mountjoy came around from behind his desk to put a hand on the doctor's shoulder and guide him to the door.

"She mustn't be permitted to engage in such excess again.

A delicate thing like her. You may tell her, your grace, that I forbid it."

"I will do exactly as you advise, thank you, doctor." Mountjoy opened the door. "You may rely on it."

He tugged at his coat. "Excellent."

"You know the way out?"

"Indeed, sir." The doctor crossed into the hallway then turned and bowed. "Give Miss Wellstone my regards, won't you?"

"I shall."

"Good day, your grace."

"Good day, doctor."

Mountjoy returned to his desk and stared at the patterns in the grain of the wood. He wanted to see Lily. Alone. He wanted to throw away all this damned correspondence and lock himself away where he and Lily would not be disturbed. He picked up the next letter in the batch he was supposed to read through. The words ran together like ants drunk on blue fire.

Half a lifetime passed and he got through precisely none of the letters. Someone knocked on the door, and he practically shouted in relief. "Enter."

His sister came in. She was a different woman since Lily had come. So young and pretty, if one could think such a thing about one's sister. "Mountjoy."

He rose and gestured to the chair Dr. Longfield had vacated. "Eugenia."

Instead of sitting she stood behind the chair, her hands resting on the top rail. "You'll think me presumptuous for this. Oh, do sit down, Mountjoy."

He did, leaning against his chair and picking up his pen. The ink had dried on the nib. "Yes?"

She bit her lower lip. "I've come about Lily."

He picked up his penknife and set himself to sharpening the point of his quill. "Dr. Longfield assures me she's in excellent health, though he warned me she's to stay out of the sun."

"He said the same thing to me. But Mountjoy, that's not why I've come."

"Oh?"

"I'm worried you'll be hurt."

"I beg your pardon?"

"Lily is my dear, dear friend. I love her better than anyone. She's amusing and intelligent and very, very beautiful."

"Yes," he said carefully. "She is all that. But I fail to see what that has to do with me."

Eugenia licked her lips. "You won't be surprised to know that other men have loved her." She gripped the top of the chair. "But Mountjoy, she never cared for a one of them, and . . . I don't think she ever will. She never led them on, she's not that sort of woman. She's like me after Robert."

"Eugenia . . ."

"Please don't interrupt, or I'll lose my nerve."

He gestured.

"I'll never love any man but Robert. And Lily, she's met the only man she will ever love." His sister's eyes were too bright.

"There is no need for tears," he said. He dropped the penknife on the blotter and offered her his handkerchief.

She waved it off. "I'm not crying."

"As you say." He continued to hold out his handkerchief.

"I'm not." Eugenia took it from him and dabbed at her eyes.

"I won't disagree with you that Miss Wellstone is a beautiful and vivacious woman."

"She is."

"I enjoy her company. Most of the time. So does your brother. I'm glad she's here, for she's done you a world of good."

Eugenia gave him a tremulous smile. "That's true."

"She's made me see that I have neglected you. I have not done my duty by you, and for that I apologize."

"Oh, no, Mountjoy. Never."

"She took me to task for my treatment of you, and she

was right to do so, but you mustn't think I'm angry with her for that."

"Angry?"

He steeled himself and said, "Is that not why you came here?"

"No." She sat on the chair, one hand over her heart. "You can't imagine how relieved I am to hear you say that." She shook her head. "You'll think me such a goose. I was worried she might have engaged your affections without your knowing, that's all."

"Engaged my affections?"

"I apologize, Mountjoy. Of course that's not happened. We all know you love Miss Kirk. It's just I've seen it happen to other men where Lily is concerned."

Mountjoy schooled his expression. "Eugenia." He laughed, and he even sounded convincing. "I am not in love with Miss Wellstone."

"Thank goodness. I am sorry, Mountjoy for jumping to conclusions about your feelings for Lily."

"You've no need to apologize." He smiled and picked up his pen. "Please close the door when you go."

Another century passed with him having given up any pretense of working. Then Doyle tapped on his office door and informed him it was time to change for supper.

He absolutely was not in love with Lily.

*Chapter Twenty-three*

❧❧

LILY CAME DOWNSTAIRS FOR SUPPER PRECISELY AT SIX o'clock that evening, much recovered from the morning's treasure hunting experience and firm in her conviction that morning activities were to be avoided at all costs. She wore her very best evening gown, a crimson silk worked with gold embroidery and a gold underskirt that peeked from the scalloped hem. She had spent several afternoons before her departure for Bitterward fashioning the trim on the bodice and hem.

One curl of her hair was loose and trailed along the side of her neck. A matching arrangement of gold lace and crimson roses was affixed below a gold-filigree hair comb in the curls pinned at the back of her head. She'd even changed the ribbon for her medallion to a red one.

From the doorway, she had a view of Mountjoy and his brother before either man saw her. Every atom of her attention was for Mountjoy. He was seated on a chair, reading a paperbound journal while Lord Nigel stood staring into the fireplace, one foot on the grate. Mountjoy was as badly dressed as ever, yet the sight of him made her happy.

She straightened her skirts, adjusted the gold lace at her neckline, and tugged on her bodice before she walked in. Mountjoy saw her first, but all he did was set his journal on his lap. Lord Nigel turned his back to the fire and gave her an elaborate bow of the sort he only gave her when his brother was around to see it. Mountjoy stood, setting his volume on the table beside him.

She curtseyed. "Good evening, your grace. Lord Nigel."

"Miss Wellstone." Lord Nigel came forward to take her hand. "I hope you're feeling better."

"I am, thank you."

"You look lovely."

As a matter of fact, she was quite sure she did look lovely. She glanced at Mountjoy, but he stayed where he was, hands behind his back. If he admired her appearance tonight more, or even less, than any other time, she could not tell.

"I hope you haven't been waiting long," she said. He was supposed to have changed for supper, but could one even be sure? His cravat, which was not sufficiently starched, was loosened, and his coat was unbuttoned. Not unforgivable, that unbuttoned coat, but his waistcoat, that was unforgivable. The garment was muddy brown silk with small red lozenges that did not hide the knobs in the weave. Silk, yes, but poor quality. The design was not bad, but the colors and tailoring were unfortunate and inferior. She made a mental note to visit the man's tailor as soon as possible.

Mountjoy approached her at last, and with a flicker of his attention to her bosom, he bent over her hand. "Good evening, Miss Wellstone."

"Your grace."

He took something from his pocket. The corners of his mouth twitched. "I have something you ought to see."

"What could it be?" She was no longer shocked at the hard thump of her pulse when their eyes briefly locked.

There was nothing astonishing about her finding another man attractive, after all. She'd reacted that way to Greer even before she'd fallen in love with him and long before Greer had let her know he felt the same.

He opened his hand and held it out. "This."

She came close enough to see an irregularly shaped circle no larger than her smallest fingernail and so dark a copper that the object, at first glance, appeared black. Her heart sank after she plucked it from his hand. "Where did you get this, sir? From a shop in High Tearing by chance?"

The twitch of his mouth broadened into a smile. A very smug smile. "I kept several of them back from among the coins Nigel and I found near the river that day. They've been in my quarters ever since. Safe from the inquisitive fingers of boys who build trebuchets."

Lily stared at the coin in her hand. She hated to lose. Abhorred it.

"I believe, Miss Wellstone," he said in a low voice, "that I have won our wager."

She would have answered, but Ginny's arrival gave her an excuse to silently return the coin. He pocketed it, still with his smug grin.

"What wager is that?" Ginny crossed the room to envelop Lily in a quick embrace. "Lovely to see you. I was worried you wouldn't feel well enough to come downstairs."

"I'm quite well now, Ginny."

She held Lily at arm's length. "Don't you look lovely?" She glanced at her brothers. "Doesn't she look lovely?"

Lord Nigel made another elaborate bow and said, "As ever."

Mountjoy said nothing, but Lily felt the heat of his gaze.

Lord Nigel coughed into his hand. "Eugenia, I have business that will take me to London tomorrow. Is there anything I can bring back for you?"

"You're going to London?" Mountjoy asked.

Ginny turned to her younger brother. "You'll be back in time for our ball, won't you?"

"Wouldn't miss it for the world." He bowed to the duke. "Yes. I've business there. I won't be long. A few days."

"You'd better not," Ginny said. "We're counting on you to dance with all the young ladies too terrified to dance with Mountjoy."

"Of course, Eugenia. Your errands?"

"Would you mind stopping at Hookam's for me? There are several books I'd like. I'll write down the titles for you." Ginny headed to the writing desk to do just that, sweeping her skirts out of the way as she sat. She wore white, and Lily thought she looked just splendid.

"Miss Wellstone?" Lord Nigel asked. "Anything for you? Books? Ribbons? Candied almonds? I know you're fond of them. When I go to London I always bring back nougat for Eugenia."

"Thank you, Lord Nigel, that would be lovely."

"Mountjoy, what should Nigel bring back for Jane?" Ginny said from the desk where she was writing her list. She looked over her shoulder. "My dear brother," she said. "Do not tell me you haven't any idea."

Lily shot a glance at Mountjoy, who stood impassive.

"Then I must remain silent."

Ginny sighed. "Nigel, bring her back some lace. I'll write down the name of the shop. Brussels lace if you can get it."

"I promise you," Lord Nigel said quickly, "I'll bring back everything she requires."

"Something for all the Misses Kirk," Ginny said, still writing.

"Certainly." Lord Nigel turned to his brother. "What have you done with the treasure, Mountjoy? It's not still in the wagons, is it?"

"No," the duke answered smoothly. "I took the liberty of moving the artifacts to the old stillroom. If you are not familiar with the location, Miss Wellstone, Eugenia can show you where it is."

"Thank you." Their eyes met again. Head-on, and she lost all sense of anyone or anything but him, and she did not often lose her self-possession. He did not look away. Or smile. Goodness, but his eyes were an astonishing green, and his hair, though worn a shade too long, suited his careless manner.

"Here." Ginny stretched backward over the desk chair, extending the notepaper to Lord Nigel, who took the sheet from her and slipped it into an inside pocket of his coat. "Thank you, Nigel."

Lily tore her gaze from Mountjoy. "We'll need a detailed inventory of what we found, Ginny. Perhaps you and I could begin tomorrow?"

"If you like. But I've just had the most wonderful idea," Ginny said.

"Oh?"

She shifted to face her younger brother. "Nigel, what if Lily and I went to London with you?" She turned again, this time to address Mountjoy. "May we stay at the town house?"

"That would not be convenient," Lord Nigel said.

"Whyever not?" She gripped the top of the chair and leaned over it. "No one stays there when Mountjoy's at Bitterward. As well open the house for one person as three. We won't bother you, Nigel, I promise."

"I'm very sorry, Eugenia," Lord Nigel said. He wiped his hands down the front of his coat. "But I'm leaving before dawn, and I'm not taking the carriage."

"A trip to London is a lovely idea, but, Ginny, I cannot go," Lily said, partly because it was true, but also because Lord Nigel obviously did not want their company. "Not tomorrow, at any rate."

"Why not?"

She sent a quick glance in Mountjoy's direction. She had so little time before she had to return to Syton House, and she did not want to spend any of it away from Mountjoy. "Your brother has produced a coin that was the subject of a wager we made earlier this afternoon."

Ginny leaned her forearm over the back of her chair. She looked from Mountjoy to Lily. "A wager?"

"Yes."

"Oh dear. You lost, didn't you, Lily?"

"Yes."

"If only you'd told me. I would have warned you. Nigel and I learned as children never to wager with him." She shook her head. "How much did you lose?"

"Alas, Ginny, I am now obliged to wait hand and foot on your brother for a period of twenty-four hours."

Ginny tried to stop a laugh and failed. "Say it's not so, Lily."

"I'm afraid it is. We'll go to London another time, I promise you. On this occasion, sadly, Lord Nigel will have to make do without our company."

"However will I manage?" Lord Nigel said.

"Fortitude, sir. A great deal of fortitude. As I must now have. Your grace," Lily said to Mountjoy, "would you not like to sit down?" She walked to a chair and, standing behind it, put her hands on either side of the back.

"I do believe," Mountjoy said, pointing to a chair on the opposite side of the room, "that I would like to sit in that chair."

"But of course. Would you care for a blanket, perhaps?" she asked as she walked across the room. He went along and sat, with great ceremony, on the chair. "Or a pillow upon which to rest your weary noble feet?"

"That stool there," he said with a wave at a round ottoman on yet another side of the room. She fetched it for him and placed it at his feet. "*Hmm*," he said in a doubtful tone as he shifted around. Lord Nigel snickered while Ginny gawped at her elder brother. "I'm not sure this one is as comfortable as I'd hoped."

Lily gave him a curtsey worthy of a meeting with the Prince Regent. "Allow me to search the house for another, your grace, for I can think of nothing but your pleasure and happiness."

The arrival of Doyle to announce dinner prevented her carrying out that plan. Mountjoy rose and held out his arm. "Miss Wellstone."

He escorted her to the dinner table, seeing her to her seat at his right. She took care to over-attend to his needs. She even unfolded his napkin and draped it over his lap for him.

"Thank you, Wellstone."

No one seemed to notice his slip, thank goodness. The food, as always, was excellent, the conversation as good as ever. They discussed the treasure they'd uncovered, what it might be, how they might clean it and whether it was Roman or something much older. Or younger. It was Mountjoy who mentioned an acquaintance at Oxford who they might call in to have a look, which Lily thought an excellent idea.

As they talked, servants brought each dish to the duke first, but to much amusement Lily made a point of examining the dishes and selecting the most delectable slice of beef, the lightest, flakiest fish. She tasted his wine for him, and when she found it acceptable, which she did because the cellars at Bitterward were first-rate, she filled his glass rather than allowing one of the footmen to do so.

"Mountjoy," Ginny said. "Since Nigel will be gone tomorrow, would you be so kind as to drive Lily and me into High Tearing?"

Mountjoy drank some of his wine and casually held out his glass for Lily to refill. She did, with the wonderful French Beaujolais that had been opened. "I am free in the afternoon, if that's convenient for you."

"Two o'clock?"

He nodded. "I should be delighted."

As the meal came to a close, the staff brought out plates of fruit and cheese, which were, naturally, arranged so they were before Mountjoy since he presided over the table. Lily took his knife and cut and cored an apple and then a pear. She arranged the fruit and added slices of cheese until the contents were balanced and pleasing to the eye. Ginny and Lord Nigel snickered while she did.

When it came time for them to leave the men to the table, she and Ginny walked arm in arm to the salon. There, Ginny leaned against the wall beside the door and laughed. "Oh,

Lily, you were astounding. Priceless. The way you waited on Mountjoy— Oh, I will adore you forever for this night."

She, too, thought Mountjoy had been magnificent. He'd played along wonderfully and made the evening much more amusing that she'd ever have expected. She took a seat near the fire and retrieved her embroidery. She was working on new trim for one of the gowns she was having remade for Ginny. Ginny brought over the lamp and placed it so she had the best light for the work.

"Thank you, dear. So thoughtful of you." She was going to miss the companionship when she was back at Syton House.

"It's the least I can do." She sat on the chair beside Lily. "What else will you do for him?" she asked. "Please torture him. It's so wonderful to see him suffer. He cannot bear being made a fuss of."

She set her needlework on her lap, smiling. "You're so very right, Ginny. I really must make him suffer. Until he begs me to stop."

"Oh, do, please do. This is much better than going to London."

"He won't last another hour."

The door opened and Lord Nigel came in, followed by Mountjoy. The duke's eyes flicked to her, and Lily's breath caught in her chest.

"What shall we do to entertain ourselves tonight?" Lord Nigel made for a seat near the fire. When Mountjoy sat, she hurried to spread a blanket over his lap. Lord Nigel snorted when Mountjoy pushed away her hands. "You look a proper old man now, Mountjoy. Miss Wellstone, I think he needs a blanket for his shoulders, too."

"No, I do not."

"I've grown accustomed to our nightly discussions of strategies and plans for finding treasure." Lord Nigel grinned at them. "Now that we've found it, what's left for us?"

"I am compelled to point out we may not have found Roman artifacts," Lily said. She retook her seat and put away her embroidery. "Nor did we uncover a foundation. No, there is yet a great deal of work remaining, despite our initial successes." She addressed Mountjoy next. "Your grace?"

He threw the blanket off his lap. "Miss Wellstone?"

"May we continue our excavation, or have you given up on that?" She pulled a skein of green yarn from her basket and held it up, squinting at Mountjoy as she did.

"Dig as many holes as you like, so long as they are filled in when you are done with them. May I ask why you are waving that yarn in my face, Miss Wellstone?"

"Ginny, what do you think of this color for your brother?"

"It matches his eyes."

"Old men need mufflers," Lord Nigel said. "Wards off the chill in their creaky bones."

"I intend to knit you a scarf, your grace."

"I don't need a scarf."

"In respect of your wardrobe, sir, you have no authority."

"And you do?" The man knew very well that she did.

"I have decided you must have something to remember me by once I've gone home. And as your brother so wisely points out, a scarf will ward you from chills. Very useful, I should think. I am contemplating whether I should work your coat of arms into this. What do you think, Ginny? Is that not an excellent idea?"

"Oh, yes."

She found the loose end of yarn and proceeded to make a neat ball. Mountjoy, however, brought his chair closer to hers and dutifully held up his hands to act as a guide for her winding the yarn into a less tangled form.

"My father used to do this for my mother," he said. He watched Lily over the tops of his fingers.

"Yes," Ginny said. "I remember Papa would read to us or recite a poem. Or sing. Do you remember that, Nigel?"

"I do."

Instead of feeling left out of these reminiscences, Lily felt as if she belonged. As if the memories, though not hers, were hers to share. She could almost believe that she, too, had grown up in a warm and loving family. They spent the next hour taking turns reciting poetry or singing or telling tales. Lord Nigel and Ginny both sang very well, Lily had a tolerable voice, and even Mountjoy wasn't as bad as he'd claimed he was.

Lord Nigel knew long passages from Milton's *Paradise Lost*, and he recited them beautifully. After that, Mountjoy fetched a copy of *A Midsummer Night's Dream* and she wanted to hug him close for remembering her childhood dream of running away to tread the boards. She did love to act out a scene. They read scenes from the play, at one point swapping the roles so that the ladies read the parts of the men, and Lord Nigel and Mountjoy the parts of the ladies, and it was great fun.

For the first time since Greer's death, Lily felt there were people on whom she could rely. People who welcomed her for who and what she was. Flaws and all. The feeling that she was wanted here, a friend even, made the evening magical. Like her time here at Bitterward, the feeling that she belonged would end too soon.

Lord Nigel was the first to retire, as he had an early day tomorrow. Mountjoy remained to talk for a while longer, and the subjects were never anything deep, just stories about how the Hampton children had grown up, a bit of politics, though not much, and then Ginny yawned and Mountjoy stood.

"Come ladies, I'll walk you to your rooms and say good night to you both. I want to see Nigel off in the morning."

Ginny's room was closest and they stopped before her door and said good night. As Ginny went inside, Mountjoy made it seem he would walk away once her door closed. But he didn't.

Lily and Mountjoy were alone with fifteen paces yet to travel before they reached her door. "Wellstone."

She looked up at him. "Your grace?"

He came close and studied her so intently she wasn't sure what to think. "Thank you for a lovely evening tonight."

"Thank you." She touched his hand. "When I was a girl, I had to read all the parts myself. It was great fun reading with you."

"I'm pleased you enjoyed yourself."

"I did. This isn't a night I'll soon forget."

"You're sure you're well after all you endured today?"

"Perfectly." She took a step back, but somehow the distance between them did not change. She took another step back and found her shoulders pressed against the wall. The distance between them still had not changed.

"I'm glad you are here with us at Bitterward," the duke said. "I can't recall the last time I saw Eugenia smile as much as she did tonight. Or when I've had my every comfort so thoroughly looked after."

"You are ingratiating yourself with me, aren't you?"

"I am," he said.

She put a hand on his chest. "You do it beautifully."

"Thank you."

"Diabolically clever of you, sir." His mouth was inches from hers, and he was stealing all the air.

"There are one or two more things I'd like from you tonight, Wellstone."

"What could that be?"

"Come with me, and we'll discuss it."

They returned to the east tower room, but, as it turned out, there was very little to discuss, and in any event, Lily was kept busy seeing to Mountjoy's every whim. He had a great many.

Eventually, she lay in his arms, exhausted and happier than she'd been in longer than she could recall. Her last thoughts before she gave in to sleep were that she'd come out the winner in their wager and that she would be very sorry to leave here.

# Chapter Twenty-four

MOUNTJOY LOOKED AT HIS REFLECTION IN THE CHE-val glass and tugged on his waistcoat. A man's clothes didn't prove much besides how much money he wasted on his tailor. Except now that he was studying himself, he wondered if Lily wasn't right. She'd been to see his tailor and there were, he was told, great events in the works. "Elliot. Are you sure this fits as it should?"

His valet hovered behind him, squinting, hands clasped in front of his heart. His graying eyebrows made a straight line across his forehead, then smoothed out. "Your grace?"

The note of resignation in his valet's response pricked his conscience. True, he'd made it clear he didn't want Elliot fussing and interfering with his wardrobe. He wanted to get dressed and go about his business. "The truth," he said. His favorite coat hung over the chair behind him. "It doesn't fit properly, does it?"

Elliot blanched. "I don't presume, your grace, to have an opinion about what suits you."

He turned around, irritated beyond belief to have his

words of so long ago parroted back at him. "It's your bloody job, man."

"Sir." He backed up a step then bowed. "Your grace."

"Elliot. I beg your pardon. That was not fair of me." Elliot bowed but his expression remained cautious. Mountjoy sighed. "The waistcoat does not fit, though I'm damned if I can tell why."

"Perhaps if you had allowed your tailor to do the additional fittings . . ."

"Does it matter when my coat will hide it?" He remembered the days after he'd ascended to his title and how Fenris and others had sneered about farmers dressing up as dukes. Mountjoy's response had been hardly more than irritation. He simply hadn't cared much for anyone's opinion of his clothes when so many other things mattered more. For some absurd reason, it mattered to him that Lily found his wardrobe inferior.

Elliot shifted his weight between his feet, and his eyebrows met again. He coughed once. "Your grace is concerned with fashion?"

"No." But for his promise to Lily, he would barely have glanced at himself in the mirror this morning. He wouldn't have given a moment's thought to the fit of his waistcoat. "Perhaps a change is in order."

"A change, sir?" He licked his lips, slowly, plainly considering what words he would use. "Do you intend something more substantial than new buttons? If I might inquire. So as to be prepared."

He tugged on the bottom of his waistcoat again. The moment he let go, the sides sagged. She was right about his clothes. "Is there another tailor you'd recommend?"

Elliot sucked in a breath. "In High Tearing or Sheffield?"

"I was thinking of London."

There was a moment of heavy silence. Elliot coughed softly. "London, your grace?"

"Yes, London."

"Oh," Elliot said. "Oh. Do you, by any chance, mean a

*Bond Street* tailor?" He whispered the words *Bond Street* as if the mere mention would bring God himself down to earth.

He could hear himself telling Elliot, not so long ago and quite possibly in a curt tone, that he was forbidden to mention the words *Bond Street* and *tailor* in the same sentence. He'd also said he didn't give a damn what he looked like, and that he didn't need any tailor but the one he'd patronized since he was expected to buy his own suits.

"We shall see." He turned back to the mirror. He'd let his prick do his thinking for him, and now he was fending off a rapturous valet. He didn't regret it as much as he ought to.

In fact, both he and his prick wanted Lily again.

If letting Lily dress him up meant he would have her again, she could put him in tassels and purple silk, and he wouldn't care. Except she wouldn't, because Lily had exquisite taste. "What about the color?" he asked.

"The color, your grace?"

His coat was green. So was his waistcoat. Why wouldn't green go with a coat that was nearly the same color? He thought of Lily's reaction to his banyan, the way she'd smoothed her hands over the fabric. She loved beautiful things. Beautiful to look at, to touch, and to taste. "Does this waistcoat go with that coat?"

Elliot, face as gray as his hair, shook his head. "In my opinion, no, your grace. Begging your pardon, sir."

Damn. The coat he had insisted he would wear today was comfortable, and he'd last worn it five days ago. Why oughtn't he to wear it again? Mountjoy walked away from the mirror and sat down, looking sideways at Elliott. The poor man was frozen in place. Elliot had once valeted the younger son of an earl. A bit of a rogue from what one heard. Elliot had elected to stay in England when his previous employer was shipped off to India to avoid unsavory rumors and inconvenient debts. Quite a come down for the man to valet a duke with no taste.

Mountjoy sighed. "You've tried to tell me."

Elliot swallowed hard and picked up the lint brush. He held it like a shield over his heart. "Your grace."

"What coat does go with this waistcoat?" He waved a hand. "Never mind. It's the one you tried to get me to wear."

"Sir."

He stood. "I suppose none of my coats fit."

Elliot clutched the lint brush to his chest and shook his head again. He looked sadder than ever, yet Mountjoy did not think he was wrong there was a glint of joy in the man's eyes. Once he had new clothes, Lily would look at him with a glint in her eyes, too.

He plucked the other coat off the top of the chair. His most comfortable coat, his favorite coat. An old friend. He threw it on the seat of the chair where one sleeve drooped to the floor, looking to him like a fair match to the olive green of his waistcoat. He was stubborn. He knew that. He'd kept to his old habits of dress out of sheer muleheadedness. Daring people to think the Duke of Mountjoy mattered less because of his clothes and not more because he'd saved the title from extinction and then done his bloody duty every day of his life since.

Mountjoy sighed. "Bring me a coat that goes with this waistcoat, then."

His valet broke into a smile. "Yes, your grace."

While Elliot brought out the better coat, Mountjoy returned to the cheval glass. He looked like himself. More to the point, he looked much the same as he'd looked when he was not in possession of a title, an estate, or the income that went with it. But he wasn't that boy. God knows he'd changed in just about every way since then. In truth, he was a bigger man, two inches taller and still as broad through the shoulders as the farmer he'd once been. Older by a dozen years. A man, now, not a boy. Not a farmer, whether by his choice or not, but a duke.

As far as he was concerned, the new coat looked very much like the old one. Except not as comfortable. His valet went at him with the lint brush, and he gritted his teeth, resisting the urge to snatch the brush away and throw the damned thing out the window. "Thank you, Elliot."

"Your grace."

He headed for the door but halted halfway there. He turned. "I will be ordering a new wardrobe presently. If there are London tailors you think are suitable, please write me a list of names."

His valet smiled. "Your grace."

"In future, Elliot, I will endeavor to listen to your advice."

The servant beamed at him as if he'd handed over the damned Crown Jewels and told him they were a gift from the Prince Regent himself. "Sir."

He headed downstairs. Eugenia had made a particular point of asking him to attend her tea this afternoon, and he had agreed. Duty and all that. Nigel wasn't due home from London for another two or three days at least, leaving him the only Hampton male to attend. Besides, Lily would be there.

The function Eugenia had begged him to attend, since Nigel's business in London kept him away, was in the Oldenburg salon, and he arrived to find at least twenty people crowding the room. There seemed to be a great deal of food either on trays or being carried about the room by footmen in livery. Everywhere he looked were dainty sandwiches, petit fours, cheese, bread, biscuits. Jellies, and cold ham and pastries he did not recognize. Three other footmen strolled through the room, one collecting abandoned or unneeded dishes, another with a tray of meringues, and the last with a salver of assorted sweetmeats. This was the sort of gathering a duke ought to have, he thought.

He recognized the vicar, holding a plate of half-eaten cake, deep in conversation with Dr. Longfield. He saw several of his neighbors. Fine men, all of them, some of whom would have traveled upwards of two hours to reach Bitterward. At least half of the people in his house were young ladies of the sort mothers and fathers liked to have introduced to men like his brother Nigel. And him. He stayed in the doorway and scanned the room for Lily without admitting that he was.

He'd been living at Bitterward for more than ten years, but he had not had a formal gathering since Eugenia was married. No dinners or fetes. He didn't hunt much, and he had never attended any of the dances in town. Other than irregular appearances at church and somewhat more regular evenings at the homes of neighbors he liked, he'd kept to himself. He knew the gentlemen but not their wives and children.

Lily stood by the window, fingering her medallion, counting up and down the gold beads worked into the ribbon. Several men were gathered around her, some more boy than man, but they all had the same besotted expression. Eugenia stood next to Lily, wearing a lavender gown. She was laughing at something, and, Lord, his sister was still young and pretty.

Good God.

Jane Kirk was here, too, sitting for now with her mother and sisters. The woman everyone thought was his future wife. He was aware he was an object of her interest and even trepidation. He stayed where he was and watched Lily while she was unaware of his presence. She'd been naked in his arms, and he'd looked into her face while he thrust into her. She'd had her mouth around his cock, and he'd had his hands on her, everywhere he could reach, and she was smiling as if none of that had happened. Lovers for a few days and nothing more? Would she return to Syton House and her dratted father and never think of him again?

"Your grace." The vicar walked across the room to him, sketching out a bow while holding his plate of cake. Dr. Longfield had joined the crowd around Eugenia and Lily. "Delighted to see you, sir."

"Vicar."

"You really must try this cake." He picked up his fork and pointed at the remains of a slice of yellow cake on his plate. "I had no idea your cook was capable of such transporting delights."

"You ought to come to tea more often," he said.

"I shall, oh, I shall. Now that you ask. And you, your grace, I hope will one day accept my invitation to tea at the vicarage."

"I will, sir." He imagined sitting there with Lily beside him.

"Lovely tea," the vicar said.

"Thank you." Mountjoy, with the vicar in tow, joined his sister.

"Mountjoy," Eugenia said. Her smile transformed her into the sister he remembered from years ago. She went to him and kissed his cheek. "Thank you so much for coming."

Lily was right. His public support of his sister mattered a great deal, but he'd rather be tromping through the fields than standing here in a room full of people he barely knew.

He glanced at Lily. Nothing could be more natural. A gentleman ought to greet his houseguest. Their eyes met, all innocence between them. Mountjoy acknowledged her with a nod.

"Your grace," she said. She was regally calm.

By God, there would be another time for them.

Lily said, "Shall I fetch you a plate of food, your grace? There is the most astounding Edam, and some delightful strawberry preserves. Cakes, too, if you'd like some."

The vicar lifted his plate. "His grace must have a slice of cake."

At Lily's confirming look, Mountjoy said, "Yes, thank you." Anyone who looked at him must surely know he'd had carnal knowledge of her. "Miss Wellstone."

Lily went to the sideboard. He contented himself with counting the number of men who stared at her. Damn near every man in the room. Including him.

"Tea, Mountjoy," Eugenia said.

He waved her off. "Not hungry."

"Dear brother. You drink tea, not eat it." Eugenia's eyes sparkled, and he tore his gaze from Lily. "I made some for you with Lily's Lapsang, but if you'd rather have the gunpowder, I'd be happy to make that for you instead."

"The Lapsang is perfect. Thank you." With a smile, he took the cup and saucer from his sister. They were using the best china today. The Mountjoy crest was painted on every piece. He took a sip of his tea. Someone had taken the vicar aside and left him standing more or less alone with his sister.

"Mountjoy?" Eugenia said.

"Yes?"

"May I ask a favor of you?"

He sipped his tea and liked the flavor even better than before. "You may."

"I'd like you to speak to Lord Fenris."

He set his cup on its saucer too hard. What he remembered was the way Fenris had asked after his sister, how quickly the man had gone to Eugenia's assistance. If he'd made himself unpleasant to her, he'd see that Fenris was sorry he'd ever stepped foot near Bitterward. "Why?"

"He's not to be trusted. I know from personal experience that's true. He means Lily no good." She put a hand on his arm. "Protect her, Mountjoy. She deserves better than whatever Fenris has in store for her. Will you promise me?"

# Chapter Twenty-five

MOUNTJOY WATCHED LILY CHARM EVERYONE. SHE wore a frock with a pink bodice and a white skirt with narrow pink stripes. Her slippers were pink.

He was aware that he might be ignoring her too assiduously. He'd left the knot of men he'd been speaking with and had made a point of moving from one group to another, the epitome of a good host. One of the young ladies from High Tearing was sitting at the piano in the corner of the salon playing Bach and doing a creditable job, too. He spoke with his neighbors, made the acquaintance of wives, sons, and daughters, and observed that his clothes were, in the main, flavorless compared to anyone else's.

At one point, he found himself in a crowd that included Jane Kirk. He should get his proposal done with. Invite her to stroll with him, and tell her he hoped she would consent to be his duchess. "Miss Kirk." He bent over Jane's hand. She smiled coolly. There was just nothing between him and Jane. No spark. He could not deny she was a pretty woman. He liked her. She was pleasant and intelligent and there was simply nothing between them. Had there been, he might have done something about the two of them when the sly innuendos about a match first began.

"Delightful to see you at Bitterward," he said to her. "My brother will be devastated to know he missed you today."

"Your grace." She flushed and didn't meet his gaze.

They stood there with nothing more to say to each other. He opened his mouth to ask her if she would like to see the roses and what came out was, "I beg your pardon, Miss Kirk. There's someone I must speak to."

He escaped the room and, taking in great breaths of air, leaned against the wall just beside the door. The sounds of the gathering carried on the air. Laughter. The clinking of cups. Mountjoy rested his head against the wall. He was no good at parties. No good at all. He would speak to Jane another time, when his house was not full of people he barely knew. He would get to know her.

"Your grace?"

He opened his eyes and saw Lily standing before him. "Lily."

She curtseyed. "Are you well?"

"I am now."

"Mr. Kirk was asking after you."

"I will find him presently."

She put her hands behind her back and rocked on her heels in that way she had. "Is aught well?"

"When do you intend to take command of my wardrobe?" he asked in a low voice. The question reminded him of the luscious curves of her body, and the sound she made when he entered her. He did not want to think of the inevitable time when she would be gone, but it killed him to know she would be. At his side, he clenched his fists then released them.

"Your tailor will need additional measurements. I trust you will oblige him." She leaned back and swept her eyes over him. "I'll be sending fabric samples and strict instructions for how the cloth is to be cut."

The electricity between them made him feel alive. He pulled at his cravat.

"Stop," she said. "You're making things worse."

"The bloody thing is strangling me. Come with me, Lily, and fix it."

She glanced at the door and then at him. "Is that all?"

"No." He took a step toward her. "You know that's not all."

"Your sister has guests, Mountjoy. I can't abandon her. Or them." She put a hand on his sleeve. "Come back inside."

"I've had enough, Wellstone." A servant came out of the salon with a tray.

"Poor man."

"You like all that. The people. The talk and noise."

"I do."

"I don't." He speared her with a look. "All I want is to be alone with you."

She smiled, and he thought his heart would break at the sight. "Later, Mountjoy. I promise you."

"Now," he said.

"You know I can't."

"I won't go back in there."

She shrugged. "Then go, your grace. You're no good to anyone scowling like that anyway."

"I've done my duty to Eugenia."

"You have."

He checked the hall again and, seeing no one, risked a touch to her cheek. "Do what you must, then. Enjoy yourself." They were so different, the two of them. "So long as you know I want you with me."

She didn't return his smile. "Your grace."

He walked away, thinking he ought to have gone back inside, but equally aware that the crowd would have quickly worn away his civility. Some minutes later he ended up in his office, which, it happened, overlooked the same back lawns as the Oldenburg salon. The guests had moved outside, Lily among them. He gazed out the window, unable to work, though there was a mountain of correspondence and ledgers awaiting his attention. He ignored it all.

She would leave him. Every minute that passed brought them closer to that moment. That had been the understanding from the beginning. If he were honest, that impermanence had, at the start, been a relief. It would eventually happen that they would go their separate ways. But not yet. Not just yet. Even from a distance one could tell Lily was the leader, the others followers, she the sun, everyone else planets in orbit around her. She was the light of any room. In a crowd, one noticed her. Exuberant and full of spirits. Passionate beyond belief. Beautiful in his arms.

He rested a hand on the sill and his forehead on the casement. He was endangering his good name and his family's trust by thinking for even half a second that he could safely conduct an affair with Lily for the rest of the time she was here. Not with his blinding need for her. How long did they have? Two weeks? Three? Could he convince her to stay for a month? What about a year?

*The rest of his life?*

Today the sun shone bright, and the guests outside were laughing and gesturing and dashing about. Someone's dog was barking, and the sound carried through the window. Two servants came out, each carrying a basket filled with what looked like apples.

Lily was now arm in arm with Eugenia and Jane, and Caroline Kirk, too. They looked well together, the four of them. Several of the gentlemen held tennis racquets. He grabbed the windowsill and stood there, staring at Lily in that pink frock that fit her like a dream. No other woman out there looked half as fine as she did.

Miss Caroline threw a stick for the dog, a spaniel of some sort. It dashed after its prize. The footmen set the baskets on an invisible line, with the guests gathered behind them. Lily began an animated explanation that involved gestures and pacing. Dr. Longfield stepped forward, a tennis racquet in hand. At a signal from Lily, he took an apple from one of the baskets.

The doctor threw the apple into the air, a wizened thing it was, and hit it a smashing serve. The fruit came off the racquet like an overstuffed Christmas goose. Bits split off and plummeted to the ground.

The demonstration appeared to have been successful, for the doctor bowed once, turned his racquet over to the next gentleman in line, and the rest of the guests lined up. Two at a time, they took turns throwing an apple or other unappetizing fruit into the air and hitting it with the racquets. From time to time one of the gentlemen would lob the fruit into the air for one of the ladies.

There were a great many misses and an indecent amount of mirth. Not everyone hit their target the first time. Whenever someone hit one of the apples particularly well, cheers and applause rose up. There was, he could see from his vantage, spirited betting going on among certain of the spectators.

His guests—Eugenia and Lily's guests—were having a splendid time. The footmen retrieved any apples that hadn't disintegrated upon being hit and that appeared as if they could be abused again. Lily stepped up to the line and accepted an apple from Jane Kirk. She tossed her missile into the air and *whack*! The fruit spiraled through the air, shedding bits until the entire thing came apart.

Mountjoy left the window. At his desk, he dashed off a quick line on a half sheet of paper and put the folded page into his coat pocket. By the time he reached the lawn, Lily had another apple and a racquet in hand. Everyone was laughing and smiling, even people who had failed to hit anything while he'd been watching.

Lily put her toe to the line again. As before, she threw her apple into the air. He could see that most of one side of the fruit was a discolored brown.

*Thwack!*

The apple shot into the air, split into several pieces, and whirled three different directions. Cheers went up.

"Good shot, Miss Wellstone!"

"Applesauce!"

Footmen ran out to retrieve what pieces of fruit they could.

He crossed the lawn, aware of a sudden silence. From the corner of his eye, he saw Jane Kirk, ashen, a hand over her mouth. Did they really think him as awful as that? "Miss Wellstone—" He held out his hand to Lily. What little conversation was still ongoing ceased.

He heard Eugenia whisper, "No, Mountjoy."

"Give me the racquet, if you please."

Lily handed it to him with only a slight tilt of her head. During the exchange, he shoved his note into the top of her glove. Racquet in hand, he turned to his left.

"We're saving the pieces, Mountjoy," Eugenia said. She held her hands to her mouth, then lowered them. "They're to be fed to the chickens and the stoats."

He stooped for an apple. It was discolored and soft. "Even this one?"

"Yes," Ginny said. Behind her, Jane Kirk shook her head. Caroline looked at him as if she expected him to bite off someone's head.

"It's hardly fit for a pig."

No one said anything.

Mountjoy tossed the apple into the air and hit it with all his strength. It shot through the air like a thing possessed, whirling and spinning and then disintegrating. Bits of apple rained down, yards and yards distant, he saw with some satisfaction, from where anyone else's had landed.

Caroline Kirk leaned over to Eugenia and said, not too softly, "Applesauce."

Jane shushed her.

Lily kept a straight face. "Well hit, your grace."

He handed the racquet to Lily. "That's how it's done."

"Indeed, your grace."

"See that the scraps are fed to the livestock." And then he stalked away like an ogre retreating to its lair.

# Chapter Twenty-six

MOUNTJOY PACED WHILE HE WAITED. HIS REGULATED life was falling to bits. Nothing was as it should be. He no longer knew how to behave toward Lily in public and it seemed whatever he did only made Jane's opinion of him worse. People were noticing a difference in him, too. Since Lily's arrival, the men he regularly met with had all remarked, in small ways and large, that he was a changed man. Eventually, he was going to say the wrong thing to Lily in front of someone, if he hadn't already, or pay too much attention to her and not enough to Jane. He'd be caught staring at Lily, not Jane, and the rumors would start.

When the door to the tower room opened, Mountjoy stopped pacing and wondered at the way his heart beat so hard. He said nothing. His life came to a halt. She had a key. He'd given Lily the key to the tower room he considered his sanctuary.

Lily closed the door and leaned against it, hands behind her. She was . . . serene. "Are you angry?"

"Not angry," he managed. He must break with her. Send

her home to Syton House now. He must say the words he had ready.

"Eugenia and Jane had nothing to do with it."

He nodded.

"It was all in good fun. I didn't think I needed your permission for a game. The new apples are already put by. We only hit the ones that no one would ever eat."

"Close the door." Heart sinking to his toes, he knew he wouldn't say what he should. He was still enthralled. The boredom would come, and then he'd break with her. But not yet. Not while she was at Bitterward. Surely, he could manage until she left. Then his life would go back to the way it was.

She did, then faced him again. Patient. Lovely beyond his understanding. "I daresay the hens will thank me for saving them from eating all the really rotten bits."

"It was your idea." He sounded a bloody fool. Hadn't she already told him so?

Her chin lifted. "Every part of it."

"I'm not angry."

"I am glad to know it." Cool as ice, she brought her hands from behind her and drew his note from the sleeve of her glove. "You'll want to burn this."

"Come here."

"I am here, your grace." God, that inscrutable expression of hers, as if nothing he could do or say could ever touch her. "At your pleasure."

"You should be here." He glanced at his feet, well aware there was a crude interpretation to his words and action.

Her mouth curved, and the last of her wariness slid from her eyes. "Maybe you should be here."

"Come here. To me."

She leaned her head against the door. "I think I will be safer here."

"Yes," he said. "You would be. Much safer. Is that what you want? To be safe?"

She pushed off and walked toward him. He watched her approach. "Are you sure you're not angry?"

"Quite."

"Well then. If you're not angry, why the imperial summons?" She waved his note.

"I thought I would go mad watching you. They admire you, all of them. Too much. Especially that damned Dr. Longfield."

"Don't be jealous," she said when she reached him. He took back his note, the dratted thing. "It's unbecoming a duke."

He drew her into his arms and brushed his mouth over hers. They fell into a kiss so carnal his initial thought of indulging just in this, just the kissing, flew off with his good sense. He pulled away. "I have a sheath," he said. "From Venice. I'm told they make the finest."

At first she didn't understand, and he felt a pang of guilt that she was innocent enough not to know what he meant. But then her expression cleared. "Oh. I see." Her cheeks turned pink. "Have you?"

"Yes."

"What of it, Mountjoy?" Her arms stayed around his shoulders. One of her hands played in his hair.

"I have it with me." He patted his chest in the location of an interior pocket of his coat.

"Convenient."

"I want to fuck you here." The words sounded crude, not what he meant at all. "Right now. With you wearing that pretty frock."

She drew in a sharp breath. "Wicked man."

He released her and walked to the sideboard to pull the salver from beneath the bottles there. He put an edge of his peremptory note to the flame of the lantern until it caught. When the fire licked down nearly to his fingers, he dropped what was left on the salver and waited until nothing remained but ashes. He also found some still water, thank God, and dropped his sheath into a glass of it so it would soften.

"Best stir the ashes," Lily said. "To be sure no one can reconstruct the note."

"It's gone up in smoke." He looked over his shoulder at her. She remained standing in the middle of the room. "No one will be reading it, I promise you."

"I can see most of the shape of the paper."

"And?"

"I once read a novel in which a spy was uncovered in just such a manner. The clever heroine was able to read the words etched into the ashes of the page."

"Balderdash."

"Upon such convictions are nations brought down." In a softer voice, she added, "And reputations destroyed."

She was right. And it would be her reputation that was shredded. There was no reason for the risk, far-fetched as it might be. He sighed and stirred the embers with his finger until all that was left was curling bits of blackened motes. He splashed some brandy on his fingers and wiped off the ashy residue with his handkerchief. Turning, he said, "Do you think we're safe now?"

"Not at all," she said.

Carrying the glass with his sheath, he returned to her and set it on the floor by the chaise. He put his hands on her shoulders and brushed his thumbs over her exposed skin. "You're right, Lily. Neither one of us is safe now."

She smiled. "Not in the least."

Taking her hand in his, he sat on the chaise where he drew her between his open thighs. He reached for the buttons along the side of her glove. One tiny pearl after another, he unfastened her glove enough for him to pull it off. He did the same with the other and draped them both over the top of the chaise.

"Thank you," she said. "The better to touch you."

He slid his hands underneath her skirts. His hands glided up her legs until he was touching the bare skin of her thighs. "The better to touch you. Like this."

She gazed down at him. "It's not wise."

"We've established that." He cupped the back of her thighs and pulled her forward. She was careful to lift her skirt, and he took care not to crush her frock more than necessary. She straddled him, knees on either side of him, and gasped softly when his fingers pressed between her legs. Soft skin, the folds of her already slick with want. Of him. He unbuttoned one side of his breeches and opened the fall to free himself.

Lily dropped her hands to his shoulders and watched him retrieve the sheath. Her skirts hid his hands sliding the lambskin over his cock and fastening the ribbon, but she knew what he was doing.

"Ready?" he whispered.

Her dark eyes stayed on his face while he adjusted them both. He brought her down on him, hands cupping her hips while he pushed up. Her body surrounded him, and as he closed his eyes and gave in to the exquisite sensation of being inside her and surrounded by the soft slickness of her, she whispered, "You feel good. So good."

When he was seated in her, pressing her down on him, he opened his eyes and said, "Say my name."

"Your grace."

He brought his hips toward hers and angled himself so the side of his cock, the sensitive head of him, rubbed harder against her passage. He pulled her forward sharply and thrust hard into her. "That isn't my name."

"Mountjoy." Her lips parted, and he disengaged his hands from her skirts and wrapped one hand around the nape of her neck. He kissed her. Hard and deep, tongue sweeping into her mouth. He moved his other hand to her belly, as far as he could reach before the bottom of her corset barred the way. He angled his fingers so he could stroke her. He knew where to touch a woman to bring her to pleasure, and he did so for her.

Lily's fingers dug into his shoulders, and he drew back from their kiss to watch her while he brought her closer to the edge. Closer. Until she shattered, and then he lay back, angled on the chaise, drinking in the heat in her eyes, the sensual curve of her mouth.

"Like that," he said. "God, yes. More."

She moved on him, rode him, sent him out of his mind with delight, and the same happened to her. When she came, she did so without reservation, and he adored the way she gave herself over to her pleasure. Her reaction made him feel potent, a lover worth keeping.

"Beautiful," he whispered as she used his body.

Her eyes opened slowly, a satisfied smile curving her mouth. "And you?" she asked.

"I'm close. Very close."

"What do you need?"

He sat up and rearranged them so that her back was to his front, her gown safely tucked up, with his arms under her shoulders, her legs spread over his thighs, and he pushed into her again. Thrust. Pulled back, thrust again, and she understood the motion he needed. His felt his reaction spiraling tight, out of reach yet closer with every thrust, with every clench of her body around his cock.

"I'm going to spend inside you," he said.

When he came, his peak hit hard, spun him out of his mind, out of his control. The only thought on his mind was more. More of this. Let him be thrown out of his mind. Inside his chest emotion quivered. He damn near let go of her because he was completely lost to his reaction to her. Releasing inside her.

Once he had his breath back, when he was back inside his body, and they'd separated, he said, "Don't leave, Lily."

Saying her name cracked his heart in half.

She did not answer.

"Don't leave me," he whispered. "Not so soon. Not yet."

"I have to go back outside before much longer."

"That isn't what I meant."

She pushed up on one elbow and peered into his face. "What do you mean?"

"Stay here." He curled a strand of her hair around his finger. "At Bitterward. At least a little longer."

She looked away.

"Why not?" he asked.

"My father needs me. I can't gallivant around the country for weeks and weeks. He gets lonely, you know, and he hasn't any friends. When he came to live with me, he gave up all that. No one should be lonely when they're old and frail. What sort of daughter would I be if I left him alone like that?"

"If he'd raised you with half the thought you give him now, you'd have had a happy childhood. He'd be the sort of man who could make new friends."

"I'll be here another fortnight. That's a long time yet for me to impose on your good graces."

"You're no imposition."

She leaned down and kissed the tip of his nose. "And when I do leave you'll think just the same. That I was a delightful guest. You'll have fond memories of me."

"More. You know that."

"Yes," she said without smiling this time. "Yes."

What would he do if, after he'd tried everything he knew, she left him anyway?

*Chapter Twenty-seven*

❦

At Bitterward's first ball, Mountjoy wore one of the new suits that had arrived at the house just the day before. He felt foolish even though he knew he looked, in some indefinable way, more like a duke than he ever had before. Everyone was staring. In the last two hours, he'd had more compliments about his appearance than he'd had in the last ten years. He accepted each surprised remark with a nod but could not help thinking he remained the same man he'd been every day before this.

The fit was as comfortable as both Elliot and Lily had promised, but his cravat had a deal more starch than he was used to. His shirt was of so fine a linen that even he, with his dislike of any change and his aversion to even a tacit admission that he had been a stubborn ass, had to admit he liked the way his coat slid on and left him with no urge to pull or tug at the parts that bunched up. Now and again, he caught sight of himself in a mirror or a fortuitously reflective surface, and he scarcely recognized himself. He looked a dandy, but without the fussiness he associated with those overdressed fools.

This was a night in which he learned he'd been wrongheaded about more than his clothes. Obviously, Mountjoy had completely underestimated the importance of social entertaining. In London he rarely went to events that weren't political or for some purpose of business, his or the government's. He had not been to a ball these five years at least and had yet to as much as hint that a voucher for Almack's would be put to use. He did not care to be turned down by the Almack's patronesses—he wouldn't be the first duke to suffer that humiliation—any more than he would actually care to attend such an affair.

He ought to have begun formal entertainments here years ago. He really should have.

Here he was. A duke from the skin out, in a house full to the rafters with what looked to him to be the entirety of High Tearing and half of Sheffield. There was a steady procession of people through the room where samples from the treasure Lily had uncovered were on display. The pieces, though they appeared to be metal parts and fittings torn or removed from centuries-vanished armor and other equipage, were nevertheless beautifully worked. With the dirt removed and what repairs the local goldsmith felt competent to make, the displayed collection took one's breath.

An hour of talking to his neighbors had cemented better relations with them than all his years of appearing at the Sessions or at any of the official or ad hoc governance meetings that had taken place over the years. A good many of the men were genuinely interested in his opinions of the management of an estate, its tenants, lands, livestock and crops, and other holdings. The men's wives knew a great deal of their husbands' interests. More than one extended a verbal invitation for a social meeting that even he, at last, understood was at least as much a business opportunity as it was luncheon or supper or tea.

Presently, he was standing at the edge of the ballroom watching the dancers in the last set before the orchestra took an intermission and his guests could sit down for an informal meal. Nigel was not yet back from London, which had caused much consternation and upset with Eugenia. The Kirk girls were here, but for Jane, which was odd. Somewhere, though not within immediate sight, was Lord Fenris, who had not been invited but who had come nevertheless.

Eugenia was dancing with the mayor of High Tearing. She was lovely in pale blue silk, happy and smiling as she had not been for far too long. Miss Caroline Kirk was dancing with Dr. Longfield. He did not see Lily anywhere. He scanned the room, expecting to find her easily and feel that rush of his pulse that happened whenever he laid eyes on her.

Her ball gown was the color of the champagne coming from his wine cellar in such copious amounts, and he did not see that so distinctive hue anywhere in the room. He stayed until the set ended, watching his guests enjoying themselves while he looked for Lily. She'd danced several times tonight, but he hadn't asked her yet. He wanted to waltz with her.

People applauded the orchestra when the members put down their instruments, and soon after couples and groups formed for the meal that would be served during the intermission. They were enjoying themselves, he thought. Young and old alike, and he had Lily and Eugenia to thank for that.

He headed for the terrace by way of his office where he kept his cigars. His office was at the end of this corridor and ought to be closed, as that was not a room intended to be open to his guests. The door was ajar, however, though there was no light inside other than the moonlight through the windows. Mountjoy walked in, reaching as he did, for the flint by the door. He did not light the lamp because the room was occupied.

"Is that you, Wellstone?"

"Your grace," she said. She was on the sofa by the fireplace. Her soft greeting was forlorn. So very unlike her on a night that was her triumph. Success in everything, the ball, the house, Eugenia smiling and in colors, and him looking like a man born to his title.

He pushed the office door closed and crossed to her. "Are you all right?"

"No," she said. "I don't believe I am."

"Tell me what's the matter." Anything. He'd do anything to keep her from being unhappy.

She didn't answer. Instead, she turned her head away from him.

"Are you crying?" He sat beside her and took her hand in his. With her other hand, she swiped at her face.

"Certainly not. I never cry." When she faced him, her features were composed. She rested a hand on his upper chest, but her voice quavered when she spoke. "Have I told you, Mountjoy, how absolutely splendid you look tonight?"

He could not bear the thought of her in tears, not for any reason. She was too subdued for him to believe all was well. It wasn't, and that tugged at his heart. "Thanks entirely to you."

"Your valet put you together very well. The success is his, I assure you."

"He was in raptures when the first of the suits arrived."

Lily opened her mouth to speak but didn't. He watched, helpless, as she simply dissolved. He put an arm around her shoulder, and she collapsed against him, tears flowing. He'd seen women cry before, some of those tears heartfelt, but the fact of Lily, confident, happy Lily, sobbing against his chest broke something in him.

"Lily. Darling, what is it? What's happened?"

She shook her head.

Mountjoy held her until some of the tension went out of her shoulders. "Can you tell me?"

She kept her hand on his chest. "Lord Fenris is here, and it's upset Ginny. She does not like the man. Not at all."

He thought of his sister, dancing with the mayor. "He seems to have upset you as well. Has he insulted you? Shall

I find him and send him away? I will if having him here pains you."

"I've never had any family." Her fingers curled around the lapel of his coat. "No one but my father, that is. And now, after all this time thinking Lord Fenris meant me no good, I wish there were a way for us to mend things between us."

Mountjoy fished out his spare handkerchief and handed it to her. He wanted very much to vilify the man, but he didn't. Though he didn't make an endorsement of him either.

"Thank you." She took his handkerchief and pressed it to her eyes. She sucked in a breath and let it out. "I've been his relation all along. Why take notice of me now? It's just that . . ." She looked at him, her eyes glittering with tears. "I should like to have family of my own. Is that so terrible?"

"Lily," Mountjoy said. He took his handkerchief from her and dabbed at her cheek. "My dear Lily."

"Ginny dislikes him. With reason, I know that. He treated her infamously, and I wouldn't for the world force her to tolerate anyone she holds in such abhorrence. I can't."

He cupped her face with one hand and could not for his life parse out what he was feeling. "You are a loyal friend to my sister."

"I told you that the day I arrived."

"So you did." He kept his hand on her cheek. "I'll talk to him for you. Find out once and for all why he's here."

She leaned her head against his chest, and Mountjoy put an arm around her shoulder, keeping her close. She held up her medallion. "If only the magic would make my relations pleasant people. Now *that* would be useful."

Mountjoy laughed. "Lily, darling," he said without thinking, "this is exactly why I love you."

She sat up, though he kept his arm around her. Neither of them spoke for the space of half a breath. The quiet was fraught. He'd never said those words before, not to anyone, not on purpose. Nor on accident. Not even when he was a green boy.

Until now.

Mountjoy kissed her to stop the quiet or her potential question, he wasn't sure which. He hadn't meant that he *loved* her, not precisely. As was always the case with him and Lily, the kiss was immediately carnal. Wonderfully, wholly uninhibited. He didn't want to ruin her ball gown nor the arrangement of her hair, not when there was still more dancing to be done, so he fetched her with his fingers and his mouth, and when he'd had the pleasure of hearing, seeing, and tasting her pleasure, he found he couldn't think why she shouldn't use her hands on him, which she did, and then she finished him with her mouth, and he clamped his hands on the sofa while she did, so that he wouldn't reach for her head and leave her hair a tangled mess.

While he came, he thought he'd be damned if he let Fenris hurt her. Damned. Not for any reason.

# Chapter Twenty-eight

LILY LAY CURLED UP IN HER BED, IN A STATE THAT WAS not quite awake yet not asleep either. Her maid tapped on the door between her dressing room and the bedchamber. She ignored the sound, including the creak of the connecting door as it opened. Her dream was vivid in her mind, and she did not want to give it up. In between lovely, slow kisses, Mountjoy was declaring himself head over heels in love with her.

"Miss?"

He'd said those words. *I love you, Lily.*

He hadn't meant them, but the effect on her had been nearly the same as if he had. She pulled the covers over her head and tried to fall back into her already fading dream. Something delicious about Mountjoy.

"Miss," her maid said. "Doyle said I ought to tell you, or I'd not bother you at this hour. Not for anything."

"What?" she said from beneath the sheets. The linens smelled of lavender and they were warm around her body. Perfect for hours more dreaming.

"You have a caller, miss."

Who on earth would be calling on her here? She stayed with her legs drawn up and the covers warm around her. "What time is it?"

"Half past eleven, miss."

"Eleven?" She groaned. She was going to have to see whoever it was. But that did not make her any fonder of mornings. Even if her maid went away this very second, her cozy half-dreaming state was over, and she would never get back to Mountjoy and his wonderful dream kisses and declarations of love. "In a moment," she said.

"It's the Marquess of Fenris himself, and Doyle said you ought to be told he's waiting."

She turned over and lowered the sheet enough to see her maid's expression was serious. Her heart thudded as the name registered. "Lord Fenris?"

"Yes, miss."

"Does Lady Eugenia know he's here?"

"She went into High Tearing this morning. With the duke."

Now that was a stroke of luck for Fenris, wasn't it? To have arrived when both Ginny and Mountjoy were out. Coincidence? Or something else? She pushed herself onto her elbows. "Did Lord Fenris happen to mention the purpose of his call?"

"Why, I suppose, to speak with you."

"Is there anyone with him?" A lawyer, perhaps, with papers to serve on her. "Another gentlemen. Probably carrying a leather case?"

"No, miss. At least Doyle didn't say. Shall I tell him you're not at home?"

She wished she weren't. "No. I'll see him."

"You ought to wear your rose frock, I think," her maid said.

Lily sighed. "Oh, very well." She was going to have to face Fenris sooner or later, if only to tell him he must leave her in peace. She might as well do so now. "Tell him I'll be down shortly."

"Yes, miss."

She folded the covers to below her chin and spoke to her maid's retreating back. "I suppose someone should offer him tea and something to eat."

"Miss."

"When you return, would you bring some chocolate and perhaps a roll and butter? Porridge if there is any."

"Yes, miss."

She groaned and stretched out on the mattress. By the time the maid returned with the food—her roll was still warm, there was honey and butter in the porridge, and the chocolate was steaming hot—she was standing in front of her wardrobe working out what frock one ought to wear while meeting a long estranged relative whose fondest wish might be to have her locked away for a madwoman, never to be seen again.

"What parlor is he waiting in?" Lily asked when she approved of the results of her hair. "The Oldenburg?"

"No, miss. He's in the Prussian salon."

"Ah." The predominant color of the Prussian salon was blue. There was, in fact, a sofa in a gorgeous shade of the blue after that name. "You're right about the rose frock. I'll wear that."

"Yes, miss."

The ash pink bodice would look delectable when she sat on that Prussian blue sofa. The hours she'd spent affixing ribbon of the exact right color to the gown, no more the exquisite Brussels lace, had been more than worth the time. The dress was brought out, and while her maid took it off to press, Lily ate her breakfast.

Forty minutes later she was outside the Prussian salon, as nervous as she'd ever been in her life. She took a deep breath to compose herself before she opened the door.

Her cousin stood with his back to her, staring out the window opposite the door. His hair was cut close to his head, so short that she wondered if he'd recently been ill. He was tall and well made with a wiry build. Not at all sickly. His clothes were once again severe yet perfectly cut.

"My lord?" She walked in. Whatever he wanted, she would soon know. Reconciliation, as she hoped? Or something far more dire? "My apologies for keeping you waiting."

Fenris turned. His eyes flicked down to her slippers and back to her face. He smiled, but without warmth. "It's hardly been a moment, Miss Wellstone."

She approached him and curtseyed while he bent over her hand. Fenris was more handsome than she remembered, with brown eyes, though not as dark as hers. She studied him and did not know if she found similarities between them because she so badly wanted there to be, or whether there really was a likeness between them. "Shall I send for tea?"

"No, thank you." He seemed to be studying her as acutely as she did him.

"My lord." She walked to the Prussian blue sofa and perched on the edge, back straight, feet planted squarely on the floor. She gestured to a chair. "Will you sit?"

"Thank you, but I prefer to stand." He was holding a packet in one hand. Her heart sank, for she was beyond certain those were legal documents.

"As you wish."

"How is your hand? Has your injury healed? I trust it was not serious."

She wriggled her fingers. "A nuisance, really. It's nearly healed now. Thank you for asking."

"And your . . . illness? The day Mountjoy carried you into the house?"

Fenris, she thought, seemed garrulous for a man who intended to destroy her life. "Perfectly recovered."

Silence fell, and she left it to Fenris to make his purpose known. If he wished to serve her with papers, why hadn't he sent an attorney to do that for him?

He cleared his throat. "I don't know how much you know about me. . . ."

She met his gaze forthrightly. "You are the heir to my uncle, the Duke of Camber. The previous duke was your grandfather and mine. My mother was your aunt, and therefore, Lord Fenris, you have the misfortune of being my cousin."

"Hardly a misfortune."

"I confess, sir, after all this time, I wonder what business you think you might have with me."

"I find myself in a difficult situation." He paced, the packet of documents still clutched in one hand.

Oh, no doubt he did. She clasped her hands on her lap. Honestly, did he expect her to sympathize with his effort to destroy her life?

"For days, I've walked from one end of High Tearing to the other, turning matters over in my mind. Wondering what I ought to do."

"A very bracing walk. I'm sure it's improved your constitution."

He stopped his pacing and stood with his hands behind him. "My grandfather, our grandfather, never spoke of your mother. Nor did my father. I was at Eton at the time she married. They told me," he said, "that she'd passed away."

She quirked her eyebrows in response.

"I had no reason to believe my father lied to me, Miss Wellstone. I was a boy at the time, still at school when he wrote with the news."

"I cannot, and do not, blame you for what happened when you were a boy."

He blanched. "Would that my own family had been as tolerant. As you might imagine, there was an uproar when we learned Great-Aunt Lily had left everything to you. That, Miss Wellstone, was when I learned of your existence."

"Indeed?"

"Quite."

She remained silent.

"I was shocked to discover my aunt—your mother— hadn't died as they told me she had, but had instead married and even had a child." He drew in a long breath. "I was equally shocked to learn I had a cousin I knew nothing about." He drew another breath, but Lily said nothing. "Everything in secret." He paced again. "I was . . . appalled by the lies, Miss Wellstone. My own father, perpetuating such a deception." He stopped walking. "Upon learning of your inheritance, my father immediately met with his attorneys."

"I am aware."

He looked sheepish. "Yes, you must be. At any rate, as you also know, the properties and the monies were Aunt Lily's to dispose of as she wished, and eventually the family lawyers had no choice but to advise my father he would be unlikely to prevail if he continued to pursue the matter."

Lily pressed her lips together. Was he about to tell her he'd secured a more favorable legal opinion? In such a case, would she not be hearing from an attorney, and not Fenris himself? Ah, but then there was that mysterious packet he carried. The one that contained legal documents. "I see."

"I persuaded him there was nothing to be gained by going forward as he wished. Other than the enrichment of our lawyers. And yours."

If he was already in possession of papers that declared her incompetent, he would he have brought the bailiff to secure her. Or was he confident she would simply go along with a heinous plan to lock her away? "Sir. I have yet to understand why you are here. Nothing you've said is anything my own solicitor has not already told me. Perhaps not the particulars, but the result is what matters, I daresay."

"True."

"Nevertheless," she said, "I thank you for your intervention with your father. You saved us both a great deal of aggravation and money."

He nodded. He was quite a handsome man. Not like Mountjoy, but appealing nonetheless. "A few weeks ago I came across letters that my aunt—not your mother, I mean, but our great-aunt and your namesake—left behind at my father's house. She kept a study there, and after she passed, my father never went through the room." He stood very straight, as a military man might.

Lily's stomach dropped. "You found another will."

"A will?" His eyebrows drew together. "No. Not at all. I found letters. From you." He held out his packet. "I thought I ought to return them to you."

Lily rose with all the dignity at her command. "There is only so much ill will I'll tolerate from anyone, even a future duke. You traveled all this way, spent all these days here in order to make the grand gesture of returning Aunt Lily's letters to me? Because, naturally, you would not wish the letters of such a woman as I am to remain in your house." She held out her hand. "Please give me the letters so that you may be on your way home."

He blanched. "You misunderstand."

"It was made very clear to me that your family—"

"We Talbots are your family as well."

"Much to my regret. Besides Aunt Lily no Talbot has ever wanted anything to do with a Wellstone." His last words penetrated and she gave a brittle laugh. "You say Talbots are my family, too? What family returns a child's letters but one that wants no association with her? For I assure you, I was a child when I first wrote to our grandfather. And to your father, too. They returned my letters unread. Now you do me the favor of returning my letters to Aunt Lily. My collection is now complete. Thank you, Lord Fenris, for it's better that I have the letters than that they stay in the hands of anyone with the name Talbot."

"My father admitted to me that he refused your letters." He briefly closed his eyes. "I hope you'll accept my apologies for that."

"Aunt Lily was the only one of you who wanted anything to do with me. She loved me, and I loved her. Not a day goes by that I don't wish she were still alive."

"Miss Wellstone. Please."

She held out her hand again, shaking with anger that he felt he'd needed to see her personally to cut off relations they'd never had in the first place. "I am happy to accept the letters and see you on your way. Thank you, my lord, and good day."

"Cousin."

"I have no cousin." She heard in her words and the manner of her saying the echo of her father. So determined to punish any slight. If anyone deserved that, was it not the Talbots?

He stared at the letters without handing them over. So did Lily. She remembered the paper, the smell of the ink as she wrote the letters, and how deeply she'd longed to meet the woman she'd been named after. Fenris spoke softly. "You weren't more than fourteen or fifteen when you wrote these letters."

"You read them?"

"Of course I read them." He lifted his chin, and the look in his eye reminded her of Ginny's opinion of him. A judgmental man, and from what she could see, the very worst sort who probably believed he was justified in his lectures and moral superiority. "They were among my Aunt Lily's effects. I found them in the house where I live."

She lifted her hands. "Keep them, then, if you feel you must assert ownership. Or would you feel better if I gnashed my teeth and wept bitter tears?"

"No."

"For I tell you, I won't give you the satisfaction."

"I wished only to tell you that it's plain from these pages that you loved her, and that Aunt Lily had a great deal of affection for you and your mother." He checked himself. "I suppose that's obvious seeing as how she made you her sole heir. Heiress. Miss Wellstone. Cousin Lily. I read your letters to her and wanted to meet you and tell you I am sorry, very sorry, that my grandfather refused to acknowledge you and that my father did the same."

She sat on the sofa and opened her mouth to speak and found she had no words. The desire to send him away still burned hot. Why should she reconcile with any Talbot after what his family had done? She stared at her lap and struggled to compose herself. This unreasoning sense of betrayal was her father's way, and she would not follow his example. She looked up. "That's decent of you."

"I wish I'd met your mother. I wish I'd known you were corresponding with Aunt Lily before it was too late. Miss Wellstone." He took a half step forward and stopped himself. "I am here because I do not wish the estrangement between our families to continue."

"You don't?"

"You *are* my relation, Miss Wellstone. Not a Talbot by name, but my cousin nevertheless. Cannot you and I make our peace?"

"What does your father think of your visit here?"

His mouth twisted. "That does not signify."

"He doesn't know you've come."

"I'm a grown man." He laughed. "I make my own life, and my father, I do assure you, is well aware of that. I respect his advice and opinion, but my life is my own."

"Ah."

Fenris tapped the letters on his palm. "I have given our situation a great deal of consideration. Yours and mine."

"My inheritance or our estrangement?"

He colored but soon recovered. "Both, I suppose. I can see, Miss Wellstone, that you are a woman of spirit, though that has no bearing on my presence here. There's no way I could have known before I left to find you that I would encounter such a striking, vibrant woman as you."

"What is your point?"

"Naturally, your letters suggest the spirit I see in you now. I never did expect to find an ordinary woman, not after reading these."

"I'm not certain you mean that as a compliment, but I'll take it as one."

"You should. It is not and never was my intention to slight you in any way. I did not come here merely to return the letters as some sort of insult to you." His chagrin was honest, she felt. Miraculous, even. "I thought you might want them as a memento of the woman you loved."

She held out her hand. "I would like that very much. Thank you."

"Perhaps it won't be necessary for me to return them."

"Why not?"

"Because you are my cousin." He went still, composing himself much as she had needed to do. "You would be welcome to read these letters as often as you like."

The tension in her melted away. His wish for a reconciliation was genuine, and that meant she had a cousin. "I should be glad, very glad, to know you."

"It is my hope, Miss Wellstone, that we will have more than an acquaintance."

"Oh?" She leaned against the sofa back. "How so, if your father and mine have not changed their minds? Do you propose we carry on a clandestine correspondence such as Aunt Lily and I did?" The idea amused her enough that she smiled at him, and he tipped his head. "We wrote to each other in care of a particular stationer's. Her letters to me were always franked, but I wouldn't expect you to do the same. That expense is now one I can bear. But to keep our secret, my lord, I could write my letters to you in lemon juice, as a precaution against them being intercepted. Your father would think someone is sending you blank papers. Imagine his confusion. You might tell him it's a new stationer you're thinking of patronizing and the paper is a sample."

Fenris blinked once then again. "There's no need for a secret correspondence or letters written in code or lemon juice."

"How disappointing."

"Miss Wellstone." He smiled. Barely. A Tablot smile, she thought. "Have you not foreseen the reason for my visit?"

"No. Since you haven't brought the baliff, I rather think I have not."

"I am here to make you an offer."

She frowned. "Of what? The letters?"

"We can right the wrongs of the past, you and I."

"I'm not sure I follow."

He went down on one knee. "Lily Wellstone, marry me. Become my future duchess."

At that point, the door opened, and Mountjoy walked in. He took one look at Fenris kneeling and his eyebrows shot to his forehead. "What the devil is this?"

Lily didn't answer because, for once in her life, she had no idea what to say when it must be perfectly clear what was going on.

# *Chapter Twenty-nine*

❧❧

ON MOUNTJOY'S RETURN TO BITTERWARD, DOYLE informed him that Lord Fenris was here and that Lily was presently entertaining him in the Prussian salon. Mountjoy went directly there. Almost directly. He opened two wrong doors first.

When he found the right room, he stopped at the threshold of the doorway, his heart hammering as if he'd returned to find his house had been robbed and he was only now understanding the scope of his losses. Lily sat on the sofa, luminously beautiful in a gown in a shade of pink that flattered her complexion. As if she would ever wear a color that did not.

What the devil was going on, indeed.

Mountjoy raked his fingers through his hair in what was probably a futile attempt to make himself presentable. He wore his riding clothes, for pity's sake, which had not yet been altered for him or sent to him new. Mud and, no doubt, unspeakable matter spattered his boots. In all likelihood there was dirt on his face. He looked disreputable and unkempt and there was nothing he could do about it.

It was bloody obvious what was going on.

That damned prude Fenris was on one knee. In front of Lily. Holding her hand and staring into her face with the sort of stunned awe he'd seen before from other men.

The fool was proposing to her.

To Lily.

She did not look angry or horrified or even mortified. She did not look like a woman who had just refused an offer of marriage from someone she had every reason to dislike.

Mountjoy didn't question the panic that washed over him. Not that he hadn't taken into account the possibility that Fenris would do this. What he hadn't accounted for was Lily's reaction. He'd assumed Fenris would be a pompous prick and that Lily would refuse him because she had better sense than to entertain thoughts of marriage to a man like Fenris. That assumption was a serious miscalculation on his part. If she married Fenris, whether she was in love with the man or not, she would have the family she'd always longed for. She would belong, and for her, that would be a powerful incentive to accept.

Fenris rose and gave him a look that took in and dismissed his well-ridden-in clothes. "Your grace."

Lily looked between him and Fenris, and he realized he had no idea if she'd just accepted a proposal of marriage from the man or whether he'd interrupted the question or the answer or both. His heart lurched.

He did not own Lily, he told himself. They had no understanding except that she was leaving before long. What had he offered her besides physical passion? Nothing. Fenris, on the other hand, had just offered her the family connections she'd always longed for. Camber himself would come to terms with a daughter-in-law who brought with her a fortune he'd had to give up for lost. For that sort of fortune, even the Duke of Camber might see his way clear to recognizing her father.

"Might Miss Wellstone and I have a few moments longer?" Lord Fenris said. One corner of his mouth twitched. "I've matters to . . . discuss with my cousin." When Mountjoy didn't move, Fenris said, "They are of a personal nature, your grace. I'm sure you understand."

If he knew anything about Lily it was that she knew her own mind, and this self-righteous prick was going to treat her as if she did not. As if her desires, whatever they might be, were of no consequence compared to his. He fought his urge to throw the man out on his ear. "Wellstone?"

Lily rose slowly. She did not, as another might have done, pretend the moment wasn't awkward. "Lord Fenris, thank you very much. You do me a very great honor. I'm deeply flattered." She held out her hand for him to take. "And taken by surprise, as you must imagine. Though I thank you for calling on me."

Fenris turned his back on Mountjoy. "Have you an answer for me, cousin? Or do you need time to consider your reply?"

Her cheeks pinked up. "No. No answer yet, my lord."
*Not yet.*

"Is there a time when I might know my fate?"

"Tomorrow," Lily said. "If that's agreeable to you."

"If I must wait, I shall. Thank you." He took her hand and bowed over it. When he straightened, he put a packet into her hands. "In the meantime, keep these. Please. To remind you of my sincerity."

The emotion that flooded her face brought a lump to Mountjoy's throat. "Thank you." She took Fenris's hand in hers and pressed it. "Thank you very much."

"Until tomorrow."

"At two o'clock, if you don't mind."

"Certainly." He brought Lily's hand to his mouth and kissed her knuckles. As he walked past Mountjoy, they traded looks. Mountjoy waited until Fenris was past him before he said, "Perhaps you and I ought to have a word. My lord."

Mountjoy turned to find Fenris had done the same. They now faced each other. "You're not her father, Mountjoy."

"No, but she is an unmarried woman staying in my house. I am responsible for her while she is here."

Lily cleared her throat, but they both ignored her.

"Your concern for my cousin does you credit. Thank you." Fenris looked past him to Lily. "Tomorrow at two, Miss Wellstone."

"Not a moment sooner."

With that, Mountjoy was alone with Lily. "Would you rather I leave?" he asked. He closed his eyes. Of all people, Fenris was in a position to know just how wealthy Lily was. It made sense to bring that money back into the control of his family. Fenris would know that a man in his position married for reasons of dynasty and that he would please his father beyond words if he were to bring back Lily's fortune. Marrying Lily was a far cheaper solution than laywers.

Would she agree?

She shook her head and sat on the sofa. She placed the packet Fenris had given her on the table beside the sofa. "I confess, Mountjoy, I am at a loss just now. And I am rarely at a loss."

He stayed where he was, just past the door. She had not given Fenris an answer yet. Not yet. But tomorrow?

She looked at him, and for once she did not seem impossibly confident of herself. She clasped her hands on her lap. "I thought he'd come here to tell me they'd found another will and that I must leave Syton House and give back everything." She gazed at him. "All this time I've been imagining the awful things he must be plotting against me. His offer was completely unexpected."

He checked the hall to be sure Fenris had really gone. "He will be a duke one day. His title is an old one."

"Oh that. Yes, I suppose so. But he is my cousin, Mountjoy. I've never had a cousin before." She twined her fingers on her lap. "And he wishes to know me. After all this time, he wants a connection between us."

It killed him, but he said, "Commendable of him."

She fixed wide eyes on him. "My father would never forgive me."

"Does it matter if you add one more item to his list of your unforgiven sins?"

"Oh, Mountjoy, you do make me laugh." She smiled. "When you put it like that, perhaps it doesn't."

"Don't let your father ruin this for you, Wellstone. You mustn't."

"But what of your sister?" Her amusement slowly faded. "Ginny will never forgive me."

"She will," he said.

"I wouldn't. I wouldn't forgive a thing like that. My dearest friend marrying the man who tried to prevent my marriage?"

He took a breath. "Eugenia will understand."

"If she doesn't? I couldn't bear to lose her friendship. I couldn't."

Her despair broke his heart. "Come." He held out his hand. "We'll walk in the garden and talk. Or say nothing, if you prefer. Or speak of everything that is inconsequential."

She walked to him and put her hand in his. She squeezed his hand. "Thank you, Mountjoy."

Not ten minutes later, they were walking side by side in the rear garden. She'd fetched a cloak and had that around her shoulders. In silent accord, they headed past the formal grounds. He held the gate for her, and they walked a path that led to the lake, the bottom of which he now knew contained a good number of Roman coins. There was a bridge at the narrowest part of the water, and they followed the gravel path that wended that direction.

"I don't know what to do, Mountjoy," she said when they'd exhausted subjects such as the weather and whether they preferred lemon tarts to sweet puddings. "I've half a mind to sneak home in the dark of night."

"Impossible. You are engaged to be here another eight days."

"Stop making me laugh when I feel so miserable."

He tucked her arm under his. "Listen to me, Wellstone, because I ask this in all seriousness. Is marrying Fenris the condition of this connection he is so suddenly pursuing?"

They walked several feet before she answered. "No. I don't think so." She looked away. "I don't know. He might have meant that." She stopped walking. "I am aware that I am in possession of some very valuable properties and a fortune the present Duke of Camber believes should have gone to anyone but me. So don't imagine I do not understand my cousin's financial incentives. He wouldn't be the first to have them."

"Believe me, I do not dismiss your understanding of anything."

She shot him a look. "It was not my impression that Fenris agrees with his father about me. At least not now."

"He's a bloody good little son, to come haring halfway across the country to propose to the woman his aunt made her sole heir."

They walked a few yards before she replied. "I wonder what he would have done if I had turned out to be an aged and wrinkled old hag?"

He drew her closer. "How large did you say your fortune is?"

"About eighty thousand. More now. Rents are up and my investments have done quite well."

"Then he'd have gone down on his knee to you whether you proved a hag or a shrew. Or both."

"There's an excellent basis for marriage." She released his arm to straighten her cloak. "Mutual ignorance of each other's character."

"Marriages have been contracted on far less than that."

"They have been."

"I thought you had determined you would never marry."

They strolled a ways before she answered. "Not for love."

Mountjoy stopped walking. "For what reason would you marry?"

Her fingers tightened on his arm. "I don't know. When he can't possibly expect me to love him. When it makes such sense."

"You think it makes sense to marry Lord Fenris?"

"Objectively, it does."

He crossed his arms over his chest. "Suppose," he said, "that I told you I could never love you and that I understood you would never do something so inconvenient as to love me in return. In such a case, would you agree to marry me?"

Her gaze burned into his. "Are you asking me under those conditions?"

"That is not the point. Our discussion is a purely academic one."

"To answer your question, no. I would not."

"Why not? If your only criterion is that there be no love between you and your husband, it seems to me that any unmarried man will do. Therefore, why not me instead of Fenris?"

"You're twisting my words."

"No, Wellstone. I am attempting to unravel that nonsense."

"All right then. For reasons of dynasty. I'd marry him for that."

"I am in need of an heir. For reasons of dynasty." He took her arm again and continued down the path. He scowled the entire time they walked. "Why would you marry Fenris but not me?"

"Because."

"Because?"

"Because marrying you would be a betrayal of Greer."

"Why?" he said softly.

"Because you're going to marry Jane."

"Jane has nothing to do with Greer. But suppose that was not the case, that I was free to marry anyone I wished."

She pressed her lips together before she answered him. "No, I would not marry you."

"Why not?"

She glared at him. "Because you are my friend."

"Your friend."

"Yes."

"As your friend, I say you ought not marry a man whose character you do not know. You needn't tell Fenris yes or no tomorrow merely because you said you would. If you need more time to decide, for God's sake take it." He took her arm again when they reached a rough portion of the path.

"But I promised, Mountjoy."

"You told him he would have a reply."

"Exactly."

"Tomorrow reply to him that if he wishes to win your hand, you must at least know him well enough to give your approval of his character. If he's serious, he'll wait for you to make your decision."

"Shall I languish in the tower of yon castle, while I ponder on the subject?" She pressed the back of her hand to her forehead. "I cannot marry any man but one who proves himself worthy. By slaying a dragon. Or fetching me a golden fleece."

Mountjoy chuckled. "I don't advise that you languish, though you may if you like. If you mean *that* tower"—he tipped his head in the direction of Bitterward—"I'd find a way to keep you occupied while your cousin performs his mighty works."

She gave a sigh and leaned her head against his shoulder while they walked. "If he turns his back on me when I tell him I cannot answer him? What then?"

He stopped walking and faced her, hands on her shoulders. "Wellstone. You are an extraordinary woman. A woman worth knowing." He wanted to be selfish and tell her to stay the hell away from Fenris, but he couldn't. It wouldn't be right. "Fenris is a damned fool if he didn't know that from the moment he laid eyes on you. Don't let anyone, especially him, make you think that's not so. If you marry anyone, at least make sure the man deserves you."

Her mouth quirked. "No one deserves me."

He chose to ignore the double meaning. "God knows Fenris doesn't. He's done nothing to deserve your love." His fingers tightened on her. "Don't settle for marriage without at least respect between you. You can't live like that. Not you, Lily. I know you loved Greer, and I believe you'll never love another man the way you loved him. But does it follow that you can never love? Does a parent love only one child? A child only one parent? May we love only one friend? You, Lily, you of all people must have love in her life. Genuine love from a man who understands the wonderful eccentricities of your mind. Accept nothing less. If Fenris proves himself that man, then marry him but not until then. That's my advice to you."

"Ginny's right about you." She touched his cheek. "You give excellent advice."

"Will you take it?"

"I should think you'd be cackling in glee at the thought of him ending up married to me."

He took a step back. "Do you find me as petty as that? I wouldn't wish that on you. I want your happiness."

"No, Mountjoy. No I don't think that of you."

"If you're going to do something as harebrained as marry in cold blood, then marry a man who understands your worth."

She pushed away from him and spread her arms wide. "Imagine the clothes I could have if I were a nobleman's wife."

"You have those clothes now."

"Yes." Her eyes sparkled. "But I wouldn't be spending my money on them. There are economies I would not feel compelled to make. I could have a dress entirely of silver cloth without feeling a moment's guilt. I should look perfectly stunning in a gown of silver cloth."

He grinned because he couldn't help it. "You wouldn't feel guilty if you had one now."

"True." They remained standing quite close. "But I feel I ought to. If I were Lady Fenris, I would feel it my duty to wear only the most fashionable and tasteful gowns and slippers. And jewels. I don't see how I could get by without quite a lot of jewels. Ruinously expensive jewels." She touched her head. "I've always wanted a tiara."

"Is that your sole criteria for marriage? Clothes and jewels? Then by all means tell him yes. When you've confirmed he's the money to keep you in the style to which you wish to be accustomed."

"If I did say yes, would I have your blessing?"

"No." The word burst from him, hard as a diamond.

She stepped back, but he followed. "Why not?"

"Because you would not be happy."

"A casket or two of fabulous jewels would make me quite happy."

"Buy your own jewels." He clenched his hands. "You have the money."

"They're so much prettier when someone else buys them." She drew her cloak around her and headed for the bridge. He followed. Of course he followed. When he caught up, she said, "I don't get many gifts, you know. And that's an argument in favor of marriage I hadn't considered. My husband would be obliged to buy me a gift from time to time. Don't you think?" She touched the medallion around her neck. "Do you know, Mountjoy, that this is the first gift I've had these dozen or more years at least?"

"A dozen years?"

"That was when my father stopped speaking to me."

"What?"

"Well, he did now and then, that couldn't be helped. It would have been awkward to refuse to speak to one's daughter in front of the vicar or one's neighbor. But I recall he once went five months without saying a word to me. Thank goodness for our housekeeper or I might have been as silent as him." She waved a hand, as if to say it no longer mattered. They were at the bridge and neither of them spoke until they reached the other side. He didn't know what to say to her. What could he say to her that would not reveal his outrage on her behalf? Her bedamned father had much to answer for.

Back on the path, she faced him while he stood at the end of the stone bridge. "It has occurred to me, Mountjoy, that perhaps the medallion is working as the Gypsy king said it would."

"It is?"

"Consider the matter." She crossed her arms beneath her bosom. "Fenris showed up here, didn't he? Completely unexpected. And he has proposed to me knowing his father will never approve. Why, it must be the medallion. No other explanation makes sense."

"You can't be serious."

She tilted her chin. "Why can't I be?"

"Because it's absurd to think magic has anything to do with Fenris pursuing you."

"Perhaps we're fated lovers, Fenris and I. Why else would he come all this way to make an offer of marriage to a woman he does not know and of whom his father disapproves?"

He'd never felt as powerless as he did right now. The world was slipping away from him and he did not know how to stop it.

"A dozen reasons."

"Name three."

"The estate is bankrupt."

"It isn't."

"You asked for three likely reasons. I'm suggesting the obvious ones. You're rich. He needs money. He means to anger his father; he sincerely wishes to mend the break between your family and his. He finds you beautiful."

"That's five."

"I can give you five more if you like."

"That would only be ten, not a dozen."

"My point, my dear Wellstone, is that any of those are more likely than a bit of metal having the power to draw your lover to you."

"You, sir, do not possess a poet's soul."

"A poet's soul?" He swept his arms wide, to indicate that

she should examine his attire. "You've been here all this time, Lily. Why the devil would you think I have anything like a soul, poetic or otherwise?"

"If I have to explain it to you there's no hope for either of us." She turned around and walked away.

"That's absurd," he called to her back. Were they having their first argument? He watched the sway of her backside and then followed. "Wellstone."

"Stop calling me that." She kept walking.

He caught up and put a hand on her shoulder. Lily turned. "What?" she said.

"This."

He kissed her. He kissed her with all his heart and soul.

# Chapter Thirty

WHEN THEIR MOUTHS PARTED, LILY STUDIED HIM IN a way that made the world smaller than it was. He hadn't meant to kiss her, not like that, but he had and he wasn't sorry.

His belly tightened. "Lily," he said softly. "Whatever are you thinking?"

"I could not possibly tell you," she said, without a trace of a blush.

"Would you if you had sufficient inducement?"

"Doubtful."

Mountjoy tightened his arms around her, and she did not push away from the closer embrace. "Perhaps if I guessed?"

Her smile turned liquid. "How amusing that might be if you did. Do try."

"You are a beautiful woman," he said. "You know that's so."

She shook her head. "Not what I was thinking. But thank you."

He was off-kilter where she was concerned. He'd only met her a short time ago, and they had embarked on an affair with the understanding that their relations would end when she departed Bitterward. No emotions were to be involved. Part of him knew that this was different, that his feelings for Lily were considerably more complicated than lust. But that did not warrant declarations from him. Hell, he wasn't certain what he would declare to her and was even less sure she would welcome a declaration of any sort from him.

Tomorrow, she might agree to marry someone else.

"I would risk a great deal for you. You know that." He didn't know where those words came from, but he'd said them and neither could nor would take them back. The words were true, and yet he felt he was deceiving himself, that there was more to this for him.

She gave him a pert smile. "Also not what I was thinking."

He ran a finger underneath her lower lip and tried again. And failed, he knew as the words came out. "We're lovers, you and I. Lovers such as more poetic souls than I can express."

Her smile faded, and now she looked as uncertain as he felt. "Are we?"

"We can at least admit that to each other."

"I admit absolutely nothing."

"Why should we give that up when it suits us so well?" Again, true words, and yet they also deceived. He was at a private impasse, unable to find words that would convey his true sentiments. How could he when he wasn't sure himself what he felt? "What reason is there for you to marry your prig of a cousin without love and at the risk of your independence?"

She lifted her chin, and he repeated the touch of his finger along her mouth. "We'd grow to love one another. That's a reason."

"No. It's not, and well you know it." Lord, she was quick to see beneath his words. Quicker than anyone he knew. "He was a soldier, your Greer was, going off to war. And you loved him." He touched her cheek, a caress, a plea for her to stay close. "I know you loved him; Lily, my love, I wish you had not lost him. But there's me now, to touch you like this and show you that you are adored and desired, and to wish for so much more between us." He stared into her eyes, thinking he might never sound the depths there. He slid his finger along the line of her cheek. "Will Fenris understand that about you?"

She did not move her head, but placed her palm lightly over his hand. "I knew," she whispered. "I knew Greer would not return. But I would not change a thing."

"Passion, once awakened, is not forgotten. Nor love. We never forget that we have loved."

"No."

"Lily," he said. He cajoled. He entreated. "Lily, come to bed with me again. And again. Whenever we so desire it. Don't leave here until you are well and tired of me."

She shook her head, but she was not telling him no. "You should not have kissed me like that." She bit her lower lip. "That wasn't fair of you at all."

"I will take you under my protection." The words came in a rush of desperation. "I am generous, you know I would be. If it's jewels you want, you may have them. All the gowns you could possibly wear. Ten of silver lace and another ten in gold. I promise you discretion. I promise you your privacy. In bed, you shall have all the passion you desire. No entanglements, no need to give up your independence." He touched his forehead to hers. "Hell, take me under your protection, if you like."

She kissed his chin. "And what gifts should I shower upon you in that case?"

"All the waistcoats, coats, and pantaloons you'd like." He kept his head near hers. His desperation stayed, took up residence in his chest. In his heart. "A set of enameled dueling pistols, if you're set on indulging my whims. A horse to ride when I am in Town. A carriage. Well sprung."

She laughed.

Mountjoy continued caressing her. "Are you insulted I've asked?"

"I ought to be, but I'm not." She frowned, but stayed in

his arms. "I suppose that is due to my nature. You're right. I don't wish to give up my independence, and Fenris would expect that of me."

"You have the means to assure your future whoever you take as a lover. For as long as you like."

"I can't leave my father on his own."

"I'll come to Exeter."

She lifted her eyes, very quickly, to his. "Would you?"

"I've just told you so. I can manage my properties from there."

"And if there are consequences, Mountjoy? If we remain lovers, what if there are consequences?"

A gentleman took care of his bastards, that went without saying, but Lily wasn't one of the demimonde, nor a woman used to such arrangements. "We'll do what we can to prevent that, of course, but if that should come to pass, I won't abandon you." His heart raced in his chest, his pulse drummed in his ears. He wanted Lily with him on whatever terms she would accept. "It happens sometimes, you must know that. Even when a man is careful. Even when the woman is careful."

She chewed on her lower lip.

"I'll find a home near Syton House and buy you a town house in London. You can come to Town when the Sessions are on. Or we'll chose someplace halfway between Syton House and Bitterward and see each other there. Say yes, Lily. Say yes."

"You've given me a great deal to think about."

"So long as your answer is not no out of hand."

"It's not." She put her hand on his arm and they returned to the house. They didn't speak again until they were in the corridor that led to her room. She faced him and said, "May I ask you a question?"

"You know you may."

She frowned. "I know why Ginny dislikes Fenris, but why do you?"

"When I was new to the title, hardly a man and rough

about the edges, he was of the opinion, freely shared, that I still stank of dirt and manure. I confess that did not endear him to me."

"I don't imagine it would."

"I was offended, as anyone might be when they discover they are disliked for themselves."

She patted his hand. "I'm sure he'd say different now."

"If I were wearing my new clothes, yes."

"So you admit I was right."

He laughed softly. "Blast you, yes."

"New clothes or not, you are completely splendid, Mountjoy." She stroked his waistcoat, one of his old ones.

He leaned closer. "Don't refuse him because I don't care for him." He hated himself for playing devil's advocate with her. "He will provide you much that you deserve." But not love. Not the adoration she deserved. "He may be a prig, but he's an honorable prig. He would take care of you." He couldn't stop himself from brushing his fingertips along the side of her face, and then along her lips.

"Now there's a recommendation. An honorable prig."

"Wellstone." Mountjoy put his hand under her chin and tipped her face toward his. She closed her eyes, and he leaned in and kissed her eyelids, one then the other, and he didn't give a fig about the possibility that a servant might come upon them. Or even Eugenia. He drew back, and she opened her eyes, and he kissed her lips this time and hers were soft beneath his. Familiar now and every bit as devastating as the first time he'd kissed her.

No chaste or tentative kiss between them. Not from the very first.

He didn't have enough sense to stop, or pull back, or keep his damned tongue out of her mouth. Or his hands from wandering. Nor his brain from shutting down any and all objections his good sense might assert.

She closed the distance between them and slid her arms around his shoulders. She kissed him back. It was a lover's kiss, he did not delude himself about that. The kiss was carnal. Wicked. A prelude to sex. She kissed with the unreserved passion she had for everything she did. Her kiss was full of life and spirit, and he didn't want to give that up.

Her lips softened under his, accepted his ardor and returned it. He'd been waiting for this for too long. Her arms slid around his shoulders and drew him down to her, accepting his greedy need. One of her hands snaked through his hair and covered the back of his head. His body went taut with anticipation, ripe with lust.

He pulled back. "I want to make love to you in a bed, where there's room for us both and more."

"My room?"

He stood. "No. Mine."

"No, Mountjoy. We're safer in the tower room. That's ours together."

He took her hand in his and wondered why her answer pained him so.

## Chapter Thirty-one

"THE BUTLER TOLD ME I MIGHT FIND YOU HERE."

Lily looked up from the garden bench and rested the letter she was rereading on her lap. "Good afternoon, Lord Fenris."

Mountjoy was right. He was a relation of her mother's, and he had reached out to her. He was family. And she owed it to them both to see what sort of ties they might form. One did not choose one's family, after all.

He stopped in front of her, hands clasped behind his back. His coat was a deep claret with a wider lapel than was usual and silver buttons embossed with the coat of arms of her mother's family. He carried off the boldness quite smartly. "Am I disturbing your letter reading?"

"I'm rereading it. Do sit." She made room on the bench. If she'd had a brother, he might have been a great deal like Fenris. "It's from a dear friend from the days when I still lived in my father's home. She's married now, the mother of two beloved children and soon a third to kiss and hug and lavish with affection."

The corner of Fenris's mouth slid up. "You sound as if you long for children of your own."

"Long for them?" She straightened on the bench. Where on earth did the man get an idea like that? "No, I don't think I long for them."

"Don't all women?"

"I've no notion what other women do. I'm not always certain what I want. Do all men long for the same thing?"

"No," he said. "But it's natural for men and women both to long for children. Don't you agree?"

She liked the easy way he asked the question. "We don't all have the life we would wish. Not everyone marries, my lord, just as not every married couple has children."

"Some things are in God's hands, Miss Wellstone."

"Do you long for children?" She wondered how they'd ended up on the subject of children. Well, she'd asked him, hadn't she?

"I do."

"Out of duty?"

He nodded solemnly. "Yes, but for more than that. I want children because I think I would love them very much. A son like me. A daughter with my eyes." He gave her a considering look. "But not you," he said, slowly.

"You must think me unnatural."

"No," he said. "I think you stopped thinking of children whenever it was you decided marriage was not in your future."

"Am I so obvious?"

He took her hand in his, and she allowed him to hold it. "What if you were to marry? Is it not possible that you would then change your mind about children?"

"Did you come here to turn me inside out?"

"I make you no reply to that," he said, and with a smile that made her notice how handsome a man he was.

She looked away and stared at the horizon. Her heart deeply misgave her. "When I was a girl I used to imagine the children I would have. I thought there was no question

I would one day have them. But then, I dreamed as well of exploring the world and discovering a comet." She returned her attention to him. She would have wanted Greer's children. If he had not died, she would have married him. "But that is not what befell me. I haven't explored the world or found a comet in the sky."

"You might yet have your friend's life. A husband and beloved children." He turned on the bench to face her. How cold of him, she thought, to offer marriage to a woman he did not know. To decide that a stranger ought to bear his children. "A proper home, with a husband to manage what is not your domain."

"I've become settled in my ways."

He nodded. "As I am settled in mine. I admit that to you. Can we not embark on the adventure of a new life together?" He gave her a quick grin. "I will buy you a telescope so you may search the heavens every night."

"Lest you think my friend nothing but what a woman ought to be, she is also a poetess of no small talent."

"Is she?" His eyebrows rose. "Many times blessed, then."

"Yes."

He said, "Even a mother's life can be more than the demands of home and hearth."

"Her powers of observation are acute, sir, and I do enjoy reading and rereading the verses she copies into her correspondence to me. Little rhymes, she calls them, but they are far more than that. One day I intend to publish them for her."

"A lady publisher for a lady's verses." He crossed one leg over the other. "You might sell a copy or two, I suppose."

She folded the letter and slipped it into her pocket. "I daresay you are not here to listen to me rattle on about friends you've never met and publishing ventures of which you disapprove and children I shall never have."

"I don't disapprove, Lily. May I call you that?" She nodded, and he turned a little on the bench. "It's unusual, I grant you that, but from the moment I saw you, I could see you are not the usual sort of woman." He lifted her hand between them.

She met his gaze over her hand. His eyes were a lighter brown than hers. "I cannot change my essential nature, sir. More to the point, I will not."

Fenris nodded in answer. "Nor I. I would be a poor man if I expected you to transform yourself into another creature entirely, just to please me."

She pulled her hand free of his and clasped her hands on her lap. In her head she heard the laughter of children. A family. A husband. Children she would love and cherish. "Don't think I'm not flattered. I am, sir. But I don't wish for such an alteration in my circumstances. I have arranged my life exactly to my tastes. I would miss all the things to which I've become accustomed."

"Such as?"

"I go where I like, when I like. If I wish to travel, I can. I came here, for example." Her stomach contracted to the size of a pinhead.

"Do you travel often?" He smiled, and she had the unsettling idea that he knew she rarely left home.

"That is beside the point. The point, sir, is that if I wished to leave England and visit China, I could."

"Without a husband?"

He was right about that. A visit to China on her own would be fraught with difficulties. "I don't want to visit China. That was merely an example. Be that as it may, I could certainly visit Bath or York or even Edinburgh if the fancy took me. I could sail to America if I wished and I could do so without consulting anyone or asking anyone but my banker for the funds to do so."

"If you had a husband, you could visit China." He rocked back on his heels. "With very little notice. You might even find that all the details had been taken care of for you and that more of the mystery of that country would be open to you simply because you have a husband with connections."

She looked him in the eye. "Well, I haven't got a husband."

"Miss Wellstone. Lily. You know why I am here."

For a bit, they said nothing.

"What are we to do, my lord?"

He leaned against the bench and extended his far arm along the top, away from her. "Marry. We ought to marry."

"Without any hope of love?"

He glanced at her and there was a world there that he was not admitting to her or, she thought, to himself. Lord Fenris, she realized, was in love with someone else. He had, for whatever reason, given up hope of winning the woman's heart or he would not be here with his offer.

"Does your father know what you're about? Asking me to marry you?"

"No."

She frowned. "You intend to bring home a bride you know he dislikes and a wife you do not love."

He turned more on the bench, until he was nearly facing her. "No, Cousin Lily. I will bring home a bride who is beautiful, charming, and unique. A bride who is an heiress and whose antecedents are, in fact, as impeccable as my own."

"And whose fortune once belonged to your family."

"It's your family, too." He took her hand in his again but this time he lifted it to his lips. His eyes locked with hers over the top of her hand. "Come now. It's a sensible solution. Marry me, Miss Wellstone, and you will make me a very happy man."

Her life stuttered.

"Everything come right at last. Our family whole at last."

"My lord." She jumped to her feet, dislodging her hand from Fenris's. He, too, stood, though more slowly. "You do not know me."

His expression darkened and again, she had the sense there was a great deal he wasn't telling her. "And you do not know me. That will change."

"What if I told you I'd had a lover?"

He clasped his hands behind his back and frowned. Not at her but at some internal thought of his. Then his attention fixed on her. "Have you?"

"All men want a virgin on their wedding nights. Well, you would not have one in me, sir. If you married me, you would not have the sort of wife you imagine." There. That flash of disapproval on his face reminded her of why Ginny disliked him, though in this case, could she blame him? The women men like him married were supposed to be pure, and she was not.

"Thank you for your honesty." He tipped his head to one side. "Are you with child?" he asked softly.

She let out a sharp breath. "No."

Fenris said nothing.

She stood her ground. She had long experience with men who disapproved of her. "I'm sorry you came all this way only to learn how horribly unsuitable I am."

"My offer stands. In any event, you and I needn't hurry to the altar. We can wait several months. A year."

She shook her head. He meant, of course, that he would marry her after the birth of any child she might have conceived. "Chivalry ill becomes you. It will only turn to resentment."

"And yet, my mind is unchanged."

"Why?"

"Lily." He took her hand again but just held it. "I don't mean to force you to accept me." He frowned. "But we will suit. You'll see."

She cocked her head, and everything Mountjoy had told her rushed into her head until she was dizzy with it. "My lord, if I were to marry, it would be to a man who makes my heart race. I want my stomach to drop to my toes, my limbs to quiver with passion."

Fenris studied her in his quiet way. "Are you convinced we would not have that?"

"I haven't the faintest notion." Her words came out too quickly, her breath too short.

"Sometimes affection between a man and a woman grows slowly, upon deeper acquaintance." He flushed, and that made her wonder if he was thinking about the woman he loved. The one who'd broken his heart. "Love is not always a fire that roars through you. It can be a flame that is small yet steadfast over the years."

"I want my husband to love me and admire me and believe he cannot live without me." She took a step away and threw her arms wide. "I wish myself to be madly in love in return, Fenris. Can you promise me mad love? Can you imagine yourself so desperately in love with anyone that you would rather lose your soul than lose her?"

He stood straighter, but she recognized the bleakness in his eyes. "Yes."

"Not with me," she said. "Can you really imagine yourself in love with me? Be truthful or there's no hope for us. None at all."

He eyed her. "I imagine there are very few men who cannot envision themselves madly in love with you."

"Can you? Could you?"

"I am not a man of public passions." He held her gaze and then smiled. "That does not therefore mean I have no passions, I assure you of that. Marry me," he said in a low voice, "and that will change. I promise you. My family will be doubly your relations. They will recognize you and accept you."

"Marry you and I'll have everything I've ever wished for?" She frowned. "Is that a threat, my lord?" She lowered her voice to a basso note. "Marry me or you will never meet your uncle the duke."

He had the audacity to laugh at her. "I wouldn't call that a threat. Quite the opposite."

"What would you call it?"

"Persuasion."

She stopped smiling. "Tell me true, if I say no, will I lose any hope of reconciliation? If I'm not your wife, is there any circumstance under which Camber will accept me?"

"No matter what my father says or does, you are my cousin. And Camber's niece. I won't turn my back on you merely because you refuse my offer of marriage. I am a man of quieter passions than you," he went on, "but not shallower ones." And then he gave her a penetrating look. "One hears that Mountjoy will soon be married to one Jane Kirk."

"What does Mountjoy have to do with this?"

"Everything."

"Why?"

"Because you are in love with him."

# Chapter Thirty-two

In Mountjoy's room, Lily pressed her back against the wall beside the door, not wanting to look away from him. Not yet. Her heart beat faster when he closed and locked the door. His room. She drank in everything about his private quarters. Every detail revealed him to her and made her heart ache. He'd brought her here where, without meaning to, he would break her heart. She knew it. He hadn't asked her about Fenris. If he did, what would she say? What could she possibly tell him that would not ruin everything else?

The curtains were open, but the sun was at the other side of the house and his rooms were cool and shadowed. The decor was reassuringly spare, as suited the man, but not austere. She stopped examining their surroundings and watched Mountjoy. He stood by the door, a hand on the latch. Silent.

Here she was. Alone in a room with a man to whom she was not married. With a man who had just admitted for them both that they were lovers now and who had asked her to be his mistress. He'd not used the word, but he'd meant that.

Still with his hand on the door, Mountjoy cocked his head and gazed at her, the faintest of smiles curving his mouth.

She said, "I'm nervous to be here with you. I don't know why. I oughtn't be."

"Tell me what I can do to make you feel better." He stayed where he was, just at the door, but with his body angled toward her. Shadows darkened the edges of his face.

"Kiss me?" She meant it in jest, but it wasn't. Not really. She wanted the comfort and steadiness of his arms around her.

He leaned over to kiss her lightly on the mouth. She raised her chin, and his mouth lingered on hers. Her stomach flew away. Mountjoy continued kissing her, softly, tenderly, but not at all politely. How strange it was to pretend during the day that she never once thought about throwing herself into his arms. The truth was she did. She was happy around him. Giddy.

Hunger rose up in her as they continued to kiss, and she found herself leaning into him. She coiled an arm around his neck.

After a bit, he drew back, one hand lifted to brush her cheek. His head stayed by hers. "A moment."

He pushed away from the door and lit a lamp which he set on a table on the other side of the door from where she stood. Across the room he locked an interior door. So that his valet or some other servant, she supposed, would not accidentally come upon them. He left the other interior door open. She presumed that one led to his bedchamber.

The lamp made it possible for her to see there were the usual things one found in a room meant for a gentleman's privacy and relaxation. In the middle was a gleaming cherry-wood table and chairs, against another wall, a cherry writing desk with gold fittings. Books, a newspaper, and several volumes of a gentleman's magazine were on the desk. One of the torques from the treasure hoard sat atop the desk. A claw-footed sofa faced the fireplace. On one wall was a landscape from somewhere in Yorkshire.

The room and its decor suited him. It was easy to imagine him sitting in here, tending to his private affairs. Writing letters. Reading. Having a drink before he retired for the night. She committed the sight to memory so that she would have the image with her always.

She left the door to sit sideways on the nearest of the mahogany chairs, one hand gripping the top rail. This was Mountjoy's private domain. His room. He lit the tapers in a branched candelabra and the room grew brighter. He seemed so matter-of-fact, going about mundane tasks while she could scarcely breathe. Next, with a glance at her, he walked to a side table. "I know it's afternoon, but would you care for a cognac?"

"I've never had cognac."

"It's time you tried, then." He picked up a decanter and removed the top. With his free hand, he turned over two tumblers and poured cognac into both glasses. He walked to her, holding out one of the glasses. The other he left on the table. "A sample, to see if it's to your taste."

She accepted the glass and took a sip. It burned going down, but mellowed quickly enough that she was able to suppress a cough. Warmth spread through her chest. She looked up at him, still gripping the top of her chair. "My."

Neither of them said anything for a while. She didn't know what to say and knew even less what might be going through his mind just now. Had she really agreed to continue seeing him? Being here with him was a deliberate enough choice that she was forced to admit that yes, they were lovers. If he came to Exeter, she would gladly continue as his lover.

He broke the silence. "Are you having second thoughts, Wellstone?"

She shook her head because words of denial stuck in her throat. They had done this before, been alone together in a room locked against intrusion. They had been to bed before. Conducted their illicit affair out of sight of family and staff. But the intimacy of being here was too real.

"If you'd rather not, I understand."

She clutched her glass. She did not want him to send her away, and yet, if he did, she would spare herself the tension squeezing her heart. "How sanguine, Mountjoy," she said. "Are you so indifferent to my presence?"

He smiled. "I would be disappointed if you left, don't misunderstand. At the same time, if you are not certain you want this, then don't feel you must be here or that you must stay simply because earlier you agreed." He gave a quick look at the ceiling. "Damn me for saying such a thing. I'm not usually so noble."

"Yes you are. You are the noblest man I know."

His eyes landed on her again. "I want you to stay. Please. Stay. Make me forget again that the world consists of anything but you and me."

"It seems different now." A part of her mind shouted that she should leave immediately, that if she did this with him here, her life would change irrevocably. Her heart would never be the same. "Why is that?"

"Have you changed your mind?"

She held his gaze. Somehow, Mountjoy had become her friend, and she did not want to give him up. "No. Have you?"

He held out his hand and waited for her to take it. "Not in the least."

She put her hand on his palm, and he tugged the merest bit until she must either resist or stand. She stood.

He took the cognac from her and placed the tumbler on the table. His fingers tightened around hers, and he pulled her close to him. Closer than was proper, but then when they were behind locked doors they were never very proper, were they?

He dipped his head to hers, not to her mouth, but to the side of her throat. "I am unbearably aroused by you. And I ask you, why is that?" His breath warmed her skin. He trailed his fingers up her arm to her shoulder. His lips touched her skin just above her collarbone, and his mouth parted. She shivered at the touch of his tongue, the kisses he dropped. "I want to see you reclining on my bed," he said. "With your hair down and your legs spread, looking at me with that imperious gaze of yours."

"Imperious? I'm sure I don't know what you mean."

"I adore that about you. The way your eyes snap with intelligence."

"I should think you ought to at least be overcome by the perfection of my figure."

He laughed. "I am. I am and hope to be so very soon."

She leaned toward him, and his arms tightened around her. "I should like to see you unclothed as well, Mountjoy."

He lifted his head. His arms remained around her. "Ah yes, you and your fondness for splendid animals in their natural state."

"Extremely splendid, Mountjoy." She kissed his lower lip. "And very, very natural."

"Your every wish is my desire. After all, you've done the same for me, haven't you?" He took a step back and shrugged off his coat. He dropped the garment on a chair, all the while looking at her. He unfastened his watch chain and tucked the watch into a pocket of his waistcoat before he undid the buttons.

"Do you require assistance?"

He kept unbuttoning his waistcoat. "Kind of you to ask, but no. But make a note, Wellstone, that you'll need to order me new riding clothes. These won't do for me at all. Not anymore." He tipped his chin in the direction of the chair she'd been sitting on. "You may sit down again, if you like."

"I'll just stay here." She leaned against the table.

He dropped his waistcoat on the chair with his coat. "Mind your cognac."

She moved the tumbler to the middle of the table.

Mountjoy undid his cravat next, exposing the placket of his shirt. He sat down to remove his riding boots. And then his buckskins. The rest of his clothes followed. He didn't hurry, but he was naked soon enough.

Lily gazed at him in silence.

He waited, arms at his sides, his weight on one leg. She

made a motion with one finger and, with a grin, he obliged her by turning in a circle. Muscle shaped his long legs, his torso, too, front and back. He had, as she knew, little hair on his body. His body, so magnificent, demonstrated the effects of the hours he spent in the saddle or working with his tenants and neighbors. He walked to her and, taking her cognac from the table behind her, drained the tumbler. Her heart sped up.

He set down the glass and took a step back. "What will you do with me, Wellstone, now that I'm at your mercy?"

"I'll worship your body."

He grinned. "Is that all?"

"Isn't that enough?"

"No."

"Greedy man."

"Lovely, devilish, clever Lily." He clasped his hands behind his head and stretched. His member was not yet erect. "Should I confess that I dream about you every night? About you being here with me. In this very room. It's unwise, I think, but now I've gone and said it."

"Do you?" She reached for her medallion, out of habit fingering the cool surface. "Tell me what happens in your dreams." She went to him and rested one hand on his shoulder and curled the other around his nape. His body warmed hers. This was what she wanted, to have someone close, to be connected with another person in the way only lovers could be. "Is it my laughing eyes and dulcet tones you dream of? Or is it my intelligence?"

"In my dreams, I call you Wellstone."

"Mine, too. What else?"

"Your soft and naked skin." He put a hand on her waist. "Your mouth doing unspeakable things to me."

"Unspeakable?" She leaned against him and slid her hands up and down his back, over the curves and valleys of his muscles. "Mountjoy, my heart races trying to imagine what you mean. Do tell me. Or, since you cannot speak of it, show me."

"We have all day," he said. "What's left of it. I've locked the door. There'll be no servants interrupting. My bed is just there." He tipped his head in the direction of the open door. "Waiting for my most wicked dreams to become reality."

"Wicked of you, I agree, but hardly unspeakable."

He took a step closer. "I'd like for you to fetch me with your mouth."

She twined her fingers through his hair. "I'd like that, too. You know I would."

"Here?" he said. "On your knees?"

She trailed her fingers down his chest. "That is very wicked, your grace." She pressed her palm to his hip, and Mountjoy cupped the back of her head, fingers tense. She wanted to caress his cock, his beautiful manhood, and so she did. He was warm, and firm, erect now, to be sure, and his skin was soft. Without saying a word, he wrapped his hand around hers.

"On your knees," he said in a low voice. Not quite a question. Yet, not a command, either.

She knew his body by now, enough to know she adored the shape and taste and scent of him. The thought of bringing him to completion in that way aroused her. She longed for the pleasure it brought him. With a glance at him, she adjusted her gown and sank to her knees, sliding one of her hands from the middle of his chest to his groin as she did. "Like so?"

"Yes," Mountjoy said. With the lamp and the candles burning she could see the green of his eyes. His body was lean and well muscled, and she could spend hours worshiping his form with her hands, her eyes, and even her mouth.

She kissed the top of his penis, and that part of him flinched. He set his fingers lightly on her head, and a thrill shot through her at the contact. She wrapped her hand around his shaft.

"You needn't be gentle," he whispered. "You know what I like. Yes," he said again when she took him in her mouth. With word and deed, Mountjoy showed her what he wanted from her, and she loved his reaction to her, the tension in him, his groan when she used her hands, her mouth, and her tongue. Before long, his body tensed, and his directions to her turned insistent. His moan deepened her arousal.

His fingers tightened around her head again, and he pressed forward. "Like that. Christ . . . Like that."

She used her tongue on him, cupped his sac, and touched, so lightly, the base of him because she remembered once that he'd told her he liked that, and he shouted, and pushed into her mouth and came. His hands lost contact with her head, then returned. She kept her mouth on him until there was no question he was done. In such moment, he was hers.

Only then did she sit on her haunches, the back of her hand pressed to her lips.

His eyes held hers. "Are you disgusted with me?"

"No." She stood, with the aid of his hand. "Are you disgusted that I enjoyed that and would gladly do so again?"

"No. God, no. Never."

She put her hands on his chest. "Perhaps your bed would be more convenient?"

His eyelids lowered halfway so that she could barely see the green of his irises. "Yes, I think it would." He picked up the candelabra and walked to the door he hadn't locked. She followed, watching his naked backside.

He put the candles on a table opposite the bed and she looked around. His bed very much suited a duke. Four posters and a canopy of burgundy silk with yellow silk tassels holding back the hangings. The duvet was embroidered with his coat of arms, red and blue and with the swan picked out in silver thread. He pushed it away then stretched out on the mattress and extended a hand to her. "Come."

Lily kicked off her slippers before she joined him on the bed. She lay beside him, on one flank, and touched his chest. He raised a knee and tucked a hand underneath his head. "Do with me what you will," he said.

Lily stroked him, watched his face and body for reactions. His nipples were sensitive, she knew. To her fingers and her kisses.

"I think it's time you were naked, too," he said after not a very long time.

"That seems only fair."

He snaked an arm around her and brought her in for a kiss. "And convenient to our purpose."

She turned her back to him, and he unhooked her bodice. Between them, sometimes clumsily, they removed her garments. She left the bed, wearing little but her chemise and stockings, and carefully draped her clothes over a chair. She rejoined him and knelt on the mattress between his spread legs when the last of her clothes came off.

"You've converted me," he said. "From liking brunettes to worshiping blondes. Loosen your hair, Lily. So I can see it down around your shoulders."

She pulled the combs that held her hair back, and he took them from her to place on a table near the bed. She shook out her hair and arranged it so most of it fell over her shoulder.

Mountjoy held out his hands and she straddled him. "Lovely," he murmured. "So very lovely." He cupped her breasts and the flush of heat through her body astonished her.

He lay her back, and kissed his way from her shoulders to her toes and back up to her thighs. He buried his face there, kissing her and finding clever things to do with his tongue and fingers until she could hold back no longer. He stroked her body while she came, whispering her name, whispering, *Lily darling, I adore you.*

When she came back to herself, Mountjoy had himself recovered. He opened a drawer in the bedtable and took out one of his sheaths, made of the finest lambskin, he'd told her. He left the bed long enough to wet it with water from a basin as the fit was more comfortable for them both if the sheath was damp. She helped him put it on and even tied the ribbon around the base of his cock.

She lay back, and he came over her, and slid inside, and

though they'd not in the past been silent lovers, they were strangely silent now. Her heart had become too big for her chest. Mountjoy's expression was intense, and his strokes in her at first were slow and luxurious. Until he pushed harder once, then again, and she felt that stroke all the way to her heart.

He pushed up on his hands and worked her harder, and she met him stroke for stroke and still they did not speak. She couldn't. Though she'd already come, and not so long ago, pleasure rushed back, the quiver built and she hovered there at the edge, holding back because she did not want to come again so quickly when he'd hardly begun.

"Let go," he said. His words were gruff. "Give yourself to me entirely."

She raised her knees, and he thrust harder and she had to reach up toward the headboard to brace herself. "More," she said.

"I oblige you, madam."

Close, she was so close to a magnificent release, and she knew Mountjoy was close himself. She put a hand around his waist and then his hips, lifting to meet him. Once again, they had no words but the words of their bodies until he shifted the angle of his cock and she spiraled tight, so close, so close.

"Mountjoy." She arched beneath him and there were words building in her too big to hold in and far too big to speak. He held her around her waist and rocked hard into her. Her breath hitched, and she forgot anything but her need to climax, her frustration that she had not reached that point yet. He must have been close himself because his thrusts came faster and faster.

And then she crested, and lost herself completely and utterly to his body, and at the last, she felt something inside her that wasn't usual, but all that mattered was that he didn't stop, that he was coming, too, and he was calling her name and she held him tight.

"Oh, Jesus, Lily."

She opened her eyes. He wasn't looking at her fondly but with eyes wide open, staring. "What's wrong?"

He pushed back and slowly withdrew from her, looking at his member as if his cock had betrayed him, which it certainly had not, as far as she was concerned. He closed his eyes tight, then opened them again. "Lily."

She put her weight on one elbow. "What?"

He did something with his sex, and when she looked, she saw the ribbon of his condom was still tied around the base of him, but she could see only part of the sheath. The rest of his member was bare. "I'm sorry," he said. "The sheath broke."

Lily licked her lips and remembered that moment when something had not felt right. "Just now?"

"No." The rest of the sheath was in his hand. "I'm sorry. I didn't know. Didn't realize." He shut his eyes then opened them. "No, not just now. I came inside you, Lily."

# Chapter Thirty-three

❧

MOUNTJOY FOCUSED ON THE LETTER BEFORE HIM. HE blinked. Was this the one about the declining output of one of the Mountjoy coal mines? Or was that the one before, and this one reported a threefold increase in sales of Mountjoy wool? There were other letters, too, all of them running about in his head without his knowing anything but that he'd read the subject matter at some point. There was a need to better fund the parish orphanage. The sheriff was concerned that the local smugglers were bold and getting bolder, and someone else had requested that he bring a pressing matter to the attention of the House of Lords during the next parliamentary session.

His concentration was broken by a disturbance somewhere in the house. The commotion appeared to be coming nearer. Footsteps thudded down the corridor—more than one man—and he heard Doyle saying very sternly, "Sir, I assure you his grace is not at home."

"Get out of my way," a man shouted. "I'll have the bloody farmer's head, see if I don't."

"Sir," Doyle said, his voice nearer and nearer. "That is—"

"Mountjoy!" His name became a roar of agony.

He started for the door, but he didn't get far before the door slammed open and Mr. Kirk burst in, his coat still on, his hat missing, and a riding whip clutched in one hand. Doyle dashed in after the man, two footmen behind him.

"Your grace," Doyle said, wringing his hands. The two footmen stopped in the doorway when Mountjoy signaled them to leave.

Mr. Kirk's eyes were wide and staring, his cheeks flushed red, but every hair on his graying head was perfectly in place. He pointed at Mountjoy with a shaking arm. "You."

"Sir." He took a step toward the man. Lord, what could this be but that Mr. Kirk had found out about him and Lily?

"You—" Kirk said. That he'd been crying at some point was patently obvious.

"Doyle," said Mountjoy. "Please bring Mr. Kirk a brandy."

His butler bowed. "Your grace."

"I don't want a bloody brandy," the man said.

"That will be all, Doyle. Thank you. I'll call you if you're needed."

When they were alone, without servants in sight, Kirk took a step forward, whip hand raised. "I want what's right."

Mountjoy was thirty years younger and a good deal larger than Kirk. He had no difficulty taking the riding whip away. He kept a grip on the older man's wrist and leaned over him to speak deliberately. "You will sit down. And you will tell me in a civilized manner what has brought you here to my house in such a state."

"She's my girl," Mr. Kirk said. He stared past Mountjoy. "My firstborn. The best of the lot of them if you ask me. She's ruined. Ruined!"

"Has something happened to Jane?" He lifted a hand palm out. "Choose your words carefully, sir."

Kirk took a deep breath. "As if you don't know, when she's pregnant with your bastard."

He blinked twice. "I beg your pardon?"

"Don't deny what you've done. All these years you've kept her from meeting a man who will marry her. Leading her into sin. Seducing her." Kirk scrubbed his hands over his face and when he looked up, he seemed to have collected himself. "Do you think we don't know your reputation when you are in London? Opera girls and ballet dancers. Do you think a father can't see his daughter's weakness? Jane loves you. She loves you enough to do whatever you ask of her because you're the bloody duke."

Mountjoy pressed his lips together. "Has she actually accused me?"

Kirk set his jaw. "Who else would seduce her? To whom else would she give herself except to the man she believed would marry her?"

"Someone besides me," Mountjoy said.

"You'll marry her," Kirk said. "You'll marry her as quickly as you can. It's only right when you've ruined her for anyone else. I'll sue you for breach of promise if you don't."

"What promise would that be? I never asked permission of you to marry any one of your daughters."

"You didn't need to. Everyone knew you'd marry Jane. Ask anyone, and they'll tell you."

"If you stand before a judge and swear that I promised any such thing, you'll consign yourself to Hell." Anger slipped into his voice because until now he'd considered Mr. Kirk a friend, and the man was here, sitting in his house, attempting to force him into a marriage he did not want. "Nor did I ever speak to Jane or any of her sisters about marriage. I won't marry your daughter, Kirk." He leaned over the man. "Drag this farmer's name through the mud if you feel your reputation and your soul are worth the lies."

Kirk blanched. "Agree to acknowledge her bastard as yours, then. The bastard son of a duke might do very well in life."

"No." He felt for Kirk's pain, for the scandal and disgrace if it was true Jane was with child. Sadly he must consider the possibility that Kirk was lying in an attempt to force a marriage. "If it's true, I am very sorry. But I am not the father. I will not marry a woman pregnant by another man any more than I would support another man's bastard simply because a distraught father accuses me."

"We are at an impasse." Kirk lifted his head, eyes bleak. "It must be you. It can only be you."

"There's no impasse, sir. I am not the man responsible for your daughter's misfortune."

"Then she's ruined and some rogue will not do right by her."

"So long as we agree that the rogue is not me." Mountjoy walked to the bellpull and called for Doyle. When he turned, Kirk was slumped on his chair, head down, hands clasped between his open knees. "Doyle will show you out."

Still with his head in his hands, Kirk said, "What am I to do?"

He held out Kirk's riding whip. "Go home to your family. Surely you or your wife can convince her to tell you who is responsible."

The man shook his head. "If it were someone who was free to marry her, she would have told my wife."

Doyle appeared, and Kirk, after a shaky sigh and a curt bow, left the room. Mountjoy returned to his desk, but he could not concentrate on the tasks at hand. He wished Doyle had brought a brandy.

Someone tapped on his door. "Come," he said.

The door opened. Slowly. Too slowly for the efficient Doyle.

He knew it was Lily before he saw or heard her. "Mountjoy?"

This should not be happening to him, that a woman's presence should make his heart pound and his body shiver with anticipation, with doubt, and with outright lust. Shouldn't, but was. He stood, though he stayed behind his desk, fingertips resting on top. "Yes?"

Lily was so beautiful it hurt his heart to look at her, yet

what he wanted to see from her wasn't that angelic perfection but the impish smile that meant she had the measure of him and intended to make him pay. Mountjoy, still on his feet, carefully, very deliberately, capped the ink and placed his quill in the stand.

"May I come in?" She gripped the side of the door. "I understand you're busy, but I'll only bother you for a moment." She put her other hand over her heart. "I promise."

He made the same gesture to the near chair as he'd done for Mr. Kirk. "Please."

She came in and sat on the chair, back straight, hands resting lightly on her lap. She wore a pale gray muslin with narrow vertical stripes of a darker gray. A fiery orange ribbon was threaded through her hair. The effect was, as ever, flattering to her, without there being any obvious reason why. "Sit down, your grace."

The door was open. If he could have closed it with a look he would have. If he could have changed whatever thought or concern had made Lily choose to leave it open, he would have done that, too.

"You heard all that I suppose."

"Yes."

He didn't sit down. "It isn't true," he said. "About Jane and me."

She leaned forward. "It was impossible not to overhear. He was quite angry." She met his eyes, and all he could think was how she'd looked in his arms last night, the sound of his name on her lips, the way she'd felt around him. "Is aught well with you?"

"I am not the father of her child."

"I know you're not."

He came around from behind the desk and stood before her. "There will be gossip."

"I fear Mr. Kirk intended that result."

He gave a dark laugh and gestured at his desk. "My responsibilities must be met. Every day. Every minute. I do meet them and have done so since the day I became Mount-joy. Duty to my family, my title, my tenants, the people who live in this parish, and those where I am an absentee property owner they know only by name. To those in my employ and to my king and country. But I do not owe Jane Kirk a father for her child."

"No, I suppose you don't." She let out a breath. "What if you married her after the child comes?"

The world stopped. His heart no longer beat. "You can't marry Fenris. Not now. No more than I can marry Jane. You know that. You know why."

"Mountjoy, don't."

"Don't what? Am I to do nothing while you marry a man you don't love? Should I marry a woman I don't love? For God's sake, you can't mean that."

She stood, too, and he closed the distance between them and the hell with the open door, he thought. He kissed her, mouth open from the start, and twined an arm around her waist to bring her close. She moved with the forward impetus of his arm, melted against him and now, for this moment, he felt right. Whole. Her arms went around his shoulders, both of them so that she was pressed against him. She slid her fingers into his hair and brought his head down to hers and kissed him senseless.

They parted, eventually, each of them breathless. They'd ended up with her backed up to a tall and thankfully sturdy cabinet that stored various documents and supplies. Paper. Ink. Letters, deeds, the last will and testament of the third duke.

"I'm not going to marry Fenris," she said.

"I'm not going to marry Jane."

"Very well, then."

"Have you made up your mind what you'll do about me?" he said. When he made up his mind that he wanted thus and such a woman, he'd never had any difficulty getting her into his arms. He'd watched other men flirt and seduce and cajole, and he had never had to do that. Until now. Until Lily. He touched her shoulders, her low back, the sides of her throat.

She leaned against the cabinet. "I can't think when you kiss me like that."

"You do want me." He wasn't a man of sweet words. To his knowledge he had no particular way with women the way other men did, just good sense about them. "You couldn't kiss me like that if you didn't."

Her impish smile flashed. "Perhaps you're right."

"I'm always right." He kept her close. "Have you changed your mind about us?"

"No. Have you?"

"No," he said. Relief blew through him, but it was followed by the unsettling conviction that he'd just made a serious mistake. Though, how could that be when Lily wasn't leaving him?

# Chapter Thirty-four

MOUNTJOY OPENED THE DOOR TO LILY'S ROOM AND slipped in as quickly and unobtrusively as he could. Lily was in bed, a single candle providing the light by which she'd been reading. She had a book in her hand, but it was facedown on her chest, and her eyes were closed.

She sat up, though, blinking when he turned from the door he'd just locked. "Mountjoy?"

He put a finger across his lips and whispered, "Don't send me away."

"I shan't." If she hadn't been asleep, then she'd been near to it. Her hair was down, but braided so that it would not tangle while she slept. Half past six in the morning and she was only now falling asleep. "What is it?"

"Lord, where to start." She was the first and only person he wanted to talk to, and he had taken a risk, coming here with the servants already up and about.

"In the middle, if you please." The curtains were drawn, but her candle and a soft morning light kept the room from darkness.

"Nigel came home late last night." He walked to her dressing room door and closed that, too. And locked it.

She set aside her book and sat with her legs curled underneath her. If he were a painter, he'd take her likeness posed like this. As if she were fresh from her lover's embrace, even though she wasn't. A frown creased her brow. "And?"

"He arrived home in possession of a special license. In order to marry Jane Kirk. Which he has done, I should add, without my prior knowledge or consent. In the middle of the night."

"Don't tell me you object."

"It wouldn't matter if I did. They are married and are even now sitting downstairs having come here to inform me I have a sister-in-law. I have just listened to my brother confess that he has been in love with Jane Kirk for months and that he is responsible for her inconvenient situation."

"What does Mr. Kirk say? Does he know?"

"Not yet." He scrubbed his hand through his hair. "Directly he obtained the special license, Nigel went to Jane. Not here. He did not come home to consult the head of his family. He went to the Kirks', got a ladder, put it up against Jane's window, and carried her away."

"He did?"

Mountjoy looked down and saw her eyes wide and, God help him, filling with tears. "For pity's sake, don't cry. There's nothing to be done now. He did not consult a soul, the fool."

She blinked, and two fat tears rolled down her cheeks. "I always cry when there's a happy ending. I can't help myself. A ladder, you say? It's so romantic."

"Romantic?" He pulled his handkerchief from his pocket and handed it to her.

"Thank you, your grace. That's simply the loveliest story. He adores her. Did he throw pebbles at her window, or was she waiting up for him?"

"I haven't the faintest idea." He resisted the impulse to

kiss her. For now. "Wouldn't it make more sense for him to climb the ladder and tap on the window?"

"I think he must have thrown pebbles." She put her book on the bedside table. "It's what all the heroes do when they carry away their ladyloves."

The tension in his chest eased because he'd just seen his future. He was looking at it now. He knew exactly what he had failed to recognize before. "You don't think it's a scandal? Eloping with the woman everyone thought was to marry his brother?"

"Of course it's a scandal. A delicious, wonderful scandal of true love, Mountjoy." She extended a hand, and without thinking, he took it. "You'll have to have a wedding party for them."

He groaned. "More people in my house."

"I'll help you plan it."

"That's your advice for me? Have a party?"

"We'll invite everyone."

"I'm not writing a single invitation."

"Ginny and I will manage everything. Don't worry. You won't have to do a thing except pay the bills." She patted the mattress, and he sat beside her.

"What am I to do about this, Wellstone?"

"Which?"

"Any of this. You." He stretched himself over her, laying her back on the mattress, then drew back with a sigh. "I haven't got a sheath with me."

"Another time, Mountjoy."

"I want you now." He kissed her and kissed her some more and only just recalled himself. "If we were married, Wellstone, we could dispense with sheaths and withdrawal. I could come inside you again right now."

"That seems rather shortsighted of you, don't you think?" Her arms were around him, and she spoke in a low voice. "Is that worth a night or two of pleasure?"

"It's morning."

"A day then. A day of pleasure."

"Do you think as badly of me as that? Why not you for my duchess? We get along. You amuse and delight me. I never know what you'll do next. And you would be a splendid mother to our children. They'd be exceptional. How could they not be with us to raise them and lavish them with love?"

"A point, sir."

He pulled her close enough that she could not fail to know he was aroused. "You see?" he said. "I want you. I always do. I have from the day we met. I won't behave anymore as if I don't adore you more than Nigel adores Jane. I want the right to touch you, kiss you, to make my life with you in public and in private."

"You're overwrought, Mountjoy. Swept away by your brother's grand gesture." She gave him a look. "Or is it lack of sleep that's made you like this?"

Mountjoy bent to kiss her forehead, then let her go and slid off her bed where he stood staring at her with his heart racing. "Will you wait here?"

"Where would I go? I should like a few hours' sleep." She covered a yawn.

"Don't sleep."

"Why not?"

"Promise me?"

She reached for his hand and squeezed it. "I don't believe it's wise for me to indulge your whims like this, but if you insist."

"I do."

Twenty minutes later, Mountjoy was outside her window wrestling a ladder into position. It scraped against the wall and listed dangerously far to the right. Several of his grounds-keeping staff watched him. He saw one of them scratch his head. One of the gardeners who'd been pruning the roses came to lend a hand. "Ground's too soft here, your grace. Begging your pardon, but that ladder will fall over, and you'll break your neck."

Mountjoy pointed. "I need it there. At that window."

"Your grace." Between the two of them and another of

the staff who came over to assist, they got the ladder into place. The top rails banged against the windowsill. He stooped for a handful of pebbles, but that proved unnecessary since the noise had brought Lily out of her bed to see what was happening.

Mountjoy climbed the ladder but before he got to the top, Lily had already opened the window. He gripped the top rung with one hand and threw his handful of pebbles at the glass. Most of them showered to the ground below, but a few ended up on the sill and one or two inside her room.

"Mountjoy?" She brushed away the pebbles that had landed on the sill. "What are you doing?"

"There's no easy way to say this so I'll just say it." He took her face between his hands. "Lily. Lily, you are mine." He knew from her frown that he'd not spoken well. "I want you to belong to me. Mine," he said. Which he knew was exactly the wrong thing to say to her, but the word fell from his lips as if it had been waiting there to send him to perdition and now the moment had come.

"Am I?" she whispered. The ladder wobbled and he had to let go of her to steady himself.

"Mountjoy?" someone called out from below.

Lily waved from the window. "Felicitations to you Lord and Lady Nigel." She closed her eyes. "And our audience is now complete, Mountjoy. Here is your sister."

"Mountjoy?" said Eugenia. He didn't bother looking. "Good heavens."

"Good morning all," Lily said. "Your brother was concerned for my safety when he saw a crack in my window. He's saved my life, I daresay."

Mountjoy looked down and saw his brother and Jane on the lawn with the groundskeeping staff. The couple held hands. Eugenia was there, too, in her night-robe. He returned his attention to Lily. "Never mind them. Come away with me, Wellstone."

"And do what? Scandalize your family and all of High Tearing?"

"Marry me," he said, and where the demand had been hiding from him all this time, he did not know. He ought to have said it days ago. He ought to have made her understand days and days ago. "We shall deal with your father."

She pressed a finger to his mouth. "It's far too soon for that. Nothing is certain, Mountjoy. Not yet. You needn't."

He reached for her again and brought her head to his and kissed her, and as always, they were immediately in lust. In high passion. She pulled back. Below, he heard a whistle and applause.

"Come inside, you foolish man, before you fall and break your neck."

"Don't be absurd. What would everyone down there say if they saw me climb into your room? No, there's nothing for it but for you to come down the ladder with me." He reached in and got an arm around her waist. "Or," he whispered in her ear, "I can go down alone and tell them it's not the window that's broken."

"Mountjoy," she said. "Oh, Mountjoy, what am I to do?"

"If you'll take my advice, fetch your prettiest night-robe and come down the ladder with me."

"I have a jade green one, with the most cunning darker stripes running through it."

"You are spectacular in green. Fetch that one." Ten minutes later, he managed to get them safely down to the lawn. "You see? You will always be safe and sound with me." He used the sides of his thumbs to brush away her tears. "What's this? More tears?"

"Impossible," she whispered. "I'd never cry over something like this."

"Marry me, Lily." He pulled her into his arms. "I want to spend my life learning about you. Being with you. Trying to make you as happy as I will be with you as my wife."

She gazed at him and blinked twice. "Good God, Mountjoy."

"Marry me, my love."

"Have you considered the negatives? You'd have me for

your duchess when I am sure to invent a ghost or two for Bitterward. What will people say?"

"That I'm a damned luckier man than anyone deserves. They'll say I climbed a ladder to propose to the woman I love, that's what they'll say. Besides, after Eugenia tells you how sorry she is you're going to have such a one as me for a husband she'll be over the moon at having you as a sister."

Behind them, someone coughed.

"Ignore them." He gripped Lily's shoulders. "Say yes, Wellstone. I'll make you happy, I promise you that with my last breath."

"It's not your duty to make me happy."

"It would be my joy. I want to. I want you to be happy." He stared into her face and understood he had not been honest yet. Not with himself and not with her. "The bald truth. I love you." He cupped her face between his hands. "You are the most remarkable woman I've ever met. I adore you. I want to be with you. I don't care how short a time it's been since we met, my life is no longer what it was, and I am unutterably grateful to you for that."

She turned her head to one side and kissed his wrist. "That is because at last you understand the value of a decent waistcoat."

"I love you, Lily. Marry me. Please make me the happiest of men." He drew a strand of her hair away from her face, and she looked at him again, her gaze serious, unreadable except that she was not smiling and had not told him yes. Or no. Or that he needed to prove himself to her. "Love me," he said. "Love me in whatever way a woman like you can love a man like me."

More tears slid down her cheeks. "Oh, Mountjoy. Don't say such things."

"If you don't love me, for God's sake, refuse me, but if you do or if you think you could, then marry me. Be my wife, and my lover, and my friend. Be the mother of our children. Let me spend the rest of my life with you, and I will be the luckiest, happiest man on this earth. I love you,

Lily. I think I fell in love with you the moment I saw you, and all this time I've been too stubborn to admit it."

She did smile, and he was grateful for that. "You are a very stubborn man, I'll grant you that."

"That I am."

She held his face. "Do you mean this?"

"Lily," he said. "I am prepared to make an enemy of your father."

She leaned her head against his chest. "Oh, Mountjoy."

"So tell me, is there room for me in your heart?"

She looked up, her eyes bright with tears. "My dear, dear man. I think I should very much like being a duchess."

"Does that mean yes?" He kissed her once. On the mouth. "You'll marry me?"

"Yes. Yes, I'll marry you."

Behind them, the servants hooted and cheered and applauded, and amid all that joy he heard Nigel and Eugenia cheering as well.

"I feel," she said, "I ought to tell you that you have Fenris to thank."

"Say it isn't so."

"But it is. Fenris was the one who told me I am in love with you." She kissed his hand. "He was right."

"About?"

"That I love you, Mountjoy."

"I've always wanted a cousin," he said.

She twined her arms around him and for quite a while they were lost to each other, and Mountjoy felt at last he'd done exactly the right thing.

# Epilogue

Three weeks later. The Anglo-Saxon church at Bitterward.

EUGENIA TRIED NOT TO SNIFFLE AS HER BROTHER, THE Duke of Mountjoy, slid a ring onto Lily's finger. Then the final benediction was over, and her brother and her best friend were married. Eugenia just couldn't be happier. It was obvious to anyone that Mountjoy was head over heels for Lily and that Lily felt the same about Mountjoy.

The wedding was beautiful, and her brother looked so handsome in his new suit of clothes. He was smiling, her brother was. Smiling. The way he'd started smiling shortly after Lily arrived, only bigger and broader and at last without him trying to pretend he wasn't. Beside him, Nigel elbowed him and whispered something Eugenia couldn't hear but that made Mountjoy grin.

She heard a sniffle and glanced across the chapel where Miss Caroline Kirk had a handkerchief pressed to her eyes. The wedding was an intimate one, with only friends and family in attendance, a fortunate thing since the invited guests fit very snugly in the church.

The location had been Mountjoy's idea and there had

been three weeks of frantic work so that the church could be used. The walls had a fresh coat of whitewash, pillows had been laid on the stone pews, and the break in the altar had been repaired. Banners with the Mountjoy coat of arms hung from the walls and another flew outside. The path had fresh gravel laid down.

Lily's cousin, that awful man, the Marquess of Fenris, heir to the Duke of Camber, was in attendance as the lone representative of her family. He'd sat quietly during the ceremony, very proper and unapproachable. If he had tender feelings for the bride as she pronounced her vows, they were not in evidence. She resented Fenris for all that he had done, but she could not, after all, begrudge him a place at his cousin's wedding. Their aunt and uncle were here as well, all the way from Haltwhistle, as proud of their nephew as any parent could be of a son. Two of Mountjoy's close friends had come up from London and Cornwall respectively. A small gathering, but Mountjoy never wanted a fuss.

Eugenia dabbed a handkerchief to her eyes as Mountjoy bent to kiss his wife. Her aunt, who was sitting beside Eugenia, pressed her hand, but she sniffled, too. Silently, Eugenia wished Lily and her brother all the happiness in the world.

Afterward, everyone walked outside into the bright afternoon sun. A few yards distant, several carriages waited to carry the guests and the Duke and Duchess of Mountjoy back to Bitterward for a reception.

She walked out with her aunt, but they'd only got partway down the path when she heard Lily call out, "Ginny!"

With a word to her aunt, Eugenia returned to her brother and her sister-in-law. She smiled and curtseyed. As any who knew Lily would expect, she was exquisitely dressed. She wore ivory silk overlaid with silver lace with tiny silver blue flowers knitted into it. "Yes, your grace?"

"Here." Lily removed her Gypsy medallion and, before Eugenia could say a word, hung it around her neck. "For you, my dear Ginny."

"But this is yours!"

Lily pulled Mountjoy closer to her. "I've all the good luck I need, Ginny. The medallion has done its work for me." She pressed Ginny's hand and they locked gazes. "It's someone else's turn now."

"I thought you didn't believe any of that," Mountjoy said.

"Why wouldn't I?" Lily asked. "The magic worked exactly as the Gypsy king said it would." She patted his cheek with her free hand. "After all, the medallion brought me you. There's no better magic than that, Mountjoy."

"True," he said, dropping a kiss on his wife's cheek.

"Thank you, Lily," Eugenia said. She touched the medallion, tracing a finger over the bow and arrow engraved on it. The metal was warm.

Lily leaned in to give her a kiss. "I'll take good care of your brother, Ginny. I promise you."

"I know you shall."

"Be sure you sleep with the medallion under your pillow."

She laughed. "I will."

"Promise?"

"I promise."

A few minutes later, Mountjoy had escorted his bride to their carriage and they were on their way to Bitterward where they were to say good-bye to their guests before leaving for Syton House and parts south.

Eugenia sniffled again as her brother's carriage rolled away from the church. At the same time she was turning to rejoin her aunt, the Marquess of Fenris was heading for his carriage. Eugenia's vision was blurred with the remnants of her tears and did not realize how close he was to her. Fenris was inattentive as well, for he collided with Eugenia on the path. If he'd not caught her, she might actually have been injured in a fall.

She found herself clasped in the arms of the man who had told Robert he was making the biggest mistake of his life, marrying her. The man who'd done everything in his power to prevent her marriage. When she had her feet underneath her, she pushed him away.

"I beg your pardon," Fenris said.

Eugenia stepped away from him. "It's nothing. I beg *your* pardon." He was her new sister's cousin, and therefore she felt she could not cut him dead. That did not mean she had to be anything but cool toward him. She didn't like him and never would. She dropped him a curtsey and returned to her aunt.

"He seems a polite young man," her aunt said when they were once again arm in arm. "And very handsome."

"The man who nearly knocked me over?"

"I didn't mean the vicar, dear."

"I suppose." Eugenia didn't bother looking at Lord Fenris or she would have seen that he was watching her. She did at least lower her voice. "But I dislike him exceedingly."

Look for the next Romancing the Rake novel
by Carolyn Jewel

*Not Proper Enough*

Coming in September 2012
from Berkley Sensation!